KINGDOM OF THE SUN
THE HOLLOW CROWN SERIES
BOOK ONE

HP NERO

KINGDOM OF THE SUN Hollow Crown Series, Book One Copyright © 2025 by HP Nero

All rights reserved.

No part of this book may be reproduced or transmitted in any form or by any means, electronic or mechanical, including photocopying, recording, or by any information storage and retrieval system, without permission in writing from the publisher. This book is not permitted to be put into any sort of artificial intelligence LLM in any capacity for any reason whatsoever.

This is a work of fiction. Names, characters, places, and incidents either are the product of the author's imagination or are used fictitiously. Any resemblance to actual persons, living or dead, events, or locales is entirely coincidental.

ISBN [softcover]: **979-8218603892**

ISBN [hardcover]: **979-8300014551**

Cover design by HP Nero

Edited by HP Nero

First Edition Printed in the United States of America

www.hpnero.com

Our greatest strength is our ability to love.

CHAPTER ONE

The sun did not kiss me sweetly with warm, rosy lips, but rather licked at me with a sandpaper tongue. I could feel its feline caress on the layers beneath the surface of my skin, igniting my veins and setting them aflame.

Despite being the daughter of a king, I was seen as little more than chattel—traded and shared amongst suitors and buyers. I suppose it was no surprise that it would be so sudden…

As my father told me daily, he could not tolerate the fact that I indulged my stomach with his food and clad my skin in his jewels. All because of the halo of scarlet hair that adorned my head, a child '*kissed by the sun*'—that is how they referred to my brother and me yet others scorned us and called us children of the damned.

I looked into my mirror for one of the last times, searching for the similarities that tied me to this throne, yet I found none. I looked more Tessiah than human, and surely that made father rageful.

The Tessiah were a supernatural species, ranging from mages to Drakkarias, which were dragons entrapped in human flesh. The Tessiah were spat on by humans, hated by them, especially in my father's kingdom.

. . .

My father was a drunken sot who gambled away every precious dime we had, yet somehow, he still managed to keep himself afloat. Father despised the Tessiah and forced them to live in secret, lest he would implicate them in fabricated crimes so that he could hang them, torture them, or keep them as prisoners. Part of me felt that I could understand him—that his rage was somewhat justified...The rage that filtered in after my mother's death, at least.

There was one Tessiah who made it clear she believed in supremacy rather than harmony, and she made sure that others knew her intentions. The Drakkarias were not *extinct* creatures, but were incredibly rare. We were told stories how they had been cursed many years ago to be forged into human flesh, skin which ensnared flames.

I was told Kaneira was a Drakkarias who tormented humans, strung them up, and set them on fire with the heat that she stomached and spit into flame.

She could trap anyone she pleased with her striking beauty and words seemingly soaked in honey. She promised chaos and destruction but did so with such a sweet tone; she could command armies should she desire them.

Then there was that fateful day when she deliberately sought my brother and me out, the children kissed by the sun...the children of one of the most powerful kings in Moterrian.

I remember that day.

I'll *always* remember that day.

I frantically pace about my chambers, looking out the windows for a gentle breeze to blow in a calming feeling. I didn't know where I would go—what would happen to me after today, but my mind could only swirl with more thoughts of dread. As much as I would have loved to be free of this prison, the remains of my mother's memory still lurked in these walls, and I wasn't sure I could do without being trapped inside of them.

I stare at the dahlias on the nightstand—the ones from her garden. I sighed at the sight of them; how her garden was once full of life, but now rots. I try not to think of that day—that *wretched* day...

My father watched as Kaneira snapped her neck, my brother and I at his side.

Kaneira was regal but cruel, unrelenting in her allegiance to herself and her kind, but no one else. Still, though she was vicious, I thought I heard a whisper of apology leave her lips moments before my mother's bones cracked beneath her hands.

I even believe I saw a softness in her that she did not show to the public—to the people. Fear was her weapon, and she wielded it like a blade.

I would never forget her face: the sapphire eyes which burned with rage and madness, the dark skin which held moonlight in the night, her long black hair which reached her waist. She was a beautiful woman, and I could not help but think of her that way even as she wrenched my mother's bones under taloned fingers.

I could hear the measured footsteps coming down the hall now, I knew those footsteps like they were my own.

It was a miracle Dracar did not hate me—did not *loathe* me. We were twins, both kissed by the sun; though mine was a halo, his was more like strokes of sunlight which scattered about his black hair. His eyes matched mine, a color which danced between a deep brown and a burgundy.

The people feared us and our existence, believing we were some special siblings with powers or abilities. We were not; we were just marked with an orange flare which donned our heads but if we had power I would have known...I would have used it...

Dracar protected me for most of our lives. He fought off my father who tried to be rid of me, and he denied suitors in my father's stead as he was too drunk or off on '*missions*' as he would call them—such an idiot he was.

Dracar felt the tether of our kingdom, a desire to preserve and protect it, but also to be rid of it entirely. He felt that way about most things, where he sat between love and hate, straddling the line that was indifference.

The footsteps grew louder as I stood in the glass door letting the wind brush salt on my cheeks from the sea.

I try hard to think of the happier memories I shared with Dracar, yet it felt impossible to do so as my doom was awaiting me in the throne room.

He knew one day my father would try to marry me off, probably just to be rid of me. There was a time when women were valued in the Tenth, or so my mother told me when I was still a child—it was hard to even pretend that was the case now.

I didn't want to leave my brother, much less to be married off to some tyrant like my father, but alas.

I was already late to marry, twenty years old was far too late.

My father should have nearly ruined any chance of suitors wanting my hand, since he would speak to the whole court of how my halo of sun was a curse.

He would pity himself for his vile children: the son who could never stomach being a king and the daughter who was a curse. Dracar and I were not special—and we were certainly never made to feel that way.

As my doors opened, a flash of black and orange flashed in the doorway, the stoic face of my brother staring back at me. I stared at those strands of fire that danced on his head—how beautiful it looked in the sunlight.

"Mirage," Dracar said at my doorway. I didn't respond to him, I was too lost in the shades of scarlet that matched my own.

"Mirage," he said again, approaching the balcony. There was a hint of warmth in his voice; his stone cold demeanor softened. I turned to face him, unsure of how I should even respond. He took in the look on my face and tilted his head at me, as if he understood my sheer terror.

"I will do what I can." He reached out a hand, as if to touch my shoulder, and as I peered back at him, he lowered it. I saw the faintest twitch of his brow before he nodded slightly, turning on his heels and walking back out of the room.

Dracar walked like a king.

He *looked* like a king.

He appeared as if he were born of autumn-touched leaves, a breath of crisp air on a warm fall morning. He was the embodiment of where the sun met the tree lines and golden flecks peeked beneath leaves to touch dewed grass. He was a perfect son, the best son any king could ask for, yet my father detested him.

His commanding presence was precisely why the Tallier family wanted him. Lady Tallier had no heirs, and they prayed my father would one day default on his debts so they could claim Dracar instead. The Talliers craved having him as the champion of their kingdom's power, but my father would never allow it.

He would never allow his throne to go unclaimed.

I especially was an unsightly heir to him; he would never risk a woman ruling his kingdom. My father would, of course, sell *me* first to pay any debts his jewels and physical wealth could not afford.

Today, he would sell me off to the highest bidder—to any prince or heir who could pay the most, regardless of whether they were kind or gentle.

. . .

As the floors groaned beneath my weight, I trembled with every step. My head began to ache with pain. It roared with anguish, sorrow, despair. I would be separated from the only person who protected me, who loved me, who would tear the world apart for me. My brother would endure my father's cruelty alone, and that too, tormented me.

When we trained together, I would occasionally get a glimpse of his smile as he knocked me down or stabbed me lightly. Likely he enjoyed drawing a bit of blood—a sense of odd triumph.

Yet, I needed his strength and poise; it helped me survive all of these years under the devastating rule of my father. Dracar was the only light aside from the sun that this castle saw.

I stared down at the sea rising up to touch the rocks which sat outside of our walls. This was a beautiful place, yet my father managed to drain it of all of its glory.

The only home I had was in the heart of my brother—and Diana, of course, who has been ripping apart my wardrobe for the last hour and a half. She insisted on only perfection, even on one of my darkest days.

Her eyes were soft and a shade of lilac I had only ever seen in nature, blossoming in the sun as any flower would. She was deeply compassionate and cherished my company as I did hers. Except this morning, Diana was stiff. Her hair was more disarrayed than usual, golden strands finding their way out of her delicate purple lace.

"How are *you* this morning, Mir?" She asked in such a hushed tone.

I simply stared.

This morning was not one I wished to ever endure, and I had no interest in discussing it. I shuddered at her touch, her delicate fingers sweeping my hair down my back. She tied the black part of my hair upward to reveal more of the scarlet halo I donned beneath. She noted my silence with a small nod, and spoke to me anyway, knowing I was too stunned—no—too terrified to speak.

"He'll stop it," she said, her eyes meeting mine in the mirror that lay before us.

I knew it was Dracar that Diana spoke of. He would certainly try, of that I had no doubt. Before he had retreated from my chambers, his eyes locked onto hers, though I wasn't sure if it was longing or a plea to somehow get me out of here.

The sun often reached this part of the room and typically lit the adornments around the mirror, sending scattering color throughout. It made my chambers feel alive every morning, I would miss that. I would miss this room—I *loved* this room.

I loved the soft green of the walls and the gold accents which glittered in the sun…

Diana loved this room too, as she often slept in it with me after our nightly conversations. We typically gossiped about castle conflicts and things she had heard the servants say.

Diana somehow knew everything about everyone. The way she moved through the castle, unseen and unheard, felt nothing short of magical.

Most of the gossip would concern my brother, in some way or another. He was always a topic of discussion—beloved by his people and catching the lustful eyes of man and woman alike, *especially* Diana's. He was a force, and that force buzzed through the castle walls like an energy.

CHAPTER TWO

When Diana finished binding my hair in black silk ribbon, she took me to the armoire and retrieved a red silk dress. The silk would brush the floor, whispering to those who looked at me with a predatory glance.

Normally, I would have liked the tight fit of the dress, the bright colors, and the jewelry that complimented my freckled skin.

Admittedly, I enjoyed being a royal; however, the aspects I did not relish were those like today, where my royalty robbed me of my freedom.

I looked like the part I had to play: rich and special, the kind of woman that young lords and princes would waste gold, rubies, and sapphires on.

The only family I had, I would lose today.

My father had finally extinguished my final light.

Hope was beyond me.

Diana continued to place jewelry all over my body, from my

waist to my ears to my neck. She smiled sweetly when our eyes met, but there was a haunting presence behind those eyes.

I sulked for only a moment as she concluded the finishing touches of jewelry, and I stared back at myself in the mirror. I feared what I would look like in a week, a month, a year—the time that would break down my soul and, in turn, my body.

I gazed out the grand window one last time and saw a raven sitting on my railing.

A beautiful creature.

Its coat was glorious in this light, the black almost appeared purple as it bathed itself in the sunlight of the morning.

When we left the room, the sheer weight of the day came pressing on my chest as if someone had been pushing down on my lungs, holding them, squeezing them. I made my way down the long hallway, walls crafted with marble and stone, and that beautiful green color that I loved *so* very much.

I was going to be sold and taken away.

When I entered the throne room, a bone-colored dais sat at its head, but as I looked upon it, my father did not stare back down at me.

It was Dracar who sat on the throne.

He had a look of impatience and irritation on his face, a hand beneath his chin leaning on the arm of the throne. I realized his agitation was not with me, but rather my absent father, who is no doubt drunk somewhere.

As I was halfway through the human sea, the doors flew open wide behind me again, my father standing between them. He was fitful and disheveled, his crown hanging crookedly on his golden head. He reached for it and marched down the aisle, the sea of flesh parting to create a path for him to stride down.

He slid briskly past me without even making eye contact, and my eyes widened at the lack of stench that followed him.

Sober.

Stone cold sober.

Such an odd occasion to deny his only friend, the bottom of a bottle.

He stalked toward my brother and gave him a disgusted look.

"Up, boy," he said, his eyes narrowing on my brother's. Dracar simply stared at him, making no gestures, no words parting his lips. He slowly rose from the dais, never breaking eye contact with my father, and sat beside him.

When I resumed my walk toward the dais, I then noticed a gleam of white in the sea of heads.

White hair, speckled with black—I could not see his eyes, the top of his head.

I finally reached the dais and sat beside my father. I felt the sun coming down from where it had just graced my brother, and for the first time today, I felt its warm embrace.

I looked for that white hair again, only to not see the stranger in the crowd. Throughout the years I had come to know most of the royals who gathered before me, but the white hair was unfamiliar to me entirely.

It *almost* excited me.

There were murmurs and laughs coming from all over the room, bouncing off of the walls as well as the insides of my skull.

I knew that a woman in my position never had control over her fate, but I was still a fool and held hope anyway.

A dangerous and pitiful thing, hope was.

KINGDOM OF THE SUN

The last time I felt it was moments before I saw my mother's fragile neck in the hands of Kaneira as she snapped it like a twig. I felt the hope burning behind my eyes as I fought down my tears. I thought to myself that she wouldn't do it—that she wouldn't kill my innocent mother.

My mother, who had also been sold like cattle, who did not ask for a marriage to my deranged father.

My mother, who sang us sweet tales of a faraway land of flowers and apples—a kingdom of eternal autumn…

Lost in the thoughts of my mother, I didn't realize Dracar's eyes on me. It was as if he were taking in my face for the last time—in case he were never to see it again.

I could fight, and I could fight well, but what if my buyer had a blade and I did not? What if he took a whip to my back while I was restrained?

Things that father did to Dracar for many years. I stared back at my brother.

It's okay.

It will be okay.

"Silence!" My father shouted whilst raising his hand. He reached it upward to readjust the crown, which seemed to misplace itself yet again. We shared little resemblance to our father. His hair was golden and long; it came past his shoulders, a length similar to my own. His eyes were a shining emerald green, and they nearly made me sick to look at.

Despite his infatuation with liquor, his body was fit for a king. That didn't change the fact that he disgusted me, for even in silence, I could hear the things he said about me: *a wretched, weak, pitiful girl.*

. . .

I recognized so many faces in the crowd, specifically that of Prince Porlend, a cruel, wicked bastard of a "king", was in the very front, his eyes roving my body from head to toe. Jamen Porlend was his full name, but his sister called him Jam.

My father made Voryn Porlend a so-called king as a gesture of his goodwill and 'kindness', but it was not a kingdom they ruled; rather they held a few villages in the far south of *our* kingdom. Voryn was an inventor—a kind man, but one who hardly ever tended to the needs of his two children. I looked in the crowd for a dash of ginger hair—his daughter Lyris—a woman I had grown fond of over the course of our lives.

To no one's surprise, Prince Porlend stepped forward. That snake-like grin spread across his face—the same grin he'd worn when we were fifteen and Dracar had broken his nose for touching me.

The crooked bridge of it had never quite healed right.

"Your highness," he began, and I could swear he hissed, "My father has offered me a great fortune so that I may claim my bride." He stared at me again with that predatory look, but I was not prey—not yet.

I held his gaze as calmly as I could, willing my terror to not show on my face. The room erupted into conversations among the many men arguing and hounding the young prince for his arrogance. He said the words as if this were settled years ago, as if he was entitled to me.

"Jamen, it is an honor, as always. May I know this fortune you speak of?" I wasn't surprised that my father only really cared about that offer. He did not care for the pleasantries and ass-kissing, just the amount of gold he would come into possession of.

"Well," Jamen quickly gave me a wink before he continued his offer, "My father made a claim long ago that you believed Porlend wine was the best in the ten kingdoms. So he has offered five hundred barrels of it and fifty thousand gold."

The room then fell into complete silence.

Some young princes and lords even left entirely, knowing they had been outbid by the very first to offer. My father's excitement could hardly be contained, but my brother gripped the arms of his throne so tightly his knuckles turned to a ghostly white.

My father made no secret of his willingness to jump at the offer, but surprisingly collected himself and said to the still bowed menace, "Is that *all* you have to offer?" My brother shot him a look with an unreadable expression. Jamen raised his head slowly, a look of clear confusion on his face, "*All* I offer?"

"What else could you possibly desire? What else could my family possibly give you for just a *woman?*" He let that last word roll off of his tongue with such a venom that I could already feel the torture he would do unto me. My father's face tightened into a wicked grin,

"Well, only a fool accepts the first offer." He raised a hand to physically cast away Jamen and hear the offers of others who milled about the throne room.

"Anyone else?" He cooed, so gentle yet firm. The words nearly sounded loving exiting his lips, but I could see through his facade.

"Forgive me," a voice came from the middle of the room, commanding yet sincere, "I come from a kingdom not of the ten, but I wish to make an offer on behalf of my master."

The white of his hair knocked the air from my lungs.

An unfamiliar face indeed, one that belonged to someone who was in some way similar to me and my brother.

"And who, pray tell, is your master?" My father chuckled lightly, clearly ready to shoot down whatever offer the stranger had.

"I come from the eleventh kingdom, your highness, one of which you are wholly familiar." The man now stood next to Jamen, dragging his eyes from his head to feet, and gave an unamused snicker.

. . .

The eleventh was not a true kingdom—but a myth—supposedly a haven for Tessiah, a place where they were free to exist as they were…free to kill as many humans as they desired.

My father made no attempt to veil his anger and disgust, "and what will *your kind* offer for a human girl, and why?"

"My master has granted me an allowance of one hundred thousand gold for your daughter, and what we do with her is none of your concern. We could torture, kill, imprison—it's beyond you once she has been paid for." The warmth left my body.

I felt as if I had been killed right there, impaled on a shard of ice, sucking any of the life left within me onto its tendrils.

Torture, kill, imprison.

The words echoed in my head and I found myself looking at Dracar, terrified.

Please. I mouthed to him from my own throne.

"Over my dead body." Dracar spat as he stood tall, his hand draping over the hilt of his sword—elegantly, but also to unsheath it if need be.

My father was nearly drunk from the excitement of the moment, he loved violence; in fact, he lived for it. Perhaps this is why he had forgone his favorite pastime, so that he could fully revel in the misery of my brother's and mine without missing a beat.

Dracar's blade was now inches from the stranger's throat, but he remained unphased. For a moment, I saw the stranger's eyes flicker to the hilt of Dracar's blade, as if he were going to reach for it.

The stranger only made eye contact with my father, as if Dracar was not mere feet away from him wielding a blade which could take his head clean off of his shoulders.

. . .

"Well, sir, do you accept my master's offer?" He asked. Such a bizarre creature, dare I even consider him human.

"It would be foolish for me to say no, would it not?" Asked King Carlisle. A rhetorical question. The stranger smiled, and offered his hand for me to take—for me to leave with him, right now.

"No." Dracar now stood between the stranger and me, sword still at his throat.

"Now now, that is very unfair. If I pay for it, I keep it." The stranger gave that feline smile, laced with amusement, to my brother.

"*Her.*" he said, his eyes not breaking once from the stranger's. I wanted to reach for Dracar's arm, to cling to him, but I had been paralyzed, unable to move an inch.

Torture, kill, imprison.

That would be my fate, sealed with a mountain of gold.

CHAPTER
THREE

The stranger stared at Dracar, his eyes cutting through the veil he placed over his soul. If my brother and I were destined for a land of eternal autumn, then the stranger was destined for eternal winter.

His eyes were sapphire blue, cold and calculating, but had a hint of warmth circling his irises. Despite his cruel words, I could not find cruelty in his features, and it bothered me deeply.

His eyes had been kissed by snowflakes, as his eyelashes were a dazzling white which accented his eyes. He had a devastating beauty to him, one that could kill if his hands could not.

Though I reprimanded myself for even thinking of him as I did, the stunning Winter incarnate was forged by something inhuman and unnatural. His gaze moved to me, and a gentle smile pulled his lips upward, and he nodded once at me again.

His words and face told different stories; his words were daggers that pointed at my throat, but his face was soft and inviting.

"Perhaps, I should have introduced myself to you both before whisking away your lovely sister." The stranger smiled and tucked his hand into a pocket as he bowed.

"My name is Hiver Snoke. My master calls me Snow, so I will allow you to do the same." He lifted his head so that I may see his eyes again, so corruptly beautiful.

"I am not sure I care—but *you* will not be taking her." Dracar held his blade at the stranger's throat again as he rose from his deep bow.

"I can double my previous offer, your highness, for your son to join us." This time, the stranger's—*Hiver's*—words dripped with venom. If my father was a snake, then Hiver was a cobra, and I fear his strike would be far more lethal.

Once I was at Hiver's side, he linked our arms and placed a soft hand onto mine. He stroked my knuckles, a soothing gesture, but it felt so wrong.

"You could offer me millions of gold, but I will *not* give up my only son, my only heir to my throne!" Father now stood many feet away from Hiver, guards at the ready to strike him. Hiver only smiled.

"Okay." Hiver turned on his heels, but he still linked arms with me to pull me through the sea of flesh, all gasping with shock and terror.

"Your gold is at the front gates, King Carlisle." Hiver said and led me gracefully through the doors. Dracar snarled and thrashed in the hands of guards; his eyes were frantic when I peered over my shoulder.

"Not with him—anyone but him!" He yelled, struggling against the strength of seven men. Hiver made no effort to hurt me, he simply strolled with a look of triumph on his face.

"You are quite lovely." Hiver whispered to me, patting my arm once. I shuddered from his touch.

As we strode arm and arm, Hiver said nothing else to me after calling me lovely. My brother and I were loved by our people, but also very feared for whatever dark presence veiled us in Autumn's attire. They were not words that belonged to us, that were *made* for us.

"Will I be able to speak to him again?" I said to Hiver, working up the courage to glance in his direction.

"Ah, more than that, beautiful..." Hiver did not return my eye contact and continued to strut forward. He was very unbothered by the cutting glares of my court.

In fact, he even seemed to relish in their hatred of him.

I tried to not stiffen around his arm as we walked, but I gazed around at the walls and beautiful things that were so dear to me. There was much to miss, and yet I still found myself somewhat relieved to be free of my father and his madness.

I was leaving, and that was terrifying.

With a passing glance, I did not notice the gold Hiver had promised; perhaps the guards already hauled it inside. My mind quickly faltered when I saw something I could only have imagined in a dream. It was a carriage which was made of clouds which were fluffed and grey, and it appeared to have snowflakes adorning it.

It was *magic*.

I had never seen magic up close—only magical people, like Kaneira. The seats were a pale blue color and were velvet to the touch.

I imagine my awe was apparent to Hiver as he leaned in front of me, "I take it you like my style?" He managed a small chuckle. I could not tear my eyes away from the otherworldly carriage.

My father had forbidden the use of magic, and if it was used in the kingdom, the consequence was usually death. However, I had my answer about Hiver; he was *not* a normal being, and not kissed by Winter in the same way my brother and I had been kissed by Autumn.

The snowflakes glistened on the clouds. They appeared to be like small pearls, shining in the sun and lulling me to come closer. I was fully entranced and did not even realize my fingers were upon them until Hiver again appeared at my side, smiling joyfully.

I again failed to read him. I heard in the back of my mind those horrible words: *torture, kill, imprison.* I could not fathom how this *thing* could take us to the eleventh kingdom, should I even make it that far.

I was fearful to meet Hiver's master—whatever creature had sent him here, and with so much gold. I could also not imagine why they would purchase me in the first place—potentially to make an example of humans? Perhaps to attempt to drive my heinous father into further madness?

They would not know that I hated him as much as any Tessiah could.

I imagined my father's expression now as he sauntered about his throne room waiting for the gold to be carried in—his sheer excitement for being rid of me finally. He no longer had to look upon my cursed face, and now he only had Dracar.

Imagining his face in my absence made my soul wither. I

pictured the pain and defeat he felt losing the only family he had, the only *real* family anyways...

"If you are done inspecting your ride, my lady, I think we should be on our way?"

Hiver stepped into the carriage before me and held out his hand for me to follow. For a brief moment, I thought about my options. I could not run, and I could not hide, so my only option was to obey.

We sat in silence for the first hour or so of the trip. I stared out the veiled window, trying to poke my hand through the soft cloud; however, I was trapped, unlike I was on the outside.

"How I do love the sea," Hiver breathed, talking to no one in particular. I looked down at his attire as he lifted his head to the window, eyes closed as the breeze caressed his face. His pants were a shade of black I had not imagined possible, dark and fading into nearly nothingness.

The tunic he wore was a dark green, almost like he had been clad in evergreen trees. As his eyes opened, he noticed my staring—I'll admit that it *was* impolite...

"I do think red is your color—*Mirage*," he said my name as if he were testing the way it felt on his tongue.

"I prefer Mira," I said, willing myself to tear my gaze from his alluring blue eyes. I could feel his gaze still on me, but he did not look at me in the way I expected; he lacked a predatory nature, even when his eyes were ravenous.

"But I love the name Mirage," He grinned.

Perhaps I was being tricked. He could very well be a wolf in a sheep's coat; it could be a part of his game. One that I could tell he would like me to play with him.

I stared longingly out the windows, a beautiful land rolled into hills before me. We were near an ocean, a lovely sea of blue and violet, and it had such a rich color that I would miss terribly. I did not know how far the eleventh kingdom was; in fact, I had no idea *where* it was at all.

I kept my eyes fixed on the ocean in the distance as the carriage rumbled against the rocky terrain...until it felt like we hit something—something very hard.

The carriage jumped violently, and Hiver's head slammed into the wall behind him. The carriage halted before nearly flipping over.

"What the hell!" Hiver groaned, reaching a hand for the back of his head.

Something hit *us*. Not the other way around.

He shot me a look that sent a shiver down my spine, like his eyes casted an ice bridge which covered every vertebrae from my pelvis to my neck. I felt that I had been kissed by Winter as he had, and it was turning my veins into slush.

He spoke softly, calmly as he kept that look on me, "Stay here, do *not* leave." He jumped out of the carriage door and walked toward the front of the carriage.

I tried to sit still, to be patient, but part of me continued to believe I would die anyway—that I should go investigate, and if whatever lies outside *were* to kill me, it would perhaps be a more merciful death than what I would face in the eleventh kingdom. I pushed through the cloud which was penetrable once more to my touch.

Before I could catch my bearings, I was tumbling from the beautiful vessel, and I came face to face with Hiver who was panting, sweat beading from his white brow. He was on his knees, his tunic shredded. Drips of blood flowed from his mouth and the ripped cloth that hung from his abdomen.

Our faces were inches apart, and my eyes widened in terror; I could not stop looking at the blood which began to trickle onto his snow-kissed lashes.

"I *said* do *not* move." he huffed, his breath tingling my skin. His scent was so strong now: pine, eucalyptus, and a hint of smoke. He groaned as his hands slid across his wounds.

"*Fuck...*" He whispered as he pulled his hands from his stomach and reached for his brow, the source of more blood.

"What can I do?" I breathed, not daring to move an inch.

"You?" he laughed lightly before immediately wincing, "*You* can do nothing, except for getting back into the carriage, please." He grunted as he pulled himself up from his knees.

"We aren't far now—no worries—just..." he trailed off, wincing once more at his physical wounds.

"Reavari," he breathed.

I had only heard rumors of Reavari. They preyed on humans and weaker Tessiah, drinking their blood as sustenance. The stories claimed they were an abomination from the Three-Faced God. I thought they were only rumors, but they walked the Earth, breathed our air, and ripped their talons through Hiver's clothing.

I felt that shock of fear again, the paralyzing terror which kept me from clinging to Dracar's arm when he stood before me.

Is this the new life which awaited me? A life of paralyzing fear?

I felt genuine fear for him—concern that he would not make it to the eleventh. Hiver noticed my stare and cooed sweetly, "Worried for me, princess?"

Was I still a princess? I no longer had a castle, a court, a tyrannical king to parade himself over me...

"I am sure it would please you to know that I was worried." I did not even think about how my words may offend him. I felt such opposing emotions about Hiver; I didn't know whether to be thankful to be whisked away from my cruel father or to fear whatever new tragic life awaits.

I could only hope his master would be quick with my death, just like my mother's...

I welcomed that sensation, no longer feeling pity for myself and fear for my brother. I did not know what death would entail, but I could only hope it was like falling asleep.

Hiver was smiling at my remark. He put his hands behind his head and retook the position where his legs spread apart, taking up as much of his seat as he could. I was poor at eye contact, and accidentally peered straight between his legs. I blushed from it, closing my eyes and looking away as quickly as I could.

"It would also please me if you were thinking other things about me." He winked and winced almost simultaneously. I could not help but slightly roll my eyes at his comment.

Hopefully, the only torture I would endure in the eleventh kingdom would be his snide and flirtatious remarks, but that was likely not the case for me. I was being delivered to a master, some higher up who commanded Hiver.

My master calls me Snow.

I heard his voice echo in the back of my mind; that seemed like a sweet nickname, not one a torturous overseer would give, though I could not know for sure.

We then snaked onto a path which sent us further into the densely packed wood. My father told us of this place—that we should never enter unless we wished to be hunted and killed by Tessiah and abandoned children of the damned.

My stomach knotted as we were led us to the heart of a forest so thick the sun could no longer breach the canopy above. I clenched onto my dress, grabbing a fistful of the silk.

The texture was cool and soothing in my hands which were slowly heating from fear.

Just then the carriage felt like it slammed through a hole far too tight for it, and the world around me rippled and tore. The thick forest gave way to lands which ran rampant with wildflowers and fruit trees.

Honeybees and birds swarmed the grounds getting drunk on the fermented fruit and lazing about the vast fields. We had just passed through some sort of a...*portal*. I reached for my chest and stomach, making sure I was still whole since I had just somehow passed through to another dimension—another *world*.

Hiver made efforts to laugh, but he inevitably coughed and struggled from his injuries, which still did not seem to be doing well. I looked out the veiled window frantically, searching behind us for the dense wood. There was only a black mass of rock, which rippled and displayed trees behind the faint sparkle in the middle.

It really was a portal.

CHAPTER
FOUR

Hiver's laughter seemed to dance on the breeze that flowed gently through the cloud carriage. He *did* have a lovely laugh; it was almost like a song which the wind carried to grace my ears. He held a hand to his stomach as he did, as if it would leak through his wounds like they were his mouth.

"So they're right—Castle Sage *truly* outlawed magic? Even ripples?" Hiver laughed, still pressing his palm to his stomach.

"Ripples?" My fingers had yet to let go of my gown, as if I feared my body coming apart in pieces from this *ripple*.

"Is that what you call portals?" I said, lowering my hands to neatly sit on my lap, confident that I would not vanish into the world around me.

"Nah, portals lead to one of the other two dimensions; ripples are *like* a portal which hides something, like this place. Allegedly, the Gods can ripple themselves, though, like teleporting." His calm was unnerving—I did not understand how in his current condition he could manage to remain so unbothered.

"Why aren't you healing?" The words left my mouth before I

could even think about them. Hiver looked me up and down before he responded, "Well, how about this: I'll answer your question if you answer mine." I could feel my cheeks heating with rage.

What could he wish to know from me?

I could offer him no wisdom, no advice, nothing. I could offer nothing other than myself, and he knew it.

"What could you possibly want to know?" The anger rolled off of my tongue, and my eyes narrowed.

He laughed lightly, and his eyes found their way to my thigh. Dragging that gaze back up to my own, he smiled lazily at me.

"I just wanted to know what you thought you were going to do with that blade—that's why you asked about my healing, isn't it? So you could kill me, or rather you could *try*." Hiver maintained that eerie calm as he winked at me.

I could feel my face turning cold—the blood being chased out of my skin by those sharp blue eyes. It was only then I felt the bite of leather against my thigh, the blade Dracar had insisted I hid under my gown this morning. He told me to always stay armed, no matter what.

I reached for it slowly to make sure that it was still there, that he did not use some sort of magic to remove it from my body.

"It's still there," he said, still giving me that lazy smile; he nearly appeared bored. He knew what I was reaching for, knew that I had the blade at all, but how?

"I don't know, should I be trying to kill you? After all, I did hear your schemes of torturing and killing *me*," I shot back at him, hand now on the hilt of the blade strapped to my thigh.

"You can certainly try, you have a good shot to take me all the way down now while I am still injured." He pulled a hand away from his stomach, his hands coated in blood, and held one up to me, that lazy and uninterested look still lingering in his eyes.

"Anyways," he started, lowering his hand back to its place to put pressure on his wounds, "Healing isn't my form of magic, so that would be why I am still bleeding. Also perhaps why it's getting worse…"

He groaned a bit as the carriage wobbled, taking us to an unknown destination somewhere in the vast fields. I had not looked out the window in some time, I instead kept all of my focus on the dying Winter-blessed man who sat before me.

I tried again to stop feeling fear for him…the fear that he may die right here in this carriage with me. I wondered if I should just end his misery now with my blade.

"Are you going to make it?" I said as nicely as I could manage, considering my irritation with his constant remarks.

"Hopefully," he snickered but then hissed from the pain. My mind was swimming with questions, and Hiver did not seem completely unwilling to answer them, so I continued to prod.

"How did you get rid of the Reavari earlier? Did you use magic?" I tried to maintain eye contact with him as I spoke.

"Lots of questions today, huh?" He smiled so sweetly, an invitation—one I was near desperate to accept. He had such an alluring charm that was so difficult to resist, but I had to remind myself of what he was, what he brought me here for.

"Apologies, I only wanted to learn a few more things before my inevitable execution, could you blame me?" He looked at me for a long moment, as if he was carefully crafting a response before speaking again.

"Inevitable, maybe, but I have no doubt you will put up a fight." He smiled and stared back down at my thigh before speaking again, "I am Winter-kissed, so I have illusion magic. A risky game to play —but I personally *like* taking risks." His fiendish smile shone in the morning sun, "What of you, princess? Do you like to take risks?" His eyes trailed again down my body, but I only stared at his eyes—not his gaping wounds or any—*other*—part of him which may grab my attention.

I scoffed at his comment; his flirtation was irritating. But something about his answer felt *wrong*, as if he were lying about how he chased off the beast. I thought it was best to not dwell on it, not now. Instead I would dwell on far more terrible matters…

In the distance I could see it: we were fast approaching a castle constructed of what looked like black glass.

The pillars looked naturally-formed, like obsidian erupted from the earth to reach for the mighty structure which radiated in the sunlight. It looked like it had the same sparkle the portal did, and I felt both awed and disturbed by it.

The castle was so antithetical to the world which surrounded it. It commanded a presence that was undoubtedly as wicked as the master who sat within. The beauty and terror consumed me and made my thoughts swim faster.

I could not fight whoever I was to be brought before, whatever creature instructed me to be purchased, whatever creature now demanded my head on a pike, no doubt.

I felt my heart sink as we neared the magnificent structure. The windows were all stained glass of every color, even colors I could never find a name to describe.

He began to trace small circles on his clouded window as he lazily turned toward me with a sweet smile pulling at his lips. But his smile did not reach his eyes…he was starting to lose consciousness.

"Hiver." I said gently, reaching a hand for him as his eyes slowly closed. He squinted at me and tried to sit up straighter.

"I'll be fine," he said in such a hushed tone I could hardly hear the words escaping his lips. The Reavari nearly ripped him apart, and it was a miracle he survived with his *magic*.

Magic.

It existed, it was very real, and I was seeing the consequences of not having any at all before me as the Winter incarnate sank slowly, barely managing to keep his eyes open.

"What can I do?" I could not stop the panic from escaping on my breath—I was heaving slightly from fear.

He loosed a wet cough and reached both hands to his stomach where the wounds still dripped, the blood blackening.

"I don't think you're going to be okay," I stated. I could not stop myself from reaching for his wounds and helping him to keep pressure on them.

"I will," his lips curled slightly, as if he tried to smile but could not physically bring himself to. I tried to keep calm for my own sake, but maybe also for his.

We continued near the castle, every minute feeling like it stretched into eternity. Hiver's breathing was labored, and he continued to cough and groan from the pain of rasping.

I didn't *want* to kill him, but I did feel like I needed to—the way one would when their arrow didn't kill the deer. I moved one bloodied hand from his wound and reached for my blade; I would kill him here, and I would run. I would run back for the portal—but could I?

Could I even escape this place before guards would hunt me down, not only for the murder of the master's pet, but for being a runaway prize? After all, the master did pay a good deal of money to have me here.

I stopped reaching for the blade and put my blackened fingers back over Hiver's, pushing with a bit more force than what could be considered gentle. I had nowhere to run, nowhere to hide. I would be a fool to think I could kill him and escape.

Gods only know what other horrible creatures lie out in that forest—definitely more than just Reavari. I shuddered slightly at the thought. Hiver's eyes still barely stayed open, and he rested his head completely against the velvet backrest of the carriage.

I could feel him losing grip of his stomach.

"No…no," I breathed, pushing his own hands back onto his wounds. If by chance I could save him, I could create an ally. I could have someone fight for me when the time comes for the noose to be thrown around my neck. He smiled again, but only once, before he was officially unconscious.

CHAPTER
FIVE

"Hiver?" I whispered it at first, but immediately reached for his neck to feel a pulse. I could feel his heart beating, but it was faint. I couldn't know if his heart beat the same way mine did, if it could pound the way mine was now.

"Hiver!" I yelled this time, shaking his shoulders mercilessly with one hand while holding my other to his wounds. It had been a few hours since the attack; it almost seemed miraculous that he held on this long...

I tried to peek out his window. We were closer now, much closer.

No running, no hiding.

I could do my best to make sure someone helped him and made sure he survived. It was the only thing I *could* do. I removed the blade from my leg; its hilt was cool against my overheating skin.

I began to cut my dress into strands to form a tourniquet—I was a fool for not thinking of the idea earlier. I held the blade in my mouth as I tried to tie the strands around his waist.

The silk from the dress was slippery, a horrible material to try to work with in this circumstance.

. . .

"Fuck." I murmured as the silk continued to slip from my blood-soaked hands. I could not even comprehend the amount of blood loss he endured already.

Hiver would die, and even worse, his fate would be brought upon him by his retrieval of a mortal woman. If my doom was not assured already, it was now.

Just as we entered the gold and black gates, I heard voices outside of the carriage.

I couldn't make out what they were saying or even just how close they were. I stayed on the ground between Hiver's legs, holding the wound and praying to the Gods my tourniquet would be enough.

I thought about screaming for help, for *commanding* someone to fix him, but this was not my kingdom. I didn't know what they would do to me if they knew I was in here, so against my better judgment, I held off until we passed through the giant gates.

I waited what felt like hours to reach the portcullis, but it could not have been more than five minutes.

Five extra minutes I allowed him to bleed—allowed him to die.

The moment the carriage halted, I leapt from it, my blade in my hand; I did not think to return it to its sheath before I jumped out.

I was now inherently threatening whoever I would be greeted by, but there was not a soul.

"Someone, please help!" I yelled, trying to resheath the blade. But I quickly discovered I cut the dress far too short, and its attachment to my thigh was now visibly apparent to any onlookers.

"Shit." I nearly cried as I tried to cover the blade with ripped silk. There was no use.

"Open!" a loud thundering voice said from above me, yet I saw no face: no mortals or Tessiah alike. The portcullis screeched terribly as it opened. It felt like it had been carved with the screams of countless innocents who had strolled to their deaths, as I was now.

"Please help." I sobbed now: anger, fear, despair, all coursing through my veins, lighting them on fire just as the sun had earlier today.

I went back into the carriage and checked Hiver's pulse…still there, his unrelenting heartbeat softly thumping beneath his flesh. I sunk down between his legs again, laying a head on his thigh and still pushing on his wounds with my hands.

I felt like all of the strength had left my body. Even if he were my enemy, I did not wish for him to die—not yet, not before he could be useful to my survival.

"Please, please, please," I whispered between frantic sobs; I had to use my blood-soaked hands to wipe the sting away from my cheeks.

Why did my tears hurt so badly? Why did they set my skin on fire?
No matter, *stupid thoughts for a stupid girl.*

It was not my own voice echoing in my mind, but my father's. I could not imagine how he would patronize me for my current state—weak and helpless.

I was always weak and helpless.

Just then, I heard hurried footsteps pounding against the stones. I lifted my head slightly to see if a face would appear in the window.

The carriage did not have any *real* doors, just pieces of cloud that would move freely when the carriage was halted. It was then I noticed the flash of lilac eyes approaching us, golden hair swaying as she ran.

Diana.

I willed myself to stay on the floor of the carriage. I tried to avoid leaping into her arms and squeezing her tightly.

"Snow!" she screamed as she continued to run full force at the carriage.

"No, no, no, no!" She yelled in a hushed tone as she reached us. I reached a bloodied hand for her cheek, and my flesh connected to hers.

"You *are* real." I said in awe and disbelief.

"What happened?" She shot me a look of terror, ignoring my uninvited touch on her cheek, which now had now been smeared in blood.

"A Reavari—I don't know," I said quickly, watching as Diana grabbed his face in her hands.

Confusion was not enough to describe my current predicament—I felt her flesh, so it had to be her, but now I've witnessed the power of illusion magic; could this be someone else posing as her? I couldn't know.

"Diana," I said softly. She ignored me, and instead reached for his body.

"What are you doing?" I asked her while reaching for her hand to stop her.

"Please, Mir." She just stared at me again with begging eyes.

"Help me lift him," she said to me, not daring to make eye contact again. I could not source the despair that gleamed in her beautiful purple eyes.

Was she too purchased by these people? Was she now a slave to whatever master lurked beyond the great walls?

I hoisted Hiver up and draped an arm around my shoulder, and

Diana took his other. Once through the gates, I saw many faces, all staring back in horror at what had been done to Hiver. I realized again my blade was in full view, praying to the Gods these people would not think it was me who carved him up.

I tried to keep my gaze straight ahead and used every bit of my strength to pull him alongside me. I continued passing looks to Diana, whose expression was entirely unreadable.

Diana heaved under his weight but continued to push on. The way she said Snow hung in my mind like the noose which would soon hang from my neck.

She knew everything about me, and yet I was starting to realize I must have known *nothing* about her.

"Diana—I—"

"Please… just—" she huffed, I could hear the fear edging in her tone.

I nodded to her and forced myself to swallow any questions which found their way onto my tongue. I urged myself to wake up from this dream—no—*nightmare* that was unfolding before me. I tried to shake the grogginess of sleep, but alas, I was conscious. I was here, *really here*.

We reached doors fashioned of solid gold, embellished with engravings of two men, each with only a single wing to match what the other was missing, and they held the Earth in their hands.

That is all I was able to make out of them before the doors swung open with a gust of wind; I realized it had come from Diana's hand. She stared straight ahead at the dais, and I turned my face up from the ground to meet a familiar set of sapphire eyes staring at me, unraveling my soul.

Another wave of nausea rolled over me, and I vomited on the floor before us, the rage and sadness all mixing within me. I could no longer stomach it.

. . .

Kaneira sat upon the dais, looking down at us. But her eyes were quickly drawn to Hiver, who was entirely unconscious and being held up solely by Diana as I emptied my stomach out onto the pale blue floor.

It looked like marble beneath me, swirling and cascading like a true ocean, like the sea that was outside of my home—my *old* home.

I fell to my knees and sat there, staring up at the woman whose eyes I could never remove from my mind.

The eyes of a monster, the woman who snapped my mother's neck in front of my brother and me.

"Snow, my sweet snowflake," she cooed, reaching her hands to his wounds. She did not so much as *look* at me, despite being just inches away—*inches*.

I reached for my blade, and before I could even think of my next action, I brought it to her throat from behind her. My hands shook.

"My darling…" she hissed, her voice sounded like coals crackling upon a hot fire. I knew that fire stirred beneath her skin—that it swirled and popped, waiting for her to call on it. I felt the sobs coming up again, and I forced them down with a hiccup.

Diana looked up at me, horror glazing over her eyes. Against my better judgement, I pulled the knife closer to her throat, pushing it just enough to draw blood.

Kaneira held her hands up in the air to keep her guards from approaching me. An animalistic sound escaped my throat as I thought to push the blade all the way in—to end her life here and now, just as she did to my mother all of those years ago.

"Please, do not be stupid, Mirage," she said to me, hands still raised above her head.

"Do you really believe you can escape? You will kill me, then what? Die?" She cackled a bit, the knife pushing into her throat as it bobbed.

"You can kill me, darling. But know it will do you no good." Kaneira's voice went cold, and I could tell she had no interest in playing games with me.

She seemed to only care about Hiver, who I knew was getting worse by the minute—minutes I continued to waste by being a fool. She was right: I could kill her, but to what end? I would be killed immediately, if not hunted down for the rest of my life. I let her go and removed my blade.

She did not turn to me as I released her. Her life was moments from ending in my hands, and her first action was not to condemn me, but to save Hiver.

CHAPTER

SIX

"Lucius!" She yelled, a pain filled her voice, and again, my heart sank as a man appeared at Kaneira's side, clad in robes which must have been fashioned of clouds. His expression was blank as he looked upon Kaneira's face.

His vibrant hair was like fire, his eyes the color of smoke. I had never seen him up close, only heard of how he was a master of many and a slave to none; yet he stood before Kaneira, a loyal servant. It seemed as if he were not fully a part of our world when he first appeared.

His robes and hair looked as if they were just sparkles and nothing more. Over the next several seconds, his body turned solid, like he hadn't been made of dust mere moments before.

"You've summoned me, Kane?" He said to her calmly, as if he did not see Hiver bleeding to death on the floor beside her.

The Stone Mage had a beauty that could only be matched with fire, though he was not a Drakkarias. He was merely a magic wielder, yet he too seemed to embody the devastating fury and beauty that came with stomaching fire.

Lucius.

The man who had helped kill my mother.

"Don't play dumb, Lucius. Help him," she aimed a shaking finger toward Hiver.

"I cannot, Kane; you know that," Lucius frowned now, his hands tucked in his pockets. He continued, "Iit would be foolish to play games with Gods."

Before I could gather any more details, Kaneira whirled around to me, fury sparking in her eyes like flames rage behind them.

"Then *you* will." She grabbed my chin and forced me from my knees next to her. She then grabbed my arm so tightly I yelped, as her long nails sunk into my skin.

I felt a trickle of blood spout from where her fingers dug in. She threw me on the ground next to him, only inches away.

I could not force the tears to stay tucked away any longer, and they fell from my eyes and down my cheeks.

"What— " I started, my sobs stifling my ability to speak. Every breath felt like my last, and I trembled before her. Kaneira then raised her hand to me, flames igniting from her palms.

I could see the power in her eyes, like they were gateways to her blazing soul. It was then she put her palm to my chest, which had not been covered by the red silky scraps that draped most of my body, and searing hot pain coursed through me.

She was burning me—setting me on fire, and I was helpless to fight her off.

I kicked and scratched, reaching for her eyes so I could gouge them with my fingers, but she held me down with a single hand that burned into my chest.

She was not going to make my death quick, but very, *very* slow. I would not be granted my mother's mercy of a quick snapping of the neck.

"Please—please!" I yelled. I tried to pull her hand from my chest, but all my strength could not move her even an inch.

My death was here.

I would die in a room with floors that mimicked the Grandar Sea—*my* sea.

I would soon see my mother, with her doe-like eyes and beautiful smile. I would see her just as she was a decade ago: young and lovely.

However, the pain just raged on and on for what felt like forever. It was then Kaneira removed her fiery hand from my chest, and I reached for the spot, only to feel... *nothing.*

No burns.
No hole.
Just solid skin.

It took everything in me not to empty my stomach again on the great marble floors. I sobbed, tears burning my skin with only half of the heat which emanated from her hands. She stood over me now, her expression a bit crazed as she peered upon my terrified face.

"Lovely," she sighed. Before I could say anything at all, she gripped my hand again and unsheathed my blade. She dragged my arm before Hiver and sliced the blade across it.

The pain radiated from my chest, despite no physical markings—at least none I could see.

She took my forearm and held it to Hiver's mouth, nodding at Diana who then parted his lips, and I watched my blood pool on his tongue.

The tears still rolled insistently, stinging and burning my cheeks, which made the sobbing worsen. I could feel pain all over my body —I could have never suspected this sort of torture.

Through it all, Diana remained utterly silent.

I could not even begin to grapple with the emotions currently coming over me.

I could not tell if I was angry or sad or anxious—my blood was being fed to another being, and the feeling of fire lingered in my chest as I burned from my eyes. I stared at Diana, not even realizing my eyes had been fixed upon her for perhaps several minutes.

The blood spilling out of my wound seemed to cease, and when I looked at where I had been injured, the slash was gone.

I rubbed my eyes aggressively again, trying to wake up from whatever horrible dream I was being forced to endure. I tried to stand, but immediately, I fell to the floor consciousness escaping me.

CHAPTER
SEVEN

T he blackness came to consume me: to either lull me into slumber or carry me into death.

Neither of which I was opposed to.

I woke up in a room that looked...*familiar*. My vision blurred with sage green and light from an entire wall of windows. I could barely keep my eyes open; sleep was trying to overcome me.

This room was not just *slightly* familiar—it had been modeled after my own.

I willed myself not to vomit again.

I knew I didn't even have anything left in my stomach to empty, but the nausea made my head swim.

"What the— " I let the thoughts surface on my tongue, but stopped myself when I noticed her standing there.

I had barely lifted my head from the pillow, propped up on my elbows as I took in the room that was so similar—yet so different from my home.

I noticed those lilac eyes staring at me.

. . .

"Where the fuck am I, Diana?" I didn't mean to snap at her, but my tone held such a venom, and I had coiled up to strike as if I were a scaly beast.

She looked guilty and afraid, like maybe I would lunge at her. Perhaps she deserved it—Gods only know what all she has been keeping from me.

She bowed deeply at the waist when I spoke to her; she was never one to curtsy.

"I wanted you to feel more comfortable here, so I did my best to remember… everything." She spoke with such a gentle tone. It was like hearing the first snowfall of winter.

She had a delicate beauty, and it bled into everything she said and did. She could use frost, a power perfectly fit for her to wield.

I was reeling from the day's events. Perhaps it was my fault that I did not notice her powers; maybe she gave me hints all along. I did not have time to consider it all: every hint, every promise, every single conversation we have ever had.

I had just enough time to ponder the words she said to me this morning, *he will stop it.*

I foolishly thought she meant Dracar—that he would save me from being sold off—but she likely meant Hiver. Was he the one who stopped my inevitable fate? One of being sold off to the Porlend family to be nothing but a body, used for breeding and torment.

My heart could not beat any faster; I feared it would burst out of my chest. And when Kaneira pressed her fire into me, I nearly thought it would…

"You know I didn't—you know what I meant." I started to rise from my bed. I felt fury rising up my throat like fire, and at first I thought to scream, but instead, I chose to interrogate.

"Why did you keep this from me? How long have you known this place was real? How long have you had *powers?*" I spat.

The fury won over any love I had for Diana, and I was now inches from her. I clenched my teeth so hard I thought they would nearly break, but surprisingly, she held my gaze.

She did not tear her eyes away from mine; she merely stared.

"That is a lot of questions, Mir."

I reached for my skin, realizing there were no marks, no scars, no blood—nothing.

"How am I—unscathed?" I asked her, still stroking the unmaimed arm, which, to my shock, was still attached to my body.

"Autumn-Kissed…" Diana began, her eyes trailing to my hair and her fingers following shortly after. She continued her thoughts as her fingers twirled around my curls, "It's your gift." She finished, and before she could remove her hand from my hair, I swatted it down.

I narrowed my eyes as I beheld her standing before me, so unbothered.

"What?" was the only word that I could manage to speak: the only word that would roll off of my tongue without protest. I could not even begin to fathom how that was possible—how it was possible that after *years*, no one could find evidence of magic.

"Kane—"

"I am not going to see her," I said before I could let another thought pass. The woman who killed my mother in cold blood and nearly killed me, too.

"Mir, I know it is complicated—Kaneira was never going to kill you, and she did not just *murder* your mother!" Diana raised her voice. Never, in fifteen years, had I ever heard her yell, especially not at me.

I could not imagine the shock that cast its shadow over my face. Diana's expression mirrored my own when she spoke again, "I am so sorry, I didn't mean to yell." She reached a hand for my arm, and I instinctively pulled away.

I did not know the woman who stood before me; the familiarity of her gentle features began to feel foreign—*she* felt foreign to me. She must have noticed the hurt and mistrust in my eyes, "We *saved* you." The word hung on past the rest of the sentence.

Saved.
Not imprisoned, not tortured, not killed, but *saved.*

Another wave of emotions came crashing over me; it felt like a hurricane was stirring in my mind. I was hurt and scared—I did not know who I could trust here, if anyone.

I smelled the alluring scent of eucalyptus and pine as Diana stiffened and turned toward the door she left ajar.

"Not the time," she said and shot a stream of frost at nothingness. I could smell his magic; I knew he was there, but I saw nothing. When the frost reached about ten feet away, a blue shimmer rippled through the air, and there he was, standing with his hands tucked in his pockets—Hiver.

"How did you—When did you—" I fumbled over the words. I could not even think how to ask. What I was witnessing was far beyond my mortal comprehension.

"What! I wanted to check on our new princess who saved my life. Thank you, by the way," he bowed deeply at the waist. Diana shot another missile of frost at his chest and he stumbled back.

"Ow!" he yelled and hissed at her. She kept her cold and unforgiving gaze on him.

"Princess," he said as he resumed his bow. This time uninterrupted by a fit of frost magic.

I felt flushed.

These people had power, *real* power. Diana could use her frost as a weapon, and Gods only know what Hiver could do. He then disappeared from in front of me entirely, and the scent became overpowering. I hadn't realized I'd inhaled it deeply when he then appeared next to me again, the shimmer casting itself around his figure.

"Hmmm," he smiled, putting a finger under my chin. I jerked it away and could not help the heat rushing to my cheeks.

"You like the smell of my magic, it seems." He purred, circling me like I was prey. I tried to fix my posture, to stand straight. I kept my eyes locked on him as he walked around me.

I did not realize I was reaching for my blade when he grabbed my wrist and pulled it toward my face. He did so with force, but not so much to hurt me.

"It isn't there. Perhaps a skilled huntress would notice the weight of her weapon missing?" He gave me a feline smile and dropped my hand gently, keeping his hand elevated as he held my eye contact.

"Quit it, *Hiver*," Diana spat at him, and the frost began to coat her fingertips. There was a vapor coming off of them, as if the warm air of the room protested the frost she summoned.

"Ouch, the full first name—" He danced around me and whispered into my ear, "That's how you *know* I'm in trouble." He giggled.

It hit me that she too had a scent when she summoned her magic. It was brisk and cool—it smelled like lilacs and fresh apples, a scent which mimicked the color in her eyes.

"Don't you want to know more?" Hiver said to me. His tone was so warm and kind, the antithesis of his cold and winter-coated exterior. He held out his hand and wiggled his fingers, urging me to take it.

It must have been curiosity which urged me to put my palm to his, and all of the sudden, the room around us changed.

CHAPTER
EIGHT

In a flurry of smoke and sparkle, I saw Kaneira sitting in her throne room, Diana and Hiver standing before her.

"I want her *here*, where we can awaken her power. They'll try to kill me if I go to her." Kaneira sighed, putting her hands together and leaning her chin over the top of them.

Her dress was blood red, shimmering in the low light of sunset. If I did not know any better, I would think that she was clad in blood, her dress whispering against the floor as a breeze brushed it against the tiles.

"We can offer some of Hiver's power in exchange for Mirage." Kaneira's smile was wicked, scheming, and cold. Hiver's smirk mimicked hers.

"What?" Diana said with an edge of concern in her voice.

"The power of illusion, *sister*." Hiver appeared and disappeared around Diana, giggling and grabbing her hair until she reached out and grabbed him by the wrist, an unamused expression on her face.

"Ow," he whimpered and rubbed where she grabbed him.

"Knock it off," Kaneira said, rising from the dais and descending the steps toward the two Winter-Kissed. She began to speak again as she approached them, "Snow, what about gold? An irresistible offer and more than what that *despicable* creature needs." She snarled.

                      I was watching the past.
               Hiver was showing me *past* events.

I wiggled from his grasp, and the world around me returned to the familiar room. I felt sick to my stomach, like I had been ripped through space and time. He stood at my side, a look of concern flickering in his eyes.

"Are you okay?" he said to me, putting a hand on my shoulder. His touch was considerate.

I had not realized I'd fallen to my knees.

                      Too much magic.
                      Far too much magic.

I heaved and reached at my chest and head again, as if part of me was left in the past. my body still shimmered, and the blue ripples began to die down as time passed.

He came down to my level, and I felt a primal fear, something I had never experienced in my life.

"This is why I told you *not the time.*" Diana's voice had an edge to it as she spoke. I could make out her silhouette and could see her disappointed posture.

<hr />

I hadn't experienced this kind of fear even in the face of my drunken father, striking a sword down on Dracar, who pulled up his own to push my father off. The clanging of metal rang in my ears as if I were reliving it again.

Fear was a part of my life, a part of *me*. This fear, though, was like nothing else I had ever felt. My entire world could be fake, *an illusion*—a borderline hallucination…

I had no sense of what is real and what is not. The gold my father had been given for me—it was all *fake*.

"He's going to kill you for that," I murmured as I continued to rest my body weight on my knees. My head spun with all of the knowledge I now had: illusion, frost, healing, dragon-fire, and Gods know what else.

Magic of all varieties, beyond what I had ever learned.

What I did know in this new uncertainty was that father would come for Hiver for that stunt.

He would execute him, mercilessly and slowly.

My palms were pushed against the tile, and I noticed they appeared to be smoking. More panic flooded my body, and I pulled my hands up from the cool tile to see the marks of black that smoldered where they had just been.

I screamed.

I could not speak or make another sound; I just screeched. Something had happened to me—*Kaneira* had happened to me.

"What did she do to me?" I managed through the beginning of a sob. I was too afraid to touch my palms to my eyes, to wipe away the tears. I was scared to burn myself as I did the tiles.

I could barely hear Hiver's voice over the ringing in my ears. I vaguely made out him saying *okay*, but hardly anything more. I felt one hand pressing into my chest, and as I looked down, I saw Diana's eyes.

She held my cheeks and stared at me with such concern, and she blew a cool breeze into my face; the last thing I knew was the scent of lilacs and apples lulling me into a deep sleep.

When I woke again, she was at my side, Hiver sitting on my other.

"*Diana,*" I said tenderly, reaching my hand to her, hoping she would take it. She raised her hand but hesitated before sliding it into mine.

"I am sorry," I said to her while stifling a sob.

They either wanted my power or my safety; either one was better than living under the tyranny of my father. If he ever did discover *any* power, he would have surely killed me.

That was a realization I was struggling to grasp.

I had magic.

I'd always had magic, but somehow, knowing made me feel like a different person entirely.

"You're safe here, Mira. We would never hurt you. What Kaneira did —was *fear*. She was running out of time." A tear twinkled in Diana's floral eyes, and she blinked it away before it could run down her face.

"It doesn't justify what she did, though; know that. She'll apologize." Diana said and Hiver stared at her, his head cocked slightly.

He didn't know what happened.
He was unconscious.

Diana shook her head slightly at his questioning gaze, as if to silently shut down any questions he had.

"We are never going to hurt you," Hiver said, offering me his hand to hold too. I realized I had been gripping Diana's fingers so tight my knuckles were whitening. I did not release her, but I did ease my grip.

I put my other hand into Hiver's and gave it a single assuring squeeze. A question rolled to my tongue as I clasped both of their hands, and my eyes shot back and forth from Diana to Hiver.

"You're siblings?" I said, still glancing between the two of them. Diana giggled and began to shake her head.

"No, not by blood," she said sweetly.

Hiver too laughed at the sentiment and said to me, "is that *all* you got from the memory?"

Such a lovely laugh.

"We will take you to see Kaneira tomorrow. Until then, rest, explore, whatever…" Hiver said, patting the top of my hand once before raising himself from the tiled floor.

I watched as he left the room, looking once over his shoulder to give me a sweet smile.

CHAPTER NINE

For a long while I sat in silence—only my thoughts permeating my consciousness until Diana spoke.

"Walk with me?" she asked, offering her arm to link with mine as I rose to my feet. I nodded again.

"What does Autumn-Kissed mean?" I asked her. The words felt so strange leaving my mouth, as if saying them was like invoking a curse.

"Well, you and Dracar were born in autumn. The season you're born in is the season your powers belong to. Autumn-Kissed are rare nowadays." We turned a corner to a vast courtyard: it looked like spring had washed over it, with bright greens and freshly bloomed flowers.

The air was warm and smelled of dirt after the rain. There were those small creatures again, jumping, hopping, singing, dancing on all of the flowers and plants.

"There are four seasons, so four types of Seaura—"

"*Seaura?*" I interjected, not letting her finish before I understood the words she used.

"Yes, Tessiah kissed by a season. Tessiah is an encompassing term to represent all the *Numortalis*—meaning anything not quite human—and anything that is human… is *Mortalis*. So really, there are only two categories: *Numortalis* and *Mortalis*," Diana said, moving her hands to two imaginary piles to illustrate her point.

"So was my mother…*Tessiah*?" I said, turning away from the beautiful courtyard of spring to face Diana.

"Not exactly—Kaneira can tell you more about that, I don't know much of it," she said.

Even though I believed her and Hiver's promises of my safety, it was still difficult for me to stomach being face to face again with the woman who killed my mother and ripped my flesh open without so much as a word to me about it.

Hiver was dying.
She needed to save him.

I tried to reassure myself over and over again, but the thought of my flesh tearing made my skin crawl, and I instinctively reached for the completely unscathed skin that she struck with my own blade. It was healed.

I was okay.

It would take time for that to sink in.

The fact that I sobbed here made my stomach turn over. I was a helpless child, crying in the face of *real* power. How utterly pathetic.

"This place is special—it is blessed ground, which is why all four seasons exist in various courtyards. The Spring Courtyard is to honor the Spring Seaura, and this…" Diana skipped a bit ahead around the corner and eagerly gestured for me to join her; I picked up the pace and trotted behind her.

Before I could fully turn the corner, bits of scarlet lit up the pillars that sat at every corner of the outdoor halls. This place was truly magnificent—it was nearly like a maze, with outdoor corridors that led you past the four season courtyards and tall black ceilings that were laced with glowing purple embers.

The fiery colors which lay just beyond my vision began to become more and more vibrant.

The Autumn Courtyard.

"Oh my Gods," I could not help but breathe the words as I hurriedly approached the center of the courtyard. The sun hung low, but not quite at sunset, and trees of gold and scarlet sprinkled their leaves about the grounds. Creatures that appeared like fireflies danced between the falling leaves.

It was Autumn here, *all* of the time.

It was truly peaceful in this courtyard. The grasses were a soft green: not vibrant like Spring, but more of a sage color like the walls of my room. In the middle of the courtyard, there was a tree of which every color of apple hung, from crimson to yellow.

"Can I eat them?" I asked Diana, unable to hide the amusement and awe in my voice. She smiled softly and nodded. I reached up for one of the apples and plucked one that mimicked the vibrant yellows of the leaves.

Diana began to speak as I brought it to my mouth, "Yes." I felt a twinge of fear sink into my stomach, and I hesitated before biting into the apple.

But it was perfect.
Truly, perfect.

I felt alive as I bit into it, and I started to eat faster. I heard Diana's gentle laughter rising above the whistling of leaves, "The Foi

Saison—that is what we call the fruits of the courtyards—they enhance your power." Diana watched as I devoured the apple.

"We eat them before we need to harness a lot of magic." I began to reach for another, this time a red one when Diana warned, "but you are not to eat too many—they can, and *will,* drive you mad." She approached me and gently pulled my hand back down from the tree, where I stood anticipating the feeling of the red apple's crunch beneath my teeth.

⁂

This place enchanted me; it made me feel a way that was pleasantly unfamiliar. *This* was the promised kingdom my mother told us of… The eternal Autumn…

Diana led me from the Autumn Courtyard and looked back at me cheerfully as every sparkle and shine caught my eye in the corridor.

"We are coming to my favorite, obviously." She said as we turned yet another corner of the vast outdoor labyrinth. I hadn't realized how quickly she'd begun moving toward her next destination, and I was practically sprinting to keep pace with her.

The cold of the courtyard brushed across my cheeks—the scent of fresh pears and a floral aroma seeped into my nose flushing my lungs. It was an intoxicating scent, the kind that could draw you in— drive you mad.

The courtyard had a far different layout from Autumn. It appeared to be endless. I imagine I wore my awe and confusion on my face as Diana turned and gave me a wide smile. It was a smile I had not seen in a while: not polite, not subtle, but a smile which reached her eyes and caressed those lilac irises.

"Why does this place go on… forever?" I stumbled over the words.

"It is snowsmoke—or the power of illusion—a Winter-Kissed Gift. The courtyards are spell-bound by the varying elements; it is what makes them feel… *alive.*" Diana sucked in a large breath before she finished her statement and led me over to a bush with a fruit on it. They appeared to be frosted cranberries.

This courtyard had many more fruits—*Foi Saison*—than Autumn. I reached out to touch a cranberry so delicately frosted by the power of the courtyard, and to my surprise, it stung me. The frost snaked its way up my fingers, and I panicked and wagged my hand.

"Ah, yes, you can't eat the fruits of other seasons," Diana smiled sweetly at me as I gripped my wrist and stared at her through wild eyes. I felt a dread coming over me—even if my skin did break, it would heal.

I would heal.

I tried to push the thought back and continued to take in the beauty of the Winter Courtyard when I spotted the familiar white hair, speckled with perfect streaks of black.

He sat on the ground with two younger boys, one with black hair, the other with pure white, and made them giggle by using his magic to make things disappear at his touch. He laughed with them and continued to take berries and pears and make them vanish into thin air.

I could smell him—even from all of this distance. It made my olfactory bulb sing—I was fully consumed by the scent, every part of me craving it. The stranger, the *friend*, the nearly dead—his scent was intoxicating and all I wanted was *more*.

Diana noticed me staring and began to speak, "We all have markers of our magic—for some it's hair, for some it's eyes, for some it is markings on the skin…" I stared into her eyes, those beautiful lilac irises, they definitely seemed magical.

I turned to face Hiver again, who was now alone, the young boys nowhere to be seen. I felt my brows furrowing as I stared at him, curiosity gnawing at me. I wasn't sure what it was that had propelled me to know more, but I had to know him intimately. Instead I decided to hound Diana with more questions.

. . .

"Why didn't you tell me about this place? Why didn't you tell me this is where you would sneak off to?" I asked her.

"I couldn't. It was too dangerous for you to know, especially without your powers. I feared that your father could torture that sort of information out of you, either with Dracar or otherwise…" She said to me in a hushed tone. I could tell it hurt her to lie to me for so long: to leave out details of such a magical place.

"Why didn't I have power back home?" I asked her.

"I'm not entirely sure. Kaneira told me that some Autumn magic can only be awakened through sunfire." I stared at her with utter bewilderment. She pursed her lips before continuing, "The Drakkarias are God-Born, meaning they all have the same father—Olym—and sunfire in their veins." Diana had an encyclopedic knowledge of the Tessiah, at least from my perspective.

I was relieved by her candor but still so wildly hurt and sad that she ever felt she needed to lie. I would *never* betray her.

But I know she would never forgive herself if she shared this place with me, and I for some reason told my despicable father of it. He would destroy this place—slaughter these people and not think twice.

My heart ached at the thought, sinking further when I imagined Dracar at home and in the presence of the cruel king—the man who would take every chance to destroy anything beautiful.

"What exactly are *your* gifts?" I fully faced Diana now, almost expecting a demonstration. A wild sparkle caught her eyes as she met mine, and she brought her hand up between us; at her fingertips, she generated frost.

"Winter-Kissed can have any two of the four abilities—snowsmoke, snowcloak, frost, and ikeer. Snowsmoke is the power of illusion; it is Snow's—*Hiver's*—only known gift. He is the only one we know of that was not granted two." I nodded at her comment and peered back at Hiver, who was sitting beneath a willow tree nearly half the size of the other giant willows that surrounded it.

"Snowcloak," she began again, "is called a wraith power. It allows me to become fluid—to pass through objects. It is not an ability you can use on animate things—like people." She paused as if to allow me to digest the information.

"I have snowcloak and frost, so I can create frost with my hands and disappear as I wish. But I cannot pass through people, only inanimate objects." She wiggled her fingers to expose some of the frost that formed on them before continuing, "Finally, the ikeer: it is an incredibly rare magic and hasn't been seen in decades. *Ikeer* is the power to reanimate the dead by binding them to ice…the *keer* form is stronger than normal flesh, but their memories and emotions are fractured. The more corpses you reanimate… the more damaged *your* mind becomes." Diana's face went solemn, but the spark of intrigue still danced in her soft purple eyes.

I was stunned. I knew nothing of their magic, the Winter-Kissed, or any of the other Seaura's powers.

"So that's how you managed to gather the gossip of the kingdom under everyone's noses?" I teased for a moment, trying to push aside the anxiety that began to grip my throat.

"Indeed," she smiled softly. If anyone was capable of easing the tension in my chest, it was Diana.

"What of Autumn's other powers?" I said, taking a seat on a grand white bench, which had beautiful red swirls that shimmered in the pale moonlight hanging above us. Diana sat beside me.

"Autumn, like all the others, has four—regeneration, unflinching, blacoeur, and fire." Diana paused for a long moment and stared at me: first at my eyes, then at my hands.

"You appear to have regeneration and fire. The version of regeneration you have is special—it is called *elixirium*." She said the word with such awe on her tongue.

"What is *elixirium*?" I asked, almost cautious of the question.

I feared it was dangerous: that I—I was dangerous.

"It means your blood can heal others, an exceptionally rare power. Kaneira knew you had it, but how she knew, I dunno," Diana shrugged.

"You *will* have to see her," she started, her expression vacant of any discernible emotion, "She can tell you everything I cannot. I don't have all the answers, but I've given you every single one I can." Her eyes returned to that lavender sea, storming over her irises. She could crush me with her stare alone.

I felt myself shrinking under her eyes—her scrutiny, her judgment—I ignored her piercing gaze and instead asked her another question, "What is *blacoeur*?" Diana's cold gaze softened, and she let out a giggle.

"Black-*core*, not blac*ker*." She loosed another small laugh. "It is also sometimes called *black heart*, a dark power—the first that was discovered in the Autumn-Kissed..." she trailed off, and I could sense a nervousness coming from her as she spoke.

"It allows you to puppeteer other *things*, using their blood—it can and *will* kill you." She let out a sigh, a tension loosening as she did, "It is one of the four dark magics."

"There's a dark magic in every season, isn't there?" I could feel my eyes widening at the thought. Dark magics, the kind that could kill you from the inside out.

The irreparable injury—an injury to the mind. It terrified me.

"There is, but no worries, even those who have it choose not to use it." Diana spoke softly, reaching for my hand, her silver robes glittered in the moonlight. She looked as if she was clad in starlight, covering her pale arms and legs; the fabric barely seemed real as it swayed in the soft breeze.

Diana herself was human starlight: soft and elegant, fierce and fiery.

"I think that is enough history for the day; I'm going to retire to my chambers. Do what you wish, Mira. You are *no one's* prisoner." She reached down and squeezed my hand gently, then turned to give me a deep bow as she exited the Winter Courtyard, her dress of starlight brushing the frosted ground as she walked.

I had always wanted to be like her—to hold myself with her grace, to speak with her kindness—but we were *so* different. I continued to watch her as she left, the snow falling gently on my hair and skin. I blinked furiously when the snowflakes found themselves tangled in my eyelashes.

I had never experienced snow.

I thought about how Dracar would react to it—the icy flakes that fell from the sky…I thought about the powers Diana had told me of. I heard of unflinching as a girl: the power to not feel pain.

A ridiculous power—one that would surely get you killed. I was glad I could feel, even if it was painful. The pain is what anchored me, made me feel that I was truly alive, as opposed to a puppet for my father to beat—but I did not take much of the beating, it was mostly Dracar.

I stared out at the slow snowfall, entranced by the cold droplets as they fell. This was a hard reality to grasp—certainly not the one I spent two decades becoming accustomed to. I put my head into my hands and rested my arms on my knees, my elbows biting into my thighs. I thought I would start to sob, but then the sting of Hiver's magic danced in my nostrils.

I inhaled deeply: it was such a *wonderful* scent…

"You look distressed," he frowned down at me. I gazed up to meet his eyes—bright blue, like the sea, and they stirred with concern as he looked down on me.

"I could not imagine why," I said to him sarcastically, the frost still tickling my eyelashes as it slowly drifted down from the darkened sky.

"She jokes!" he said excitedly as he took a seat beside me. I continued to look forward, but I could feel his eyes on me. I could feel my cheeks heating up.

"She *blushes*," he followed up, and I turned to face him to find a smirk drawing up the corners of his lips.

I knew then that it *definitely* was not magic heating my cheeks.

I gave him a quick smile, unsure of what else to even say. I felt a sensation of which I was unfamiliar. A craving would be the right word, but I have never felt it for another person the way I do with Hiver. It was bizarre—I had hardly known him, yet every time I smelled his magic, I became further enchanted.

"Did you see all of the courts, then?" Hiver said, fully facing me now. I shook my head; I had not yet seen Summer, nor did I know of Summer's powers, or Spring's for that matter.

"I take it you may want to finish my tour?" I began to rise from the bench. I was now looking down at him. He smiled at me and rose to stand several inches above me; he was merely a foot away.

I was breathing his air, and I could feel his warmth in the cold of the courtyard. He stared down at me for a few moments longer before taking to my side and offering his arm.

"Do you spend most of your time in Winter?" I asked him.

"I do." He turned to face me as we strolled about the frosted land.

"You have an incredible power," I smiled at him, a genuine smile: I meant what I said. He returned a thankful grin, and we wandered for a few minutes in silence. I took in the vast expanse of the Winter Courtyard—its magnificent smells, sounds, and feels.

I could smell others' magics as they used them, but no scent was the same, all different fragrances; in some I smelled roses—spices in others—an incredible mixture.

"Does my magic have a scent?" I asked him.

"I don't know—when your magic was being used, I was unconscious." He stared off into the rolling hills of frosted lavender and beautiful willow trees that lay in the distance.

"I did not expect Winter to have so much lavender. Why does it?" I reached down and crushed the frosted petals in my hand. A delicious aroma escaped from the purple dust.

"I assume it's because lavender needs frost in order to grow." He joined me in my petal crushing. After a beat of silence he spoke again.

"I assume you will start training tomorrow," he said as the purple dust flowed from his hands. I shot him a glance.

Training? Why would I need training?

I then allowed my thoughts to breach my consciousness as I spoke them to Hiver. He cocked his head to the side as if he almost did not understand my question.

"Why *wouldn't* you get training? You have magic…"

"I suppose…but why train it?"

"So you don't kill everyone and burn the place down." He replied.

"So what has training taught you?" I teased, and his face lit up. I was greeted by the pleasant fragrance of his magic, and he pulled me into him, putting a hand just under my throat onto my chest. I felt like I was being sedated, like the world around me no longer mattered—that I would drift off into a state of unconsciousness at any moment. It was an eerie sense of calm draping over me like a soft blanket. It was as if…nothing mattered…

He could make me *feel* things—he was capable of psychological *warfare*.

"I'm not going to hurt you, you know—just showing you my power." He shrugged and placed his hands into his pockets. I was breathing erratically.

These *people* could take so much from me—most importantly, my autonomy.

"I'm sorry," he spoke gently, regret settling in his eyes which were previously sparkling with excitement. He began to turn on his heels and walk away.

Despite his invasive method of showing me his capabilities, I was not yet ready for him to leave. I think it was apparent he was not trying to hurt me or kill me, but it was still in my favor to be cautious.

"Take me to see the other courts," I breathed. I was surprised he could hear me, but he stopped and peered just barely over his shoulder before snapping back around to me and offering me his arm to intertwine with my own.

We exited the frosted landscape and set out for the Summer Courtyard.

CHAPTER TEN

"Summer's four magics are mostly elemental—water, earth, and air—but the fourth, and most dangerous, is *desicara*." Hiver led me around a large corner in view of the Summer's courtyard... it was breathtaking.

There were flowers of every color that accentuated walkways made of bricks, and there was what appeared to be an ocean in the distance. It had a similar effect as Winter, somehow feeling endless. I was sure it ended out at the sea, which shimmered in the sunlight.

It was brightly colored and so animated. Similar to Winter, there were many people and children—milling about, playing, laughing—in a beautiful harmony. In every courtyard I was struck with awe, the beauty and wonder of it all: a place that could have every single beauty that this world had to offer, and it was safe from humans and their hateful souls.

My once hateful soul.

"*Desicara* is the power to drain water from things that they touch—including people. They could desiccate someone with the brush of a hand, but the consequence is that they too will wither over time." He physically shuddered at the thought.

"What a terrible power." I couldn't help but shudder as well as the words left my lips.

Who would want to desiccate themselves just to desiccate another?

Perhaps I had no idea what true hatred was—and what it was capable of. The three dark magics I had been told of were truly terrible indeed, each causing great damage to the user and the victim.

I could not imagine wielding such power—being torn apart from within. My mind was my temple, my sanctuary, and I could not fathom destroying it.

We walked for a while in silence, following the path down near the sea. I tried to take in all of the sights and sounds: the water swayed obediently at the hands of young Tessiah who were no doubt blessed with the power to wield water.

Children played with one another and used their magic to splash their friends. It was a beautiful sight, and one I was certainly not used to. In my kingdom, the children were fearful and hesitant; they did not play freely and laugh and sing as these children did.

In the tenth kingdom, the Tessiah were hunted, raped, and murdered. They were made examples of, their heads spiked in front of the castle. No magic was to be wielded in the tenth, and my father made sure of it.

Legions of soldiers were deployed to see to it that magic was punished, enacting whatever heinous crimes they saw fit before capping things off with a gruesome end.

A wave of relief washed over me since I now sat several hours from the wicked kingdom I had once called home. I no longer faced the guards who cast predatory and hateful glares at me as I walked past them.

A terrible place... with terrible *humans*. Apparently, I was never among them: never a human, never the person I'd believed I was...

⁂

There was a long stone edge that sat above a small body of moving water. I took a seat on it and stared out at the flowing gardens of flowers and fruits—so many fruits. A peach tree hung over me.

I could hear whispers beckoning me to take the fruit from the branch: whispers that became so loud I could hear them echoing inside of my soul.

> *Bite the flesh, cure the crux,*
> *Inside the depths the Clariflux.*
> *Cer undar veris, yaru da payer*
> *For truth, you become the soul's betrayer.*

It sang in a beautiful tune and spoke again... and again. Hiver milled about behind me, gathering rocks to skip into the waters on the other side of the walkway.

I did not speak the tongue of the Tessiah, the ancient language they used hundreds of years ago.

I hardly even noticed the peach I now held in my hands. It was soft to the touch, and the song became louder now, shouting at me, yet maintaining its beautiful, sweet tune.

I could not control it.
   I could not stop myself from bringing the fruit to my mouth.
   I bit into it.

It hummed a tune into my ears, a tune so delicious I nearly tasted it on my tongue as I did the peach. It was delightful and juicy.

KINGDOM OF THE SUN

Clariflux pour dar soluar.

It finally said to me, and all of the whispers stopped. The tune it hummed ceased to drum in my ears. It was entirely silent, and before my vision went black, I could hear Hiver's voice—his sound getting closer, his footfalls becoming quicker.

"No! Mirage!"

The world fell black, and all of the sudden I was consumed into a vision. It felt like a memory, hazy and cloudy.

I heard voices, but I could not assign them to people; I could not assign faces to the commotion, but then it all surfaced.

I was staring back at myself, except I was ten years younger, terrified—shaking and crying. I saw my mother's limp body before me. Her eyes were gently closed by Kaneira's fingertips, something I did not remember as a child.

I sat on the ground, screaming and crying. My father had fallen to his knees just a few yards from my mother's body, tears welling in his cold eyes.

He did not love much, but he *did* love my mother.

He loved her dearly. She was all he cared for—if he truly cared for anything aside from himself at all. She seldom left the castle walls, and she became thinner and paler with each year of our lives.

My father was convinced we were driving our mother to sickness: that *we* were somehow responsible for her slow decay. I saw flashes of other moments clouding the vision, images of my mother touching portraits of her and a woman whose face I could not make out. I watched my mother's fingers trace the dark contours of the woman's skin... her black thick hair. Then, I saw her pulling back the floorboards and rifling through a book.

I caught her once as a child, secretly flipping through the pages of the leather-bound tome. The images came too quickly for me to understand them.

I was snapped back into the vision—a vision of being whisked away by Dracar into a rather small gangway between castle walls. He wiped his tears before they could touch his cheeks, and he silently begged me to come swiftly.

I was completely petrified.

I was reliving that day—that terrible day...

My mother passed us a brief smile, one that held both pain and promise, and her gaze dropped as she looked to the ground. In her final moments, all she saw was the stone beneath her.

More flashes of images passed through my consciousness, and in those images, I could hear a shrill scream from my brother, and I felt a pressure of a hand on my chin, "I will be back for you, my dear—just not yet."

I heard the voice of the peach again, gentle and lovely,

The cost of truth, the lover's oath,
A fate together which binds you both,
No longer choose your own desire,
The betrayed heart, reforged through fire.

A symphony of whispers began to rise as the voice concluded its statement, urging me to open my eyes, and in a moment I was back in reality.

My eyes strained from the bright light of the Summer Courtyard. I sat up slightly to see Hiver sitting beside me, my head rested on his thigh. My eyes fluttered for a moment, struggling to focus on the world around me, and the voices halted as my eyes fully opened.

His concerned face loomed over my own.

"What did you see?" was his first and only question. For the first time, he did not immediately ask me if I was well.

"No concern about my well-being suddenly?" I sat up slowly, my head aching from the voices which pounded on the sides of my skull.

"Did you *really* believe you were eating regular peaches just now?" a wicked grin spread across his lips.

"Tell me Mirage, how many peaches have you consumed that sang you a pretty little song? Hm? Bidding you to sink your teeth into it—*begging* you to?" He spoke to me with a sarcastic tone and loosed a brief laugh.

He hovered a hand over my cheek, as if he wished to touch it. I couldn't help but scowl. I shot up and stormed out of the Summer Courtyard. Whatever answers he had were not worth being belittled by him for.

I heard him rise behind me, no doubt to follow me. I did not stop; I did not turn around.

"Mirage." He caught me after a full sprint and grabbed my arm. I whirled around angrily to see his face: it was unreadable.

"Don't run from me," he panted, disappointment gleaming in those eyes. I grimaced as he held me, but I didn't pull away.

"I'm tired." I said softly, and he gave me a half-hearted smile.

"Tonight you sleep…*but*…tomorrow night is the Solarian Ball." He said cheerfully.

"What is that?" I questioned, wondering what party was going to be had and why.

"Tell ya later, there's still so much to see!" Hiver said, excitement twinkling in his sapphire eyes.

Diana wandered into the courtyard, a soft smile pulling her lips.

"I've been looking for you, I wanted to ask if you'd like us to draw you a bath?" She gave Hiver a glare of warning.

"We're busy," he replied, linking arms with me, making my cheeks heat.

"He will exhaust you if you let him," Diana teased.

"You are bitter because you're no fun." Hiver then gave her a vulgar gesture. Diana met it with a scowl.

"Ready?" He held out a hand to me, his grin wide and wild.

"Actually," I started with a smile, "I think I *would* like a bath." I frowned down at the clothes with dried blood that stuck to them.

"Fair choice," Hiver said, giving me a curt nod and bowing deep at the waist before kissing my knuckles and leaving the courtyard.

CHAPTER
ELEVEN

The scent of roses and chamomile wafted up from the warmth of the tub. Chamomile was my favorite tea back home; I drank it nightly, and Diana nearly always accompanied me.

I inhaled it deeply, and the more of it that entered my lungs, the deeper my heart sank. I thought again of Dracar, then of those wild visions and images I saw in the Summer Court. It almost felt like a nightmare, with the sights and sounds moving far too fast to understand.

I sank into the tub.

The water was waving back and forth at my chin, and I decided to go completely under. The water felt softer than back home. It was tinted a pinkish color, like it had been dyed with rose petals. It felt so warm and clean against my bloodied skin.

When I popped back up, I decided to try the word on my tongue —the word that was currently plaguing me.

"*Clariflux*," I said aloud as I splashed the water onto my body to clean it, contemplating the fruit and its cryptic visions.

I didn't even want to begin to imagine the consequences of eating such a fruit, but my mind felt intact, and I physically felt okay, so I tried to hold on to some sort of relief.

The further time strayed from the moment I consumed the Clariflux, the less of the memory I retained. I was starting to forget how the voice sounded. It was both cruel and comforting, like ice that melted to the touch.

She had an edge to her—a confidence I could not place. I could no longer find the voice; I could only remember the words she spoke, *"I will be back for you, my dear—just not yet."*

Who would come back for me? Why would they come back for me?

There wasn't a single logical thought that could point me in the direction of the woman—no—man? Person? I had lost their voice entirely. I had already forgotten what it even sounded like.

"Fuck." I threw my head back against the tub, immediately regretting it as pain surged through my skull. I growled at the sensation of stabs shooting down my neck. I sunk back down into the water; it was starting to become cold. Surely, now would be a good time to summon the burning that scorched the floor previously.

I hadn't a single clue how to conjure it—the fire that was hot enough to char but not to ignite my skin. I put my hands under the hardly lukewarm water and tried to focus on the feeling of the cold surrounding my hands. I had no idea how to surface the flames, but I could try.

Nothing.
No flames, no heat, nothing.

I tried to feel sadness, anger, fury—whatever emotion could elicit a strong enough reaction to encourage the fire to rise to my palms.

I thought of my mother's neck cracking, I thought of Dracar holding the blade to Hiver's throat, I thought of him patrolling my chambers at night to ensure I was safe.

I felt it all.

I felt the pain and suffering mixing into one. I closed my eyes and felt my hands floating in the water. All of the sudden, heat rushed forth from my hands and forced the water to shoot from the tub. A large splash fell onto the tiles, and I let out a loud shriek.

I could hear the patter of running steps coming closer to me. I feared how loud I had been—loud enough to alert someone of my self-testing.

"Mirage?" Diana's concerned voice echoed over the wooden door.

"I— " I started looking back down at my unscathed hands and then to the puddle beside me, "I'm fine."

I started to rise from the tub and reached for a soft robe the maids had left for me before they finished drawing the bath.

"I'm coming in." Diana's voice came through the door muffled, and I could soon hear her fiddling with the handle. We had been raised together from age five.

She was taught to care for me, to dress me, to love me; it was her job, and she did it well. She was a best friend that I was practically given—better, a sister.

She burst into the room, a judgmental look on her face, and sunlight came rushing in behind her. I had nearly forgotten it was daytime. I looked at her and smiled briefly as her eyes fell to the puddle on the floor.

"What's that?" she looked quizzically to the water that glittered on the black and gold tiles of the bathroom floor.

"Nothing."

I lied.

She knew I had lied.

She crossed her arms and looked me up and down, an expression I had grown used to in the last fifteen years.

"I tried to use my magic," I confessed, and before I could say another word, she immediately countered me with "Don't try again." This time, her words were cold instead of comforting. She was genuinely upset with my confession.

"Why?" I squeezed my hair to remove the water from it. I didn't expect her to scold me for attempting to use my magic.

"It's dangerous. *We'll* teach you how to use your magic. You may heal, but that doesn't mean others do." She cast a gaze down at my hands, which I was using to fasten the robe around my waist.

"*You* also still feel pain." She again gave me that disapproving look that she saved for moments like these.

"I was just— " Again, before I could even finish, she said, "We will teach you."

I simply nodded; I didn't want to fight her any further on it.

"Let me know if you need anything, Mir." Diana shot me a look that indicated that there would be consequences if I tried to use my magic again. She then turned on her heels and exited the room.

I noticed that her clothes had drastically changed since we came here—she dressed like royalty. She was always beautiful, always dressed in impressive robes provided to her by the palace. She was a woman of shadow, a ghost, somehow never noticed and never seen.

Here, though, she *sparkled*. She was always clad in robes and dresses that glittered in the sunlight. An unearthly aura surrounded her; she was the moon and stars in human flesh—well, not *quite* human.

I stared at the tub before I pulled the plug from the drain. I decided to stop wasting thoughts on the voice that spoke to me all those years ago. Instead, I thought about the Solarian Ball.

KINGDOM OF THE SUN

I had been to a few balls in my life, but we were not allowed to celebrate the Solstice; my father claimed that it was a Tessian holiday where they sacrificed humans to their Gods.

I knew the Summer Solstice was coming, so I could only assume that's what the Solarian Ball was for. Most of my beliefs about these people from my upbringing were false, so I can assume they *didn't* sacrifice humans as my father claimed.

Or perhaps they did and I was to find that out firsthand.

I thought about sneaking back home. Taking a carriage during the Ball and going to see Dracar, maybe even convincing him to come with me.

I exited the bathroom and paced beside my bed. I would need a plan, and a very good one at that to not only escape this place, but to survive the journey to palace. I knew it wasn't far—it only felt like a few hours passed with Hiver in the carriage. It was a terrible idea, but then again, something told me staying *here* was too.

Then I felt my stomach begin to rumble. They said I could parade about this place freely; I didn't need a chaperone—maybe I didn't need one to eat either. I decided to put on one of the dresses Diana likely left in the wardrobe.

I spent my entire life being royalty, being dressed like I was royalty, I thought I had seen every fabric, every pattern, and every texture under the sun. Yet, as I stared into the large cherry-wood wardrobe, I knew I had seen nothing.

I reached for the dress that jumped out at me the most: a scarlet, red, and yellow fire weaved into fabric. It shone, and the flames of it rippled in the midday sunlight that stretched across the great floors.

These were not dresses—they were *art* in the form of beads, glitters, and cloth. I let a sound of awe climb out of my throat, and my eyes widened at the many outfits that shimmered in the wardrobe. This palace—this kingdom—had many treasures: both within the walls and out.

"Wow," I said softly as I caressed the fabric flames that gripped the bodice of the firelit gown. Most of the clothing in the wardrobe was fashioned around the elements, with a strong emphasis on fire. I then thought about how Diana was constantly clad in what appeared to be starlight; she dressed like her season—like her *power*.

Hiver was typically clad in forest colors, hues of dark green and black, with his white hair and blue eyes always accentuating his otherwise dark appearance. I continued to rifle through the dresses, in awe at every single one. I had three in my hands, all lovely. Some fashioned of flame, some fashioned of a color that resembled blood.

The crimson dress was a thick and soft velvet, adorned with black glitter that ran about the bodice like veins under the bloody velvet skin. I couldn't imagine how these dresses were even made—with colors I could not describe and precision that was supernatural.

The beads—*the beads*—I investigated further and put them between my fingers. They weren't beads at all; they were *real* jewels.

Rubies adorned the dress of fire and flowed all the way down the center of the dress, cutting through the colors of flames.

"*Holy shit,*" I whispered to myself as I investigated the gems. I noticed black guardite—the most expensive gem on Earth. It glittered on the blood-red dress, making up all of the veins. Black guardite had an immortal sparkle—it was a gem associated with the Gods.

How much money do these people have?

I thought to myself as I continued to gawk at the black jewels that glimmered with traces of red in the sunlight.

After a while of staring at all the gowns and jewelry, Diana bursted into the room, and began to comb through my hair. She told me more about this place and its inhabitants, and how divine the food was.

I was *starving*.

Once she had felt satisfied with the work of my hair, she proposed we get some lunch. I nodded and followed her out of the room, and I was beyond eager to eat something.

CHAPTER
TWELVE

There truly was no end to the wonder of this place. We entered a great hall that had wooden tables and benches all around it. The walls were dark, and the lighting was a warm white that scattered around the room. The lighting was soft, like that of candles, and the smell of fresh bread and fruits warmed the air.

Hunger began consuming me from the inside out, and I quickened my pace. There were tables of freshly prepared food at the front of the room, many Tessiah milling about, eating, laughing, and chatting with one another.

Plenty of them bowed as we passed—it took me a moment to realize they were not bowing for me, but Diana.

"You're a *princess*," I breathed. I felt so foolish at that moment. She smiled sweetly to me and said, "Not really, but since I am Kaneira's, people will treat me like one." She nodded a bit.

Diana's heart was truly made of gold, and it shined through every part of her.

I started approaching the table, which was covered with the best food I had ever seen. Then a man who looked slightly familiar turned and stood in my path. I slowly raised my gaze to his, and he stared back down at me with a predatory smile.

"The princess," he said with a biting venom in his voice. I took a step back and instinctively reached to my side, where there was no longer a knife sheathed. His hair was close to the color of wine; strands of it hung to frame his face, but the rest was tied up.

He had vibrant golden eyes that nearly made me uncomfortable to look into for too long. Something about him felt…off, so I refrained from saying a word, when Diana stepped beside me.

"Get out of the way, Jesper," she said sharply, moving a hand to push him gently aside, but he grabbed her hand and shifted his wolfish gaze to her, a sinister smile spreading across his cheeks.

"What if I don't?" he asked, still smiling down at her. She pulled away hard, and I watched the frost gather at her fingertips.

"Then I'll *make* you," she said coldly, a tone I never heard her use. She was angry. I started to get the sense that this man was not a good one.

"Don't you want her to know her people? You can't hurt me—not here, anyways," he snickered before waving his fingers a little bit, and a few droplets of blood swirled around them.

"You would lose if you tried," he sneered again before splatting the small bit of blood on her face. She hissed at him and grabbed my arm to drag me away.

He quickly pulled me back and whispered, "Hello little firebird," He cooed smiling at me sweetly. His grip was oddly gentle as he wrapped his fingers around my bicep.

I jerked away and followed Diana to the food table.

"What is his problem?" I turned to Diana, who was still seething; her face had turned pale.

"*Jesper*—he's also Autumn-Kissed," she said quickly, appearing exasperated by the conversation. I stared at her, as if silently urging her to tell me more.

That was why he looked familiar: we had passed him upon entering the Autumn courtyard. I was curious to know more about him—if he had power like mine.

"He is a blacoeur user—cursed with the '*black heart*' as the Tessiah call it. He uses blood as a weapon…" Diana closed her eyes, and I could see a quick shiver shoot down her body.

"Why is he allowed here then?" I questioned further.

"He's useful sometimes, but just a terrible pain in the ass. Just stay away, please?" Diana turned to me. Her plate was loaded with fried turkey, cankerberries caramelized in lime sauces, and strawberry pattisaire. I stared down and nearly felt the saliva falling from my mouth.

"I am going to take a seat; join me once you've gotten your fill," she said before facing away from me and greeting a group of Winters that sat nearby.

I looked at the massive array of foods. Cankerberries were banned in the tenth kingdom for being associated with the Gods, but they were delicious little fruits that only came from Ekelwood trees.

My father burned down every Ekelwood tree within one hundred miles of our home because they were a beacon of unity and mortality for the Tessiah. They would gather around them to pray for their dead and to celebrate the inevitable—our end…

I decide to grab exactly what Diana had taken. We only had pattisaire for holidays—it was a soft and flaky pastry that was both glazed and stuffed with fresh strawberries and cream. It was a delectable dessert that I deeply missed, as the last time we had it was at Mother's mourning rites.

I searched for Diana in the sea of people—so many *normal* people—all with powers that were beyond my comprehension. They laughed and smiled with one another and made the atmosphere warm with their joy. The people of my kingdom were frequently grim, typically terrified of my father's next stupid and usually cruel action.

I saw hair that was white, and gold, and black, and red—even some that shone a deep blue. The markings of these people were so noticeable, it made me shudder thinking about how my father's guards would kill them for just that alone.

I felt so wrong amongst these people, these people I deeply misunderstood for so long. I felt like a predator to them—that I embodied all the prejudice and hatred directed toward them.

Diana could tell me that I belonged here and belonged among them, but I was not sure I would ever truly feel that way.

I eventually spotted her sitting at a table in a far corner. She sat with two men: one who had blood red-colored hair with black streaks and another who had bright white hair with beautiful sage eyes.

I smiled at them before sitting. The boy with the deep red hair smiled at me, his greenish black eyes following his lips in its upward motion. Diana motioned to him first.

"This is Stygian; he is also Autumn–Kissed." He rose from the table to take my hand and shook it warmly, placing his other palm on top as he grinned.

"It is lovely to meet you, Mirage," he said before sitting back down. I then locked eyes with the other one whom I did not recognize, a deeply beautiful man who seemed as lethal as he was alluring.

"This is Natsu. He is Summer–Kissed," Diana said. He also rose to shake my hand and lightly kissed my knuckles. He then bowed before sitting back down on the bench.

"It's lovely to meet you both." I smiled and bowed my head. Diana's smile was wide and chaotic, and she stood from her chair to greet another woman who came sulking over—her hair was night black, and her eyes were a terrifying shade of blue.

I felt like she could devour my soul with just her gaze. She was like a black hole—the personification of a star collapsing in on itself. She held the kind of beauty that would strike fear and awe in the eyes of the beholder… and that was I.

"And this!" Diana began as she pranced up to her side; the woman locked her gaze onto mine, fear and curiosity dancing in her icy blue eyes.

"Is Samira!" She sat her down beside me.

"It's lovely to meet you, Samira," I said to her, but I did not dare reach out my hand; she continued to give me a crazed look.

"Samira is a frostwalker," Natsu began, "and one scary bitch." He nodded softly to her and offered her a slice of his cinnamon cankerberry pie.

"It's her favorite," he said to me with a welcoming smile spreading across his cheeks. She warmed at the gesture, a bit of color surfacing to her too pale cheeks.

"Why would you introduce her that way!" Diana snapped, scowling at him.

"I mean, what else do you want me to say? You want me to *lie?*" He widened his eyes and giggled at the sentiment.

Stygian tossed a Cankerberry at him and he laughed harder. I stared past them at Jesper who had stood in the corner, a beautiful girl at his side. Her hair came to her shoulders and swayed as if it were made of ink. Diana must have noticed me observing her, a woman who was the embodiment of dusk—the moment the sun is consumed by the horizon.

"And *that,*" Diana pointed with her fork at the woman beside Jesper as she smiled and laughed with him, "is Araya, a Solarian—someone born on a solstice."

Solarian was a word I had heard before. These solstice-born Tessiah were welcomed into a secret society to be taught magical talents and gifts.

"She was never invited to the Order of the Solarian, though—at least not yet," Diana said while putting the pattisaire into her mouth.

"Hate that guy," Natsu added, continuing to shovel down the pie that he had so generously offered to Samira. She smiled when he spoke.

"Don't we all," Stygian scoffed, keeping his eyes on the group and not bothering to cast a gaze in Jesper's direction.

The group Diana sat me with continued to talk amongst themselves, with the exception of Samira. Her cold and lifeless eyes would occasionally meet my own, in which moments I would immediately throw my gaze back down at my food.

The flavors were so rich and diverse, things I had not experienced much even as royalty—it was a bizarre thought, that these people who lived here were truly equal.

It was then I caught her gaze again… but this time, she dropped it first. Natsu looked up from the pie he had left all but crumbs of, glancing to Samira.

"It's rude to stare, Sam," he said briefly. before fiddling with the other foods on his plate. I looked back to her, those eyes focused on me once more; if I had not known any better, I would think she was terrified of me.

I heard faint conversation, but I couldn't make out the words. Then, Natsu threw a small carrot at Stygian, who growled and gripped Natsu's hand. A flame crackled in Stygian's eyes, but he was met with a small blast of water to the face.

Natsu laughed at his transgression, and Stygian simply glared back. Even as I was merely feet from the action, everyone's laughter felt so far away.

It felt like I was underwater almost, like the waves muffled the sound and slowly carried me away from the table. My head felt heavy, and my mind was fuzzy.

I blinked furiously to break the feeling, but my head only felt heavier with every effort I made. I slowly pulled my gaze upward and found her eyes staring back at me. Samira's cold, frosted eyes shot daggers through me.

Then I heard a voice in the back of my mind.

"Who are you, Mirage?" it said in an eerie tone. I tried to reply, but I felt my soul smashing back into my physical body. I yelped and gripped the table.

"Mirage?" Stygian's eyes were wild and searching. I felt his hand touching my shoulder.

"What the hell, Sam?" Natsu scowled, standing from the table and gently shaking her. I could not fully make out the scene between them.

"She's not like them—she isn't one of them!" Natsu insisted, gently shaking her, but her gaze did not break from me; I could feel frosted talons sinking into me somewhere inside.

"Mira," Diana said, placing a chilled hand onto my cheek. Her eyes were flooded with concern.

"What?" I croaked. If they didn't know any better, they may think me drunk at this moment. I was still holding Samira's gaze.

She tilted her chin up at me before making eye contact with Natsu instead, and for the first time in several minutes, I could breathe again.

"What was that?" I asked Diana, whose kind gaze still looked down upon me. I then turned to Stygian, who was also searching my eyes for any sort of damage.

"The power of a frostwalker," Stygian said coldly; he even shivered a bit at the words.

"What does *that* mean?" I questioned him, slowly steadying myself back into reality.

"She tests your soul—she can see the kind of person you are, the kind of power you have." Stygian still stood tall over me; the shirt he wore did little to obscure his muscles.

"She gets nervous with newcomers, that's all," Stygian reassured me as he offered a hand to help me up from my seat.

Natsu looked emotional as he peered into Samira's frosted irises, the sharp blue that felt as if it could physically cut.

What a terrifying woman.
A soul tester.

Something I had only heard myths about, cursed women who could reach inside of your soul and see all of your worth. But what was she testing me for? I decided to gain the courage to ask.

"What did he mean, not *one of them?*" I asked, and I felt a sudden chill shoot down my spine.

"Samira has not been very *welcoming* to all Tessiah..." Diana started, trailing off as she tucked a piece of golden hair behind her ear. Stygian cast a gentle gaze upon Diana, a kind that was both loving and respectful as she spoke.

"She feels it's her duty to protect us from people who may be like...her family..." he trailed off, eyes locked on Natsu.

"Like her family?" I echoed, sure that she could not hear me from her position.

"The last known Ikeer..." Stygian whispered to me.

Stygian peered down at me, a frown tugging at his lips. He crouched down closer to my ear so that he could keep his voice down as much as he could, "Her parents used Solarian knowledge to gain access to the dark magics; you wouldn't trust after that either." I could feel his breath on my cheek; I would be lying if I said it didn't make me blush. He continued to speak softly to me, his voice so low and delicate I could barely capture his words.

"When they forced her to kill an innocent, Rainier sought justice and cursed her to be a frostwalker, a less cruel punishment than her parents..." his words faded away into the air. I looked up at him as he finished; his eyes were a deep-emerald color and glittered in the midday sun.

He possessed a brutal sort of beauty, the kind that Death itself wore. We stared at one another for a moment in silence as I took in his haunting words.

I had a wicked father, a truly evil man he was, but I could not envision him demanding I bring down a blade on an innocent, though he did it himself daily.

Samira was clearly haunted; the ghosts of her parents and her past seemed to hang over her. She constantly appeared to look a little mad, a vigor in her eyes that encapsulated both fury and fear, as if she was waiting for a soul to come to her that she deemed fit to strike down.

"If I failed her test, would she have killed me?" I decided to break the tempting silence which floated between us.

He chose to not answer me but instead nodded softly.

A few moments more of silence passed between us. I felt as if I could lose myself in his eyes—the eyes that held the forest and all of its terrible secrets. I thought of the woods outside the eleventh kingdom, riddled with Reavari and Gods only knew what else lurking in those woods.

I could not pass the fact that Stygian was also like me.

Autumn-Kissed, as I was. We were some of the few that were left. I thought about the fire that swelled with every breath, the flames that sat beneath the surface waiting for him to call upon them. It was the same fire I too possessed. I needed to know why there were so few of us—*how* there were so few of us. He still stared at me, concerned about dancing in his bright eyes.

"What happened to us?" He blinked with surprise at the question, as if he could not have imagined I would ask him.

"*Us?*" He said softly, not breaking the eye contact we had held now for what felt like eternity—an eternity I certainly would not mind.

"Autumn-Kissed?" I said back to him, searching his eyes as if they would reveal the answers before his lips could.

"War," he said simply, as if that single word would answer every question I could possibly have regarding our kind, our people.

"What do you mean, *war*?" Diana now inched closer to us, listening to the discussion that unfolded.

"I mean, when you can heal yourself, others, and also feel no pain, you become a good candidate to be stolen and sold into the military…" He raised a hand in front of my eyes and allowed a spark to escape from his fingertips, "Firepower isn't too bad of a weapon, either." I smiled from the warmth of the sparks on my cheek.

Then I smelled his magic.

Lavender and peppermint, a combination that was violent yet sweet on the senses. It completely overwhelmed me and pleasantly stung my nostrils. He gave a shy smile as I leaned in for more.

I began to speak before I had even realized what I was saying, "I absolutely *love* the smell of magic." I immediately felt the rush of embarrassment flooding my cheeks as the words tumbled out, and Diana let out a giggle.

"Yeah?" he said softly as he let more bits of sparks trail from his fingers; I could feel them crackle on my skin, but they didn't burn.

The scent of his magic hit me again: strong waves of the sharp and sweet scent.

Something about his presence felt *right*. I was entranced by him, by the scent of his magic, by the fact that we were somehow bound to one another through the favor of a season—by the kiss of Autumn —the gift of shared magic.

I stared at him for a few extra moments before Diana gently tugged at my arm. I turned to face her and was met with an expression I was not expecting—grief.

For whom that grief was for was unclear.

I felt my brow harden in response to her expression. My mouth parted to ask, but before I had the chance, she broke the silence.

"I think it's time we spoke to my mother," she said softly. Her expression was hard and her skin paled.

"Why don't I join you?" Stygian said warmly. He placed his palm underneath my own and gave me a gentle smile.

"I think you shouldn't." Diana met the tender eagerness in his tone with her own kind gestures. She reached her hand around his free one and gave it a light squeeze.

Diana nodded at me, signaling that we would depart to meet that wicked woman she called a mother.

I looked at her in fright, and I felt my chest tighten.

CHAPTER THIRTEEN

Diana led me past Jesper and I felt the edges of my dress brush against his calves. He did not bother to move as we passed, instead staring down at me as if I were a rabbit—he a wolf.

I would not be shocked if fangs appeared when he smiled, but I only saw human teeth when he did. His golden eyes followed me as I walked, and I held his stare.

I would not be prey here.
I had power.
I too could be a predator.

Araya also made eye contact with me, but she did not emanate that same hungry nature that Jesper did.

"Why does she allow *them* here? I mean, doesn't *his* presence endanger everyone? Being a dark magic user?" I said to Diana in a hushed yet hurried tone. Her pace was quick and purposeful: she was clearly eager to speak with Kaneira.

"They were just kids, too," she said with a bit of an edge to her voice. I was hesitant to push the conversation beyond that point. They must have been orphaned like her.

We passed a corner where there were incredible markings along its column. It looked as if the marble was etched with the symbols of the seasons: snowflakes, leaves, water, and flowers. I knew we were nearing that grand and awful throne room.

I reached for the spot on my arm that all of the sudden felt tender. A few visions surfaced in my consciousness from that event—her ripping my skin… feeding my blood to Hiver.

Her son.

We finally reached those grand golden doors again, and this time I was able to see more of the story I previously could not.

The two men, seeming to each be missing a wing, stood holding the Earth in their hands. Above them was a woman who wore a crown that appeared to be fashioned from the galaxy upon her head. Her hands touched both of them on the shoulder of which their wings shadowed.

"What does this mean?" I asked Diana as I stroked the engravings on the door.

"It's the story of us," she breathed softly, tracing the man in the image who had the moon carved into his chest: the other had what appeared to be the sun.

"Ready?" she finally said after a few more strokes of the moon-carved man.

I nodded.

I suppose this was as ready as I would ever be to face my mother's killer.

CHAPTER
FOURTEEN

Diana pushed open the great doors, and I peered into the flawless throne room. It was marvelous and grand, far beyond the beauties of our throne room back home. I then saw her sitting upon the dais, a black dress hugging her body.

It appeared like she was shrouded in night as the fabric glittered at her curves. She tapped her fingers on the dais and waited for us to approach.

"Hello dearest," she hissed from her dais. I found Hiver sitting about thirty feet away reading a book.

He did not even look up to greet me. She began to rise from the throne she sat at, and Diana smiled as she did.

"Don't call me that." I hissed back at her. It was against my better judgment to challenge her, especially in her own throne room; I just couldn't help the words coming out of my mouth.

"I am not your enemy, Mirage. I have *never* been your enemy." I could not ignore the venom in her voice, the pure evil that she laced her tone with.

If I hadn't at least trusted Diana a little, I would think she was being satirical this entire time…

"Let me show you," she said, offering me her hand, "Snow, come," she looked in the direction where Hiver sat, still entirely consumed by his book.

He gave me a polite smile as he crossed the floor toward us. I watched him take every step toward me as I continued to sit on the floor—I nearly counted them. When he reached me, I did not hesitate to take his hand.

"I can show you the memories of others, and I can show others *your* memories with my power. You just have to let me in, okay?" He smiled softly and guided my hand to his cheek.

"Touch me here," he said, and I simply nodded.

Terror was an understatement for what I felt, but something urged me to trust Hiver. I felt something in the pit of my stomach that allowed me to leave my hand pressed against his cheek: a feeling of connection, of trust.

Kaneira came to sit beside me, and she placed a hand on my own; I flinched from the sensation of her warmth. I attempted to pull away, but the weight of her hand increased, pushing mine down into the black velvet chair.

"I told you, I would come back for you," she said to me, and before I could react, Hiver's palm pressed to her head and the other to my own, and she placed the hand opposite mine on his other cheek, completing the circle.

Images and sounds flashed before me, disorienting me until I found myself looking at three people sitting in a field together.

. . .

"You cannot go with that bastard!" a familiar voice said sharply, Kaneira's unmistakable black hair rising from the green blanket of grass that swayed in the wind.

"He paid for me, what else can I do? My parents have already agreed!" A woman with long brown hair yelled back at her; her back was facing me. Hiver stood beside me and placed a reassuring hand on my back.

Kaneira turned to face the woman who sat on the ground, fury rising in her eyes—the fire beneath crackling in the sunlight.

She was terrifying to behold in her rage.

Another man sat next to the unidentified woman, a hand resting on her thigh, but he said nothing. She reached for his hand and briefly held it, but did not brush him away.

The hair that sat upon his head, the fiery locks of hair that fell from his skull, could belong to no other—that must have been the Stone Mage. As I stared at him, I heard Kaneira snap again, this time tears flowed from her eyes.

"Then you shall take me with you—you will *not* go to that horrible place alone." She violently wiped away the tears that fell from her eyes. It was evident she was plagued by hysteria; she clearly cared for the faceless woman who sat before her.

I looked to Hiver who still stood at my side, and as he spoke, his voice was warped and echoed, as if it had stretched across time to reach me here, "You can move closer, but they won't see or hear you. It is just a memory." The words echoed off of the walls of my skull as if he had streamlined them directly into my brain.

I did as he suggested and neared the trio to get a glimpse of the face that was hidden from me. As I approached, I caught some of the discussion that unfolded and stopped dead in my tracks when I heard her name.

"Please, Aramore...Please just let me go with you. Let me

protect you," Kaneira said again through tears. The more she cried, the more the flames physically sparked in her eyes.

I was not imagining it—her power was dripping through her with the emotion that poured from her body.

My mother.

She now stood up to reach for Kaneira, and I stifled a sob.

"*Mother,*" I managed to whisper as I quickened my pace toward her.

"*Mom,*" I whispered again as I neared. Her back was still to me and I could only see her long brown locks nicely swept into braids. She wore a pale pink dress.

I noted Kaneira's eyes, which held so much emotion—fury, love, hatred—all stirred up to coax a liquid fire.

I watched Aramore join Kaneira. She first put her hands on her shoulders, she then pulled her into a tight embrace.

"I will see if I am to take a handmaiden," my mother sighed heavily as she pushed herself into Kaneira, "but if he finds out who you are —*what* you are—I do not know if I can save you."

Kaneira pulled away, the whirlwind of emotions melting into one I could identify easily—*love.*

"I was never the one who needed saving," she said as she grazed my mother's arm with her hand.

I could no longer stifle the sobs, I could no longer keep my distance, I ran toward my mother and made sure I could see her face—to take it in again. She was beautiful when she was young— she was beautiful when she was older…she was timeless.

I could hardly see her through my tears; I began to wipe them away as they came. My mother: alive, young, and with the people she *loved.*

She loved Kaneira.
　Kaneira had loved her.

I struggled with the reality I was facing.

Why would Kaneira kill her? Why would she snap her neck?

I stared into my mother's soft sage-and-hazel eyes. They glowed like molten amber, encapsulating a warmth that could rival the sun. She was the embodiment of it, a ray of sun made flesh.

Her skin was olive colored, and she wore jewelry that was unfamiliar to me. A chain that stretched from her nose to her ear: a beautiful gold chain that was adorned with—*it could not be*—black guardite...

My mother wore a gem that was for the Gods, a gem that exuded power, status, and wealth. I looked now at the dress I still wore, the dress fashioned of fire, with the same black guardite adorning its impossibly-made flames.

I touched the gems on the dress as I stared longer at my mother's face. Nothing could have prepared me for the scene I was to witness next.

Kaneira spoke through a sob, "It's not fair; we should be together. A woman should not be bought with gold." Kaneira looked away from my mother, who reached a hand to her cheek and pulled Kaneira's maddened gaze to her own.

My mother's other hand rose to her other cheek and pulled her into a kiss. I felt a confusion settling over me—I had mistaken the events I saw before—this was not the love I shared with Diana but something *entirely* different.

"Love finds a way," my mother said gently as she pressed her head to Kaneira's. The Stone Mage sat still in the grass, the wind blowing his hair in the breeze.

When I faced him, I was shocked to see his expression—happiness. A smile that was warm and welcoming; he was radiating a joy that was foreign to his person.

They were all friends.
My mother's killers were her confidants.

I reached out to brush my mother's cheek with my hand. I just wanted to feel her again, to have her warmth spill over me like the morning sun pouring through my windows.

As I reached for her, I was ripped out of that memory of the field and thrown into yet another.

Many years had passed at this point, and I saw her again. This time the jewelry she previously wore was absent from her face, and she was paler—more sickly.

"Please, Lucius, I cannot save them myself. I don't know what else I can do." My mother sobbed, and I could see the bump she had, carrying my brother and I.

She was relatively far into the pregnancy at this point. She had her hands on her stomach, and she softly rubbed the sides of it. Her hair was matted with sweat and rain; it was pouring outside.

Kaneira sat on a barrel in the dimly lit shelter. It was hardly a room—or a house, for that matter.

It looked as if they were taking refuge in an abandoned barn of sorts, just outside of the castle's walls. Kaneira was bloodied, and white scar tissue appeared to be forming on her neck, contrasting her dark skin. The blood matted into her thick black hair, and she was picking her nails as she sat with a foot up on the barrel in front of her. Her stance was nonchalant, and her eyes were tired.

In her beaten-down state, she still held that aura of fury and madness; it radiated off of her in the dimming sunlight.

. . .

"It is a risk I am unwilling to take, Ara—there is a great cost for using their practices." Lucius had scars on his neck as well, in similar places to Kaneira.

"Please. They are all I have left," my mother pleaded, her hands still on her stomach. Kaneira's eyes glowed with that blue fire in the pale light as she stared at my mother.

"Kane, I— " my mother started as she approached. Kaneira wore an unbothered expression and turned away, not making eye contact with her as my mother placed a gentle hand to her face.

"You're freezing," Kaneira said as she lightly brushed away my mother's hand. She still looked away from her, refusing to meet her pleading gaze.

"I never meant for you two to suffer," my mother said with a sob. She sat upon a barrel and allowed the tears to flow freely from her eyes.

In the previous memory, her eyes were bright and full of life, but now they were merely embers that could barely maintain their flame.

She was dying, and it was clear *we* were dying too.

"I put us in danger, not you," Kaneira said, her frenzied eyes catching my mother's stomach.

"I put *all* of us in danger," she continued with a sigh as she stood from the barrel. She leaned against a post and stared out at the vacant stone streets before her. She too was covered in rain and sweat. From the looks of it, they had been on the run.

I was then sucked through a series of events that I could only catch glimpses of.

My father burned Tessiah at the stake and placed their heads on pikes. The scenes passed quickly, but that did not spare me the horror of them.

I saw him gloat to his people about the murder of these innocent magic users—of all types. I saw other Drakkarias at the stake, their hands pinned to crucifixes with ice nails. I closed my eyes at the tragic scenery. Nothing could cleanse my memory of this nightmare…

I was now in a new memory. It was in a grove of Ekelwood trees.

The last Ekelwood trees.

"This will hurt, Kane," the Stone Mage said as he spilled his blood on her head, tracing it into the formation of a symbol I did not recognize. It appeared to be half of a sun with an arrow through it, but I could not tell—I was too far away.

I began to approach the scene, but as I did, Lucius began chanting words unfamiliar to me, and a concentrated ray of sun came down on Kaneira's body. Her eyes glazed over and were a bright white color.

She did not speak, but her body *did* move and writhe under the beam of sunlight. After a few moments, Kaneira stood from the ground, her eyes still aflame.

"Lucius, Lucius, Lucius," she tsked at him, but her voice was warped and distorted.

"Did you tell my daughter *exactly* what this price was?" Kaneira's garbled voice said to him, her arms now crossed as she stared. He shook his head and let it hang to face the ground.

"I couldn't… you know that, Olym," he said with such pain in his voice.

Olym.

My jaw fell open as I stared upon Kaneira's possessed body. The God, Olym—the God of the Sun—had taken her body.

. . .

"You are lucky I want more children," Olym said as he knelt to my mother who sat on the ground nearby, her stomach even larger than in the previous memories. Kaneira's warped voice spoke again as she gently caressed my mother's bump, "My *beautiful* children…were *you* told the price, my dear? The price you and my Kane will pay?" Olym thundered through her when he spoke.

Kaneira was truly a terror of a woman as it was, and with the God inside of her, she commanded a presence that felt like it could bring entire nations to their knees. My mother only nodded at the question; she did not let even a breath escape as she did.

I had never seen her afraid. Even as Kaneira's grip tightened upon her neck, my mother's eyes held no contempt, no fear—only love.

Olym spoke so rigidly—so *bizarre*—I was told that I spoke in a similar manner—*rigidly*. I watched as Olym cut through Kaneira's flesh, and the blood fell onto my mother's stomach. Then, the God raised a hand to my mother's mouth and had her drink from Kaneira's open wound.

Olym stood tall over her as he did this, letting no emotions present themselves upon Kaneira's face.

"Upon the birth of your children, I will collect your life at Kaneira's hands. Life for life," Olym said apathetically as he wiped the blood from my mother's face then cleaned Kaneira's arm.

Just then, her body shook, and Olym's calm demeanor tore into a rageful cry from Kaneira's throat.

"No!" she yelled, gripping her possessed flesh as she began to combat Olym's power.

"You want me to kill her! To kill the woman I love!" Kaneira roared and fought against Olym's grip of her physical body. His voice came through her again, "The cost to embody a God: the life of the person you love the most."

Lucius still hung his head, truly defeated. The look of despair on his face was all-consuming; I was sure that the damage had touched his soul. He had betrayed one of his closest friends. Lucius took refuge in the grass, and tears began to roll down his face. He did not sob, nor did he make a sound, but the tears fell silently from his cheeks to coat the blades of grass like morning dew.

He had chosen a side, and he had chosen my mother's.

Kaneira roared again, her eyes still glowing from the God's power, "How could you, Lucius? How could you do this?" She screamed and approached him where he sat. She did not hesitate to pull him up by his robes and hold him to face her.

She was strong as it was, but *this—this* strength was immeasurable.

"I should tear you to shreds!" she growled as she raised a hand, claws protruding from her fingers.

Long black talons took the place of her dark and scarred fingers, and she lifted them to his throat.

"No! Please don't!" my mother shouted from her position on the ground. She was still sickly, too weak to move from her position without help.

"Kaneira, no!" she yelled again, fighting to stand up.

Kaneira briefly looked in her direction before slashing her claws against Lucius's chest—she easily tore through his robes, exposing his flesh, and she let his body hit the ground before her.

"I should *kill* you for that," she said. Fangs took the place of her regular canine's, and two great black wings protruded from her back.

A dragon—a real dragon...

Olym's voice took hold of her again, and her talons retracted.

"But you will not," he said matter of factly through his distorted voice.

"The children within Aramore will be Autumn–Kissed; I will claim them as my own. They will have my powers, and one will have the capacity to heal, therefore healing you of your sickness, Aramore. For now, your blood may also heal Lucius." Olym used Kaneira's hand to point at Lucius, whose blood was already blackening.

"My blood?" Aramore said to the God. He simply nodded in response.

"Your daughter's blood will heal herself and others, *so,* as long as she is a part of you, *your* blood will heal too," Olym said as he leaned down to her, gently cutting her arm with precision and care.

"I guess, I should say *our* daughter." Olym corrected.

It was a far less wicked scene than the one I had endured with Kaneira, but I noticed he cut my mother in the exact same spot I had been.

I touched the area that was completely healed: no scar, no bruise, nothing. Evened skin, as if it had never been touched. I looked in horror at Lucius and his injuries; his blood was spilling out of him with the force of a river.

My memory snapped back to Hiver, who was cut open by Reavari in a similar manner—deep cuts that stained his blood black.

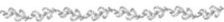

I turned to find Hiver, and I stared at him for a long moment, until he offered himself to me, opening his arms to allow me to settle within them. I rushed at him and threw myself against his chest, the sobs erupting uncontrollably. I hardly hugged him back, but rather bunched his tunic into my fist and allowed my tears to soak it.

I felt his hand gently rest on the back of my head, softly stroking my hair, and the other hand was wrapped around my shoulders to pull me into him.

"It's okay," he whispered. He said nothing more. I could not will myself to break from his grasp; I would rather suffocate in my tears than turn to face the images that unraveled before me.

The betrayal.
The horror.
But worst of all—the future.

I broke from Hiver's comforting embrace when I heard more

roars coming from Kaneira. She tore at her own flesh with the talons she unsheathed once more, cutting at her skin and ripping open her chest.

She sobbed and screamed through it. I assumed that since I had turned away, Lucius had been healed by Olym.

Rather *I* had healed Lucius.

Kaneira's screams rippled through the air—her wails were so sharp I was sure they would cut through the wind itself. I covered my ears to stop the blows of her shrill cries through my skull.

"I won't do it! I would never do it," she shouted as she eviscerated her flesh.

"Release me!" she thundered as she continued to rip off the skin from her stomach, her chest, and her arms.

"Would you rather lose all three of them? Hmm? Would you prefer to lose your lover *and* her legacy? Her children that will carry your lover's blood? Children who you can raise?" I felt the power of his voice coming through her deep in my bones; his presence shook me to the core.

Kaneira then dropped to her knees, eyes still bright with the power of the God, and she placed her palms to the ground as she heaved.

"Just release me, Father," she said, defeated. To see her back down—to fall to her knees—was a jarring sight indeed.

"As you wish, my dear," Olym retreated into the ray of sun that was cast upon her to allow him to take her form.

I could see his essence physically leaving her body and returning to the sky. The light left her eyes, and in its place, her blue, maddened gaze remained. She sat on the ground still, her knees to the earth. She heaved, the tears continuing to fall from her face.

"How could you do this?" she whispered; her voice cracked upon the words. Her eyes stayed focused on the earth beneath her—at her bloodied hands, which starkly contrasted the lively green grass.

Her question was met with silence as Lucius was still panting from his injuries, his expression grim.

"How could you do this!" she screamed and slammed her fists down upon the earth. Fire came out from her balled fists and swirled up into the air as she hammered down upon the grass.

Lucius sucked in a labored breath before he spoke.

"We could be free," he said softly to her, placing his hands over his wounds, which were healed over now.

"At what cost?" Kaneira said softly; any trace of warmth was lost in this last sentence of hers, as what came next made me shudder.

"I was going to die either way, Kane," my mother said, still sitting with her hands on her stomach.

"Please, just promise me when the time comes, you will care for them. It *must* be you." My mother's voice was so lovely and soft when she spoke, it was as if her sentences fell into the lull of a song.

Kaneira did not rise from her spot. She merely breathed as she gripped the ground with her hands. A true madness had befallen her unlike what she previously exhibited. Kaneira pressed her head to my mother's and kissed her forehead softly.

"I will care for your children, but that does not mean I won't make them fatherless." Kaneira sniffed and wiped away the final tear —the last tear I'm sure she ever shed.

"I love you, Kane. I will love you until the garden claims me," my mother said softly, gently caressing Kaneira's cheek.

Kaneira simply stared down at her; the frenzy in her eyes only flickered for a moment as she said to my mother, "I love you too, and I will love your children even more."

CHAPTER FIFTEEN

Just as Kaneira's voice rang through my head, I was sent through another onslaught of horrifying memories. I saw Kaneira ripping out the hearts of guards, pulling their throats out with her talons and breaking their backs with her bare hands. She went on a rampage—

killing all of my father's men that dared to touch the Tessiah. Like before, I could only see glimpses of the scenes, but the imagery would stain my consciousness for eternity.

Just before reaching consciousness again, I saw her standing outside of the gates of the castle, holding my father's brother, by his shirt as she ripped his throat from his neck.

She smiled when she did it.

It was one of the last memories I had with my mother: her grabbing me and covering my eyes in that tall window moments before Kaneira tore out his throat.

My father locked her up the next day for her crimes, and two days later, she would be freed to snap my mother's neck as Dracar and I watched.

I was forced back into my body, my *real* body, as I lay beside Kaneira. It appeared she had reached consciousness before me, her hands nicely folded in her lap as she stared down upon me.

My eyes were heavy with sleep, and I looked at her for the first time in my life.

I actually saw her this time.
I saw the kind of person she was.
I saw *her*.

"You loved her?" was all I could manage before erupting into sobs. I could not stifle the tears from coming down my face; I could only writhe in my despair and misery.

She did not say anything to me, but instead she inched closer to put her arms around me and squeezed. I could not see her face, but I felt a single drop of water hit my back.

I made several efforts to speak, but the sobs were too much to overcome. I had so many questions, yet none of them would surface to my tongue.

It seemed in that moment she read my mind because she pulled away and stared into my eyes with the most sincere expression I have ever seen another being wear spread across her face.

"Olym threatened to have you and your brother turned into Reavari if I did not fulfill my end of the deal..." She squinted at me, as if to force back tears, but she continued, "We managed to push back her fate a decade before Olym sent down his threat—I had a fortnight to accomplish my task, and I waited until the last few days." She stopped again and crinkled her nose; this time, she could not stop the tear from falling. She felt remorse for her actions—she was bound by a Godly pact.

"There's a reason Solarian gifts are only shared among the few of them. They come with terrible costs...but I didn't know—" Kaneira sucked in a breath, and a slight squeak came from her throat as she did. I could tell she too was stifling sobs.

This moment would weigh on me for the rest of my life.

I would have never predicted my next move; it was as if I moved on an instinct, an animalistic urge. I could not control myself as I flung my body into her and placed my head under her chin, onto her chest. I could hear that fiery heartbeat rattling beneath her warm skin. I closed my eyes and hugged her.

I now made a decision I never thought myself capable of: choosing mercy, choosing pity, choosing *love*.

This woman was the bane of my existence. Upon meeting her for the first time in this throne room, I had brought my blade to her throat, and it had taken every muscle in my body to pry myself off of her back. Every single nerve singing a song of warning, coaxing me to make the correct decision and remove my knife from her. It took a symphony of sorrow and anger to allow myself to step away from her body.

I had the opening to kill, and I was more than willing to take it, but in that moment she had been correct: I would not have made it far, and I may have let Hiver die.

I saw the Tessiah as my enemies, but the entire time, the true enemy was always looking back at me in the mirror. It was those who were like me, the hateful mortals who saw Kaneira in her crazed state and thought it was the product of magic—but in reality, it was the product of *love*.

The words came up from my throat like more of a croak than a coherent sentence, "I'm sorry," I managed to say to her.

I could taste my tears. They began to burn my skin as they did the day of my taking. I felt as if the streaks were leaving physical burns upon me as I cried, but even though I could feel the searing pain, I could not stop the tears from flowing.

KINGDOM OF THE SUN

This is what I imagined it felt like as the sea bit the land, the salt lacing itself into the rock and degrading it over millions of years.

The great rocks that sat at the seaside would eventually give way to the minerals of the ocean, and that was just as I felt now: I felt myself giving away to the salt of the sea.

I had thought the last few days here were overwhelming—that I was suffocating on information, intoxicated by magic—but it was the last few hours in this room that truly broke me.

I could not imagine waking up tomorrow and feeling the same flesh I felt today. Feeling that my soul was the same one entrapped in my body as it was just mere hours ago.

Kaneira was the last piece I had of my mother.

I remember overhearing as a child how father meant to kill one of the twins—this had to be how he did it...he had to make her ill.

We hated our father enough.

We did not need more excuses to hate him, so we never truly dwelled on the fact that *he* caused our mother's illness.

"My children and Lucius are all I have left," She whispered to me. She said it in such a low tone I doubt Hiver could make out her words despite being just a few feet away.

"And now *you*..." She squinted at me again, as if to stop the tears from flowing. I simply nodded at her, unable to say another word. Sorrow clung to the sides of my throat, and if the Gods willed it, I would have sat and apologized to her for hours if I could.

I would have told her how heinous I was, how awful it was that I hated her so vehemently—that I would drag my blade to her throat. I remembered again that moment in the throne room. She instantly went to Hiver's side; she did not make an effort to reprimand me. I had tried to kill a queen—*the* queen of the eleventh kingdom.

The ruler who would die for her people—*kill* for her people.

She was both a savior and a cold-blooded killer.

I stared at her for a long moment. I did not say a word, nor did she. In our moments of eye contact, I believed we understood each other.

I understood her madness, and she understood my hatred; but now I was hers. There was only one more thing that I needed—that *we* needed: Dracar.

CHAPTER
SIXTEEN

I noticed now Diana and Hiver were not in the room with us anymore, and I was not sure when she would have left, but it was just Kaneira and I sitting in this large chair. She looked off to a giant frosted glass window engraved with the symbols of the seasons.

Flames coiled up from my finger tips, like bracelets and rings, adorning me just like jewelry would. Kaneira raised a brow at the magic flickering at my hands.

"You will need to train, but that can start after the Solarian Ball," she said very seriously.

I stared at her for another moment, taking in the full beauty of her face—her cruel and brutal features, the white scars which adorned her skin like jewelry. She made no effort to hide the marks of her battles, the scars she wore so proudly across her chest and neck.

After a moment of silence, she rose from the chair and stood over me, "You have no control of your magic…and you're going to have to learn," she said matter-of-factly as she pulled my wrist up to her face, and I stared at the flames. She snuffed them out with her own hand before leaving the throne room.

. . .

Kaneira did not say another word to me as she left, but I could hear the quiet chatter erupting between her and Lucius in the corridor beyond the doors.

I did not dare move from the chair.

I decided to lie down.

I tried to force out the traumatizing memories that were now in my mind. However horrible they were, I had not lived them—Kaneira had.

I sat there for what felt like hours reliving the scenes; I saw my mother's face, I saw Lucius's, and Kaneira's—they occasionally all blurred into one, and I saw their love and their sorrow mingling together.

I fell asleep on the soft velvet chair. The world slowly spun around me as my eyes closed, making me feel as if the chair was slowly ascending toward the skies to deliver me to my creator: to the God who made me with his blood—with Kaneira's blood.

I could not tell how much time had passed, but I had slept for some time.

I was not plagued by nightmares.
I did not see horrors when I rested my eyes.

When I floated back into consciousness, I noticed the sun was no longer shining through the great frosted window. There were pale lights lining the walls, but otherwise, the room was mostly dark. I slowly sat up, and that was when I noticed him.

Hiver.

I was shrouded in a translucent cloud of white dust; it sparkled like snow in the very pale light of the room. I saw him sitting, but his eyes were not open—he was asleep too. I had no idea what time it was at this point, but night had fallen. I stared at him for a moment.

Perhaps it would be unsettling for him to open his eyes and see me looming over him, watching him sleep. However, I was more curious to understand how his magic was emanating off of him while he was not even conscious. I reached a hand out, attempting to touch the cloud of snow and dust that surrounded us both, but it stretched with me.

I then tried to reach upwards to breach the opaque layer of magic, but as I moved, it moved. It formed to me and would not allow me to touch it.

I felt a spark of terror rising in my chest; I feared being trapped. I did not wish to wake Hiver, as it was evident the cloud of magic did not have any interest in hurting me.

Slowly, I reached down to him, my hand reaching near his cheek. As I got closer, the magic surrounded me and molded into the face of a wolf. It snapped at my hands and forced me to take a step backwards, nearly making me lose my balance. The snow-coated wolf disappeared as I distanced myself from Hiver.

Was it an illusion?

I decided to dedicate my efforts to hoping that's all it was, and I approached Hiver again; this time, I accompanied my touch with a whisper. The wolf appeared again, but before it could snap at me, Hiver shot his hand at mine and gripped me so tightly I could swear I heard skin tear.

He pulled me down into him and made an effort to pin my arm.

"Hiver! I'm sorry!" I yelped. He released me slowly a realization dawning upon him, and I sat over the top of him, holding myself up on the long chair he lay on.

Our faces were just inches apart as I panted from the pain. We stayed like that for a little while, neither of us saying a word.

"I'm sorry," he breathed; it was hardly even a whisper that escaped his mouth. He sat up in the chair, but I continued to lie there holding the part of my arm that he nearly broke with his raw strength.

"What was that cloud?" I asked as he kept his back to me. He turned to face me slowly; sleep had softened his otherwise hard features.

"I'm sorry," he said again, and he began to rise from the chair. I reached for his arm and tugged, an effort to keep him sitting in the chair.

"I didn't dismiss you." I teased, a slight smile pulling my lips.

I felt that I could see him contemplating his next action—him deciding whether to sit again, or to walk away without another word. It was the former that won, as he eased back down into the chair.

"I used my magic to help you sleep…" He trailed off, only for a moment glancing at my face.

"I know it was wrong, but after what you saw in there, I thought I could maybe give you one night of peace before those scenes haunt you forever." He sighed and placed his head onto his hand.

"Thank you," was all I could muster up. I gained the courage to say one more thing before he could leave, "You can stay." I sucked in a deep breath as the words left my mouth.

He stopped dead in his tracks and slowly turned to face me. He had only made it a few paces from the chair at this point.

"You want me to stay? *Here*... with *you*?" The surprise in his tone almost made me blush.

"I didn't have any nightmares," I regretted my words immediately—how vague they were, "I want you to stay, yes," I corrected, attempting to sound more confident in my request.

He waved his hand outward as if he were throwing some sort of dust from his hand, and the white shroud appeared again.

He went to lay on my old chair instead of the one that I now sat on a few paces away. I did not want this distance between us; I wanted to feel his warmth, smell his magic.

"We can share?" I proposed it as more of a question than a statement, and I felt the heat of embarrassment rising in my cheeks.

"Oh?" he said, sitting up and raising a brow at me questioningly. He positioned himself to take up only half of the chair and opened his arms with a slight smirk.

"You take the reins, princess," he said with a playful tone. I stood up and came over to his chair, laying down beside him.

I reached for his arm and pulled it over me, an action I surprised myself with.

The full intoxicating scent of his magic hit me as if it had been blown into my face. My back was to him, his arm laid across my torso. I felt the urge to turn and face him, but I fought myself not to.

His scent lulled me into a state of calm I had never experienced before. My existence became mere bliss; I felt my soul falling through the earth to be laid to rest.

I noticed him move to bring himself up to my face, and he whispered against my ear, "Goodnight, princess." I shivered from the heat of his breath against my ear. I felt his lips brush my cheek—*a kiss*.

I sucked in a breath of his air and whispered back to him, "Goodnight, Hiver."

There we slept—side by side, the soft melody of his magic lulling me into a restful slumber.

CHAPTER
SEVENTEEN

"Gods! I am not sure I even *want* to ask questions!" Kaneira's voice echoed throughout the throne room, jarring me awake from my deep slumber.

Hiver too sat up with an urgency coaxed out of him by Kaneira's thundering voice. Despite the haziness from sleep still hanging over me, I noticed the shimmer of magic burst around us, and the cloud fell to the floor, dissipating into nothingness.

I watched as the sparkles scattered about.

"Why wouldn't you have returned to your chambers?" she asked Hiver, primarily. She gave me a disapproving glare as she spoke, but her attention was far more fixated on him.

"She asked me to stay with her," he shrugged at her and gave me a wink.

"I— " I began to protest but immediately stuttered as I tried to explain.

I truly did not have an explanation.
I would not tell her that I craved him.
That a primal part of me wanted to feel him everywhere.
Instead, I would tell lies of omission.

"He took away the nightmares, so I asked him to stay."

She raised a brow at me, but chose to not say a word. I shared in awe at her.

She was pure power.
Sunfire confined to mortality.
The daughter of a God.

Right in front of me stood a dragon made flesh, and for the first time in my life, I did not feel afraid. Kaneira raised her hand to her face and made a disappointed gesture.

"Up. Now," she said, raising her hands in an upward motion, bidding us to follow her commands. I rose up from the chair immediately, but Hiver groaned and lay flat on his back for a moment which earned a glare from her.

It was clear he had a rebellious soul, but that soul would bend to Kaneira's will if she asked him to. Kaneira stood with her arms crossed, her gaze hard upon us as we stood at the edge of the long chair.

"Well why have grand chairs that can accompany two if we aren't to use them?" Hiver said to her, his irritation and sarcasm bleeding together as he spoke.

"We have a long day ahead of us...on with you—*both* of you." She spoke as a general would, as if she were commanding soldiers as opposed to her children.

Hiver began to walk away from the chair to the throne room's exit, but after a few paces, he turned to me. He smiled and offered me his arm.

"Shall I walk you to your chambers?" he smiled sweetly, but his tone remained sarcastic.

Kaneira violently rolled her eyes at the sentiment, but I could also see a smile cracking away at her otherwise cold expression. I happily took his arm, and we exited the throne room together.

We did not say a word to one another the entire way to my chambers.

I was at a loss for words; I could not express to him every feeling that welled beneath the surface. I previously saw him as a wolf and I a lamb, but even if those sentiments held true, I would wish for him to ravage me like I were his prey.

"Diana is going to be furious when she discovers you slept in that dress," he said to me as we stopped in front of the chamber doors.

He looked me up and down, his eyes roving over where my body naturally curved—where the dress bit into my skin.

"Shall I tell her who kept me in it?" I said back to him; I immediately felt the heat rising to my cheeks and warming my stomach. I had only once experienced that sensation at any point in my life—and here it was again.

"Oh?" His face contorted to reflect a genuine question.

"Perhaps you can just ask, if you'd prefer I undress you." He paused for a moment, a smirk pulling at the edges off his mouth before he continued his sentiment, "A lady's consent is truly her highest praise," he said too nonchalantly.

I felt my insides burning.

I blushed, but I could not muster up the courage to speak back to him, so instead I smiled politely. I bowed to him, keeping my eyes fixated on his. He watched me move downwards and snickered,

"Ladies don't bow, you know."

"I know," I giggled in response, and he returned the bowing gesture.

"I will see you tonight," were his final words before he turned away and walked down the magnificent stretch of hall to where I imagined his chambers were located.

As I entered my room, I slunk down to the floor and held my hands to my chest.

KINGDOM OF THE SUN

I felt so alive.

My heart was both full and heavy—seeing Kaneira pay the ultimate price to save us.

Love was the wager in every battle I witnessed.

For a moment, I believed I heard a clattering of items in the bathing room and perhaps footsteps making their way toward me. However, I dismissed them as potential hallucinations or perhaps maids drawing up a bath.

I was too tired to investigate, to try and engage with whatever—*whoever*—should be milling about my chambers. My mind was busy, racing with the events of the last twenty-four hours.

I sat with nothing but my thoughts for only a few moments before Diana burst into the room from the bathing area.

"Where have you been?" she yelled it more than asking.

"I have been waiting for you since dawn—I even checked the courtyards for you!" She sounded both scared and upset, but it felt like her fear was winning the hold of her tone.

I merely stared at her.

There were very few moments where I felt like I had control—that I was not reacting out of fear or necessity. The moments I felt pure peace were in the presence of the other Tessiah who lived here, the people I once feared.

I thought of my time with Stygian in the food hall.

The night I spent with Hiver.

Chatting with Diana as she fixed my dress.

That moment of vulnerability where I threw myself into Kaneira's arms...

"You have to get ready for the Ball!" Diana said, her usual cheery voice returning, breaking me out of my prolonged thoughts. She held a hand down in front of my chest as an offer to pull me up from where I sat slouched against the door. If she had spoken to me in the last few moments, I would have heard nothing.

"Yeah—right. So what do we do at the Ball?" I asked her in all sincerity. Her first response to my question was a giggle.

"We dance, we drink, we eat, we *love*," she said and walked in a circle around me, imitating dancing. I giggled at her movements; I watched her nearly skipping to the armoire.

"Shall we see what Anathena has fashioned for you?" Diana smiled and clapped her hands eagerly as she opened the armoire doors.

"*Anathena?*" It was a name I was not familiar with.

"The seamstress. She was blessed by the Goddess, Kyren, to make armor for the Gods when they went to battle—she was also blessed with immortality." I looked at Diana with a raised brow.

"*Kyren?*" I shook my head. I had not known much of the Gods and Goddesses, only Arudia because of the stories my mother told Dracar and I when we were young.

Arudia was the Goddess of the Flame—a mighty force in battle and a ferocious woman. From the stories my mother told, I would have thought she was just describing Kaneira.

Arudia was deeply passionate and driven, but fierce in her own right. She was commonly a symbol of war, a symbol of chaos—destruction. My mother told us tales of her battle with the mortals hundreds of years ago: how she would ride into battle on a horse whose legs were made of fire and whose eyes were hot coals.

She wielded a whip made of flame that crackled upon impact. She was the character of bedtime stories mostly, but in fact, she was real and existed in this realm—something I once thought impossible.

"Kyren is the Goddess of the Silk, or so they call her. She has the power to imbue armor and cloth with magical essence. When she spun thread into cloth, she would weave elements into them. She gave her favor to Anathena, who can imbue fabric with magical essence too." Diana rifled through the wardrobe as she spoke, and after a few moments she stopped and stared with glee; I could swear I saw her eyes physically sparkle at her excitement.

"And this..." she started, pulling out a grand dress from the wardrobe. I caught a glimpse of it as it exited the structure, and I too was awestruck at what I saw.

"Is *it*." She held the dress in the morning sun, its light scattering about the room.

It was a dress fashioned of the universe, woven with stars and layers of moonlight. It looked as if Anathena pulled the heavens down in the dusk and spun them into fabric. It was as if the universe only existed here—in the layers of silk and tulle of this dress.

I imagined my eyes glittered in anticipation to put it onto my body, to have the light of day scatter its beauty onto the world around me. I would light up the room, *literally*.

For a moment, I faltered; I felt like I did not deserve to wear the fabrics crafted by the blessed.

I struggled to come to terms with what I did and did not deserve. Perhaps I shouldn't be parading myself around a ball while my brother sat in that *prison*—while what I now knew as my people were being hunted and slaughtered by the despicable creature I called a father. Even in the event that I did not deserve to be here, I was... and I *wanted* to be.

"Isn't it gorgeous?" Diana asked as she floated it just inches off the floor. I could hear the bottom of the dress hissing as its fabrics just barely reached the marble. She spun and swung it around her, smiling at me as she came to face me once more.

"I think I'll have you try to get it on—*alone*," she said in a playful tone.

"You cannot be serious," I said and gestured to her to help me get into the remarkable piece of clothing.

"So, truly, where were you last night?" Diana asked as she pulled the dress past my hips.

"I slept in the throne room."

Another lie of omission...I was playing a dangerous game. Diana was sharper than any dagger I had beheld.

"And for what reason would you find more comfort in the throne room than in here?" she said, gesturing to the room she had made sure looked like the one I inhabited at Castle Sage.

"Hiver took me into Kaneira's memories…" I thought carefully of the words I would choose next.

"I saw *horrible* things, and I suppose I just felt the weight of exhaustion fall upon me, so there I slept."

Another lie of omission—or perhaps the wholehearted truth; I myself could not tell.

I knew Diana better than I knew myself; her mind was no maze to me, but rather a labyrinth of mirrors, all reflecting her truth into me.

"You'll be okay," she finally said. It took the will of a God to command my tears to remain in the ducts of my eyes. She read beyond the lies and saw me struggle to come to terms with the weight of my mere existence.

Somehow, Diana had known just what to say to ease the burden of my torment.

For the second time now, I did not think but merely threw my body into her, squeezing as tightly as my muscles would allow. This time, even a God could not prevent the tears from streaming down my face and onto her silk dress. I buried my face into her hair and pulled her into me. I merely sobbed.

"Thank you," I managed to croak. She returned my squeeze with her own inhuman strength.

"I love you Mirage, always." She said softly, giving me a light stroke on the back.

"I love you too, Diana," I wept. For a long while, we sat in silence—our touch spoke for us. I sometimes forgot Diana and I shared no blood; we still maintained the unbreakable bond of sisters.

I am unsure I could have managed to navigate the darkness without her light; and Diana possessed a light that could eclipse the sun itself.

A true good.

"Luckily, I have not yet marked your eyes, or else it would have all come off just now," she said to me, putting a finger under my chin to force my gaze onto her own. That word had caught me—*marked*.

Markings used to be worn by Tessian royalty—way back when. They were golden sparkles that came from the bodies of Spikestar beetles: beautiful creatures that could glitter across an entire room, almost like this dress could.

They were a rarity now, especially in the tenth kingdom. They sought refuge in the Ekelwood trees, and when those disappeared, so did the Spikestars.

I had seen one when I was about age four; it crawled across my windowsill, and I watched it scurry in the low light of dawn. My mother sat behind me telling me how they possessed a magical essence called *Spiridium*—a substance that mortal royals would put up their noses as a form of "*medicine*".

Spiridium would intoxicate the user in a pleasant way, making it a popular substance at royal balls.

"You're going to mark me?" I asked. She nodded sweetly and spoke even sweeter, "You're Tessian royalty."

Those words hit me with such a force I nearly fell.
Perhaps I was.

I was at a loss for words, but not a loss of thoughts. My head swam with memories. I had always been *this*... yet I feel that this was a new part of me. I wore the markings of an Autumn-Kissed, the scarlet streaks in my hair and my matching eyes; I had always looked like one of them, but I never had their power. In fact, I *still* didn't.

I was prone to rumination, fearing my next words would be met with retaliation. It was possible that aspect of me was the result of my father's abuse. He made sure to inform me how absolutely useless I was. I was well read, though—my mother saw to that even beyond her death.

I don't know what defines—*me*.

I don't know who I am.

I sat down at the vanity and Diana began to pull my mess of hair into clips that glittered gold.

"Your mother left these for Kaneira so that they would one day find their way to you." Upon closer inspection, I noticed the clips were crafted to look like Spikestars.

"They're beautiful." I had meant it, too.

"Was my mother wealthy?" I asked Diana, since this was the second item of jewelry I saw from her—the image of the black guardite still hung in my mind. I imagined seeing it upon her face again at this moment.

"I don't know... I only know that Kaneira loved her, but not much more," Diana said in earnest. I had wondered what information she *did* know, like when it came to this place.

"How do people make it to the portal to get here?" I asked Diana. She gave me a puzzled look.

"You mean the ripple?" she corrected. I nodded: I did mean the ripple. I had completely forgotten that was the word they used to describe the entry point.

"Kaneira mostly led people through, but she has not brought anyone new in years—apart from you. The majority of us have been here since we were children. There are many more older adults that reside here." She continued to pull my curls through smaller golden clips as she spoke.

"And what of those who were not led through?" I questioned—there was no way Kaneira guided every soul into this place.

"Some were sent by Alysara—her general would bring them to the ripple."

Alysara?

"You mean *the* Alysara? The queen of the eighth?" I was completely dumbfounded. Diana nodded.

"She is the only Tessian leader in the modern realm... but we are the only ones who know that," Diana confirmed.

※※※※※

Alysara was not much older than us, probably twenty five at the most. She ascended the throne upon her parents' death at the Battle of Bandur. Both of them were warriors and did not trust a general to lead their army into battle, so out they went—and there they died.

The eighth kingdom was the only matriarchy in the modern realm. Her mother Aroteria was the queen prior to her death. She was a true beacon of power and prosperity—she believed in progress and honor. The eighth was the only kingdom in the lower five that did not butcher the Tessiah.

Alysara was bold like her mother, always outgoing yet precise. She spoke only what she meant, leaving few details to the imagination. She, like her mother, was truly beautiful: her face full and radiant, complemented by warm brown eyes which apparently guarded some of the largest secrets in the realm.

"What *is* she?" I needed to hear more. There was a Tessian woman—no—a Tessian *queen* living amongst us all this time, and I had been none the wiser.

"She is not Season-Kissed like us." Diana began snaking her way around my chair to gather loose pieces of hair into the clips.

"She is a Veritongue—have you an idea what that is?" She paused and stared at me in the mirror, awaiting my reply. I shook my head.

"The Veritongue are truth-bound shapeshifters. They *cannot* lie, but that does not mean they don't know how to shuffle around the truth."

"*Shapeshifters?*" I questioned—I hadn't a clue they even existed. Then again, I think I knew little of the Numortalis entirely.

So many creatures, so many powers.

I imagine my expression clearly conveyed the thoughts which ran through my mind at this moment as Diana began to frown at me.

"It *is* a bit overwhelming," She said softly, snaking her away around the chair yet again to face me.

"You will eventually get used to it all, but I have no doubt it will take some time." She put a hand under my chin.

She reached back toward the vanity and pulled out a white box from the drawer. I had to admit, I did not investigate my new chambers thoroughly; I had no idea it was even there.

The box was pearlescent: it looked as if it had been retrieved from the sea. I watched her open it, and inside was a mass of compacted gold glitter.

It was the powder from the Spikestars.

I watched her dip a finger into the powder and she brought it to my face.

"Close your eyes!" she said cheerfully. I did as she said and let my eyes drift shut. I could feel her bent over the top of me, and as she pressed her finger to my eyelid, I felt a shock move through me. A voice echoed in my consciousness.

Mirage.

The voices mingled and mixed, but in distorted tones. I was unable to place a gender on them; they all collectively whispered.

"Do you hear that?" I panicked and pulled away from her.

"Hear what?" Concern coursed through Diana's eyes as she looked upon me; I felt sweat beading on my brow. I looked around the room to potentially find the source of the voices.

Again they whispered.

Mirage.
Mirage!

It was almost too much to bear.

I let Diana continue her streaks across my eyelid, and she moved onto the next. I could feel her attempts at precision, moving her fingers on my eyes with varying pressure.

The Firebird has come.
The Firebird seeks us.
Mirage.
Mirage!

The entirety of the time she pushed it onto my eyes, I heard the thousands of voices calling out to me. I then felt her hand on my lips; she parted them vertically from my cupid's bow to my bottom lip.

She then moved to my collarbone and traced her fingers where it met my skin. I kept my eyes shut through the entire process, trying to force the screaming to stop. I felt that my consciousness was being consumed by a haunting melody of voices, my name the chorus.

"All done," she said softly, and I realized I no longer felt her fingers on my skin. The moment she stopped, the voices did too.

"What a horrifying ritual," I murmured as I leaned toward the mirror. It was as if the voices never existed at all—that I merely imagined the whole thing.

As I looked into the mirror I hardly recognized the person who stared back at me. The gold was stunning in its box, but on my body, it shimmered. It appeared that the skin underneath it also glowed; I could feel it coursing through my veins—the power of the Spikestar beetle.

They were not myths…I continued to focus on the gold sparkles in the mirror, I noticed my eyes themselves also had flecks of the shimmering gold.

"What…" I began as I rose from the chair to get even closer to the mirror. I opened my eyes wider to observe my now gilded irises.

"What happened to me?" I asked Diana, who seemed unamused by the change in my appearance.

"It's the Spiridium—it's magic," She said softly, "Too bad the mortals used it as Mercurial Powder." She rolled her eyes at the words.

"Substances used for revels and soirees," she clarified upon seeing my questioning expression. I nodded in understanding.

"This stuff supercharges magic—it blends with *you*," she pointed a finger to my golden lips and looked at me with a kind smile.

"Like the fruits?" I asked.

"Hmm, not quite. The Spiridium physically changes you—the fruits only change your magic. Well, maybe…I actually don't fully know," she beamed at me before continuing.

"Okay, I shall see you later then? You can spend some time in the Courtyard?" She gave me a quick squeeze and brushed her hand down my cheek before turning away to the door to leave my chambers.

But before she fully found herself outside of the door, she turned to me and said, "By the way, Mirage… you look absolutely gorgeous." She winked before finally exiting the room.

I stared for a few more moments at my golden-flecked eyes in the mirror. I could feel the supercharged magic coursing through me; it was as if every drop of my blood was now laced with the Spiridium.

I could not imagine what this did to mortals—no doubt my father dabbled in the *Mercurial Powder* before he removed the Spikestars' habitats from the kingdom.

Sometimes, mortals were pathetic creatures.

CHAPTER EIGHTEEN

Pride was not normally something I felt.

Despite my royal status, I was a victim to my father's relentless torment. It was part of his vicious game to make us feel powerless—if only he knew we were just the opposite.

Carlisle fancied himself a predator, but beneath the roar was no lion: just a coward. Perhaps he would hate to see me now, fashioned in the cloth which held the universe and all of its stars.

Perhaps he would hate to see the royal in me, the leader that somehow prevailed even when I was the one being led. The castle was always suitable for Dracar, but never I.

Despite being the wealthiest in the ten kingdoms, we were one of the least respected. The advantage of the sea gave us access to riches other kingdoms could physically not acquire.

The other lower kingdoms followed my father's hateful lead so that they could find themselves in his good graces—his wealth...

So it was now I decided to feel pride.

To feel pride in my changed heart—*my evolved soul.*
To feel pride in *belonging.*

I decided to take Diana's offer of spending some time in the Autumn Courtyard.

I made my way down the labyrinth of halls, touching my hands to the beautiful engravings that were truly *everywhere*. If the throne room's doors held the story of our creation, I could only imagine these hundreds of artistically crafted engravings told the stories of many. I saw one particular etching that caught me dead in my tracks.

I had seen *this* tale with my very own eyes.

It was Kaneira—with two Gods placing a hand on each of her shoulders. Except that was not the scene I had watched unfold. I saw the Gods touching her, their opposite wings indicating just which Gods they were: Rainier and Olym.

The engraving showed her rage and sorrow as she screamed to the Heavens—it was the moment she realized that she was to kill my mother. I ran my finger along the engravings, taking in the scene made permanent into the stone walls.

I had stared for what I imagined was five or so minutes when a voice came over my shoulder.

"I make a great effort to document all of our sacrifices," Lucius said.

The Stone Mage.

I whirled around to face him, unsure of how long he had been standing behind me.

"You made these engravings?" I asked, staring at his expressionless face. He simply nodded.

"All but the one on the throne room's doors—that pre-existed us all." His hands were buried beneath his robes, making them invisible to me.

At that moment I had a realization.

"This is why they call you the Stone Mage?" I questioned.

He nodded once more.

"I have dedicated a great deal of my life, learning our stories and being sure to record them. Books will burn—get lost even—but the stone of the earth is permanent." He, too, reached a hand to touch his works of art that spread across all of the walls inside the castle.

"I take it you recognized this one?" he asked; I thought I hallucinated the brief moment a smile began to take form on his face.

"I recognized some of it—but why Rainier?" I asked, still staring at his work of art on the wall.

"Kaneira has become a symbol of unity—of *power*—so I may have added some artistic touches to this moment." He stared at his work when he spoke.

I slowly moved down the wall, finding more moments frozen in time.

"What of this one?" I asked Lucius, who trailed shortly behind me.

"That is the Battle of Death's Chalice." Lucius remained with his gaze fixated on his creations; I stared with him.

"I am not familiar," I said.

He hummed knowingly.

"The Goddess Arudia was seeking to kill the Three-Faced God, Sabaa—or the God of Curses—for blighting one of her blessed." Lucius now reached forward, touching the carvings in the wall.

"Arudia knew she had only one chance to fell a God, and that was Death's Chalice—a *Talis* item—one enchanted by the Goddess Tasalisence—"

"That is why we are called Tessiah?" I blurted, stopping him mid-sentence.

"Precisely," he said, breaking his gaze with the wall to look at me when he spoke.

"Tasalisence is the Goddess of Existence…birthing two sons, Olym and Rainier. The other God who predated this universe with her was Vidhi, or the God of Fate. Vidhi and Tasalisence created the Talis items: five objects that could kill a God—as Vidhi believed *all* life must end."

I stared at him in awe.

"How did you learn this? What exactly is the Chalice... is it just a cup?" I didn't mean to hound him, but my understanding of history was dwarfed in the face of a man who was seemingly all-knowing.

"The Solarian scripts hold all of the universe's knowledge—except for the creation of mortals..." He sighed, seemingly flustered by the unattainable knowledge.

"The Chalice's existence was confirmed by the Solarian scripts; in fact, I have seen it—it is indeed a cup. To drink from it is to reach Vidhi: an outcome we all face yet fear all the same—death." The Stone Mage now wore a grim expression, tracing his fingers around the outline of the cup. He continued, "Tasalisence is the beginning. Vidhi is the end. They are the eternal heartbeat of the universe, its first breath as well as its last." He traced his works as if he were carving them for the first time.

"What are the other objects?" I asked, curiosity choking my restraint.

"Death's Chalice, The Eternal Harp, Arakos's Star, The Shard of Aetheris, and the Veil of Phantasm. Only one object remains in the care of the Solarian; the others have been seen few times throughout history..." He trailed off as he continued to walk down the hall, hand still touching various carvings. He eventually stopped and turned to face me, a seriousness overcoming his expression.

"However, over the years I have heard rumors of someone *hunting* the items...what for, I could not know."

I felt my stomach sink.

To have such deadly objects in existence and able to be retrieved by *anyone*...Lucius let out a low grumble: what I imagined to be his version of a chuckle.

"I would not worry much of it, Mirage. The Chalice is the worst of them, and it is in good care with the Solarian." I nodded.

I supposed that a group of people who prided themselves in magic and knowledge would not let such an object fall into the wrong hands.

"I must be on my way now. I ought to ready myself for tonight's occasion; it is my birthday after all," Lucius said in a tone one *could* mistake with excitement.

"Happy birthday!" I exclaimed to him as he walked away. He raised a hand in what I could assume was a motion of thanks.

I had not heard myself be willfully cheery in some time.

I looked forward to tonight's ball... the ball I had previously aimed to flee from.

I walked down the halls, taking in all of the carvings both brilliant and horrifying: the stories of creation, destruction, and existence.

I eventually found my way to the Autumn Courtyard, the leaves painting the sky like an eternal snowfall of Autumn's colors. It was empty in here now: no Tessiah, no other beings.

I walked to the tree I had pulled the fruit from before and gazed upon it. A truly beautiful sight—nature's arm shooting from the ground to deliver nutrients to the Earth—nutrients that strengthened my power. I reached up to touch the apple. Part of me was tempted to eat it, just to see what would happen if I did.

I reached my fingers to touch the outer flesh of the apple, and as my fingertips met it, I heard a voice from a few yards away.

"Wow... You look stunning," Stygian said. I turned to face him; he approached me with his hands buried in his pockets. He was wearing a blood-red cloak, adorned in a variety of gems which made it shine in the low sun of the Autumn Courtyard.

"And you as well," I smiled at him and made my best effort to curtsy.

"A bit rusty on your royal manners already?" he giggled at me.

"But I see you have been marked—perhaps I should have bowed to *you*." He extended a hand past me and reached for the apple I had nearly touched and plucked it from the tree.

"Delicious, aren't they?" He said whilst taking a bite into it, the liquid dripping from his lips onto his hands. I nodded politely.

Stygian pulled the apple from his lips and smiled sweetly at me. He outstretched his hand, an offering for me to also take a bite.

"Go on, I would like to show you something." He had a charming darkness about him. His smile was consuming—inviting. I suppose that some of us enjoyed playing in the dark.

Maybe I was one of them.

Without another thought, I took the apple from his hand and sunk my teeth into it.

My skin began to hum.

The places where Diana had marked my skin had begun to tingle, and I noticed a faint glow coming from my collarbone.

"Oh no—" Stygian said softly, and he reached a hand toward my neck. I felt like I was losing control of my body: that I was slowly descending into madness.

I felt like I was sharing my consciousness with another person—another me. As Stygian's fingers met the part of my collarbone, I grabbed his hand, and fire erupted from me.

"I can't—" I struggled to get the words out, and he fell backwards. I lifted my hands to my head, trying to regain control of my body—my magic.

"I just wanted to show you—to—" He stopped speaking as the flames nearly consumed me.

My arms now had flames spiraling around them from my wrists to my shoulders, blazing in what seemed to be rings around my flesh. They climbed up my arms, and I could feel them behind my eyes.

All of me was on fire.

"Mirage," Stygian said, holding a hand up to me as if to ask me to stop, but I continued to approach him. He sat a few feet away from me on the ground.

"Mirage!" he yelled again, his hand still extended. His own fire leapt from his hand, but it did not reach me.

The fire surrounded him—it was like a shield.

"What is happening to you?" I could hardly hear his voice; my thoughts were corrupted with the familiar eerie tones: *Mirage, Mirage.*

I continued to approach him, every step warranting a full stop as I reached for my head to try and silence the voices.

"*Please.*" I managed to whisper to the cacophony of voices— genderless, faceless, voices all yelling in terrifying unison at me.

Reach for the fire
Be burned by the flame
Die upon the icy spire
Forever in the Gods' game.

They screamed at me, the words so foreign—so *odd*.

Stygian rose from the ground and began to back away slowly toward the courtyard's exit, his face to me.

"Please don't make me fight back," he said, the softness in his tone melting into caution.

I could not collect my thoughts; I could not even speak to him. The words that found their way to my throat were melted down with the fire that erupted from inside of me. I stared down at the spirals around my arms—the fire that warmed my skin, but did not burn.

I then noticed that Stygian's back came into contact with another body.

I would recognize those golden eyes anywhere now.

Jesper.

"Move," Jesper said to him, peering down with those wicked golden eyes.

"Don't go near her," Stygian shot back, now fully facing him.

"I'm afraid you won't do any good to help her, *Sparky*," Jesper said, flicking a few drops of blood onto his face. For a moment, I thought I saw shadows erupt from Stygian, coming out from behind him like tendrils of darkness that reached out for Jesper, but he quickly pulled away.

I watched Jesper's fingers flicker, and Stygian stopped moving. It was as if his insides had turned to stone, rooting him into place.

Stygian yielded, despite the clear irritation flickering in his eyes.

"*Drasickar Blerium,*" Jesper said, and he moved his hand in a twisting motion. Suddenly, I felt my insides tightening. I could no longer move my body—*I was paralyzed.*

I fell to the ground onto my knees, unable to use my arms to catch the fall. I noticed it then as I kneeled motionless in the courtyard—Jesper's other hand faced the ground, his palm in the direction of the earth, and coming up from the grass was a faint series of golden twinkles.

He was somehow channeling the magic of the courtyard...

"What are you doing to me?" I choked; it seemed my throat, too, was tightening.

"I am helping you," he replied and closed his eyes—chanting the saying three more times as the earth twinkled up into his hand.

The voices ceased in chanting my name, now resorting to shrilling screams. I had no ability to cover my ears—to make any physical motion to ease the screams in my head... I screamed with them. Tears welled in my eyes, but I tried to not let them fall down my cheeks.

Jesper now stood over me.

"Release," he then said, both of his palms facing the ground.

The screaming stopped.

I had control again.

I sat on my knees, heaving from the events that just unfolded; I could not catch my breath. I could feel the nausea surfacing—it took all of my effort to not empty my guts on the ground.

As I sat, Stygian rushed over and fell to his knees beside me. He put his hand under my chin and forced my gaze to his; his eyes searched mine, as if looking for evidence of my sanity.

"Perhaps you should be more careful, darling," Jesper's eyes were vacant as he spoke, his wine-colored hair falling around his face to frame the sharpness of it.

"Okay, Jess. You can leave now," Stygian huffed, turning his attention from me and unto Jesper.

"You're welcome!" Jesper mocked as he turned away from us.

"Of course you want your dick sucked for one good deed—*thank you,* Jesper!" Stygian spoke sarcastically.

"Wait!" I yelled, but he did not even turn to face me.

"How did you know I was here?" I screamed to him, my voice raw from the shrieking.

"Like calls to like..." he said without turning or stopping.

I frantically looked around the courtyard, searching for any damage or signs of the magic that he had snuffed out of me.

. . .

"What did he do to me?" I asked Stygian, horrified at what had just taken place.

"Blood magic, it's sort of his *thing*," he said softly. He put his hand to my cheek and moved it slowly down to my jaw.

"Are you okay?" His gaze softened as he looked at me. I nodded.

For the first time in several minutes, I noticed the positioning of his hands. He nearly cradled me: one of his hands on my face, the other under my back to support me.

I stared where Jesper was just a few minutes ago, his hands to the earth, drawing on its power and somehow binding me. I was almost fearful of the consequences. My blood no longer felt like my own, almost as if he had reached his hands inside of me.

Something just didn't feel right.

"Is the gold still in my eyes?" I asked Stygian, peering into his. I felt that I could see his soul through those eyes. That I could feel his quiet—his calm.

I felt like I could see the shadows that swelled under his skin, the ones he used just moments before. There was a darkness in those deep green eyes. He nodded at me, putting both of his hands to my cheeks.

"What is going on?" he asked me, his thumbs tracing circles on my skin.

"I don't know what he did—how he did…" I trailed off, tearing my gaze from his eyes and again looking to where Jesper stood.

"Jesper has *different* abilities—but there's no way he can take away power. You're okay." He pulled me into an embrace, squeezing me tightly.

. . .

Then I felt it, the tears slowly trickling from my eyes and onto his coat. When he pulled away from the embrace, he reached a finger to my eye and wiped away the tears. As he did, he gave me a warm smile. I pulled my gaze back to his, and for a moment we just stared at one another.

"I am so sorry; I didn't even think about the Spiridium," he said.

For a moment, I thought I could get lost in him.

Lost in his warmth.

"What were those shadows?" I asked him, still concentrated on the forested color of his eyes—the deep green that sparkled in the low sun. If I did not look as closely as I had, I would mistake his eyes for black.

"My mother was a Tenebris. My father was Seaura—Spring-Kissed." He looked off to the apple tree as he spoke.

"What is a *Tenebris*?" I asked.

"The Tenebris are shadow users. They also like to keep *to* the shadows; they aren't the most social people…" He trailed off and his gaze followed as he seemed to scan the courtyard.

"You can have more than one given power?"

"Not frequently. The Tenebris aren't born, they are chosen by Skadira—the Goddess of Shadow. She blesses generations with power. So when I was born, I was blessed by her to also wield shadow magic. It did not matter that I was born Seaura—because my mother was a Tenebris. If that makes sense…" He reached for the back of his neck, almost seeming nervous at the interaction.

"Incredible," I murmured.

The Tessiah encompassed so many amazing gifts, it was both awe-inspiring and terrifying.

For a moment, I thought I noticed him blush at my words.

I did not think much before I spoke—before I moved. The way his hands felt on my cheeks was like a delicate burn that woke something deep within me. All I could think about was pressing my lips to his—to taste him.

And so I did.

I pushed myself into him, nearly mounting him in the courtyard, and I pressed my lips to his. He was soft and warm. He tasted like smoke and peppermint.

I felt him push back into me, his tongue finding its way into my mouth, begging for entry—further, deeper. He pulled me on top of him, burying his hands into my hair and drawing me in tighter. I now straddled him as the leaves fell around us slowly.

His breath caught as I moved against him, the world around us fading into nothing but the sensation of his hands gripping my waist, firm and desperate, as his shadows found their way out from underneath him to surround us.

The crisp air of the courtyard was a stark contrast to the heat erupting between us, a fire kindled by every press of his lips, every graze of his fingers.

I could feel his heart pounding beneath me, matching the erratic rhythm of my own. His lips left mine only to trail along my jaw, down my neck. I moved my hands down his chest and frantically pulled away his coat, searching for the bare skin that heaved with every breath.

I wanted to feel his fire.
Become it.

He whispered my name, his voice low and strained, filled with something between restraint and surrender.

"We shouldn't—"

"Then stop me," I whispered to him, still pulling his buttons to reveal the hot skin beneath his clothing. His grip on me tightened, his fingers digging into my hips as though grounding himself to reality, but I saw his eyes flicker and a smile parted his lips.

"I think I just might have to." He pulled me back down into him, and kissed me forcefully again, his hands moving down my collarbone and to my chest.

The shadows around us seemed to grow darker, closer, as if the night itself conspired to hide us. He pulled me tighter, his body pressed against mine, and I could feel every inch of him, including the erection that fought to release itself from his pants.

For a moment I had hoped the shadows would conceal us entirely, leaving us to become nothing more than heat and hunger, a tangle of limbs fighting the urge to tear off each other's clothes entirely.

I then felt him slowly lifting me off of him, but he did not dare remove his lips from mine.

"What the hell?" I moaned as I now sat on the blanket of leaves that nearly served as a bed. He chuckled and pushed one of the loose curls behind my ear.

"Right in the middle of the courtyard?" He laughed a bit harder and began to button his shirt.

"The only *real* threat to our discovery would be Jesper," I said back to him. This time he howled with laughter.

"I think Diana would have my head if I ruined this beautiful dress of yours…" his hands found their way to my cheeks again as he continued, "or anymore of this beautiful face." He pressed another kiss onto me. He reached a finger to his lips, and a bit of the Spiridium powder came off.

He was so warm, so inviting.

"Because I am a gentleman, I think you should allow me to escort you to the Ball tonight—perhaps a real date of sorts before you rip off my clothes?"

"So *I'm* the problem?" I laughed and crossed my arms.

"You *did* kiss *me*," He uttered quietly.

"Shall I do it again?" I moved closer to him—my face now an inch or so away from his. I felt my eyes drifting to his lips.

"Definitely yes, your *highness*." He threw himself back into me, laughing as he pressed his lips to my own but released me quickly.

There was a power I felt when I pushed myself into him. The power to choose for myself to be reckless—unafraid— and it was an intoxicating feeling.

Stygian rose from our place on the leaves, fixing the remaining buttons of his top and staring down at me. He offered me his hand and pulled me up from where I sat, a fire igniting in his eyes—but not one even I could quench.

CHAPTER NINETEEN

Stygian led me through the labyrinth of halls to the ballroom. We chatted with one another about our lives before coming here. I learned about his mother, Shadu and how magnificent she was in life.

He informed me that most of the Seaura were orphaned—by my father or other kings. I told him about Dracar and how deeply I missed him. We then arrived at a set of obsidian doors: they were grand and carved like the throne room's. The story they told must have also pre-existed the Stone Mage.

I could make out a few figures on the door, but I had no names to give them. I imagined Vidhi was one of them—the figure who was like shadow and surrounded by blackness—death himself. Beside him was a bird-like creature, with fire for wings. Before I could take the scene in more, Stygian pushed open the doors, revealing the ballroom to me.

The ceilings were adorned with constellations and stars as if we were merely yards apart from the heavens themselves. The large stained-glass windows were carved with the symbols of the seasons.

Large curtains hung from the ceiling with threads that shimmered as if they were laced with Spiridium—it was possible that they could have been. The air was thick with the scent of wines and spices, mingling with the heat of too many bodies in one space.

Stygian offered me his arm, so I took it, and he led me to the table of drinks. The wine glasses built a pyramid, the liquid pouring down them like a fountain: certainly the work of magic.

"This is amazing!" I said to Stygian as I watched the wine cascade down the glasses, filling the ones that sat beneath.

"Isn't it?" Natsu said, coming out to reveal himself from behind the glass pyramid.

Natsu reached a hand over the wine glasses, breaking the flow for a moment so that he could pull a glass out to drink from.

"So it *is* magic?" I asked as I watched him restore the flow again.

"Of course it is—everything here is magic," Natsu peered over the glasses of wine and champagne at me as he spoke. He eventually made his way around the table to us and smiled, placing his drink down.

"I haven't seen markings on anyone but Alysara in years…" he said as he reached for the powder on my eyes; I did not move or chase his hand away. He touched the Spiridium on my eyelids, and he shot backwards a few inches as he recoiled from the touch.

"Amazing!" he said excitedly.

He reached again for the drink he had put down, taking a swig before saying, "That dress is incredible by the way—Anathena is truly an artist." He raised the glass to me.

Natsu then looked past me—I also turned to gaze upon what made his eyes sparkle.

In all her glory, clad in snowflakes that seemed to cascade down her sleeves… The gown looked as if it had been spun from frost rather than thread. As the fabric reached the bodice, it formed into a constellation of diamonds, glittering brilliantly under the warm light. It was Samira who stood before us, decorated with frost and starlight.

"What did I say? A *true* artist," Natsu said as he slowly approached the frostwalker.

I too stared at her in awe as she approached. Natsu reached her before she could arrive near the drinks table where we had been lingering. I watched as her dress swayed with her step, until Stygian broke me from my thoughts.

"Hungry?" he said as he pulled out one of the unmistakable apples from the Autumn Courtyard.

"I hope you are joking," I said back to him, nearly nauseated by the sight.

"I am—none for you, your highness," he said, taking a bow and continuing to bite into the apple. I shook my head and allowed a giggle to escape my lips.

"Let's eat, though," he said, holding out his hand, and he guided me through the never-ending sea of bodies.

They moved and swayed with the rhythm of the music, their breaths rising and falling like waves crashing against a shoreline.

Eventually, we made it to the outskirts of the room, where food was sprawled across six grand tables. The dishes—like the wine glasses—were arranged in pyramids and precise formations, with plates of solid gold beneath turkey legs and mountains of desserts.

I began to pile a variety of foods onto my own platter, and Stygian occasionally looked back at me and chuckled at my eagerness. Perhaps he was used to the grandeur of such an event—I was not. I was nearing the end of the tables when someone approached me with an anger in her voice that was jarring.

Alysara.

"What are you doing here?" she questioned angrily. My eyes immediately found the markings of Spiridium she wore on her face.

"And why are *you* wearing that?" she reached a hand to my collarbone and brushed off some of the golden dust.

A man stood just inches from her—a man that could easily be mistaken for a mountain. He stood tall over her, his black curls tied back as if he were already set for battle.

He wore a mixture of fine clothes and armor, as did Alysara. The golden armor sat upon her shoulders and came across her chest—as if to protect her heart. The man who stood behind her wore a similar set of armor: golden shoulder guards that also came down to cover his chest.

She wore a dress that looked to be fashioned of smoke—as if she were merely the consequence of flame.

The eighth was not only progressive but also a notorious war kingdom.

Castle Ironshade.

Alysara was inches from my face now; I could nearly taste the venom on her breath when she spoke. She would kill me and not think twice: as far as she was concerned, I was her enemy.

I was taken aback by her accusations—that she deemed my presence a threat to her—and I had failed to defend myself from her verbal assault. She reached quickly down to her hip where a sword was fastened to her belt, and she pulled it up to my throat in a matter of seconds.

"Alysara—stop!" Stygian had his hand against her blade now, doing his best to push her back from me. I could feel the steel biting into the lower part of my jaw where the bone met my throat. I felt a drop of blood come down onto her blade.

The look in her eyes at that moment was ferocious. She was not only ready to kill me—she was more than willing. Her gaze sharpened upon mine, her sword finding its way deeper into my skin with every passing moment.

"Please—" I managed to strain. I was too fearful to speak as the blade was so close to cutting me enough to where the healing would cease to be useful to me.

"Kokonos, stop her!" Stygian barked at the mountainous man who stood behind Alysara. He said nothing, but he touched the hilt of his sword in response to Stygian and peered down at him.

"You need to take a step back," Stygian said, fire blazing in his eyes as his shadows sat around him now, waiting for him to call upon them. I felt his hand wrap around my waist as he gently pulled my hands away from where she cut me.

It did not heal.

"Fuck," he huffed.

Alysara merely stood, the rage still stirring in her eyes as she cast her hateful gaze onto me. Her knuckles were turning white where she tightly gripped the blade.

"You brought a Sifrune sword into a ball full of magic users?" Stygian yelled at her. It seemed the room had gone entirely silent with the exception of our current commotion.

"Why isn't it healing?" I asked him, terrified at what she had done to me.

"*Sifrune*," she said blankly—no apparent emotion penetrating her cold gaze.

"It is anti-magic to stop Tessiah from using their powers," Alysara said as she resheathed her sword, my blood still glistening on its surface.

"In the eighth, we use more than just Sifrune, though." She said the words as if she were offended that Stygian didn't know better.

The man who allegedly went by the name Kokonos still remained silent, but he kept his hand wrapped around the hilt of his sword—undoubtedly also enchanted with this anti-magic.

I then watched the crowd begin to part as someone made their way toward us, and rather quickly. I then saw her face appear over the shoulders of the nearest bystanders.

Kaneira.

Her dress was like liquid sunlight, a cascade of golden brilliance that was spun from the very fire that crowns the sun; the silk embraced the curves of her body. There were yellow gems adorning the bodice which shimmered under the warm white lights of the ballroom.

The queen.

"Alysara—what have you done?" she said frantically, and came in a near full sprint to my side. Her face was also marked with the Spiridium powder.

"Why is *she* here, Kaneira?" The venom still coated her tone.

"Because she is like us, like *you*. We took her from Carlisle," Kaneira said as she touched the cut on my neck.

"Jesper!" Kaneira thundered into the ballroom, waiting for him to part the crowd.

Like clockwork, he found himself pushing to the front of the crowd, that wicked, coy smile parting his lips as he approached me.

I watched him move his hands into gestures I did not recognize as he approached, and again, he put his palm to the ground; the world beneath him glittered and rose up to greet his hand.

I physically recoiled from his touch upon my neck. He ran his thumb over the cut, and it sealed as if I had healed it myself. However, unlike when *I* healed, this left a scar—I could feel the raised skin under my fingertips.

"I'm not quite as *equipped* as you are, but it will do," Jesper said as he rose from my side and offered me a hand. I stared at him for a long moment, my eyes narrowing upon him.

His lips curled into a soft smile, one that was almost inviting. I denied his hand with a subtle shake of my head.

"Fine, stay on the floor then," he smirked, then found his way back out into the large ballroom.

Kaneira made an effort to thank him, but his back stayed to her, and he raised a hand as if to acknowledge her. She ran her hands over my cheeks, a sign of affection.

"I apologize, Kaneira," Alysara said, sincerity in her voice. Kaneira shot her a disapproving glare.

"Apologies, *princess*," Alysara gave me a tender nod. She seemed genuine in her apologies—that she truly deemed me to be a threat.

Kaneira rose from her place at my side, and the crowd that had been watching the events all bowed to her before scurrying away to the various activities of the Ball.

"Have fun—and try not to get yourself killed," Kaneira whispered, casting down a look of both sincerity and disapproval.

"Everything is fine...back to your snobby discussions and overindulgences," Kaneira nearly laughed at her own comment, but managed to keep it down.

I was overwhelmed by what had just transpired before me.

Sifrune?

A new word to add to the expansive dictionary of Tessian language.

"Mira, are you okay?" Diana's voice rang out, managing to dissipate my thoughts as if they were made of nothing but smoke.

"Yeah, I'm okay," I said to her; this was the first time tonight I had seen her.

. . .

Her dress was like the heavens captured in cloth—a masterpiece woven with threads of starlight. Her hair, like molten moonlight, spilled over her shoulders, blending seamlessly with the aura of her gown. She held the essence of lunar beauty and grace—the moon and all of its stars pulled together to form human flesh.

"Diana—" I breathed upon seeing her. I took her hands into my own as I spoke to her, "You look stunning!"

She smiled sweetly and gripped my hands, "As do you, *your grace.*"

"Ah!" She cheered and clapped her hands together upon noticing my company.

"You came together!" she gestured at both Stygian and I. I nodded at her, a blush gathering on my cheeks.

"How marvelous!" she said cheerily. "Well—eat, dance, *love!*" She said the last word with a specific emphasis, and Stygian offered me his hand.

"We must do as she says," he said with a smile.

"Yes, you must!" She winked before spinning off to dance with Natsu and Samira. He pulled me into him, close enough that I could feel the heat coming off of him. He whispered into my ear, "Dance with me." His words tickled my skin pleasantly.

The faint music swelled, its melody slow yet provocative—and intoxicating as if it too had Spiridium melted into it. He pulled me closer, impossibly so.

His hand was firm against the small of my back, the other cradling mine with deliberate care. Our bodies moved together, but I wished for a closeness not achievable while our clothes still hung from our bodies.

His steps were precise, yet there was an edge of wildness to his movements. I felt it in the way his hand pressed against me, guiding me through each turn, each sway—as if the entire ballroom had vanished, leaving only the two of us in its place.

. . .

"You dance well," I murmured, though the words felt insufficient, unworthy of the heat simmering between us.

Every place his fingers touched me, I nearly felt like I was burning alive. I wanted to close the distance between us...to be consumed by him—to feel his flesh upon mine.

"You're not terrible—but I expected a bit more *flare* from royalty," he replied, his voice low and teasing, brushing against my ear like a spark igniting a flame.

"How rude! Do you think my drunkard father bothered to teach us to dance?" I playfully pushed away from him for just a moment, but he pulled me back in, just as I pushed away.

"No, no..." He said with a wolfish grin, "I'm not going to let you put space between us now." He pulled me back into a spin, the kind only stories told of. In a thousand lifetimes, I never thought that this sort of moment would be possible—not for me.

"You know, I never would have foreseen this the day I was taken," I said, my eyes finding his as he continued to spin me.

"And why not?" He pressed, his eyes softening as he looked down on me.

"Because the day Hiver came to retrieve me, he used the words *'torture, kill, imprison'*...I thought—" I stuttered.

"I thought that was my fate," I sucked in a hard breath.

"You are royalty, Mirage. That would have *never* been your fate," he huffed, amused at the comments.

"Not here."

"*Here*, you can be whatever you'd like. You can be royal, you can be—" he spoke with an effervescent cheer, the words tumbling out in bursts of excitement.

"You can be... *you*," he finished, joy flickering on his face.

"What if I don't know who that is?" I asked in a very serious tone. Maybe I had just destroyed this perfect moment with the hasty movement of my tongue.

"How about I tell you what I see," he twirled me once and dipped me low, hardly able to contain his amusement.

"I think you are fiery, demanding—" He raised a brow as he pulled me in tight again.

"I think you're a bit...*avant-gard*e." He pulled me around again, making me giggle and squirm as he would intentionally touch me in places that made me tickle.

"Stop it!" I chuckled and wiggled beneath his touch as he pulled me in tight again, restricting my ability to fight him off.

"*Demanding!*" He hung onto the last consonant and subtly rolled his eyes, hinting at the inner amusement—a knowing, almost conspiratorial acknowledgement of how he truly saw me.

"I forgot—beautiful, lovely, exciting..." he giggled as he spoke, hardly getting the words out.

"Oh why don't you just kiss me already," I teased, tilting my head to the side.

"I would love to do more than that."

"Like what?" I asked, my mouth staying half open to expose my teeth as I looked up at him.

"I want to feel your fire, Mirage—let it burn me." He moved his lips to my neck and kissed me softly. He then whispered into my neck, "Show me where you burn the brightest." His lips found their way back up to my jaw and to my lips.

He kissed me with such a force, an intensity that I could not match even if I had hoped to. We both possessed the gift of fire—and I could ask for nothing more than to let his absorb me entirely. His hands gripped my waist, pulling me impossibly closer, and I could feel the raw strength in his hold—the kind that begged for my surrender, that demanded it.

I felt the world blur around us, the swirls of gowns and the clink of glasses fading into the background. His body moved against mine in perfect sync. I had to again resist to take him right here in the middle of the ballroom.

I wondered if anyone else in the room could feel the fire that threatened to consume us both.

"Since you possess fire—I can only wonder if you fuck like it too," I said to him silently, only willing my lips to separate from his to make the statement.

"Wouldn't you like to know," he said, pulling me into him yet again, so tightly I could feel him growing hard against me.

"I think you'd like to know too," I said to him and reached a hand down just to run my hand over his erection. I would not dare tease further in this setting.

"Careful," he whispered to me, grabbing my hand and pulling it back up to his shoulders. I burned where his hand touched my wrist.

"Oh, like you'd risk it," I laughed at him and his smile turned more eager than it was before.

"Oh, who said I would make you pay for that here." His fingers found their way to the curve of my hips—then lower, his touch firm and possessive, igniting a fire wherever his fingers skimmed.

"Now who's a bit *avant-garde*," I shook my head and rolled my eyes at him.

"Your fault, your highness." He squinted at me, crinkling his nose.

"Shall we leave here, then?" I asked him.

"Ah, that is not very proper decorum—even if you are a princess." Before we could make it from our spot in the dancing area, Diana joined us.

"Are you enjoying yourself?" She asked me. Her eyes were dazzling in this light; the soft purple flickered in its warmth.

I nodded and Stygian did as well. I was almost worried that she would have seen our interactions just moments before she joined us.

"Have you seen Hiver?" She asked us after a moment of smiles and silence. Her expression of joy melted into something that resembled worry.

I hadn't even thought of him.

※

I felt my stomach drop upon her asking—how I did not think to look for him, to see him, despite all he had done for me. I shook my head to respond, Stygian did the same.

"Have you checked winter?" I asked, and Diana shook her head.

"I can go find him if you'd like?" I suggested and Diana smiled at the sentiment.

"Thank you," she said softly and touched my arm before turning away and fading into the crowd.

"I'll be back," I said to Stygian. I kissed his cheek, but he pulled me into a tight embrace and kissed me hard on the lips before smiling and letting me depart.

CHAPTER TWENTY

I stopped frequently to look at the marvelous creations that the Stone Mage had worked on. I would trace the many stories that were carved into the rock and obsidian of the walls.

I may have been lying to myself about *why* I meandered in the corridors.

There was a feeling of guilt seeping into my bloodstream. It was making me feel as if I were overheating, that the air around me was becoming heavier.

Why did I feel so guilty?

I tried to ease the anxiety by feeling the cold stone beneath my fingers. Eventually I found my way to that lovely courtyard—the land of eternal winter. The snowflakes flurried down softly upon me as I entered a place where dusk never fades into night.

"Hiver?" I called out, not seeing a soul in the vast courtyard. I walked over to the tree where I watched him play with the boys just days ago, crouching down to that very spot.

I reached a hand out to touch the fresh snow that had accumulated in it, when he materialized over me and grabbed my hand.

I whirled around to face him and saw his outfit, undoubtedly also fashioned by Anathena's skilled hands.

He wore a dark blue linen shirt with golden buttons. On top of that lay a coat that was crafted from the night itself—with streaks of gold that outlined constellations. The shadows flocked to him, gripping the navy blue of his shirt.

I realized that we matched *perfectly*: both of our attire forged from the night sky. Anathena wove the stars into our cloth—into the buttons which fell along his shirt. We both stood, wrapped in shadow and dusk. His eyes were illuminated by the pale light of the moon as he looked upon my face.

"Wow," I muttered. Without thinking, I reached out to touch his coat; I was stunned by the similarities in our ensembles. As I neared his coat, he dissipated into thin air as if he had never been there.

"Forgive me," he said from behind me yet again, "but the last time we touched, I think I got the wrong impression."

"Hiver...I–"

"No, do not think about apologizing, or explaining yourself. You owe me no justification for your desires." His whole body seemed to sparkle in this lighting.

His eyes seemed to darken to form a stormy blue color, like twilight falling on the ocean.

"Hiver—"

"I don't want an excuse or apology, *please*." He looked at me with such pain radiating in those eyes.

"I— was just getting to know you...I didn't—I don't—" I choked on the words; they struggled to come off my tongue.

"I have always known *you*," his voice was soft as he spoke.

"What?" I gasped at his comment.

"For fifteen years, I have been told all about you: I know your favorite color is sage green, I know your favorite flower is the violet,

I know you have nightmares almost every night, I know you have… *fits*…you can't control—I have seen you. *I know you.*" It sounded like he struggled to get the words out.

"I don't understand," I managed as tears fought their way from my eyes.

"I know you only sleep with silk because the sensation of it calms you. I know that Dracar taught you how to wield a blade. I know your soul is passionate and fiery." He continued, his voice raspy as he spoke.

"How—"

"Diana loves you. She always loved you; Mirage—" He closed his eyes and sucked in a deep breath.

"And here you came…then I couldn't help but love you too." He swallowed hard.

"Hiver I—"

"Goodnight, princess," he interjected as he dematerialized into nothingness. He faded into the twilight of winter; not even the sparkle of his magic remained.

"Gods," I whispered to myself.

Guilt had become me.

I knew why it tugged at my chest when Diana said his name.

I did not know how to feel—*what* to feel. I had betrayed someone I cared deeply for. Someone who had slowly become my friend. The other night in the throne room, I had craved something more from him, something intimate. I had wanted him to remove my clothes, to touch my skin—the way I felt about Stygian too.

My mind buzzed with guilt, desire, and rage.

I was a mess.

"Hiver!" I yelled into the empty courtyard.

"Hiver!" My lungs burned from the frost that found its way

inside of them. I retired to his spot beneath the tree and put my palms to my eyes.

I began to sob.

Many days worth of emotions spilled from me.

Rage.
Fear.
Sadness.
Desire.
Love.

It all mingled and forged my tears; they singed my skin.

"I'm sorry—I'm so sorry," I cried into my hands. The Spiridium stuck to my eyelids like a second skin, hardly coming off onto my fingertips.

I didn't think of Hiver in my blind desire—*but should I have? Should he have crossed my mind? Did I want him out of convenience or out of connection?*

At that moment I was unsure of what I wanted—*who* I wanted.

I burned for both of them.

I sat for a few more moments in my misery, the tears soaking my skin; I would be devastated to lose Hiver. My sobs echoed faintly in the courtyard, swallowed by the stillness of snowfall.

I didn't know what was eating away at my soul more: Hiver's absence, my own reckless desires, or the tangle of emotions I couldn't begin to unravel. The tree above me stood as silent witness to my turmoil, its branches heavy with frost.

I found myself staggering for the exit to the Winter Courtyard; my legs felt heavy beneath me. As I trudged through the fresh snow, my tears melted small areas of the white fluff beneath me.

I made my way back out into the corridors of the castle, tracing those lovely designs left by the Stone Mage. Eventually, I ran into him, carving a new design into the stone.

. . .

"Hello, my dear," he frowned at me.

"Hello—" I started, and I so desperately wanted answers that I didn't give another thought to the words before they tumbled from my tongue, "How did you and Kaneira make up after what happened with my mother?"

He lowered his hands from his work and merely stared blankly.

"I'm sorry, I—" Before I could continue, he spoke.

"We cannot always perfectly mend what we break," he pulled a hand out from his robes and touched the raised skin left in the wake of Jesper's magic.

"We can heal the skin, but the scars remain." His tone was somber and deliberate when he spoke.

"I made a mistake—and I don't know how to fix it." Lucius stared at me, his head turning to the side as if he was making every effort to truly hear the words from my lips.

"Most of our mistakes are born of love—there is no greater doom than passion," he said softly, his head still tilted as he studied my expressions.

"I suppose it does come from a place of love, but I do not know how to apologize—"

"No, no," he interjected, "the moment you find sorrow in the tales of your heart is the moment your story begins to unravel—no longer your own to tell," he murmured.

A fresh set of tears poured from my eyes, tickling my cheeks.

"Now, child," Lucius said, his grim expression still dominating his features. He reached out to touch the tear with his finger.

"To love is to live." A smile finally cracked his otherwise stone-cold expression.

"To live is to fail," he said while catching another tear with his finger as it fell. I nodded up at him, the smile slowly fading from his face.

Such a rare spectacle.

"Live freely my dear, love recklessly, fail frequently—it is our destiny." He put a finger under my chin and gave me an affectionate gaze before returning to his work on the walls.

I found myself wandering to the familiar courtyard, and I looked into the eternal land of falling leaves—the space that existed between life and death.

The stage of the year where the leaves would fall and perish, and lean into the icy death that was winter. Perhaps I too existed in a stage between progress and tradition—the constant battle between the familiar and the unknown. That was what Autumn encompassed; it was a point in time between the familiar and the inevitable untold.

I went to the tree and sank down its trunk, sitting on a bed of leaves and staring out at the beautiful courtyard: serene and empty.

It was a devastating reality that this space was always so deserted: the one season with so few Tessiah—so few people milling about in the vibrant leaves. The silent hum of the fireflies and fairy-like creatures filled my otherwise ringing ears.

The anxiety was rising in my chest, creating a consistent metallic droning in my ears. Though I felt confident in the rightness of my decision, I still feared facing Hiver.

What could I even say? How could I even begin to explain the moments between us this morning and the ones I just shared with Stygian?

Perhaps I deserved neither of them—their lust and love alike. An apple fell from the tree to my feet; it was a brilliant shade of crimson. If I hadn't known any better I would think it to be covered in blood. I reached for it and gazed upon its exterior, the shiny and tempting red color bidding me to bite into its flesh.

I thought to just bite into it, to simply roil in my misery. I turned the apple over in my hands for a few moments and decided to throw it as hard as I could into the Courtyard. I let out a frantic scream, followed by the beginnings of a sob as I watched it hit another tree many yards away. I saw it roll to a stop, tears beginning to blur my vision.

Then, I noticed a hand reaching down to pick up the apple.

Jesper.

I watched him lift the apple to his mouth and take a bite, no emotion showing on his face as he did.

"You have something I really want, *Mirage.*" He tossed the apple to the ground and approached me slowly—approached was not the right word, he *stalked* toward me.

"What could you possibly want?" I scowled; I was emotionally exhausted and hardly able to continue this interaction.

"Well… for starters your royal status would be nice." He gave me a predatory smile, the kind that was meant to intimidate.

"Hah! You already parade yourself around like you are," I scoffed at him.

"Perhaps." He flashed me his teeth when he smiled.

"There's something else I could *really* use from you, though," he said with an almost gentleness in his tone.

"What is that?" I asked as the tears streaked my cheeks.

"Your most precious blood." He was now standing over me, one hand in his pocket, the other extending toward me as if to help me up.

"No," I said through tears, but the well had started to dry.

"Tsk tsk tsk…" He rescinded his offer to take his hand.

"You don't have a choice." I felt my body tense at the words, and I realized it was not a natural reaction but rather his magic inside of me.

"Why do you want my blood?" I cried out.

"*Zertost*," he said, and before I could react, the world turned black around me—I slowly fell unconscious.

CHAPTER
TWENTY-ONE

"Ahh, good morning beautiful!" Jesper towered over me. The world around me was still too hazy; I could not even begin to fight back—not to mention, I had been restrained.

"Morning?" I murmured, my body aching from the slumber. I heard a sound of agreement leave him, and he came to the side of the table where I had been restrained.

I didn't recognize the material that held me: it was like elastic stone, a truly bizarre element I could not have even crafted in my imagination.

"I'm almost done," he said to me in a very serious tone. My eyes began to focus on the world around me, and I was able to make sense of the various shapes and contraptions around me.

I was in some sort of alchemy laboratory.

"What is this place?" I managed groggily, and I attempted to reach for my eyes to wipe them, helpless under the bindings.

"Nowhere of interest to you," He said nonchalantly as he pulled a tube from my arm.

"Ah!" I let out a small yelp from the twinge of pain where he removed it.

My skin didn't heal after the tube was been removed.

Jesper said something softly under his breath before moving his finger over the wound and closing it—just as he did my neck. Like before, the healing left a scar.

"Sorry, you can't heal under those," he said, nodding and gesturing to the bindings that held me to the table.

He moved things about a small surface, clinking and clattering as he went; I hadn't a single clue what he was doing—and more importantly, *why*.

He took a syringe-like item from the table and stuck it into the flask of blood, extracting some of it and putting it into a bright green solution. It nearly glowed in the light of the laboratory.

"Why do you look afraid?" His tone was sincere and kind when he spoke, as if he truly could not understand my fear.

"Why do you think!" I spat at him, pulling again at the Sifrune restraints.

"I would never hurt you—not in any notable way…I suppose the cannula might have pinched a bit." He reached for the little tube and waved it in the air a bit before setting back down on the small table.

"That *is* the thing: I would *never* hurt my own people. That is why I am doing this, to save them." He reached for the restraint that held my legs and undid it. I stared at him, completely puzzled by his decision. He moved up to the next restraint and removed that too.

"What stops me from killing you the moment that last restraint comes off?" I said against my better judgement.

"Mostly your lack of training," he scoffed.

"Though I welcome you to try." He crossed his arms and smirked at me from over the table.

My cheeks were burning with rage.

He was right.

KINGDOM OF THE SUN

I did not know how to use my magic at all.

"Though I do find you incredibly unpleasant..." I started to say to him. I thought this time about my words before I continued, and even still, I continued anyway.

"You don't appear *entirely* deranged—just a bit." I said to him; he gave me that wolfish grin again and as he did, the door flew open.

"They're looking for her, Jesper," Araya said, the morning sunlight beaming in behind her.

"And I'm letting her go now." Jesper undid the third binding.

"I wouldn't run if I were you." His tone was serious and stern.

"You lost a lot of blood, you'll surely faint," Jesper said as he undid the last strap. I shot up from the table and made an effort to bolt, but a few feet away from the table, I felt the world turning dark around me—consuming me.

"Please catch her, Araya," Jesper said nonchalantly.

"Jess—you vex me sometimes..." I heard her voice, and I felt hands grabbing me as the world went black yet again.

I woke up to the familiar crunch of black velvet.

"Are you out of your mind?" Kaneira boomed. I turned my head slightly and found my gaze upon a set of familiar lilac-colored eyes.

Diana.

She stroked my cheek gently with her hand as she looked down upon me. I raised my hands to my eyes and rubbed them; my entire body ached.

"You want to keep hiding! You want to keep running!" Jesper was now yelling, a fury overtaking his tone.

"Is that what you call it, *running?*" Kaneira spoke with a particular edge, as if she was fighting between whether to be furious or devastated.

"I am protecting you—*we*—" She gestured to an ever silent Lucius, "are trying to protect you! We aren't *running*!" Kaneira snapped, a madness overcoming her features.

Her eyes blazed with a mania that I had never seen in anyone else; it was a frenzy unique to her.

"Protection only goes so far, Kaneira. The only way out is through—*war*." Jesper wore a solemn expression, his golden eyes blazing in the late morning sunlight.

"We are outnumbered, and the majority of you are young. I won't risk the lives of my people for—"

"Freedom." Jesper cut through the tension with his interruption. He crossed his arms, his nostrils flaring.

"Freedom comes through patience, strategy…if we rush in blindly because we have magic we will be slaughtered." Kaneira gathered her calm.

Lucius continued her sentiment, "Freedom is taken with the precision of a scalpel, not the recklessness of a hammer."

I sat up straighter so that I could see more of my surroundings—and then I saw him, sitting on a chair near the throne.

Hiver.

I knew I couldn't walk to him: the lack of blood in my system made it challenging to rise too quickly from my current position. I debated crawling to him.

He sat in his same attire from the night before, the same night sky ensemble. He looked disheveled, unlike his usual self. He did not look at me; his gaze stayed trained on the golden hair claw he held in his hand. He tossed it back and forth, occasionally making it disappear entirely. It was a Spikestar beetle claw—one of them that must have fallen from my head.

"I refuse to let them die in vain," Jesper croaked; it seemed he was holding back tears.

"I am sorry about what happened to your parents. I am sorry that they died—"

"Murdered—they were *murdered*," he corrected. Kaneira nodded sympathetically. Jesper shifted impatiently.

"The scripts tell of a way to make elixirium blood into an anti-healing agent. I can coat swords, arrows, spears, and more with it; it will stop the wounded from healing." Jesper's eyes now flickered with something that resembled excitement.

"You're not an alchemist—you're an artificer," I murmured. He turned to face me, his golden eyes blazing with enthusiasm and passion.

"The Solarian are many things," Jesper said with a smile.

"Except you are not Solarian," Lucius responded in his typical vacant tone. Jesper's features burned with a fury that could only be matched by the fire blazing in his eyes.

"No, I'm not...but *they* were," he said with such venom, I could nearly feel its sting. Jesper turned again to me, the sincerity taking hold over his furious expression.

"I would never hurt you, but your blood is one of our greatest weapons. We can actually win a—"

"No. You may not fill her head or anyone else's with your idea of battle. To go to war is to lose—even if you believe you have won," Kaneira seethed when she spoke.

"We've *been* at war. Since Carlisle started killing us, we *have* been at war," Lucius said. Before another would could be spoken, Kaneira raised a hand as if to silence the argument, and she left the throne room, Hiver in step behind her.

"Hiver!" I yelled, my voice seeming to echo off the walls of the largely empty room. He turned to face me but yielded no expression. I felt my heart sink.

Diana still sat beside me, a hand resting gently on mine. She had not said anything since I opened my eyes. I stared at her for a long moment; it was now only us and Jesper in the room. She gave me a polite smile before turning to Jesper with a grimace.

"Why would you do this?" she erupted.

"I'm fighting for you, too," Jesper said, not matching her fervor. Diana ran a finger over where the tube had been just hours before. The skin was raised—scarred, now.

"And who will you hurt to win that fight?" Diana's voice was hollow, echoing her sadness. Jesper merely stared, his expression haunted.

"We paid the price once—my parents paid the price with their blood. Taking a few ounces of hers is a small price to pay." Jesper said, his tone laced with melancholy.

He carried himself in a manner that displayed his maniacal nature. He was plagued by the loss of his parents—now martyrs for a war that was forever sitting on the horizon. I agreed with them both: Kaneira *and* Jesper. That it was unfair to stick to shadows because the light would seek to burn us alive.

Jesper was unhinged at best, horribly psychotic at worst—It seemed that he consistently toed the line between madness and irredeemable insanity. Diana merely shook her head, a silent gesture of disappointment. Jesper took that as his cue to leave.

"Are you okay?" Diana finally said to me, her eyes searching my face for any noticeable distress.

"I'm okay—just a bit sore." I reached to my arm where the skin was now raised. Diana gently patted my hand before rising from the chair and also exiting the throne room. I stayed where I was.

Misery.
Anxiety.
Helplessness.

The current cocktail of emotions I drank in the form of tears. I could taste the salt on my lips—on my tongue. I felt like I was drowning and every time I was allowed to breathe, something pushed me right back under.

I lay there until dusk came.

I did not eat.
I did not move.
I simply lay.

The hurricane of emotions melted into numbness. Right before I found myself falling into the embrace of sleep, the throne room doors opened very slowly. I decided to not move. I heard soft footsteps approaching me, and quite quickly. I eventually decided to sit up, and I came eye to eye with Araya.

"Come to take me again so soon?" I asked her, too exhausted to put up a fight if she *had* come for that purpose.

"No, not at all." Her tone was sincere and questioning.

"I came here to apologize to you—for Jesper." She decided to sit beside me. I had to resist the urge to move and put more space between us.

"He really does want to do what is best for *us*." She gestured between herself and I.

She had a very expressive face; she wore every emotion on her skin—in her lips, in her eyes. I could tell she was being sincere because of it. In this light, her hair blended perfectly into her surroundings—the inky midnight color that came to her shoulders. Her eyes were the color of ancient Ekelwood trees: a rich brown. They were warm like the earth, smooth and deep.

"I was told you were a Solarian." I brought my gaze to hers as I spoke.

"Yes and no." She spoke softly; her voice had the essence of honey—thick and sweet. I noticed then the sharpness of her features: the way her cheek bones made her cheeks indent, the sharpness of her nose.

"I am solstice born, but have not yet been invited to the order. One day, soon..." I could hear the hopelessness in her voice.

"When would they invite you?" I asked her.

"My 21st birthday—which passed four months ago..." She trailed off, a deep sadness consuming her features.

"I'm sorry," was all I could manage.

"It's war," she started, rising from the chair and making a half-hearted shrug.

"I see," I murmured. She stared at me for a long moment, her expression becoming worried.

"I am sorry for what happened to you—I wasn't going to get in his way, but maybe I should have." Her eyes watered when she spoke, but a tear never came rolling down her cheek.

"It's okay," I said plainly. I meant it, but I was overcome with fatigue.

"Sometimes we do things we aren't proud of for the people we love." I pursed my lips as I said it, almost regretting the words.

She gave me a courteous smile and showed herself out of the throne room. I would spend another night in this room—but this time, it would be alone.

His words hung in the back of my mind.

He knew so much about me, but to me he was just a stranger.

CHAPTER
TWENTY-TWO

I frantically grabbed at my chest and arms as I rose at the brink of dawn, the sun kissing me as I had known it to.

I heard the loud whispers of voices coming from outside the throne room's doors, the sound of footfalls becoming louder and quicker as the voices approached.

I sat and waited to see who would come through the doors, hoping it would be Hiver. When they opened, it revealed the final members of a once lovely trio—Lucius and Kaneira.

"Ah, good morning child," Kaneira said as she approached me, her usually crazed expression absent from her face. Lucius simply nodded to me as he approached. Kaneira's ensemble caught my eye; she wore a golden helm that covered the top of her face, exposing her mouth.

It had scratches and carvings on it, indicating that it had seen battle. She wore all black, tightly-fitted clothing that appeared thick and protective. On top of it rested golden armor that looked to be crafted by the Gods themselves. The armor, like the helm, had been scarred from previous battles. Knicks and scratches adorned it like a set of jewels would a dress.

"Are you going into battle?" I said with sleep still coating my tongue.

"No, you are." Kaneira gave me a wicked smile and clapped her hands.

"Up now." She gestured toward the throne room's grand doors.

"I figured Diana had told you that today you would start training. That is why I was so pleased to see you at this hour, but I can tell it maybe was *not* by choice." She looked me up and down.

She led me down a corridor that felt to be more like a labyrinth, every moment a new turn and twist. I felt terribly lost as she guided me down it. She finally stopped in front of a large, ancient slab of wood.

This was no ordinary door, but one that was truly *alive*. The door seemed to take large breaths, and the great wood creaked with every inhale and exhale.

"Open, Torvain. I must access the armory."

The door then did the unthinkable: *it opened its eyes.*

"I do not recognize the new one," the door said, its voice thunderous and ancient.

"Mirage Darakyn, the Princess of Castle Sage—an Autumn-Kissed Tessiah," Kaneira said.

"*Hmmm,*" was the tree door's only response.

It was an unsettling sight. A wooden door, breathing—somehow *living*.

"*Nihiryn,*" the door said and opened for us to enter.

"Thank you, Torvain," Kaneira said, stepping into the massive room. I must have worn my mortified expression on my face as Kaneira leaned down to me and said, "Do not be afraid. Torvain is an unequivocal good."

I was completely awestruck yet again by what I saw before me.

The armory was unlike anything I had ever seen—it was the intersection of brutality and elegance, forming a space that could only belong to her.

The room stretched wide and high, its vaulted ceilings adorned with intricate carvings that told the stories of battles past—Tessian warriors, etched into the stone like immortal guardians.

In the center of it all was the tub—though to call it a mere tub would be an understatement. It was carved from dark stone, large and rectangular with steps leading to its center. Steam rose lazily from its surface, curling into the air and creating a faint mist that softened the hard edges of the armory.

I could not take in the scene any more vigorously.

I wished to touch every armor set, to wear them, to wield the great blades in the room. *It was mesmerizing.* I reached for the armor set closest to the tub when Kaneira reached for my hand and swatted it down.

"Bathe first," she pointed at the vast pool of water that steamed and hissed in the morning light.

"Right now?" I did not even look at her, but rather kept my eyes focused on the beautiful set of armor. I could not even envision it on a battlefield; it was too grand—too marvelous to see the brutality of the blade...

"Yes, I'll find you armor that should fit." Kaneira quickly disappeared among the many armor pieces arranged with a deadly precision.

As I neared the hot pool of water, its scents pleasantly tickled my nostrils. The smell of ginger and cedar created an aroma both invigorating and grounding. I watched the steam roll off of the water slowly, and I felt a twinge of excitement as I dipped my foot into the pool.

"I found a set for you," I heard Kaneira's voice echo from somewhere behind a mass of armor stands. I could not even bring myself to open my eyes.

I heard her grumble over me, so I reluctantly opened them.

The set of armor she had pulled for me was incredible.

It was in pristine condition: a black set of armor that looked to have veins of sunfire coursing through it. The pauldrons flared slightly, their edges kissed by the same burning veins, and the chest plate bore the faint image of a rising sun, its rays barely visible beneath the coursing fire.

Even the gauntlets shimmered, each finger tipped with a faint glimmer of flame as though the wearer could channel raw power with a mere gesture. The armor itself seemed to be forged under the God of the Sun, his touch emanating in every crevice.

"For me?" I asked, truly breathless at the creation she held before me. She simply nodded in response.

"Now hurry up, child, we have work to do." Kaneira placed the armor on an empty stand outside of the tub for me with a fresh set of clothing similar to hers—the tight black suit.

She left the armory then, but before she stepped through the terrifying door, she turned to me and said, "Meet me in the throne room when you are ready, the others will be waiting." She then exited through the door—*Torvain*—I suppose its name was.

I stayed under the water for as long as I could until it felt like my lungs would burst. I ran my hands through my hair, making every effort to undo the knots which had formed.

I looked out of the tub at my ball gown which sat strewn about the floor—a hard contrast to the intensity of the surrounding armory.

I thought again of the grim expression Hiver wore in the courtyard as he spoke to me. There was no hatred in his eyes, but a deep sadness stirring in his icy gaze.

I decided it was time to get out of the tub.

I nearly dragged myself out; I felt the aromas gripping my skin as I rose from the bath, clinging to me as the steam rolled off of my body. I looked down at the neatly folded ensemble beneath the Sun-Kissed armor.

I ran a hand over its molten veins. I could not believe she wished for me to wear this—that she sought out this piece for me.

To be called Sun-Kissed back home was an insult—we were children that had the wrong features—the wrong hair, the wrong eyes—and onlookers were sure to let us know of this.

Here, though, Sun-Kissed was a gift, and not even the proper word.

I pulled the black suit over my still-steaming body. The towels were able to remove the physical essence of the water, but the aromas and steam seemed to linger—like they had become me.

I could feel the tingle of ginger on my body, and the water seemed to hum with an aura of life. Even the final drops, sliding down my body, felt alive—breathing their last into me, urging me to pull myself out from my misery.

The black suit was thick against my skin; it had been made with a fabric meant to sustain the sharpness of a blade. The cloth was thick and woven in such a marvelous pattern.

It fit me tightly, leaving no shape of my body to the imagination. I could not recall a time where I wore pants. I stared down at the form of my legs under the black fabric—a truly bizarre sight to behold. I had never seen fabric take this shape on me.

I stared at the helm which was truly magnificent; it had golden spikes coming from its back, as if to mimic rays of sunlight from the back of my skull.

I wandered down the vast expanse of hallway until I stumbled upon the throne room. Truly, I thought it was an impressive feat that I had made it back here without proper guidance.

As I pushed open the golden doors, I saw several of my friends in the room, all adorned in customized armor like my own.

Diana and Hiver's stood out the most. The metal their armor was made with was a pure white, with dark blue and silver outlining the moon on each of their chests.

The entire suit seemed alive, as though it carried the weight of the heavens within its folds, wrapping them in an aura of celestial power. Diana's helm was very peculiar, covering her eyes entirely and stretching out to form what appeared to be horns.

I could not fathom why she would fight without the ability to see, or what purpose that served.

Stygian wore armor carved of fire like mine, but the sun was absent from his design. He did not have the same molten veins which traced my armor; instead he had golden engravings that seemed to spell out incantations of some sort.

Natsu's armor looked to be made of the ocean itself. A rich blueish-green color coated his armor, with white rifts that appeared to create the illusion of waves. His armor followed the curves of his body as if it truly were water clinging to his frame.

The only person in the room who did not wear any armor was Lucius.

"Why is Lucius without armor?" I asked out of curiosity.

"Because Lucius doesn't need it," Kaneira said, and without hesitation, she then swung her great blade at him—but before it could connect, he vanished into a cloud of smoke and sparkle.

"A warning would be preferred," Lucius grumbled, now standing behind her. She merely laughed and pointed her blade toward the floor. Lucius looked disheveled as he swept his hair out of his face. He stayed behind her now, his mouth twisting into a frown.

"Begin," Kaneira said while she paced back and forth in front of the throne.

Diana dashed for me, throwing her gauntlet into my chest.

I fell to my knees and coughed violently.

"Gods..." I croaked, a metallic taste filled my mouth.

"Up, child," Kaneira growled. "If this were a real battle, you would have died."

"Great—I'm thankful it isn't," I groaned.

I tried to rise from the floor, but the world felt unbalanced beneath me. I rose shakily, the armor weighing heavier with each passing moment. Diana's horned helm caught the light, her figure towering yet familiar. She had come at me with unrelenting force, but never malice. Still, her strike had left me breathless, my ribs aching from the blow.

"You must fight back," Diana said gently, her voice cutting through the tension like a blade, dulled only by affection.

When she held up her hand, I noticed her palm was exposed beneath the gauntlets.

Her gauntlets flexed, and the faint shimmer of frost began to gather at her fingertips, creeping up her arms like ivy made of ice. Even as she spoke kindly, her movements were precise, calculated. She wouldn't allow me to falter without consequence.

I barely had time to register her next move before she surged forward, the air around her biting with cold. She swept low, the frost from her magic leaving twinkles of ice in her wake.

I tried to step back to dodge, but her fist collided with my chest plate, the impact sending me staggering.

I gasped, the cold cutting into my lungs as I steadied myself. But before I could fully recover, Diana was looming over me again. She moved like the winter winds—unforgiving, unyielding, but with a beauty that could only be admired in the briefest of moments before they overwhelmed you.

This time, frost laced her strike, a trail of shimmering ice blooming against my armor where her gauntlet connected. I stumbled back, the world tilting beneath me until I found myself upon it, desperate for more air to reach my lungs.

"Enough!" Kaneira barked, her blade slamming into the ground with a deafening clang. Diana halted immediately and stepped back, her frosted gauntlets lowering as she waited.

I struggled to rise, my limbs trembling; but I could feel the heat building in my chest, the embers of my magic stirring beneath the surface.

I closed my eyes, trying to grasp hold of it—to summon the fire that had always sat directly out of my reach.

"*Feel it*, Mirage," Kaneira said, her voice quieter now but no less demanding.

"Emotion is what guides our magic."

I raised my hand, emboldened by my raging emotions, and flames burst forth, wild and untamed.

But they were reckless.

Diana summoned her frost, snuffing out the heat before it could reach her. The flames sputtered and died, leaving only the faint charred scent in their wake.

I clenched my fists, anger and shame bubbling to the surface. The fire responded, flaring again—but just as quickly, it fizzled out, leaving me breathless and empty.

I tried again to summon the fire, but my body was trembling, exhaustion settling deep in my bones. The flames sputtered weakly, barely illuminating the space between me and Diana.

"Enough, child," Kaneira said. The disappointment in her tone stung more than any blow.

"I am becoming exhausted just looking at you."

I collapsed to my knees, my chest heaving as I struggled to catch my breath. The throne room fell silent, save for the faint crackle of Stygian's armor and the steady hum of frost still clinging to Diana's gauntlets.

"It's okay," Kaneira said finally, her voice cutting through the stillness like a dagger.

"You are going to keep fighting, or you'll die trying."

Her words hung heavy in the air as I stared at the marble floor, my hands trembling against the cold surface. I had failed, and the weight of it pressed down on me like the glorious armor I had yet to honor.

"Your turn." Kaneira motioned to the three remaining.

The air in the training room crackled with tension, the faint hum of magic saturating the space like an impending storm. The three of them stood apart, each calculating the other's first move.

Diana's frost-coated gauntlets shimmered faintly under the pale light, while Hiver lingered at the edge of the vast room. Stygian stood between them, his molten armor casting an ominous orange glow, with the fire in his veins simmering just below the surface.

Natsu took a seat beside me, not joining in the fray.

"Why do you not fight?" I asked him.

"I do, but sometimes I love to watch them try to kill each other." He laughed, and I stared at him with horror.

"Oh dear, they won't kill each other. No worries!" He placed a reassuring hand onto my shoulder.

"I'm worried," I grimaced as I made eye contact with him.

"But doesn't Kaneira get upset if you just *watch*?" I questioned.

"My primary magic is water, so a bad matchup for Styg. Diana can freeze my magic, so a bad matchup for me," he answered.

"What if in a real battle you have to fight a frost user?" I pressed.

"Then I fight like hell—or I dessicate them." He passed me a grim look, but only briefly.

"You're a *desicara*?" I asked with a bit of fear lacing my tone.

"Unfortunately… I don't use it though, obviously," he laughed. Natsu was like joy in mortal form; it was difficult to catch him without a smile painted onto his face.

Natsu continued to speak to me as they fought before us, asking me about m family and sharing information of his own. He was a wonderful companion—I was starting to see just why he could break through Samira's cold exterior.

I looked up to see Hiver managing to steady himself and swinging at Stygian, who stopped his blade with his molten gauntlet. The metal hissed and steamed as the heat clashed with the steel. Stygian shoved Hiver back with a burst of flames, sending Hiver several feet across the floor.

Diana seized the opening, and her frost magic surged. She managed to generate a freezing torrent; it exploded outward, a blinding storm of ice and snow that engulfed them.

Stygian cursed, his flames struggling against the sheer intensity of the cold. Hiver vanished again, his illusion no match for the freezing wind.

When the frost cleared, Diana stood tall, her chest heaving and her armor frosted over but intact. Blood trickled from several parts of her flesh under her white armor; still her stance was unyielding. Across from her, Stygian's flames sputtered back to life, his molten veins flaring brightly as he stepped forward.

Hiver continued to stagger backward from him as he slowly approached; blood fell from his mouth while he stumbled over himself. Hiver eventually fell entirely to his knees a mere few yards from Stygian, heaving and hacking up blood onto the floor beneath him.

His labored breaths and bloodied coughs were an indication of his concession.

I swore I saw a tail just beyond Hiver's ragged form—that of a wolf's. I gasped upon seeing the white coat of the beast from behind him, but when he raised his hand, it vanished.

None of them spoke. The only sounds were their labored breaths and the faint crackle of Stygian's flames. Each of them was battered, bruised, and bloodied, but only Hiver had apparently yielded.

"Heal him, Mirage." Kaneira handed me a small but sharp scimitar dagger, its hilt decorated with engravings of the sun and moon. I had known why she handed it to me—so that this time, I could cut open my own flesh.

Hiver heaved and coughed up alarming amounts of blood onto the marble beneath him. He did not even look up at me as I stood over his body.

I hissed as the blade tore through my flesh, the sharp sting igniting every nerve. It hurt, but knowing it would heal him seemed to dull the edge of the pain.

I reached my bloodied wrist to his mouth, but he did not eagerly drink from me.

"You have to take it," I said sternly, a mix of emotions manipulating my tone.

He slowly raised his gaze to my own, his blue eyes icy and cold. He looked at me as if I too were going to fight him.

He did not speak and instead spit another small puddle of blood on the floor. He then reached to his shoulder and pulled out the spike of ice that had nearly gone through him just a few minutes earlier. A sea of red flowed from his wound.

The blood almost appeared to be black.

He raised a hand to put pressure on the area where the spike had shredded his skin and underlying tissue. He groaned and winced as his palm made contact with the wound.

I decided to cut open my wrist again.

"Drink, or I will make you." I held out my bloodied wrist to his mouth again, and he hung his head. I then decided that of the two of us, I likely had more strength in this moment.

I dashed behind him and wrapped an arm over his chest, pulling him tightly into me. I forced his head to look upwards and pushed my flesh into his mouth. I could feel my blood soaking his lips, and finding its way to his tongue. I saw a look of relief wash over his previously miserable expression.

"Thanks," was all he managed. He stared at me for a long moment, and I almost believed he would say something else to me—*anything*. He pulled off his gauntlets and left them on the floor as he made his way toward the exit.

Diana scoffed at his leave; Gods know how she even knew he was gone as her helm still sat dutifully upon her head, obstructing her vision entirely—*or so I thought.*

"Diana, how do you fight with your eyes covered?" I asked, genuine curiosity prompting my question.

"I am a wraith," she said simply…as if that sentence could even begin to answer my question. She must have known the irony of such a response, as she giggled and removed her helm.

"I do not need to use my eyes to see. I can sense every movement within about a twenty foot radius of me—projectiles become a bit more challenging than hand-to-hand combat, though. I only have a few seconds to dodge or deflect those," she said, a smile spreading across her red and bloodied face.

"Why cover your eyes at all?"

Kaneira then chimed in, intrigued at the discussion, "It is a battle strategy to stop your enemy from predicting your next move…" She trailed off, spinning her sword about her hands. "Your eyes hold your decisions, your thoughts. If you cover that window, it makes your next move all the more surprising."

I nodded.
I felt like a fool.

I had truly believed that the habitual practices I had with Dracar would provide with me with some sort of defense.
Truth be told, I had none at all.
Diana could have killed me in only a few hits, I had no doubt of that. Combine her physical strength and reactions with her magic, and I would have surely met my doom.
"Let's eat!" Diana said cheerfully, sobering me from my self-loathing. Just past her, Stygian too gave me a warm smile and giggled at Diana's somehow unscathed enthusiasm.

CHAPTER
TWENTY-THREE

The dining hall was bathed in the warm glow of midday light, filtering through high-arched windows that stretched toward the heavens, casting a myriad of colors about the room.

The laughter and chatter of Tessiah mingled with the faint clinking of cutlery, the room just as alive as its occupants. Despite the general good aura of the atmosphere, the weight of my failure made the air feel heavy against my skin. I kept my head down even as I gathered food onto my plate.

When I took a seat beside Diana and Natsu, I still did not dare to make eye contact with them, nor did I say a word.

I was too ashamed.

Worse—I was too pathetic.

I had hoped my vow of silence would go unnoticed amongst the group. I watched Diana and Stygian engage in discussion, but I heard none of the words they exchanged. I watched Stygian throw his arms up, his gestures overly animated, and I heard the occasional bursts of laughter come from them both.

I stared at my plate for a few moments before tearing apart the warm sourdough bread in front of me. In the end, I only ate a single scrap of its soft interior, the rest scattered across my plate.

"Not hungry, eh?" Natsu's voice was gentle, cutting through my haze. His eyes sparkled like the ocean's shallows—a seafoam hue, soft and ethereal. He embodied the ocean itself: calm and playful, beautiful and deep.

"Not really," I said softly back to him, hoping Diana would not hear, but I could feel her gaze burning on the back of my skull.

"Is something wrong?" she chimed in. Her voice rang softly like that of a bell.

"No," I said quickly. Surely my misery was evident.

The interaction also warranted a searing gaze from Stygian's forested eyes. His eyes narrowed upon me, almost as if he could see the turmoil within me.

The shame.
The humiliation.

Beyond that, I could hardly bring myself to look at Hiver. I wished to just speak to him—to tell him that I was sorry, that I had felt *something*. I just felt…*confused*. The men here weren't monsters —at least, not *all* of them.

Diana continued to speak, her words becoming lost in the space around us. I could make out bits and pieces of her practically scolding me to eat food, but my eyes remained locked on Stygian.

"Did you hear me?" I finally heard Diana say through the mental fog that almost clouded me physically, too.

"What?"

"I said maybe go take a bath? Clean yourself up? It'll make you feel better," she said with a gentle yet stern tone. I nodded and rose from the table, looking back toward Stygian who gazed upon me affectionately as I passed him. I half dragged myself to the door and swung it open with my last bit of strength.

I knew I had healed, but my ribs still groaned from where Diana's gauntlets connected. I reached a hand to my aching bones, tracing the outline of them with my fingers.

<hr />

I turned down a dimly lit corridor; several of the torches were merely coals, not even embers burning upon them. I decided to take a moment to collect my calm, to try and stop whatever stirred within me from potentially exploding into flame.

I felt it surging beneath my skin, begging to burst out of me; I wanted to burn it all down, but why? What possessed me to feel so *angry*? My breaths came shallow and uneven, the weight of exhaustion and fury pressing down on me. I closed my eyes and made an effort to slow my outbreath.

"I thought you went off to bathe?" Hiver's voice cut through the silence.

My eyes snapped open, and there he was, leaning on the wall opposite me. His navy tunic clung to his form, the gold-threaded constellations catching the faint light like distant stars.

"Do you need something?" I said with an edge, the rage sparking in my chest.

"Apologies for wondering how you were doing—perhaps sulking in the dark would do you better than a friend," he huffed, his lips fighting to not form a smirk.

I could feel fire igniting behind my eyes; I feared I was going to lose control entirely.

Somehow, this was worse than failing in the throne room.

Feeling my fire under my skin—as if it ran through my veins instead of blood—and having no ability to call on it, even in the face of danger. Yet here, where no threat loomed, it chose to try and claw its way out.

"I think you should leave," I growled at him, the flames finally breaking free from my skin, erupting in my palms and climbing up to my wrists like ivy. Just like they did in the courtyard. This time, I wasn't sure if Jesper would come to stop it.

He did not move.

He cocked his head to the side, taking me in entirely.

I felt my breaths grow frantic as I struggled to keep the fire from erupting from every part of me.

"Hmmm, nah," he said, reaching for me. I pushed myself as far as I could into the wall behind me, trying hard to create space between us should I lose control entirely.

"Hiver—" I began, but his hand came to rest under my chin, tilting my face up to meet his gaze. The intensity made my breath catch. My eyes flickered between his, frantic and full of confusion. His gaze hardened and he stared down at me, his expression consumed by insatiable desire.

"Tell me to stop," he murmured, his voice so quiet I barely made out the words.

I didn't.

My mouth slowly fell open to come up with a retort, anything. But before any sound could escape my throat, he closed the space between us, his lips finding mine with a force I didn't think him capable of possessing.

At first, I did not kiss him back; the shock of the moment rendered me incapable of returning the gesture. I knew it was wrong to let this consume me, to kiss him back with the same hunger and ferocity, but I did anyway.

It was tender and slow, yet it burned with a quiet intensity that turned the air in my lungs into frost. He parted from me for a moment, and I looked at him, desperate and frenzied.

He reached his hands around my thighs and lifted me up against the wall, my legs wrapping around his waist. My hands found his chest, the hard lines of his muscle beneath my fingers. I pressed my lips into his even harder, now desperate—*yearning*.

He moved his lips from mine and kissed my jaw, labored breaths escaping his mouth in between kisses.

"So beautiful," he murmured into my neck, his lips leaving an icy burn in their wake. I could feel his teeth grazing my neck, as if he wished to bite into me—to taste my tender flesh.

I wrapped my hands into his hair, pulling him harder into me. Our bodies moved violently against each other, both hungry and longing. He tasted like his magic, the intoxicating eucalyptus and pine.

The flames from my wrists sparked and sputtered, but he did not yield. Instead he pushed into me harder.

"Hiver—" I managed to moan, but I could not find the words to follow up.

"Say it again," he commanded, his voice thick with desire.

"Hiver." I whispered against his ear and he devoured me again with an all-consuming kiss. His tongue searching—begging for more of a taste of me. The flames merely climbed higher now, reaching up to my elbows. He did not seem bothered by the fire that crackled beneath him.

This was not the apology I had hoped to give him, but I suppose that this could speak louder than any words I had. Yet I still felt riddled with guilt, so much that it nearly surpassed the longing.

I didn't want to admit that I *wanted this*.

"Hiver—we shouldn't—" I managed to break from his lips only for a moment to say the words.

"Of course we shouldn't, but it's so much more fun," he purred, his voice low and rough. I giggled for a moment as he playfully bit into my neck.

"That's a lovely sound," he smiled briefly before kissing me again.

I felt myself burning more and more until the flames came around my neck, dancing across my collarbone. I started to fear that heat—the flames that sought to consume us both. He pulled away as they ignited his cheeks, sobering him from his frenzied hunger, and I saw clarity flash through his icy gaze.

"If someone—if Stygian—" I started, not daring to continue my statement.

"Gods, I—I didn't think…" Hiver inhaled deeply, regret flashing across his face.

"Mirage—" he said softly, his tone laced with affection and remorse.

"It's my fault too," I said quickly, pushing myself off of him and allowing my feet to touch the floor again.

"I'm so sorry," he said gingerly, fixing the buttons that had come undone beneath my fingers.

"Don't be," I said softly, my face just inches from his.

I wondered if he could see it in my eyes. The overwhelming desire burning me hotter than any flame could.

For a moment, he hesitated before putting his back completely to me.

I was still burning.
I needed a release.

I let Hiver walk away, but I wish I hadn't let him. I should have reached for him, begged him to stay—if at least to talk. I don't know what it was about him, what made me want more than I was allowed.

Was I now Stygian's?
What have I done?

I stormed down the corridors to the throne room.

I found my armor still neatly laid at the foot of the dais, and Kaneira was nowhere to be seen. Surely she was out and about somewhere with Lucius. Maybe they were even discussing what a disappointment I was today—how my magic had miserably failed me.

I reached for the armor that I had lain upon the throne's steps and put it back on, the streaks of blood still contrasting the black metal of the armor. The sun emblem had been smeared with the crimson liquid.

I managed to stifle a sob.

In every facet of my life, I would only know defeat.

I picked up Kaneira's sword, the great blade that she swung so effortlessly, and felt its thick hilt against my skin. I made an effort to swing it but nearly threw it across the marbled floors.

"Nope," I huffed, putting the sword back down in front of the throne.

This was useless.
What did I even plan to accomplish here? Did I come here to lash out? To try and train myself?

It all began to feel like a fruitless endeavor.

As I thought more about the moments that just passed with Hiver, the flames erupted brighter, hotter.

Emotion.

The more I allowed myself to feel, the more my magic reacted.

I fell to my knees and sat there, the weight of all of my emotions pressing down on me, simultaneously stunting and encouraging my magic to flourish. Perhaps this was more about controlling my turmoil than my magic. The throne loomed over me—its golden inlay catching stray beams of sun.

I heard the heavy creak of the doors behind me. My body tensed, my pulse quickening as I had feared Kaneira would see me wallowing in my misery before her dais.

I refused to face her.
I refused to face the humiliation that awaited me.

"Mirage?" A familiar voice rang about the grand room, but not one that belonged to Kaneira.

"Stygian?" I said, turning to find his silhouette halfway covered by shadow.

"What are you doing here?" he questioned, his voice carrying an edge I couldn't quite place.

"What are *you* doing here?" I asked him, the flames still clearly unruly as they coiled around my limbs.

"I was just going to grab your armor for you—bring it back to the armory." He gestured to the armor that I now wore on my body.

"Oh," was all I could manage.

More embarrassment.

"You summoned your flames," his tone was laced with encouragement.

"I can't control it." I managed to stop the stream of tears from falling down my face.

"Your emotions are high…" He trailed off, the distance between us now mere feet.

"You need to target what is weighing you down. Your magic will follow…"

"I don't need to target anything—I need release!" I snapped at him. Guilt immediately rose to my cheeks, burning them hot as if I had swallowed flames. Stygian took a step back, a puzzled expression taking over his face.

"Release?" Stygian's expression shifted as I stepped closer, the flames licking higher around my arms as I came to him. His eyes flickered with something unreadable: curiosity—and maybe something a bit darker.

"Use it," he murmured.

"I'm afraid I don't know how," I confessed, as if my performance was not indicative enough of that.

"You do." He stepped even closer to me now; he was just inches from me, his face looming above my own.

I saw shadows behind him—wavering in the sunlight when they reached for me, driving me backwards. Stygian's shadows slammed into me, a force that felt like a tidal wave, knocking the breath from my lungs as I stumbled back. My flames remained around my arms, climbing higher in response to the onslaught of shadow.

When I met his gaze, his eyes were dark, a dangerous smile pulling at his lips.

"Come on," he taunted, his shadows eager to knock me down again.

My frustration boiled over, and the flames surged, bursting from my arms in a wild arc toward him. He sidestepped effortlessly, his shadows swirling around him like a protective storm, swallowing my fire as if it were nothing. The smirk that spread across his face ignited something deeper within me—a mix of rage and humiliation.

I snarled at him and allowed another flame to swell out. It formed what looked like a whip from my hands, allowing me to use it like a weapon. It snapped on the ground before him, but his shadows intercepted it; they coiled and twisted around it like living creatures, smothering the flames before they could even reach him. He rushed toward me again, his shadows gripping my wrists, forcing them to remain at my sides.

"Wow, you're a natural," he teased, his grip firm but not cruel. I writhed beneath his hold, a frustrated yell escaping me as I strained to free myself from his unyielding grasp.

Instead, I stopped to meet his gaze, "Do you mean that?" I questioned.

"Absolutely not," he laughed, reaching a hand under my chin and caressing me for just a moment before throwing a fist into my stomach.

I nearly vomited on the floor.

Somehow, I summoned the fire whip again; it snapped out toward his legs, wrapping around his ankle. My chest heaved as I tried to pull the whip back into me.

I could not control it.

It stayed wrapped around him, but I could not force it to return to me. Even as I tugged at the whip in my hand, it was almost as if the fire had a mind of its own.

His shadows managed to untangle my flames, allowing him to stand upright again.

"My turn," he murmured, the smirk ever present on his face. His shadows came forward toward me again, one taking the form of a serpent, slithering toward me on the floor—I was completely awestruck by it.

The serpent's eyes were ablaze with an orange and black fire, unique to Stygian. It surged toward me—sinking its teeth into the arm I raised to deflect the creature. Its great fangs were made of flame, burning my skin as it tore into me.

I screamed at the intensity of the pain, my flames igniting in response. I tried to fight off the creature, but like Stygian, it managed to maneuver skillfully, dodging me entirely.

I was burning from the inside out.

I threw a fist at the large, shadowy body of the creature, but again it slipped underneath me.

I fell to my knees.

"I yield," I huffed, my skin still healing from the deep wounds of the serpent's fangs.

"Oh that's no fun." Stygian frowned as he approached me, but the flicker in his eyes indicated he wasn't finished. I could not respond to the shadows locked around my hands, refusing to let them move.

"I never asked *you* to yield," I said to him as I looked up at him. His eyes burned with a ferocity—his gaze was heavy and sharp. The faint glow of my flames illuminated his face.

He was a weapon, honed and lethal, but there was a devastating allure to his movements. The way his hand caressed my jaw, the way his fingers traced the scarlet halo of my hair.

The sharp angles of his face made him look as though he had been forged by a blade—like a God of Death.

"Tell me Mirage," he purred, crouching for a moment to reach my level, "What *would* you ask me to do?" His gaze felt as if it were devouring me.

"More," was the only reply I could muster.

I was frustrated sitting here.

My flames still remained coiled around my arms, roaring in response to the sexual tension that flourished between us.

"Hmm," he said before standing over me again. The shadows released my hands, and I shot up to him. I crashed my lips to his and began fumbling with the buttons of his tunic; I couldn't remove his clothes fast enough, nor could he mine.

Stygian's hands roamed over my body, undressing me with an urgency that matched my own. The cool air of the room nipped my skin, but it was quickly replaced by the warmth of his touch.

KINGDOM OF THE SUN

I came back down to my knees and took him into my mouth. My tongue swept over his cock, savoring the rich, earthy taste that overwhelmed my senses.

I couldn't get enough of him.

I could hear him groan in response to me driving him in deeper. His hands tangled in my hair, pulling me closer to him, pushing himself far enough so that he could feel the back of my throat. The sensation of him filled my mouth entirely as he moved.

"Fuck, don't be a tease," he said, pushing me gently. I watched his erection slip from my mouth, dripping and wet.

"I want *you*," he whispered as he pulled me up from the ground —covering my lips with his own. His hands were searching my body, finding their way to my exposed breasts, then my hips. It felt like he could not grab enough at once.

He guided me backward, pushing me to the pillar that stood a few feet from us. He brought my arms above my head, and his shadows wrapped around them.

"You asked me not to yield," he said playfully. He began to tease my nipples, already hardened by the sensation of his touch.

"Don't be a *tease*," I said breathlessly, moaning under his searching hands.

I was voracious for him; I wanted to feel him inside of me.

He reached for my thighs and pulled me upwards, forcing my legs to wrap around him.

He hesitated.

He kept me there so that I could feel his erection pressing against me, but he refused to enter. Instead, he kissed my breasts, taking my nipples into his mouth and sucking them gently while he held me up.

I felt his body tensing against mine, just as desperate as I.

"Come on," I croaked, the feeling of his cock teasing my core was driving me into a state of madness. I wanted to grab him, to coax him into me, but my arms remained strapped by shadow above my head.

He hummed in response, a faint giggle escaping his mouth and warming my flesh.

"Just fuck me!" I cried out—the longing in my chest was melting into a mixture of fury and frustration.

"Beg me to." He licked my skin and brought a hand down to my center and teased my opening with his fingers.

Part of me wanted to remain stubborn—to resist giving into him.

But I craved release more than control.

"Please," I nearly shouted at him, my voice raw with need. A dark and teasing laugh escaped him, and he entered me with a hard, swift thrust. He groaned, the sound low and primal, his chest tightening with his quick and deep movements. The sound of his pleasure made my chest vibrate, making me tingle with anticipation. Each thrust was like a wave crashing into a shore, relentless and powerful, making me quake with its intensity.

His shadows now coiled around me, teasing and deliberate, tugging lightly at my breasts and wrapping gently around my throat, applying a soft pressure. His mouth crashed into mine, devouring any sound that attempted to escape.

"I love the taste of you," he said, breaking away for only a moment.

My body shuddered beneath him, unable to endure the intensity any longer. I could feel him release inside of me as he pulled away, his cock throbbing and dripping before me.

"Release me," I commanded.

He did as I asked and vanquished his shadows before allowing me to touch the ground again. I hadn't noticed the flames winding their way up my arms and neck until I reached up, my fingers brushing against the tendrils of fire that had formed a structure atop my head. I cold feel the heat of the flames at my back, but before I could turn to see where they burned, Stygian reached to my head, almost reverently—to touch where the flames shaped themselves into a blazing crown.

I threw myself into him, yearning to taste him and feel him more.

"Lie down," I said, guiding his chest and torso with my hands.

"Okay, your highness," he chuckled, his dark eyes glittering with excitement and anticipation.

I mounted him, allowing him to slide inside of me until he was entirely encased within me. He ran his hands down my hips, gripping me firmly. As I closed my eyes, I for a moment thought of someone else beneath me—someone else's hands gripping my thighs…

"Fuck me," he moaned, his eyes hazy with lust and exhaustion. The sound of his voice snapped me out of the thought as I gazed down at him, his dark red hair flayed out behind his skull like blood.

"I believe I am," I gathered enough breath to speak to him, and he made an effort to laugh, but instead groaned beneath me. I could feel my knees digging into his sides as I pushed myself onto him harder and faster.

I was reaching my absolute breaking point.

I eventually collapsed onto his chest.

"I yield," I whispered shakily.

"You are very good at giving up." He quipped. I exhaled weakly at his departure.

We lay there for a moment, our bodies breathing in perfect unison. The flames that climbed up my arms previously had vanished.

"As much as I would *love* to stay like this…" Stygian said lazily, running his fingers down my spine, "we need to dress before someone finds us here."

"Up." He tapped my shoulder blades, gesturing me to rise from his chest.

I sighed and pushed myself up, gazing down at him. His eyes held a warmth that glowed in the sunlight that cut his face, casting half of it in shadow.

Before I could fully remove myself from him, he reached for the back of my neck, pulling me back down into one last kiss before allowing me to rise from him completely.

I think he took his time clothing himself.

"From the way that you're looking at me, I'd think you want more," he snickered as he buttoned his tunic.

The overwhelming feeling of lust turned into *guilt*. I felt the need to tell him about Hiver—about that moment in the hallway…about how for just a moment I pictured white hair under my hands instead of his.

Instead, I clothed myself.

"I am going to bathe," I said to him, a feeling of anxiety washing over me.

He smiled at me lazily.

"No invitation to join? I am shocked, truly." Sarcasm laced his tone.

I rolled my eyes and picked up my armor.

"Actually, I may need you to help me with something," I said, realizing Torvain may not willingly allow me into the armory.

"I'm not sure I can take much more, Mirage." Stygian let out a low chuckle and I returned it with a smile.

"I don't think Torvain will let me through alone," I admitted, a bit of shame bleeding into my tone.

"Ah, I see. No problem! Living wood *loves* me!" He gestured to the exit of the throne room with the nod of his head, and I followed him.

When we reached the door, it groaned open, and before us stood Hiver.

CHAPTER
TWENTY-FOUR

His sharp blue eyes flickered between Stygian and me; the silence in the corridor only lasted a moment, but it seemed to stretch unbearably.

"Hello, Princess—Stygian," he said coolly.

I could not even muster a response. Stygian nodded and smiled.

"You two have been busy, eh?" Hiver said nonchalantly.

Panic began to consume me.

I felt like I might vomit on the floor.

Did he know? Could Hiver somehow sense the happenings of this room just moments before?

"Busy is an understatement," Stygian replied, his tone infuriatingly calm.

"We're off to the armory, if you'd like us to take yours, too?" Stygian offered.

The way Hiver's eyes pinned me made it impossible to focus. His gaze roved over me, but he maintained his composure. I couldn't figure out if he was suspicious or annoyed.

"I'll take it myself, later." Hiver said before moving aside so we could leave.

. . .

I followed Stygian out of the throne room, but I quickly cast a glance at Hiver before fully leaving. When our eyes met, his expression softened and I saw a flicker of pain in his eyes. I opened my mouth to say anything to him—instead, I left the throne room in silence.

"Hmm… it seems you make him more *feral* than normal." He chuckled low and quiet, and when I glanced at him, there was something smug in his expression, "Oh trust me, I don't blame him."

"What?" I managed. We came to a full stop a few yards before the great door.

"Oh, you think I don't notice the way he looks at you? I would think he's trying to fuck you with his eyes." Stygian laughed again—he seemed entirely unbothered.

"Oh," I said softly. I could not snuff out the panic that rose in my throat.

We eventually reached Torvain, at which point he grumbled, "Mirage Darakyn, Enemy to Tessiah."

"Kindly stop referring to me as an enemy," I said, the heat of embarrassment rising to my cheeks.

"Torvain, please allow us into the armory," Stygian said with detached ease—he was unphased by Torvain's hostility.

"At once, *Nihiryn*," Torvain bellowed, and the door creaked open slowly.

"What does *Nihiryn* mean?" I asked him softly, hoping that Torvain could not hear us.

"It means *open* in old Tessian—the language is largely dead…" His words trailed off as he hung some of my armor on an empty stand near the tub.

"The Solarians use it, the Clariflux use it, and Torvain uses it—but that is pretty much it," he said, adjusting the chestplate so that it sat straight.

"Why do the Solarians use it?" Curiosity constantly ate at me in this place.

"For ritualistic magic," Stygian said as he turned to me, unbuttoning his tunic.

"Ritualistic magic?" I asked, watching his hands carefully undo the buttons of his tunic. He stopped right at the top, not letting the last button release to reveal his skin.

"Well—there's natural magic and ritualistic magic. What you and I use? That is natural magic. What the Solarian use from their scripts? That is ritualistic magic." He undid the final button of his shirt then, letting it fall to the floor behind him.

"Is that what Jesper uses? Is that why he says those words?"

"Correct." He now reached for his pants.

"Can I ask what you're doing?" A smile spread across my face as his pants fell to the floor below him.

"Bathing—don't you wish to do the same?" he smirked and his voice dipped low; each word felt like it was brushing against my skin.

I nodded and decided to place the rest of the armor I carried onto the stand then also undressed myself.

"And if someone comes in?" I stared at his exposed body.

"They may, but this is a big tub. People bathe in here together all the time." He watched me with a lazy grin.

I stepped into the tub—it still felt invigorating on the skin. He followed me in, and the warm water enveloped me, sending a soothing ripple over my skin that contrasted starkly with the tension that coiled in my chest.

"You seem on edge," he observed, his voice was low and nearly teasing, but there was a thread of concern woven in it. I turned to watch the water slosh against the edges of the tub, averting my gaze from his.

"I'm fine," I murmured—I suppose lying was not my strong suit...

Truth be told, I was overwhelmed with guilt and anxiety.

I did not want to hurt Hiver, but it seemed that was inevitable, especially since I'm apparently reckless and desperate for physical touch...

"Tell me, Mirage, do you always lie this terribly? Did Diana ever fall for it?" He leaned back, draping his arms over the rim of the tub; his posture was incredibly relaxed.

"I am not lying!" I snapped, regret washed over me the moment I raised my voice at him. When I brought my eyes back up to his, I expected to see pain, but instead I saw a flicker of amusement.

"Hmmm..." He stirred his finger in the water and sunk himself under. Right before his head came back up, I heard Torvain's faint growl, and the door slowly creeped open.

I turned toward it, anxiety coursing through my veins, making the water feel hotter against my skin than it should have. The creaking of the door seemed to shatter the fragile tranquility of the bath.

I saw Hiver's unmistakable silhouette fill the doorway; his blue eyes swept the room. He stared for a long moment at Stygian, whose head just breached the water to the surface.

"Oh, you again," Stygian said as he pushed back the hair from his eyes.

Hiver merely cleared his throat in response.

"Thought you might want the gauntlets?" he said, holding them up.

My heart pounded under the weight of his gaze, and the heat of the bath pressed down on me, suffocating me.

"I'm sorry I left them..." My voice faltered, dwindling away as his intense eyes stole the rest of my words.

"Perhaps you should be more careful with your things, Princess," Hiver said, his tone sharp but measured.

"Oh come on, Snow, you came all this way just to scold her?"

Hiver's jaw tightened, and for a moment, I expected him to yell at Stygian. Instead, he straightened and fixed Stygian with a cold, unyielding stare.

"You're right, I came to bring my own armor—I thought I was being courteous," Hiver shot at him, his words laced with venom.

"Well surely you'd like to come in, no?" Stygian gestured to the water that rippled softly from his movements.

Hiver's gaze fell back upon me.

"Sounds like you just want to see me naked," Hiver said back to Stygian, his voice softening.

"Certainly! It wouldn't be the first time anyway," Stygian chuckled back. They both shared a brief smile, amused at the other's comments. I felt the knot of anxiety easing in my chest.

"I'll leave you to it," Hiver finally said, giving a gesture of good riddance before fastening *his* gauntlets to the rest of his armor. Stygian reached a hand under the water and splashed it at Hiver, who sucked his teeth in response. A smile breached that cold exterior, and before I could say another word he left the armory.

Only a moment of silence passed before Stygian was booming with laughter.

"What is it?" I asked him.

"The awkwardness of it all—he's so clearly into you it is beyond entertaining." I rolled my eyes, and as I did so, he started to swim toward me. He stopped a few feet away, splashing me with the water, another howl of laughter erupting from him as he did.

"Terribly rude of you to do," I said back to him, my arms crossed.

"Oh, come now, Mirage." He continued to approach; for a moment, I thought his movements held an ulterior motive, but he then splashed me again. This time, I dove for him, pushing him under the water.

He came back up, his laughter still booming off of the armor that surrounded us. He grabbed and shoved, splashing intermittently.

I could do this for eternity.

The sound of my own laughter felt almost foreign to me.

I began to fall in love with the person I was becoming here—someone braver than who I used to be.

CHAPTER
TWENTY-FIVE

Weeks passed in an instant.
Kaneira had been working us ruthlessly: days of Diana beating me down until I had no choice but to yield. The whips I could summon, but never control. It felt that I was somehow making no progress. The most I could do is deflect the attacks of Diana and Stygian.

This morning, it seemed Kaneira had a new game for us to play.

"Snow and Mirage, you will fight against Diana and Stygian..." She paced in front of her throne as she often did when she was giving out commands, "Well...go on!"

As always, Diana moved first. She would charge directly, seeking to use her hands the most in combat, so the only solution was to avoid her. She was fantastic in hand-to-hand combat and weaved her magic in between blows—she was the perfect balance of raw and magical power.

───

I spent a lot of time watching the three of them spar: studying their movements, their style of fighting. Diana usually wielded two karambit daggers; they would sit in sheaths at her thighs for easy access. I barely had time to think before the flash of horns assaulted my vision.

I jumped to the side, managing to stabilize myself before Diana dashed again, a blade at the ready. Her blade came down fast, glittering in the dim light of morning. I had no other option but to brace it with the arm guards I wore.

The frosted blade clashed loudly with the metal of my armor, jolting me so hard I thought my teeth had shattered. The impact sent a spray of shards and icy mist into the air, cutting my face repeatedly. Before I could make another move, Diana kicked at my chest, sending me backwards into the stone pillar of the throne room.

I coughed violently upon hitting the floor, blood spurting up as I did. Diana stalked toward me, her blades back in their sheaths. I was too weak to fight her; I needed a few moments to regain my bearings.

When she reached for my chest, I tried to use my hands to stop her. I pushed against her with every drop of strength I possessed, but to no avail. Her hand phased directly through my armor and onto my chest.

She began to freeze me.

"Diana!" I yelped, trying to remove her hand, but I was simply not strong enough. I could feel the frost spreading across my skin, seeping even deeper into my organs and making my heartbeat slow.

"I won't kill you," she said coldly. When she was in battle, her warmth disappeared.

"Diana, please!" I wailed at her, pressing and kicking against her—

but I knew I could not stop it. Hiver then crashed into the back of her, forcing her hand out of my armor and to the hilt of her blade.

"Are you okay? Yeah? Okay, get up," Hiver quickly said, pulling me up by my forearms. The world around me spun as I gathered my footing.

Hiver then created many illusions of the two of us: in some I sat on the ground and coughed up blood, in some Hiver pulled me up, and in others I reached unconsciousness. It was the last that grabbed Stygian's attention away from battle.

"Mirage!" he yelled, finding his way to an illusion where I was completely unconscious. He darted over, reaching for me, his eyes full of concern.

As he reached down to my body, it disappeared, and before he could react, Hiver's fist connected with his jaw, sending him back. Diana for only a moment put her back to me, and I summoned the flame whip and tossed it out at her, snapping against her wrist.

I managed to pull it into me, forcing Diana to move with it. She made no sound, but I could see the flicker of pain pulling at her exposed lips. I could see the fire burning her skin.

※※※※※

The other two continued to brawl with their fists; Hiver was over the top of Stygian landing blows, but Stygian's shadows surfaced, throwing him off. I heard the thud of Hiver's body hitting the ground, and it broke my attention from Diana—who had frosted over my whip, and shattered it. She threw an ice spike into my shoulder.

It had impaled me completely.

I fell to my knees again as the force of it stole the air from my lungs. I stayed there for a moment, hardly able to breathe, before I pulled it out. The wound closed very slowly, letting the suffering linger. I used my other arm to summon another whip, lashing it at Diana once more, but her blade parried it.

"Fuck," I huffed as she approached again; not being able to see her eyes *did* throw me off. I started to believe she truly wanted me dead. I could hardly register her quick movement, but her blade came slashing toward my throat.

I jumped backwards, the edge missing me by inches, and I tried to counter her with a burst of fire that erupted from my palm. She jumped back, a layer of frost forming on her skin as it fought against the heat of my attack.

I could see past her that Hiver was under Stygian, shadows about to consume them.

"This is a team exercise—fight as a team!" Kaneira roared from her throne as she watched. I was distracted by Hiver writhing beneath Stygian, and Diana threw two more spikes through my stomach. I hit the ground.

My vision blurred as Diana towered over me, her gauntlet about to come down on me. Hiver had managed to throw Stygian off and darted for me; he threw himself into Diana, causing her to lose her footing.

"Up," Hiver's voice cut through the mental haze, sharp and commanding. He grabbed me by the arm and pulled me to my feet. His touch was grounding; he reached for the ice spikes that protruded from me and yanked them out.

I placed my arm around his neck to stabilize myself as he did.

"Ah! Fuck!" I screamed as he pulled them from me and blood gushed onto the floor. When the spikes were removed, I could feel my magic surging to life, knitting the skin back together.

"Come on, you're alright," Hiver said, reaching for my cheek to force my gaze to his. His eyes sparkled in the sunlight. Stygian's shadows came forward, and for a moment I was able to summon that fiery shield that he so often used to deflect.

Stygian charged me, throwing me to the floor and straddling the top of me. His shadows restrained me, his hand gently resting on my throat: a threat that he could push it in harder. He raised a brow at me as he held me there—and winked. I scoffed and squirmed beneath him, unable to match his physical strength.

As I writhed beneath him, a great white beast had come running at Stygian, shoving him off of me, and pressing his back into the ground. The wolf growled, eyes ignited with icy flames. There seemed to be a net formed over Stygian from where the dog's paws pressed against his chest—restraining him *and* his magic.

Meanwhile, Diana slashed at Hiver, her blade connecting with his midsection. He fell to the ground in front of her, heaving and holding his hand to the wound. That was not the first she had given him…

"Enough!" Kaneira thundered, and Diana immediately ceased her stalking toward Hiver.

I almost forgot that I too wielded blades—one that came here with me, and one that was given to me by Kaneira. I pulled it from my hip and sliced open my wrist. Hiver heaved on the floor before me. This time, I did not need to force him: he drank from me willingly.

"Thank you," he huffed, coughing up blood as his gash healed.

"Are you okay, brother?" Diana approached us, removing her helmet.

"Fine," he snarled at her. She flashed him a look of surprise, and her expression became very solemn.

"Even if you fight well—you do not fight together. That will be your death when we go into a real battle," Kaneira said, rising from her dais. Her words sent a chill down my spine.

"Glacien, come." Hiver croaked and the great white dog came happily running over, disappearing into nothingness as Hiver continued to hold his slowly healing gashes.

I could not fathom a real battle. Especially since I could hardly last against my own friends.

The others were going to go for lunch as we always did after training, but I hung back.

"You are getting better, child," Kaneira said to me, a warmth in her voice I did not often hear.

"It doesn't feel like it," I said back to her, taking a seat on the steps that led to her throne.

"It won't for a while—especially against Diana and Stygian. They have been a bit more… *aggressively trained*, compared to Snow."

"Why put us together if you know we are weaker? It feels like you want Diana to kill us..." A sadness had come over me as I spoke.

"Battle is about more than your physical strength; it is about how you care for your fellow soldiers, too. You and Hiver also seem to have a *special* connection," She said with a tone I could not reasonably place.

"If Hiver is weaker because he only has one power, why not give him Solarian scripts? Why not give him an advantage?" I questioned. Kaneira shot me a look of disapproval, her nostrils flaring a bit at my suggestion.

"The scripts are dangerous and only made for Solarian eyes." Her tone cut the air like a blade.

"But Jespe—"

"Jesper is truly corrupted because of those scripts. He will never see the world the same way after them. That knowledge is for the Solarian and the Solarian *only*." Her tone was cold.

"But he can use the dark magics without harming himself... They taught him control—they gave him an advantage!"

"No child, you are mistaken." Kaneira paced in front of me as she spoke; her posture was militant.

"The consequences that should befall *him* instead befall the world around him. He channels this place to use his magic, slowly killing it. The eleventh kingdom was created by the Gods. It is plentiful with magic, a never-ending well, if you will. You can channel *anything* with magic, which makes him all the more dangerous because—"

"He can channel other Tessiah, too..." I interjected. The thought made me shudder.

"So he can only use his magic here, then?" I asked.

She nodded in response.

"If he needs to, he will use you as an substitute for this kingdom; his magic is only effective if there is a source he can drain to use it."

I stared at her for a long moment. I was not only terrified of what lay beyond these walls, but also what was being held within them.

. . .

"Do not be afraid, child…" Kaneira spoke with an uncharacteristic gentleness.

"You learn to fight to protect yourself from *all* of your enemies, whomever they may be." She said.

"Why do we train so rigorously?" I asked.

"War is coming and it spares no one." There was an edge to her voice as she said it. I nodded before leaving to return my things to the armory.

When I reached Torvain, I expected the usual struggle, but this time it said something different.

"Mirage Darakyn, if you find yourself to be a liar, the heavens will fall down upon your head." Torvain thundered.

"I don't understand…" was the only response I could muster as the door stared at me, its eyes wide and scanning.

"I am threatening you. *Nihiryn.*" Torvain slowly creaked open, allowing me to pass through into the armory. This was the first time I was allowed to pass without another Tessiah asking for entry.

I walked to the stand I typically placed my armor on and took my time placing it down. I gazed at the blood which now stained my chestplate, my gauntlets, and my arm guards. The blood was a painful reminder of failure.

I stared at the armor for a moment; the dried blood dulled its gleam, catching in the grooves where blows had cut a bit too deep. I traced where the blood had dried—I could almost feel my vulnerability in the red lines.

I could see my reflection in the mirror that sat behind my armor. I thought of that vanity again, and how I destroyed it in my bout of rage. I thought of Dracar—how in my absence, my father had only one child left to torment.

I frequently pictured him, holding the shard of glass as he yelled at our father. I tried to think of less turbulent memories, as I could feel my blood heating up.

Like the moments with Hiver—the ones I dared not dwell on too long. Like when he held my face and looked upon me with those sparkling eyes…

I was constantly riddled with guilt and fear: a powerful combination to generate utter despair.

I left the armory in a hurry, the weight of the day's failures pressing heavier than usual. I found myself rushing to the dining hall when I nearly collided with Diana.

"Mira! I was just looking for you." No longer in the heat of battle, her jubilant demeanor had returned.

"I was just in the armo—"

"You must be starving!" she exclaimed, bringing me to the dining hall to sit with our usual group. However, Samira was absent.

"Where is Samira?" I asked to no one in particular, but Natsu's attention snapped to me.

"With Alysara it seems—new recruits—etcetera…" He trailed off, picking at his food. It was apparent how enthralled he was by her; how her absence seemed to crush him—he seemed eager to change the subject.

"I hear you're getting better with your magic?" Natsu said, a bit of his typical charm resurfacing.

"Better is an overstatement—" I avoided making eye contact with him, fearful he would see my shame.

"Diana is the only one of us who was truly a natural with her magic. The rest of us…struggled." Natsu spoke with a reassurance that almost made me feel better.

"Oh, speak for yourself, I was a natural too." Stygian bragged, leaning back in his chair, a devilish grin spreading on his face.

"Oh, right. Should I tell your lovely little princess how badly

Samira beat you when you first sparred her?" Natsu snickered, beginning to pick at his food a bit more; Stygian growled at him in response. Diana erupted into laughter, "I remember that!" She slammed a hand into the table and nudged Stygian with her elbow.

"Gods, that was a shitshow," Hiver chuckled at the far end of the table where Samira usually sat.

"What happened?" I asked, amusement dancing my eyes as they met Stygian's.

"Samira's parents taught her a spell to create frost gauntlets—unbreakable and hurt like a bitch. She also can wield frost like Diana..." Natsu said, trailing off to examine Stygian's reaction toward his comments; I could see him turning red, perhaps embarrassment was setting in.

"She is also ridiculously fast—supernaturally so. She could hit faster than he could react; the frosted gauntlets ripped him apart. I almost thought he was going to die right there..." Natsu said, a bit of amusement dying out of his voice.

The scars I had seen before we became intimate. The scars that wove over his flesh like threads of silk, pale against his tanned skin.

"Jesper had to patch him up," Diana added, averting her gaze from Stygian who appeared to be burning in his cheeks.

"You couldn't heal it?" I was deeply unsettled learning that Jesper had to heal Stygian—since he *had* the power to heal.

"Heal from a frostwalker? Hah! No chance..." Natsu cut in.

"What? Why not?" My curiosity only grew.

"The damned inflict wounds that cannot heal—something something Vidhi—something something," Natsu continued, his voice very nonchalant.

"Are the Reavari damned?" I asked, remembering Hiver's wounds.

"Mhm," Natsu responded.

How did I heal him then?

"Jesper can *sort of* heal—but as you know, it leaves a scar,"

Natsu gestured to the scar I had on my throat from Alysara's blade. I reached for it and felt the raised skin.

Something felt off.

I glanced toward Hiver, who met my gaze with an equal confusion. Neither of us decided to share the fact that I could heal his wounds from the Reavari without the Solarian magic Jesper used. I started to feel uneasy; I rose from the table quickly, looking down at Diana. Her eyes widened at my sudden movement.

"I am not feeling well, I think I am going to retire to my chambers," I said, shooting up from the table. Diana's gaze was suspicious as she examined my face.

I burst out of the dining hall into the corridors, finding myself struggling to pick a direction. I felt my heart roaring in my chest—anxiety or maybe fear.

Were they not supposed to know that I could heal the wounds inflicted by the damned?

It appears Hiver's incident was not announced to the group. I walked briskly to my chambers. The corridors felt endlessly long, never seeming to end. I was just outside of my chambers when I heard footsteps quickly approaching me. I turned and burst a flame out—I did not even mean to do it...

"Ah, fuck!" Hiver yelped as the fire connected with his chest.

"Gods! I am so sorry, Hiver," I ran to him, investigating the damage I had done. His tunic was incinerated, his skin burned. I still carried the dagger at my side and went to slice my wrist.

"It's okay," He huffed, his nostrils were flaring from the pain.

"Why did you follow me?"

"Because I hadn't even thought about what had happened to

Stygian—I knew you were freaked out upon learning that…" he trailed, his eyes fixated onto mine.

"Are you scarred?" I asked. He lifted his tunic to reveal his midsection: it had completely healed over, no scars were visible to me. I reached for his abdomen, where I knew the Reavari had clawed through him.

"It is probably something to do with elixirium," he said softly, it sounded as if he was trying to suppress his panic.

"I'm doubtful—Stygian heals too…that just doesn't make sense to me."

"But I guarantee it makes sense to someone else… *Jesper*." Hiver's voice dripped with malice as he said his name—as he continued speaking his aggression became more apparent, "Do not talk to him, do not go near him, okay?"

"What? Why? What is he going to do?" I asked.

"I don't know why you were able to heal me, and I have sincere doubts that Jesper was only using your blood only for anti-healing weapons. I am certain he knows something we don't, which makes him far more dangerous than usual."

"What could be in those scripts?" I asked him, too curious to know what Jesper might want with me and why.

"Gods know—we would have to ask Lucius." Hiver let out a deep sigh when he spoke, his eyes focusing on mine as he did.

For a moment, we stayed that way, inches apart, just staring at one another. Eventually, Hiver's hand found my own and he held it tightly. I gazed down where he held me, and he tensed.

"I wouldn't let anything happen to you—whether you chose me or not." It felt like an admission almost, as if he *needed* to get that off his chest.

"Hiver, I—"

"Please no—no apologies, no excuses." He squeezed my hand tighter for a moment.

"Okay," I said quietly, the word barely audible. I didn't want to fight him; I couldn't bear to hurt him more than I already had. But before I could stop myself, the truth slipped from my lips: a secret that swam in my consciousness, always nearing breaching the surface.

"I don't know what I want," I whispered to him, my eyes locked onto his. His eyebrows crinkled in response.

"I—I don't know why I said that." This moment would continue to play in my mind for eternity; I had no idea what possessed me to say it. He reached for my cheek and ran his fingers down my jaw, but he didn't say a word.

For just a moment, I thought he would kiss me again. When he didn't, a small part of my heart seemed to wither.

We walked to the throne room together.

CHAPTER
TWENTY-SIX

H iver threw open the golden doors of the throne room and shouted, "Lucius!" Yet I didn't see him *or* Kaneira anywhere.

"Lucius!" Hiver yelled again, scanning the room for any semblance of his presence.

"Lu—"

"Twice is enough," Lucius materialized from his typical cloud of magic, cutting off Hiver's third attempt to yell for him.

"Sorry," he mumbled.

Lucius's gaze flickered between the two of us suspiciously.

"Is there something you needed from me?" he said, burying his hands into his robes.

"Why was I able to heal Hiver's wounds from the Reavari?" I decided to waste no time.

"Oh, dear," Lucius said, his smoky eyes widening at my question.

"What do you know?" Hiver's tone was sharp—impatient.

"Who knows that she was able to heal you?" Lucius's gaze narrowed on Hiver now.

"I don't know. Diana—maybe?" Hiver was growing irritated.

"Do not tell a soul," Lucius warned; he now towered the two of us, his eyes glimmering with a deadly seriousness.

"Why?" I asked.

He sighed and scanned the room as if looking for prying eyes.

"Only a God's blood can heal the wounds inflicted by the damned… We suspected that your…*creation*…may have led you to possess Olym's blood…" His eyes searched the throne room again.

"When you healed Snow, that confirmed it." Lucius's voice grew quieter as he spoke, nearly reaching a whisper.

"If that was true, why could Kaneira not heal him? She *is* the daughter of Olym, right?" I pressed.

"She does not possess elixirium. It is a God's blood that permits healing, yes, but natural magic is a very sensitive thing."

"If I have God's blood in me, why am I not a Drakkarias, too?" I questioned.

"I assume Olym made you what you are so that he could also save your mother. When you were connected to her, you were able to heal her, but once you were born it seemed you needed to be treated with sunfire to reactivate your powers."

I flinched at his comment. I felt the pain in my chest again from when Kaneira held me down and nearly burnt a hole through my chest.

"Do not tell a soul that you have God's blood. It will make you a target, if you aren't already…" Lucius trailed off, his warning made my stomach turn.

"What exactly does that even mean—to have God's blood?" I pressed.

"It means you are effectively a demigod, like Kaneira. Clearly, something happened when we performed that magic, which led to you being a Seaura…" Lucius had a frenzied look in his eyes.

"It is my understanding you and Dracar are the only ones of your kind." Lucius looked down on me, something grim clouded his expression.

The weight of Lucius's words hung in the air, oppressive and suffocating.

Demigod.

The term felt foreign, as if I were trying to wear someone else's skin. My mind reeled, spinning in a thousand directions.

"So what do we do?" Hiver asked, his voice tight.

"You do nothing—you *say nothing*. For now, at least. We do not want to risk putting Mirage in any more danger. Children directly descended from the Gods have been rare in the last few decades." His tone left no room for argument.

"I do not fully know what that means, either. So forgive me," Lucius sighed.

I shot a look to Hiver. Concern and fear were gripping my chest. He reached for my arm, a gesture of reassurance.

"Sounds like I am on bodyguard duty?" Hiver said with a bit of excitement in his tone. Lucius raised an eyebrow at him.

"If you wish," Lucius said; it almost came out as a question. Hiver turned to me and gave me a smirk—a devilish one that hardly concealed his ulterior motives. I locked eyes with Lucius for a long moment, trying to somehow communicate without words that I was utterly terrified.

CHAPTER
TWENTY-SEVEN

I spent most of my afternoons in the Autumn Courtyard, exploring and practicing my magic on things that could not fight back, such as the fruits. I did not know what day it was—or rather how many days passed—or weeks?

The air of the courtyard was thick with the scent of ripened fruit and falling leaves. The magic I practiced here felt safer, smaller. The fruits and vines couldn't feel the flame, couldn't scream, couldn't fight.

A burst of flame bloomed from my palm, curling around an apple that sat before of me. The flames licked its flesh without burning it—the magic had responded to my command to not burn the fruit. It was here where I felt I had the most control, but it was always fleeting.

"That's new," Hiver's voice called from behind me, startling me so that my flames burned through the apple, leaving nothing but ash. I turned to find him leaning against the courtyard wall, arms crossed and his usual smirk firmly in place.

"Must you sneak up on me?" I stared at him; his features

contrasted so harshly in the Autumn Courtyard. I loved the stark white of his hair against the hues of orange and yellow. I loved the perfect curve of his lips—and the way he stared at me with those hungry eyes.

I hadn't spent a lot of time with Stygian recently. I couldn't tell him what kept me so on edge, but he knew something had been gnawing at me. I recalled the way his gaze burned into me when he noticed my avoidance. His dark green eyes clawed at my soul, begging to be let in on the secret Hiver and I were sworn to keep.

"May I ask what you are doing?" Hiver gestured to the apple, now burnt to a crisp before me.

"I *was* practicing, but you seem to take your bodyguard role a bit too seriously," I laughed.

"I more so meant the point of your little trick." He now approached me to take a seat on the grass before me.

"I am trying to teach myself control. The more calm I remain, the less the flames burn the skin." He gave me a smile of amusement.

"Lovely—but why use flames that do not burn?" He placed his chin into his hands, gazing at me.

"I don't know," I admitted, a bit of shame washing over me. I had not the talent nor the restraint that the others had. Kaneira had told me Hiver was weaker than the others, yet he could still beat me with his eyes closed—Diana *literally* already does.

"Is this where you run off to everyday?" he asked, a gentleness warming his tone. I simply nodded in response.

"Mmm." he hummed. He gazed up at the apple trees that surrounded us, watching as their soft leaves fell to the grass. He reached for one of the leaves as it floated down, his fingers brushing its edges as though testing its fragility.

"You know, we all struggle with control," he said, twirling the leaf between his fingers.

I scoffed in response.

"I mean, sure. But that doesn't mean it is any less obvious how terrible I am comparatively." His eyes locked with mine then, the blue hues soft yet piercing, as though he could puncture the veil of shame and irritation.

"Control is about your emotion—"

"Tell me something I don't know!" I interjected, my face getting hot from anger.

"Okay—Diana has frozen over the entire throne room in a burst of rage, losing complete control and allowing Stygian to best her. Kaneira loses her temper and rips out the throats of your father's soldiers. I get too flustered, and I completely lose control of my illusions…"

"Okay," I responded; my tone was harsh. I looked away, my gaze falling on the ash where the apple had once been.

"It *is* okay," he said, resting a hand on my thigh. I burned where his fingers touched.

My eyes widened as they met his again, my heart drumming in my chest. It felt rhythmic, like my heart beat to a tune that only he could hear, willing him to come closer.

"I shouldn't—" he murmured, but the words sounded more like a plea than a statement as they fell from his tongue.

He began to remove his hand from my thigh, but I reached for it. I wouldn't let him walk away again.

"Then don't," I said, though the breathlessness in my voice betrayed me.

"Oh princess, you don't mean that, do you?" his smirk returned as he spoke, the teasing in his voice made my breath catch.

I didn't mean it.

I hadn't an idea why I felt so drawn to him. His hand came up to my face, brushing a strand of hair that fell in front of my eyes, his fingertips grazing my skin. His touch made my heart drum faster, harder. The air around us felt as if it were growing heavier—that it was somehow pressing against my skin, urging me to stop him.

My eyes searched his, scanning for any restraint, hoping he

wouldn't stop but also wishing he would. Then, his lips brushed against mine—soft at first, tentative as though he were waiting for me to push him away.

I couldn't.
How could I?

The kiss deepened, his hand sliding to the back of my neck and pulling me closer as his other hand rested lightly on my waist. His touch was firm yet careful, his movements deliberate as though he were savoring every second. I found myself inching closer to him and soon found myself on his lap.

He was intoxicating.

I could taste his magic on his tongue: that lovely combination of pine and eucalyptus. I felt his breath hitch against my lips, as though he were surprised by my position. The kiss shifted, growing more urgent. His hands settled at my waist, pulling me closer into him; he rolled my hips on top of him so I could feel him growing hard against me. My hands found his chest, and I frantically fumbled for the buttons of his tunic. I undid the buttons slowly as our lips crashed together, my tongue searching for more.

I wanted to feel *all* of him.

He then reached his hands to mine, stopping me from pulling more buttons apart.

"Are you sure?" he asked, breathless from the kiss.

I smiled at him, an excitement electrifying my entire body.

"Definitely," I murmured as I pushed his body to the ground. I straddled him now, gazing down at his face.

The sharpness of his jaw, the striking blue of his eyes—I craved it all. I fell back down into him, kissing eagerly as I undid his tunic.

"Easy, you'll rip it completely!" he laughed beneath me—something I am not sure I had experienced from him.

I had heard him laugh his low chuckle of amusement, but this was something else entirely. Perhaps a giggle of comfort, a playful laugh that danced on his tongue—a melody to my ears. I stopped for a moment, staring down at him, his face glowing from the charming smile he wore.

"That's new," I smiled back at him, hungry for more—but yet couldn't continue until I savored the moment of that radiant smile.

"What's new?" he almost giggled again when he spoke.

"That smile—I don't know if I've ever seen it on you," I said softly, inching closer to his face now. His gaze hardened a bit at the comment: an unexpected response, and I watched his cheeks turn a pinkish color.

A blush.

Another entirely unexpected reaction from him. I leaned back down and claimed his lips with my own; he pressed back into me, warm and demanding. I slid my hands down his bare chest, feeling the contours of it. He pulled me harder into him—the heat of his body seeped into mine, and the smell of his magic filled my senses. My eyes opened for a moment, and I could see the faint snowfall of glitter around us.

"Is this that lack of control you were talking about?" I teased, pulling only inches away from him.

"Are you going to keep talking or are you going to kiss me?" He chuckled again—such a pleasant sound.

I felt his teeth graze my bottom lip, a teasing pressure that made me shiver. A soft sound escaped me, and he responded immediately, his kiss growing deeper and hungrier. He then flipped me over him so that he was now above me.

His fingers slid beneath my chin, tilting my head to give him better access to my jaw as he kissed down to my neck. The warmth of his breath against my skin sent a wave of heat coursing through me, my body arching toward him.

"Ever the impatient," he whispered against my collarbone as he pulled down the sleeve of the bodysuit I wore. He must have undone its back as I sat on his lap—I hardly noticed.

His hands fell to my chest, pulling off the clothing that cloaked my skin; his movements were desperate and lacked his typical restraint and deliberance. His touch ignited a fire that coursed through my veins.

Gods did I want him.

He continued to kiss up and down my neck, his hands moving freely about my body when a voice rang out; shock and surprise laced her tone.

"What *the* fuck!" Diana yelled toward us.

"Gods, what the hell are you doing?" She approached but covered her eyes at the sight of us.

I immediately felt shame and regret washing over me—the realization now hit me in full force that I had done something terribly wrong. The last encounter I had with Hiver in the hallway left me riddled with guilt and longing, but it seemed that only now—with Diana's disapproving gaze upon us—that I felt the true weight of my betrayal. Her lilac eyes sparkled, not with delight, but with unmistakable horror.

"Well, I'll tell you what we aren't doing now that you're here," Hiver said, his voice carrying a note of irritation in it—though I could still hear the roughness lingering in it.

"Ugh, just dress yourself, you whore," she said to him, still averting her eyes from his halfway-undressed body.

"Mirage," she said to me softly, the disappointment in her tone stinging.

"Yes?" I said to her, the unbearable pain shaping into an audible quiver.

"What are you doing?" she whispered, but not so quietly that Hiver could not hear.

"Oh, don't be that way, Diana," he growled at her, noticing the shame that must have overtaken my expression.

"Don't be what way, exactly? You were about to full on fuck in the middle of the Autumn Courtyard! What about Stygian?" Diana thundered at him; her voice was raw with emotion, a sincere distress overcoming her.

"I—" Hiver started, but Diana spun to face him, completely cutting him off.

"Out, now!" She boomed, pointing at the exit to the Courtyard. Hiver's eyes narrowed on her, but he did as she commanded.

"As you wish, *sister*." He spoke with such bitterness as he left the Courtyard, not even daring to make eye contact with me as he left.

Diana's soft eyes fell upon my face.

"I just don't understand," she said gently, a hand coming to rest on mine as I sat on the bed of grass, completely disheveled.

"I don't either," I huffed, unable to even think of how to continue this discussion.

"You can trust me with anything, Mira," she said, brushing my knuckles with her fingers.

"I don't know what I want. I suppose I have never really had the freedom to choose…" I was unable to meet her gaze, which burned into my flesh.

"You are free here. But that freedom does not mean you can hurt the people who care about you—the people *you* care about," her soft purple eyes looked almost grey in the lighting of the Autumn Courtyard.

"Choose who you wish, make mistakes, be reckless—sure, but don't be like *her*." Diana made no secret of her distaste as she mentioned Lyris. I hadn't thought much of her since moving here— of the girl who would play with feelings for fun. I grimaced.

"Come now, let's get you cleaned up," she rose from the ground and offered me her hand—and off we went to my chambers.

CHAPTER
TWENTY-EIGHT

The next morning came too quickly—*far* too quickly...

It was only me, Hiver, Kaneira, and Samira—she stood in the middle of the room with that typical crazed look in her eyes. The blue of her irises was piercing and vicious.

"You will fight Samira, and you will do *whatever* it takes to win," Kaneira said. I could hear in her voice just how bloodthirsty she was. She wanted to see what the God gave me, and I prayed to him now that it was more than just blood.

Samira's armor was exactly as I had imagined it.

A blue set that looked to be made completely of sapphires—raw and untamed, a natural yet precious stone. Her armor was streaked in silver, running down her arms and legs. It looked as if she had ice snaking up and down her—like her veins were made of it.

Her pale skin nearly glowed in contrast to the armor, her eyes illuminated by the radiant sun that spilled in through the windows.

. . .

"Go!" Kaneira boomed.

Samira began to mumble something under her breath, a flurry of frost climbing from the floor onto her fists.

"Frost gauntlets," I said breathlessly.

"Fight to kill, Mirage," Hiver shouted. His magic danced around his hands, climbing up his arms and exploding into dust around him, creating a cloud.

For the first time I got a good look at the wolf that protected him when he slept. From the dust, the white-coated wolf leapt out at Samira, charging at her through the mist. Its jaws clasped around her arm, ripping it apart with a ferocity that was terrifying. The wolf retreated, and Samira screamed at the sight of her skin barely hanging onto to her muscles.

It was a sickening sight.

The beast found its way to my side as I stared beyond in terror. It circled me once, staring at me. It was already covered in blood; its teeth held some of her flesh as it growled before completely fading into the dust. Samira frosted over the wound, creating what looked to be a cast of ice, and then she barreled toward me.

The gauntlet smashed into my chest, knocking the air out of my lungs. I felt something wet on my clothes as I reached down and noticed I was bleeding—but the healing was not happening quick enough.

I fell to my knees, not an unusual occurrence for me...when I saw her frenzied eyes glowing above me.

They actually glowed.

One of the gauntlets came down upon my face, ripping open my cheek; I could feel the flesh hanging down. I reached for it with a trembling hand. I was certain she had broken my ribs, maybe even my sternum as I struggled to breathe. A fear consumed me like nothing I had ever felt before—when Hiver shot out of the mist behind me, his sword cutting at Samira's midsection.

She yelped and threw a fist into him, but he managed to dodge it. I hadn't seen him move that fast before. His slashes were deliberate and precise, hitting her in specific places; he dodged every blow. I was told Samira was quick—supernaturally so—but Hiver kept up with her.

I made it back to my feet with a stumble and tried to wipe the blood from my mouth and cheek, but so much of it had come down. My head was humming with a throbbing pain that I fear wouldn't subside.

I felt like I was not healing.

"Mirage!" Hiver yelled to me from the mist. I could not see him, and I could feel myself growing frantic. I searched for him, for the source of his voice, and I fumbled through the fog that spread about the room—when a chain wrapped around my legs.

The frost that coated it bit into my skin, burning my flesh. I screamed in pain. The chains yanked me to the ground, the marble floors ripping open my skin.

Everything was healing slower.

The pain was completely disruptive, making it impossible to think, to even move.

This all happened much faster than in typical training; Samira moved quicker and she was far more bloodthirsty than the others. I could see her glowing eyes in the mist, as I was being pulled toward her, I grabbed at the floor, which was covered in my blood.

Her silhouette came into view: she towered over me, her inky hair pooling around her head as if it were alive. She continued to yank me into her, those sapphire eyes gleaming—her expression ruthless.

She was a monster.

Damned was not a strong enough term.

She was brutal.

I saw her wind up her frosted gauntlet, ready to let it slam down upon me as I sat helpless before her. Then out of the fog, that terrifying creature leapt onto her again.

The white wolf.

It tore at her, and Hiver burst from the mist yet again. He brought his blade down upon her, but she was so fast she dodged his attack entirely. I heard her mumble something under her breath before a shield of ice sprouted up to take the brunt of his blade.

He reached his hands to her temples and pressed them, and her eyes glazed over a milky white color as she stared out in front of her. He seemed to be struggling, though she didn't move a muscle. She was entirely still, eyes empty of thought as she gazed outward, but he flinched and grimaced. After significant struggle, she reached up, eyes back in their glowing blue state, and threw him off of her. He heaved on the ground next to her, his blade positioned toward her.

I decided to summon the flame whips. I casted them out to grab her, and they did. They clasped both of her wrists, pulling her forward into me. I yanked her toward me, her great armor hitting the ground as she dropped to her knees. She tugged back at them and nearly pulled me from my place.

The blood didn't seem to stop flowing—*for any of us.*

I didn't even know if I was healing at all by this point. I couldn't feel my tissue welding itself back together.

She eventually stopped pulling, but I knew better. A woman with this much power didn't stop because she was weak—she stopped because she had a plan.

The whips frosted up to me, biting my skin where I held them. I cursed under my breath as the frost climbed up my arms; my flesh turned frostbitten, and my breaths came out labored and cold. She was freezing me.

Not in the way Diana did when she pressed her hand through my armor—this was faster and far more painful. I could feel the frost creeping into my lungs, slowing my breathing—

no, *stopping* it.

I was choking.

I fell to my knees, gasping for air, but it wouldn't find its way into my lungs. The frost was consuming me, turning me into pure ice. I was rasping now, no oxygen making it into my throat.

"Enough!" Kaneira boomed, and Hiver instantly willed away the fog. The clear air revealed the blood covered floors; and even worse, pieces of flesh.

"Hiver!" I croaked. I half dragged myself over and fell to my knees before him. I was too weak to move; I didn't have the strength to even reach for my blade—I couldn't cut my arm to give him my blood.

I could feel the consciousness fading.

"You're okay, you're okay," Hiver cooed. He stroked my cheeks as I sat helplessly before him, then he pulled my head to his chest and wrapped his arms around me. I would usually burn under his touch—something in me would start on fire at the mere grace of his fingers. But now, I only felt *safe*.

I looked past his arm at Kaneira who slowly approached us. The look on her face was not one I had ever seen before. Her eyes softened, and her lips pulled into a soft smile as she looked upon us.

"Love is power," she whispered, so low I hardly heard the words leaving her lips. I felt something tighten in my chest, but it wasn't entirely unpleasant.

I was too weak to move—too weak to even return her smile. I just allowed him to hold my head to his chest, to stroke my hair as his cheek rested atop of my head. I felt as if I could fall asleep here in his embrace…and that I did. I didn't know how long I lay there, but when my eyes opened, I was still in his arms. I reached for my face, feeling the closed wounds.

I sighed with relief.

Then I noticed the cannula that sat in my arm: that same tube that Jesper had put into me. I shot up, terrified that I was in a nightmare—or even worse, back in the possession of Jesper. I jolted Hiver awake, but only for a moment as sleep reclaimed him. I reached down for the tube, and pulled it from my arm when Lucius spoke.

"Your blood is the only way we could heal them," he frowned at me.

"How long have I been here?" I turned to face Hiver.

"You've been here a few hours—not long." That emotionless tone Lucius used prevailed over his disappointment.

I looked at Hiver's body, pulling up his tunic to be sure the gashes had disappeared.

"He's healed," Lucius said. Though I couldn't see his face at that moment, I could hear the smile on his lips. I allowed sleep to consume me in the safety of Hiver's embrace.

The next time my eyes opened, it was moonlight that spilled into the throne room. They had allowed us to sleep in here for the remainder of the day.

I wondered if Hiver always slept with his magic still alert, as the beautiful sparkles of magic surrounded us—just as they had the last time we slept in this room. I saw the moonlight casting a gentle glow over his features, which seemed so much softer in sleep. I could almost picture his radiant smile—that lovely laugh that escaped his mouth in the sun-kissed land of Autumn. I reached a hand to his cheek and caressed it softly, hoping not to wake him from the peaceful slumber he had fallen into.

I couldn't describe the feeling that washed over me. It was something that consumed me—it gripped my heart and my mind with such a force that I could not think clearly. I must have jostled him, as his eyes opened lazily, the blue color hardly peeking from under his eyelids.

"What're you doing?" he smiled at me: that gentle smile that felt safe.

"Nothing," I said to him, unable to stop myself from grinning back at him. He did not say another word but opened his arms, gesturing for me to fall back into him—to sleep at his side. Instead, I found my curiosity winning over my exhaustion.

"Where's the wolf?" I asked.

"Huh?" he said in a lethargic stupor.

"The *wolf*," I whispered.

"Glacien?" he groaned drowsily.

"*Glacien?*" I responded.

"He's my protector," he grumbled, adjusting himself against the chair, his eyes fully opening now.

"What?" I said breathlessly. "So *he* is real? It's a real wolf?" I gasped.

"Uh—kind of? The children of Rainier are given a protector at birth, but snowsmoke can physically manifest it," he explained nonchalantly.

"So it was real?"

"Yeah, he's real," he chuckled.

With the wave of his hand, he summoned the creature—Glacien. His coat now white again and no longer drenched in blood. The dog's tongue flopped out of the side of its mouth and stared at me.

"Well? Pet him!" Hiver urged, reaching his own hand to the dog's fluffy head. I did as he did, reaching for its great coat. The wolf collapsed beneath my hand, exposing its stomach to me. I giggled as he rolled back and forth, tongue still not quite fitting in his mouth. For a few moments we pet Glacien in silence, not really saying much as the dog happily rolled around.

"He would never hurt you…just so you know." Hiver whispered before pulling me back into him. We stayed on the floor for the remainder of the night, his arm lazily draped around me as his back was pressed against the chair.

"Did I miss the 'no training' announcement?" Stygian's voice rang. The sun pouring in through the windows was painful to my eyes; I held up a hand to block the light as I made eye contact with him. Hiver groaned and moved a bit, still drowsy and unwilling to enter reality with the rest of us.

"I know how rough Sam can be…I understand just passing out afterwards." Stygian approached Hiver now, giving his arm a squeeze—a gesture of affection.

I found Diana still staring at me with such an intensity I felt my skin burning from her gaze.

"Sit out today, Mira," Diana spoke in a gentle tone.

"I suppose you can sit out too—but I appreciate you offering to train with us, Snow!" Diana playfully spoke to him, shoving him as he groaned and covered his eyes.

"I'll see you later," I said and decided to leave the throne room to spend some more time in the Autumn Courtyard.

CHAPTER
TWENTY-NINE

The whips crackled to life in my hands, the golden flames writhing like living creatures tethered to my will. I threw them around tree branches in the courtyard and watched them crack and fall to the ground, their fruits following suit.

"Wouldn't you like to know more about those, darling?" The silky cadence of his voice wrapped around me, suffocating me.

Jesper.

I lost control of the whips, and they began to sputter, their golden light flickering.

"Is there something you need, Jesper?" I tried to keep my voice steady.

"Is there something wrong with just wanting to be your friend?" He tilted his head and stalked toward me, "don't you want to know more about yourself? What makes you able to wield such *precious* weapons?"

"I think ignorance will be my salvation if that information needs to come from you," I shot back at him.

"Would you like to know what is at the core of Arudia's whips?" His lips curled into that familiar feline smile.

"*Arudia?*" I said—my curiosity must have been overwhelming my features as Jesper's smile widened.

"The Goddess of the flame? Daughter of Olym? Hmm, you really don't know much, do you?" He reached for my chin and tilted it up toward him. I didn't try to pull away, but I did narrow my eyes at him.

"Arudia's whips are made with blood and fire—the core of your whips is blood, but you probably didn't even notice that." A vicious grin painted his face.

"How do you know anything about me *or* my magic?" I spat at him, the fury rising up to my throat again.

"Because I've gotten a taste of it," he said, pulling a vial from his pocket.

He began to whisper in a language I did not understand, and I could only assume he was summoning something sinister.

Fleurara a flamber
Duskani aum ember
Ehl podor aum God detdet me sur finir

He said before drinking the contents of the vial—my blood. His eyes started to glow as if he were possessed. I pushed my back into the bark of the tree as he stood tall over me.

"Isn't it incredible?" He gestured around him.

"I can channel *you*." His voice was sinister, low and dark.

"You have no idea what kind of power you possess…" He spun himself in a circle.

"You have no idea what this power can do for *us*…" He trailed off and turned back to face me; his eyes were a solid gold color.

"What is the point? I can't even control it!" I snapped, and the fire reacted, forming in my palms and wrapping around my wrists.

"Do you know why you can't control it? Because like the young Goddess, you inherited that chaos—that *rage*—that *passion*," He said the words so intently, "Did you know Arudia is also the Goddess of Passion? *Ahh*, I'm sure you didn't," he began to ramble, excitement lacing his tone.

"That doesn't make any sense," I shot back, averting my gaze from his golden eyes.

"Of course it doesn't—because you were never told." He still stood over me, his expression hungry, his eyes roving over me.

"I can help you use that magic—teach you some of the scripts. Let me," Jesper said with an uncharacteristic kindness in his tone.

"I don't trust you, Jesper," I said breathlessly. I struggled to look at him when I spoke; I feared he would read the terror on my face—that he would use it against me.

"I am sorry I *took* you." His apology dripped with sarcasm, lingering on the word took, as if it pained him to say it.

"I still don't trust you." I hoped the harshness in my tone would be his sign that I wished for nothing more than this conversation to end.

"Okay, fine. If you ever want to know more about your magic, you can always come find me." He left me in the courtyard by myself, a blessing from the Gods.

His words still hung in the air despite his absence.

He had compared me to a Goddess.

I tried to shake off his words as meaningless—possibly even lies; I couldn't trust Jesper or anything that managed to escape his tongue. I thought of him drinking my blood: the immediate glow in his eyes and the excitement that coursed through him—I thought of being bound again to that table, the Sifrune straps inducing a nauseating sensation of helplessness.

Panic poured over me.

I decided to pull my knees up to my chest.

Tears began to swim down my cheeks, the salty taste of them settling on my lips. I didn't bother to wipe them away, instead I rested my head on my arms and stared out at the slow falling leaves.

. . .

"It's late, you know," Stygian's voice drifted to me.

"Oh no, Mirage, what's wrong?" he said upon getting a closer look at my face, which I imagined had become red and splotchy under the tears.

"I'm not sure," I sniffled. I tried hard to suppress the tears that fell from my eyes—to will them to stop flowing like a sea.

Stygian dropped to the ground beside me with a graceful ease; he settled close enough to me for his warmth to brush against me. His deep green eyes fixed on me, sharp yet tender, as though he were studying every single tear-streaked line that etched itself into my flesh.

"Would you like to talk about it?" he asked, his voice quiet— lacking that usual excitement he wore like a mask.

I shook my head in response, unable to begin to sort the words into coherent sentences. He didn't press, instead he reached into his coat and pulled out a piece of cloth; wordlessly, he wiped away the tears from my cheeks with it. I stared at him through glassy eyes, unable to say even a word.

"You don't have to speak," he said softly.

I looked upon his face just to see the way his eyes illuminated in the low sun of the Autumn Courtyard.

He was breathtaking.

"Why did you take an interest in me?" I whispered, the question slipping out before I could stop myself.

I watched his lips turn into a small smile: one that was polite and inviting.

"You're perfect, that's why. I could see that when I first met you."

His words struck a chord in my chest as if he were playing me like a harp. I suddenly felt a stir of emotions that I could not identify —maybe it was more than lust, maybe it wasn't, but at this moment I couldn't decide. I reached for him, brushing his hand with my own. He froze for a movement, his eyes darting to mine, but he didn't pull away.

"Stygian, I—" I began, but he interrupted me.

"I know you think the same of me; I mean look at me," he laughed while motioning to his face. I allowed a giggle to escape my lips too, and he leaned in closer. I loved the almond shape of his eyes—the way they crinkled when he smiled at me...

I hardly had time to register his movements, but suddenly his lips were on mine: warm and insistent, as though he had been waiting for this moment since he sat down. His hands found my cheeks, pulling me closer as he kissed deeper. His hands felt strange on my raw skin. The way his fingers felt against where my skin streaked red from tears—it almost felt *wrong*. But the way he kissed me was so soothing—so *right*.

He began to undo the suit I wore, that stitched black fabric—I realized I had not changed my clothes in more than a day.

"Um—" I pulled away, a smile pulling at my lips as I looked at him, a bashfulness settling over me.

"I think I should bathe first. I haven't since fighting Samira." I lowered my head to avoid him seeing the redness that enveloped my cheeks—the heat of embarrassment made my skin burn under the salt lines from my now dry tears.

"I don't care—" He whispered to me before playfully biting at my neck and ear. Something about him set me on fire, made my veins burn hot with desire for him.

"Do you want to join me?" I was shocked at the words as they left my mouth and he nodded enthusiastically before falling into step behind me.

<hr />

When I opened the door he followed me in—but stopped right at the entrance.

"You know, I wasn't trying to take advantage of you in the Courtyard. I realize how my actions might have portrayed something different..." he sounded distressed now, an emotion I never saw from him.

"What?" I almost laughed at the thought. Stygian was kind and gentle—and from time to time a bit cocky—but never the kind to take advantage of another.

"I never want you to believe that I don't deeply…care for you, Mirage." The softness in his voice became him; his eyes, his face, his everything became more gentle as he spoke. A genuineness overtaking his expression.

The collision was violent.

My feelings were a tempest: a hurricane of love, lust, rage, desire, sadness, and anxiety all colliding together to create a storm. I wished to turn them off, to lose myself in Stygian's fire—the all consuming, the raw magnetic force that lured me to him.

I began to run the water to the bath and remove my clothes. As I did, Stygian cocked his head at me, watching the fabric hit the floor.

As the water filled the tub, I slipped in, letting the heat envelop me completely. I decided the only way to reconcile the impossible contradiction of my emotions was to sink into the rose-scented water that caressed my skin like a soft embrace. After a moment, Stygian joined me. We sat in silence, the steam weaving a fragile veil between us, easily pierced by the intensity of his curious gaze.

"Show me your candor," his voice was soft like velvet, the words a warm invitation.

"I think I lost most of myself," I started and immediately felt ridiculous. I shook my head and rolled my eyes at myself.

"What do you mean?" He asked. His hand skimmed the water, but his eyes didn't leave mine.

"The world shifted so dramatically around me, and I think I was forced to adapt too quickly. Now, I'm not sure I even recognize who

I used to be. I'm still terrified." The words continued to come out almost against my will.

I gestured frantically in the tub as I spoke, sending small waves crashing against his skin. He came closer to me and pulled me into a tight embrace.

"You haven't lost yourself—you *found* it." He pulled away and caressed my cheek before pressing his lips against my forehead.

"What if I don't like what I found?" I looked up at him.

"None of us do at first. You grow into yourself—we all did." He gave me a wistful smile.

"What if I don't?" I felt embarrassed for asking.

"What if we all died right now because the Gods decided to pull the sun into the Earth?" I giggled at his sentiment.

"Okay," I smiled.

His lips met mine, gentle at first, and the warmth of his mouth and the soft press of his lips was so inviting. The water rippled around us as he shifted closer, his hands pulling at my waist. His chest touched mine and his heartbeat drummed to the same rhythm as my own, its soft thumping igniting me further.

My fingers found their way around his shoulders, and he pulled my naked body onto his. His kisses found their way down my jaw and my neck; his lips eventually made it down to my chest.

"Why don't we leave the bath?" I said to him, and without hesitation he lifted me from the tub and carried me out to the bed.

"Stygian! We are still wet, you're going to soak the sheets!" I squirmed and giggled beneath him, but he had me entirely restrained.

"Oh no, what will you do with wet sheets?" His laughter erupted, rich and unrestrained; his energy was contagious and vibrated through his body.

"Stygian!" I squealed.

"So you want me to stop?" he whispered against my ear, nipping and tugging on my neck.

"Of course not," I grabbed him and pulled him down into me hard. I kissed him with aggression—longing was consuming me.

I wanted him.

But for just a moment, I had wondered if the hair between my hands would look better if it were white.

CHAPTER
THIRTY

It felt as if we woke up in the middle of the sun. Its blinding light casting no shadows, reaching every corner of the chamber.

"Up! Now!" Diana's voice radiated with energy as she finished opening all of the windows.

"Diana, what the fu—" Stygian began, but she quickly interjected.

"It's *Summundor*? Hello?" She frowned at our shared confusion.

"Stygian, what the hell is your excuse? You have lived here almost your entire life!" She yanked the sheets off of us now, and we sat almost entirely exposed before her.

"Come, up!" She clapped her hands as she wrapped around the bed to raise me from it. I looked at her with confusion and a bit of anger.

"Hate me later—we are going to be late," she said, a certain edge to her tone.

"Diana, so lovely to see you at this hour. No good morning, no how are you?" Stygian teased.

"I've seen more of you than I would have liked at this hour. Out you go!" She smiled a bit as she gestured for him to leave.

"Have a good morning, Diana!" He saluted to her sarcastically before winking at me and taking his sweet time to rise from the bed.

"Out, Stygian!" She laughed, grabbing the top of her nose between two fingers as she shook her head.

Stygian pulled on his clothes and gave me a polite smile before exiting my chambers to ready himself for the apparent occasion.

"What's *Summundor*?" I questioned as she sat me down to begin untangling my hair.

"Right before summer ends, everyone eats the Clariflux together for their truths to come to light!" I looked at her with a deep fear settling into me; that fruit showed me visions of one of the darkest times in my life.

"What's the matter?" Diana looked at me in the mirror with a particularly concerned expression.

"The last time I ate—"

She cut me off quickly, "The last time you *what*? You ate one of the fruits? When?" Diana couldn't help herself.

"With Hiver in the Summer Courtyard—that's when I got a vision of someone telling me they'd come back for me the day my mother was murdered," I said solemnly.

"Oh my Gods. Did Hiver tell you what that fruit actually does? What did you see?" She cocked her head to the side, her soft purple eyes glittering in the blazing sunlight.

"What? No. It gave me visions and then some sort of song? Spell? Poem?" I couldn't find the right word to describe the final moments of the visions.

"What did it say?" She prompted again, her curiosity piqued.

"I don't really remember—only the last line, '*The betrayed heart, reforged through fire*' or something like that…"

"Hmm," she hummed.

"The fruit is meant to show you the truth you seek. It can be very cryptic."

"I think I figured out what that meant, though, after speaking to

Kaneira." Though I almost felt like I was lying—that I didn't figure it out at all, despite the answer seeming obvious.

"Perhaps. We'll just have to see what it shows you today." Her lips curled into a gentle smile as she spoke.

"What if I don't eat it?" I asked.

"You sort of have to; it's tradition. There's nothing to be afraid of." She met my gaze in the mirror as she resumed her place behind me.

"Okay," I murmured, not extraordinarily pleased with that answer.

"Let's see what else Anathena's left for you, eh?" Diana squealed and drifted over to the wardrobe to pull out the masterpiece.

The gown looked to be crafted of flame and silk. It looked as if Anathena had captured the light of dawn stretching out on the horizon. The vibrant orange hue deepened into amber at the hem, as if the gown were dipped into gold. My eyes were fixated on the dress. Diana helped me get into it, and it formed to me like a second skin. The bodice was adorned with rubies and a stone I didn't recognize.

"What's this one?" I touched the yellow gems that mingled so perfectly with the rubies.

"It's Thalorite, the gem of Vulkram," Diana said softly, smoothing out my dress around my hips. I shook my head in response—I was not familiar with all of the Gods, only a few and Vulkram was not one of them.

"Vulkram? The God of the Forge?" She spoke like it was obvious, but it was not to me.

"So these were made by the God of the *Forge*?" I touched them softly with my fingers.

"Yeah, they were made in the Aurenyx—that's the name of

Vulkram's forge—Gods only know where Anathena gets them." She was on her knees before me, straightening out the dress.

It was a sight I couldn't forget: a princess kneeling before me.

Not just any princess, but the strong kind.

The brave kind.

I could never fight for my people the way she could.

Our people.

"I must ready myself too. I'll see you in Summer!" She vibrated with a contagious energy as she left my chambers.

I twirled in front of the mirror and stared down at the lovely hues of orange. I exited my chambers with a thrill. As I walked down the beautiful corridors, I traced my fingers once more along the Stone Mage's craftsmanship.

I decided to walk toward the Summer Courtyard, but I felt a sense of fear dawning on me as I did.

It was thrumming with the energy of many bodies. I navigated the crowd to that familiar area where I took a bite of the fruit with Hiver just feet away from me. I stared at its soft flesh from this safe distance, wondering what would happen this time.

As my eyes drifted out to the water that lay beyond, I caught a glimpse of him. His attire was a masterwork of elegance, and it appeared to echo me. The coat was a deep orange, the fabric shimmering slightly as though it were woven with threads of molten copper. If I were the dawn, he was the moment the sun kissed the horizon, ushering in the light of day. His hair was bound into a piece of silk, but a few strands fell artfully around his face—the white of his hair a hard but beautiful contrast to his fiery attire.

Hiver.

His eyes widened as he saw me, and he looked me up and down with a glint of what almost appeared to be panic in his eyes. He approached me swiftly, gently pulling my arm.

"We match," he said breathlessly. It almost came out as a question.

"I see you look—" I stopped myself from continuing that statement; something I hardly ever did was bite my tongue. Yet, when I was in the presence of a man who could easily look to be a God in this moment, I couldn't even breathe in his presence.

"That brooch—" I noticed the sparkle of gold catching the summer sunlight and reflecting it into my eyes. He wore a brooch that was a sunburst; it looked like the helm I wore. I reached for it, feeling the hard metal between my fingers as I gazed up at him, a confusion overcoming me. Everything he wore exuded boldness and refinement, a symbol of power and unity—though that unity seemed to center entirely on me.

"Wow, did I miss the memo?" Natsu said over my shoulder, and I turned to face him.

"Magnificent, both of you," he said cheerfully, but his attention seemed to be more focused on the crowd—surely he was looking for Samira. He didn't seem surprised by our matching ensembles, but I feared what Stygian may think upon seeing it.

Hiver reached for my hand and squeezed it, a gesture I appreciated in the overwhelming chaos of the ceremony. Natsu happily skipped alongside us as we walked, searching desperately for Samira in the crowd.

"Have you seen her by chance?" He finally asked. Hiver and I both shook our heads—I hadn't seen her *or* Stygian in the sea of people.

Somehow, this ceremony was more grand than the Ball. It was a symphony of tradition and enchantment, an event woven with both reverence and quiet dread. The air shimmered with the soft glow of suspended paper lanterns, their flames flickering like captive stars in the never-ending light of Summer.

Unlike the Ball, there seemed to only be fruit and wine at *Summundor*. Then I saw *it* in gilded bowls upon the long stretches of table—a fruit whose flesh I could never forget. I could almost taste its soft skin on my tongue, the juice that coated my mouth and sent me into a vision of the past.

"You gotta go eat one Mirage—it's a gesture of goodwill!" Natsu beamed at me.

"How is that a gesture of goodwill," I scoffed, remembering my experience with the fruit. He cocked his head at me, a genuine perplexity settling over him.

"The Clariflux shows you your truths—something you seek yet you do not know. For most people, it provides reassurance—love, happiness, joy—where they least expect it." He smiled now and pulled me toward a tray of scarletberries.

"What did you see?" I asked, unable to focus on the food but rather only on Natsu.

"I saw my sister and my mom playing in the stream that used to run past our home. My sister splashing around and using the water to make arcs above her head. She was Summer-Kissed too…" A soft smile pulled at his lips, and he turned to face me. His eyes sparkled with something different now, a bittersweetness that I could not begin to understand.

His family had been killed.

"I'm sorry, Natsu," I managed as I pulled him into an embrace. I could feel him pressing his head into my shoulder as we sat there for a moment.

"I'm *so* sorry." I stifled a sob of my own. I could feel him squeezing me tighter, as if I were the last remnant of his memory that he wished to cling onto.

He eventually pulled away, a single tear running down his cheek.

I reached for it and wiped it off with my finger, giving him a gentle smile that he returned.

"I took it for granted, I think. That memory." He closed his eyes tightly.

"Even if—they never deserved to die," I said softly, my voice hardly breaching a whisper.

"We don't deserve much from this life, except maybe its end." He pursed his lips as he spoke.

"Well that's dark," Hiver mumbled.

"Something my mom used to say," Natsu smiled sweetly, "Well anyway, I am going to indulge myself in scarletberries and pineapple now. Enjoy the ceremony!" His usual cheer made an effort to seep back into his tone, but he was overcome with melancholy.

I watched him work his way down the table, mingling with other Tessiah. Hiver then came to my side and gently stroked my arm to gather my attention.

"Have you seen my sister?" he said to me—his eyes flashed a bit of concern.

"Not since this morning, no." I admitted.

"She isn't the late type...but I am sure she's fine—assuming she helped you get into *this* glorious creation." He looked down at my dress and smiled at me.

"She did indeed." I managed to smile back at him; I had to fight the whirlwind of emotions I felt for Natsu—for losing his family to hate.

I then noticed Kaneira at the end of the table with Lucius at her side. They indulged in the various fruits, smiling and talking to those who crowded around them. I watched her dismiss those who surrounded her, and she approached me.

She moved with a certain grace, her steps fluid and silent; it appeared like the air itself parted to let her pass. Each motion of hers was effortless, yet she demanded attention without a single sound, and the crowd was more than willing to devote themselves to her.

She was a true leader.

Before I could even greet her, Kaneira had gripped my shoulders, steering me toward the fruits.

"Your turn, child," She said with a gentleness I had still not grown accustomed to. I nearly protested her as she presented me with the Clariflux fruit. Instead, I bit into the sweet flesh of it, and as it wet my tongue, the world began to ripple and blur around me. I would enter another memory, and Gods—I hoped it would be a pleasant one.

As the world gathered around me to form images, I was able to make out the scene before me, and my hopes were too high.

My uncle's funeral...
My father's brother, Catalan, was a general in life.
He was also the first person I had known Kaneira to kill.
The first time she had touched my life in a meaningful way.

> *A muffled hum - a sacred warmth,*
> *A moment in time sets your life off course,*
> *The blackest trenches - the brightest sky,*
> *The fateful sleep, its sweetest lullaby.*

The fruits chanted in their eerie song-like tone.

I looked up to see my mother next to me and Dracar at her other side. She frowned toward the casket where Catalan was being laid to rest, but she otherwise seemed unbothered by his untimely death.

However, it wasn't her lack of sadness that caught my attention —rather the veil that she wore. It looked to be woven of shadow, yet translucent simultaneously. As I stared, Dracar reached to touch it as it glittered in the low light of morning.

"Karo, honey—don't touch." Her voice was soothing and soft as she spoke, reaching down to Dracar to remove his hands from the veil.

I looked around the room as the light spilled in through the windows, casting terrifying shadows about the throne room. I was terrified of the shadows.

"Little bird, what's wrong?" My mother cooed to me, placing a hand under my chin. I felt the tears wetting my face now—I was crying from the silhouettes cast about the room. I tried to look into her eyes, but somehow the veil made them impossible to see.

I just wanted to see her face—her beautiful face—and yet I could not.

I reached for the veil so I could take in her features one last time, but the memory rippled as I did. For a moment, it looked like *my* face beneath the veil; I reached for the scarlet strands of hair that were unmistakably my own. But soon enough, I could make out the face no longer. It slowly faded as I desperately attempted to take in the entire memory.

"No!" I cried as the world around me began to blur. The shadows came down on me now; their darkness was thick and suffocating, like living entities. They moved unnaturally, their edges flickering and shifting as though caught between forms.

I tried to swing at them, and my hands passed through them. Yet they managed to cut my skin, repeatedly slashing at me with claws formed of darkness.

I wasn't healing.

The shadows then buried themselves into my flesh, creating markings across my skin. My veins turned black underneath their talons. After what felt like eternity, the world went entirely dark, as if the shadows had consumed me entirely.

Mirage.
Mirage.

Mirage!

The Clariflux screamed at me now, the shrieking bouncing off the walls of my skull making me suffocate. My breaths became labored, as if the voices were stealing the air from my lungs with each chant of my name.

Reality will fade under the shadow's grip,
The fleeting sensation, an illusory slip
The cost is hidden, the truth a pyre,
Your newfound heart reforged in fire.

I broke back into reality with a shriek. The world around me was still collecting itself as the objects and faces began to form around me.

"What happened?" Kaneira hissed. Her expression was unhappy and fitful as she spoke.

"What do you mean, 'what happened?' The last time I ate one of those things I had to relive my mother's death. Why are you surprised!" I snapped back in a frantic whisper. Her nostrils flared at me, her eyes closing.

"I had to know what you saw dear," she said sternly, though I could see behind her manic eyes that she was fearful for me.

"Well, it was a scary memory from when I was a child! I wasn't healing in it either, so if you could imagine, I was frightened!" I spoke in an aggressive whisper to not let those around us hear the hysteria I was afflicted with.

"It's—fine, just go and get a breath of fresh air." Kaneira motioned outside of the courtyard, and I half dragged myself out. Exhaustion was dawning upon me a I paced incessantly outside of the entrance to Summer.

CHAPTER
THIRTY-ONE

I tried to focus on the memory: the way my mother's face looked, the way Dracar looked, the shadow's silhouettes... yet I could understand none of it. I wanted to believe the fruits were showing me my mother's lack of distress at the funeral of my uncle—that they were showing me Kaneira was not evil. It made sense; it *had* to make sense.

I could feel myself going mad as I paced the perfect marble floors.

"Mirage?" Hiver's voice floated to me, and my attention snapped up toward him.

"What happened to you? Are you okay?" His hands immediately found my cheeks, his warmth seeping into my skin.

"I'm okay, it was just a weirdly distressing memory."

"What of?" His eyes searched mine for answers that my tongue did not have permission to give.

"A funeral from when I was a child. Another memory of my mother..." I looked past him into the eternal land of Summer. I could see the waves in the far distance crashing on a shoreline I was unsure even existed.

"I'll admit mine was a bit odd too…" He trailed off but kept his eyes focused on my face.

"And more recent than I would have expected," he continued.

"How recent?" I asked.

"When I retrieved you from your kingdom—the moment Dracar's blade was held up to my face. The hilt caught my eye; it was adorned with a *strange* jewel. It caught my attention at that moment, and I just saw it again." He shrugged when he spoke, seemingly unbothered by the cryptic nature of the fruit.

"Well, what did it say to you?" I questioned.

"Something, something, *finality and eternity, a fate intertwined, primordial existence with the spark of divine*? I don't know, something of that nature." He was entirely unphased.

"I wonder if it had something to do with you," he smiled faintly, breaking eye contact for a moment as he gazed down at my dress.

"Perhaps," was all I managed to say.

I was beginning to lose myself in the folds of his attire. He complemented me perfectly.

I too wondered if his truth somehow led to me.

"I wouldn't worry." Hiver's expression softened.

"Okay." I nodded and for a moment we continued to stare at one another, the orange hues of his ensemble captivating me. I could not tear my eyes off of the sunburst that flawlessly matched my helm.

It could not have been an accident.

I couldn't stop the smile that parted my lips.

"What could I have done to deserve that beautiful smile," he came closer now, his hands finding their way down to my waist. I studied his face as he held me there: the curve of his lips, the sharp blue of his eyes.

"Being you," I murmured, allowing his face to inch closer to mine. His lips curved into a smirk, but his gaze softened, the intensity of his blue eyes tempered by something warmer, more tender.

"You flatter me," he murmured, his fingers tightening around my waist.

"I'm not sure that I do…and perhaps that's my problem." I spoke as if I were in a trance.

I meant that I didn't deserve him…

"I'm not sure what you mean," he said softly, his grip loosening around me.

"I—uh," I faltered, hardly able to collect my thoughts. I had been truly entranced by him in that moment, speaking purely out of instinct without thought.

"I am going to take a walk through Autumn… if you wish to join me?" I offered my hand for him to take, and he responded with a wide smile.

"I have to find Diana first—I'll join you later?" He took the hand I outstretched and placed his lips to my knuckles, grazing my skin with a warm kiss.

"Okay," I said softly before departing from him.

As I made my way into the Autumn Courtyard, I had realized I had not crossed paths with Stygian today, and I was eager to see what Anathena had cloaked him in. I entered the Courtyard and planted my back against the familiar tree, beginning to play with my whips as if they were toys.

I could not shake Jesper's words: calling them *Arudia's whips*. I had to assume he was lying, since he was everything but trustworthy. The fiery threads of the whips danced in the air as I twisted them into arcs. They crackled as they snapped onto the tree branches that always regenerated after my visits here.

The stillness of the Courtyard was a welcome feeling. The leaves fell lazily to the ground around me, their vibrant hues decorating the grass as if they were nature's ornaments. I watched them fall slowly as I cracked the whips outward.

That stillness was soon pierced by a familiar voice.

"Ah, how you've grown fond of your whips." Jesper stepped into the shade that I sat under, staring down at me with his hands behind his back. He moved like the shadows, his approach a predatory stalk shrouded in impossible silence.

"Grating—your voice is grating." I replied.

I noted his blood-colored ensemble. At the waist he wore a leather belt with what appeared to be a raven on the buckle. On top lay a silky black undershirt that he chose not to button at the top. The fabric of his tunic appeared to be almost velvet—thick and rich.

"You wound me darling. You do know that I too belong to this Courtyard? That I *too* have been graced by the Sun?" I gazed up to find his lips curling into that maddening smile he so frequently wore —the charm that veiled his menacing intentions.

"The Courtyard is large enough for us to not have to borrow space from the other. Consider finding a different area to skulk in," I said flatly, letting the whips fade out so that I may fold my arms across my chest.

"Ah, but I have so much to share with you." He extended a hand to me, and I stared at it before allowing my eyes to reach his.

"You cannot be serious. How else can I express to you my disinterest?" I shot at him.

"I only wish to talk, Mirage," he said as he offered me his hand.

I knew the decision I was about to act on was poor, but I needed to be rid of him. Perhaps allowing him to explain potential truths and lies to me was one way to afford that luxury. I took the hand he had extended to me, allowing him to help me lift myself from the ground.

"Oh, lovely," he purred, tucking my arm under his and giving my hand a gentle pat. His tenderness continued to surprise me, but it did not facilitate trust.

"Do you know that you and your brother…" He trailed off, looking for me to finish his statement.

"Dracar," I said with an irritation in my tone.

"Yes, *Dracar*," he hummed his name at a frequency I didn't appreciate.

"That you and *Dracar* are the only two Seaura to ever be descended of God's blood? The rest are *Darotalis—special* variants like the Drakkarias." He looked at me briefly as if to gauge my reaction.

"You're the scions of Olym's two first-born children—the Godly children, that is." His voice held that familiar feline lilt.

"*Scions?*" My desire to have answers eclipsed the risk of letting him be the one to provide them.

"Scions, yes. It means you exist to carry out their mortal wills—to serve them. You are Arudia's scion, hence her whips being at your disposal. Your brother is likely the scion of Vulkram; it only makes sense."

"*Scions…*" I echoed, taking in the beautiful scenery of the courtyard as we walked arm in arm.

"Powerful creatures, yes," he hissed as he spoke, that snake-like presence becoming apparent him.

"Yes, yes, the both of you…the power you possess is incredible—*infinite*," he gestured with his free hand to the world surrounding us.

I was growing convinced that he *loved* was the sound of his voice.

For a few moments, we walked in silence. The leaves drifted down around us like Autumn snow; they painted the air with their vibrant hues like a quiet kind of magic.

The skeletal fingers of the branches above us clawed toward the sun as if to pull it down from the sky. The sunlight filtered through the branches, casting an unearthly glow onto Jesper's face—illuminating those hauntingly beautiful golden eyes.

For a moment, the world turned upside down, and Jesper seemed nothing more than another Tessiah—another man. After a prolonged silence, he spoke again.

※※※※※

"Well little firebird, perhaps it's time you paid that powerful brother of yours a visit?"

"I don't understand—"

"Oh, my darling, you don't need to. *I* understand." I turned to face him, panicked, and that wolfish grin had consumed his features.

"*Zertost*. Shh, shh," he crooned softly, and my body began to weaken beneath me; I lost all of my strength. I could feel myself in his arms, as he mumbled under the weight of my body.

CHAPTER
THIRTY-TWO

I could faintly hear her voice as she screamed and pounded at the door. Araya's desperate screams breaching the walls between us as she cried for Jesper.

"Jesper, don't do this!" She howled, and I could hear more pounding of what sounded to be her fists.

"I will return for you—stop banging on the door." Jesper spoke to her nonchalantly as he scurried about.

"Jesper, please. This is dangerous." She continued to hammer on the door, her voice straining as she cried out to him.

"Do you fear for me, my love?" He laughed, but it was not cruel.

"Everyday, Jesper—it isn't funny." She banged harder now. I truly thought the door would come down under her fists.

My head was throbbing, and the world around me was a blur.

"Good morning, Princess! We have a long day ahead of us, so try not to cause any unnecessary pain, okay?" The cheeriness in his voice was off-putting. I noticed then those familiar Sifrune straps were holding me down, and I was completely helpless.

"Let me fucking go!" I yelled at him, the throb of my head making it difficult to struggle against the restraints.

"I will...*soon*." His voice dripped like honey.

"If you're going to keep taking me for more blood, I'll just start giving it to you," I shouted at him, making weak efforts to remove the straps from my body.

"I did need more of that, yes, but that is not why you are here. We are going home, you and I." His lips curled into that vicious smile, the typical charm completely absent.

"What? Home?" I gasped.

"Yes," he continued, "that lovely kingdom surrounded by sea, that home? It is a necessary resting point before I reach the ninth, so you can pay your family a quick visit." His voice was entirely impartial to his suggestions.

"You think we can just walk into the castle and nothing will happen? You don't think they'll try to kill you?" I snapped at him, aggressively pulling at the straps that held me.

"Oh, they will certainly try—and they will certainly fail." That predatory grin stretched about his face.

For a moment, I had believed him to be human—at least the essence of one. I had, for just a second, placed my trust into him. And that had left me tied down yet again, unable to fight back.

"My father will have both of our heads spiked in front of the castle, do not be a fool!" I yelled, ripping and pulling at the Sifrune. He merely chuckled in response, low and cool, as if the thought did not plague him.

"Your father?" He chuckled again, "Doing that requires him to be there, doesn't it?" He gathered things into a bag, and pulled one of the straps from underneath me.

"What?" I gasped, unsure of what he had been insinuating.

"Your father is not currently at Castle Sage. He is out: gambling, whoring, who knows what men in power do in their free time."

"What if I refuse?" I said to him, a softness in my voice that I did not recognize. I couldn't make sense of why I chose that tone—why I made an effort to appeal to his empathy.

"You don't have a choice." He brushed his fingers against my jaw, and I jerked away from him.

"I'd rather die than be a prisoner," I shot at him, hoping that he could see the hatred that rimmed my irises.

"No, no—not a prisoner: my lovely accomplice!" He began to unstrap me from the table.

He was going to free me.

This moment was all too familiar—I thought of running, of fighting, of screaming. However, when the final strap came undone, I did none of those things.

I didn't fight.

I didn't run.

I sat up and stared at him, unsure of how I should react. I knew I couldn't win against him, especially since he was powered up on Gods know what sort of magic—or even my blood.

"Impressive, no retaliation?" His lips curled into an unfamiliar smile: one that was warm, one that lacked his typical wolfishness. He extended a hand to me, offering for me to walk with him. When I did not take his hand, he instead handed me a sheath, and in it rested the blade that I came here with.

I thought it was best to not ask him where he had gotten it, though I knew the answer. He had gone into my chambers and taken it. I grabbed the blade and stared at him for a long moment. I appreciated the gesture, though I don't think I could ever bring myself to thank him.

"I am going to go with you, and we are coming back with my brother. I'll do whatever you need me to in order to ensure that happens." I almost shocked myself from the words that left my lips. I never could have pictured myself agreeing to enact Jesper's will—to exercise my power for him.

"Oh my, this will be *thrilling*." Excitement laced his voice, and he pulled my arm under his and led me to a door opposite the one Araya had pounded on.

"Are you ready then, my darling?" His tone was soft and warm, such a contrast to his usually *abrasive* personality.

"As ready as I'll ever be to be carted away with a villain," I said to him with a contempt in my tone I only hoped was detectable.

"A villain?" He chuckled, the amusement was clear when he spoke, "No, I think I am going to be your hero when this is all said and done." That arrogance found its way back into his tone, but he was gentle when he held my arm.

⁂

When the door opened, we found ourselves in an outdoor area near the front of the castle: somewhere I had not been since arriving. I saw those gates that did not open for me when I screamed and cried for someone to save Hiver.

Hiver.

I couldn't spare him another thought as my mind was racing with the thought of seeing Dracar—of seeing him happy and well. I knew those expectations were rooted in delusion, yet I had hoped for them anyway. I thought of that last day I saw him: how defeated he appeared, how his eyes betrayed his facade of calm.

The carriage was sleek black. Its windows were darkened, and the body of the carriage looked to be adorned in carvings that seemed almost like the ones that covered the castle walls—but they looked to be made of blood.

. . .

"Why such a daunting carriage?" I asked, running a hand along one of the carvings.

"The carriages reflect our magic. This is what mine manifests as." He gestured to the grand black carriage adorned in crimson markings. He opened the door with a flourish, gesturing for me to enter.

"After you," he said, his voice honeyed and sharp. For a moment, I hesitated. I thought one last time of running back to safety—to my friends, to the place I now called home. I had started to feel a sense of belonging here, and I was about to return to a place where I never belonged. I managed to force myself to take the step up into the carriage, Jesper offering me a hand that I declined.

The carriage carried the scent of leather and cedar. A pleasant combination, and not one I would have associated with Jesper.

As it swayed, it cast shadows across Jesper's face, softening the sharp angles of his jaw and cheekbones, yet failing to disguise the primal gleam in his eyes. I turned to face the window, trying to focus on the horizon. I didn't wish to look back at the castle—to let it sink in that I was leaving it behind without telling a soul.

"Pensive, darling?" Jesper's voice broke the stillness, smooth and taunting.

"I really don't have much to say to you... other than to stop calling me that," I replied curtly, my eyes still fixated on the horizon.

"What a shame," he said, leaning forward slightly. His golden eyes cut into me as he stared, "I'd hate for this journey to be dull."

"I'll remind you of this once, and only once. I am not doing this to forward your mission of being a terrorist—I am doing this for my brother." Jesper let out a laugh, and it echoed off the enclosed walls of the carriage.

"There's that defiant young princess. I was almost worried for a moment. You know, you are cursed with her *passion*," He spat the last word and gestured into the air mockingly.

I could feel my jaw tightening. The space between us felt stifling; his presence consumed the carriage as though it were alive, feeding off of my anger and irritation.

I decided to let it get the best of me.
The rage, that is.

"Tell me Jesper, if you were so desperate to kill yourself, why not allow me to do it for you in the comfort of the eleventh? Hmm? Why drag us back to my home so I can watch my family slaughter you for amusement?" The venom of the statement coated my tongue. I could feel it poisoning me slowly: my anger, my fury.

"You amuse me," Jesper said, pulling out a canteen from under the seat. He took a swig of it, but his eyes stayed fixated on me as he did, as if he wanted to be sure I would not flee right then.

"Yes, actually, I think the Reavari may rip you apart first." I said to him as stoically as I could.

"Those *dogs?* Hah!" His laughter bellowed this time, a genuine laugh, "No, no, no, my darling. I know what those beasts desire, and I brought plenty of it." He offered me his canteen then, and I declined.

"What does that mean?" I questioned, my gaze focusing on the canteen in his hand.

"Reavari are insatiable. But you can temporarily give them a bit of a reprieve," he chuckled again.

"Which is what, exactly?" I pressed.

"Gods' blood—they *love* it—and of course, I know everything, so I brought enough to keep those *things* off of us." His posture was relaxed as he spoke, one arm draped casually along the back of his seat. His eyes continued to watch me as though he could read the thoughts clawing through my mind—as if he were waiting for me to turn on him.

"*My* blood?" I asked after a few moments of tossing his words around in my mind.

"Obviously," he scoffed.

I watched as the fields of flowers and soft grass slowly turned into a mass of trees. Soon, we would go through the portal—the ripple, rather. I knew it was coming now; I could see the thick of the forest inching closer. Just moments later, the carriage violently shook and tilted as if it were being *ripped* through the portal.

"Ah, fuck!" I yelped as my head hit the hard black wood that lay inches behind my skull. Jesper let loose a giggle of amusement at my pain. I began to reach at my body again, just as I did the first time, to ensure I was still all there. I could feel we were back on solid ground, crashing through the woods at a speed I didn't feel was possible.

"Why are we moving so fast?" I asked, gripping the seats as if they would fall from beneath me.

"My magic propels it, and I want to get past these woods quickly." Jesper had a slight edge to his voice, something I did not recognize—perhaps it was fear?

"I don't believe I've seen you fearful before," I said to him mockingly.

"Oh, it is not me who I fear for. It is *your* blood they desire." He smirked as the carriage bobbed and weaved through the thick of the trees.

"Why did they attack Hiver then if they wanted me?" I questioned, breathless as the carriage continued to move violently.

"Not sure."

After that, the hours passed mostly in silence.

That was until we reached the front gates of the castle, which were unguarded—an odd site.

"How does it feel to be home, princess?" His expression was unreadable as he spoke.

"It feels like I am putting one foot in the grave," I replied, my voice barely breaching a whisper.

"Where are the guards?" I asked him in a hushed tone, as if he would know.

"If I had to guess—following around your brother and drunkard father," he huffed, a lack of humor in his voice as he spoke.

My chest burned as I realized I hadn't a clue what I would say upon seeing Dracar, nor what I should tell him first.

Jesper leaned forward then, his voice low and almost gentle, "Don't look so terrified, darling. You're not the weakling you were when you left this place." He smiled when he finished his statement. I grimaced at him, but he continued to beam at me, an authenticity taking hold of his features.

"You may not be able to beat down a trained Tessiah, but you can kill mortals…should you choose to." His voice was a combination of wickedness and sincerity, as if he were giving me that option—as if he wanted me to kill.

When the door then opened, and Jesper stepped out first, extending a hand to me.

"Shall we, princess?" I hesitated for a moment before taking it. His grip was firm and grounding, and I hated myself for the faint comfort it brought. We reached the gates hand in hand, and they groaned open under his touch.

Jesper then released me and led the way, his stride confident and unhurried. I followed with a dread and determination in my chest as I approached that fateful castle I once called home.

CHAPTER
THIRTY-THREE

We found our way to the palace's entrance. It loomed before me, the horror gripping my chest as we walked through. Somehow, the castle felt darker than I recalled.

The air was heavy with the scent of stale wine and salt, the kind of smell that burrowed deep in the walls and refused to leave. Shadows danced about the long hall, casting visions of flame upon the walls.

I heard the clatter of armor and a rhythmic marching that could only belong to guards. Jesper grabbed me, his hand covering my mouth as he pulled me against the wall.

"Do *not* make a sound," he hissed, holding his hand over my mouth as we cloaked ourselves in the shadows of the hall. The guards passed, completely unaware of our presence. We stayed that way for a few moments before he released his hand from my mouth. I shoved myself from Jesper and shot him a look of disapproval.

"What the fuck? Did you think I would yell for them to save me or something?" I could taste the leathery scent from his hands on my lips, and I spit a little to try and remove it from my tongue.

"How could I be so sure you wouldn't do something rash? I

know how you feel about me anyway." He sounded almost sad for a moment.

"The reputation you hold was entirely crafted by *you* and *only you*," I shot at him.

"My reputation of wanting what is best for my people? For *you*? For Diana? For Stygian? For Hiver?" He approached me now, towering over me, his voice was laced with rage.

"Your reputation of willing to crush whoever stands in your way of being a martyr!" I nearly yelled at him now. He backed away from me, his eyes darkening with shame and anger.

"I'll crush whoever seeks to kill my people—*your* people," he spat back at me and pointed a finger to my chest. I felt like I could taste his fury as he spoke. The space between us was little, and every inch of it was filled with hatred in this moment.

"Come now, we don't have time for petty arguments," he huffed, gripping my arm gently as he coaxed me along.

I hated to think that I might have understood him.
That I might have that same maddened rage in me, too.
I think I would kill for Dracar…for Diana…for Hiver…

Gods…Hiver.

I think I too would kill for them all—and my hands were now made to do just that.

We continued to walk until we reached the large garden that sat at the center of the castle. The garden was half outside, and stretched out before us was a haunting blend of beauty and decay. This garden used to be my mother's pride and joy, a place she spent hours tending to.

Its dark stone pathways were now cracked and weathered,

dividing patches of untamed greenery that spilled over their boundaries. The trees grew tall and gnarled, standing like sentinels over our heads.

"I'm sure this place used to be beautiful," Jesper murmured while picking at the ivy which choked the dead trunks of the trees.

"It was when she was alive." I reached down to touch the dahlias that managed to survive the lack of love.

I shuddered from the wind that blew through, and began to pick up the pace toward my old chambers. Dracar had spent as much time as I in here, so when I threw open the doors I was slightly disappointed to not see him standing there.

Everything was in place, untouched.

The one exception was the freshly picked flowers that sat beside my bed; I reached to touch the hemlock and poppies that sat in the vase that had belonged to my mother.

The sun had fallen from the sky now, casting darkness over my room. The rest of the castle had already suffered from the darkness of the evening. Jesper milled about the room looking at my things, which were left in their perfect condition.

"The flowers are an odd touch, but this is a beautiful room." He reached down and touched the sheets after me, following my every step.

"Reminds me of the one you currently have…Diana's doing, I assume?" He continued to follow me as I walked around my old room.

"Of course," I sighed. This room hardly felt like my own without her in it.

"And should I assume you saw it when you went to steal my blade?" I gestured at the sheath he had returned to me earlier.

"Steal is a strong word, I *retrieved* it for you." He smiled at me.

I walked to the armoire, and as I reached for it, Jesper hit the floor next to me.

Someone had snuck up on us.

I turned as quickly as I could, reaching for the hilt of my blade—when they crashed into me, kicking my chest. I fell against the armoire, my head smacking against it. I growled and tried to rise to my feet. I looked to Jesper, who appeared to be unconscious.

"Jesper!" I yelled as the guard's blade came down upon me. I hardly managed to dodge it as it cleaved down onto the wardrobe above my shoulder. I reached for their body, slamming them into the ground. Then, the guard flipped me over onto my back: one arm pinning mine to the ground, and the other raising the blade.

The dark of the room made it difficult to see the armor. I reached my free hand to the helm of my attacker, attempting to knock it off. I struggled with them, grabbing at their chest—anything I could get my hands on to offset their weight.

Jesper threw the stranger off of me. I staggered as I regained my footing; Jesper quickly grabbed my arm and pulled me upright.

"Are you okay?" He asked, without looking at me. He kept his eyes trained on the stranger who had also regained his footing.

"This won't be pleasant," Jesper said to me in a hurried manner. He adjusted his grip on my arm, his fingers digging a bit into my flesh. I looked at him with horror in my eyes as I feared what he was going to do.

"*Drasickar Blerium, Fordaseur Lockardis.*" Those familiar words parted his lips, and I felt the life draining from me where he touched. I cried out and fell to my knees.

He was stealing the life from me.

"Jesper," I croaked. The pain was clawing through my flesh; I felt like I was being ripped apart from within.

"Jesper... please..." I cried from my knees, but he did not stop.

"I'm sorry," I heard him whisper between the foreign words. I pulled myself from him, heaving on the floor. I could feel the bile rising to my throat, and I had to will myself not to empty my guts onto the floor before me. The stranger charged forward despite it, his blade at Jesper's throat.

"Kneel," the voice said sternly from under the helm.

I was too weak to move.
Too weak to fight.

Jesper still stood, huffing from the draining magic.

"Kneel!" The stranger thundered—a familiarity in that tone. Jesper did as he was told, and dropped to his knees before the armored man.

"What the—" Jesper gasped as he reached for the hilt, and the stranger stepped backward a pace.

I knew that sword.
Even in the grasp of shadows, I knew that hilt.

"Dracar!" I shouted and ran at him. He turned to me quickly, but didn't remove the blade from Jesper's throat.

"Mirage?" Dracar removed his helm with his free hand and stared at me in disbelief.

"This is the fucking Shard of Aetheris! Do your reunion later!" Jesper cried out, his hand now fully touching the hilt of Dracar's blade.

"What?" I turned to him, not able to fully digest the words he had just spoken.

"The Shard! Your brother has the Shard!" Jesper almost sounded excited as he spoke, and he ran his fingers along the jewel that sat in the hilt of Dracar's sword.

"You are Vulkram's scion. You have his blade..." Jesper stood touching the blade with his bare hands, completely unafraid of the sharpness of it.

"What are you talking about—who are you?" Dracar turned to him again, raising his blade defensively.

"Calm down little prince—I'm a friend." Jesper made an effort to bow to Dracar, but couldn't dip too low as the blade rested right beneath his chin.

I clung to Dracar, fearful that if I let go, he would slip away again.

"How do you have that blade?" Jesper gestured toward it, his eyes glittering.

"It was given to me by my father," Dracar said plainly.

"Your father—your *drunkard, pathetic* father—got access to Talis items?" Jesper spat, his voice laced with vitriol as he spoke.

"What? What's a *Talis* item?" Dracar turned to me now, his arm still draped over my shoulders.

"Oh Gods, I don't even know where to begin." I stared at Jesper and reached for the blade Dracar still held steady at his throat. I forced him to lower it by pushing my hand down on its hilt.

"Where are all of the guards?" I asked.

"Around—they won't leave me alone, but many went with Father, though."

"Jesper, you were right." I ignored Dracar and looked at Jesper, whose face had stretched into a wide smile.

"How do you know anything about my father? Or my castle?" Dracar was growing more irritated with every passing moment.

"I know many things, little prince," Jesper cooed and reached down to the blade once again.

"But one I do not know is how you managed to get your hands on this." His golden eyes slid up to Dracar's, and he pulled the blade from his hands completely.

"Do you have any idea what this can do?" Jesper ran his fingers along the shard, and I could feel an energy thrumming from it and finding its way into him.

"Jesper," I said sternly.

"Give it back." Dracar's eyes narrowed upon him. Jesper chose not to respond and instead took a few steps back from us both, still running his long fingers against the jewel in the hilt of Dracar's sword.

I could swear I heard a growl escape Dracar's lips as he lunged for Jesper, but Jesper was nimble—quick. He managed to avoid Dracar entirely, sidestepping with an ease that appeared unnatural.

"I can't…" Jesper's eyes fell upon the blade, and he began to say something under his breath; the magic from the shard physically found its way up his arms, coursing through him like blood. His eyes glowed in the same way they had when he consumed my blood.

"What *is he*?" Dracar stayed a distance from him now; he raised an arm cautiously in front of my chest to keep me away too.

"A Tessiah—like *us*." The words felt almost foreign the way they fell off of my tongue. It felt like I was speaking a language that I had not fully understood.

"*Us?*" Dracar asked as Jesper continued to pulsate with an energy unlike the kind he had possessed before.

"Jesper, drop the blade!" I yelled at him, but he continued to stare into the distance, his expression vacant.

"What the fuck is happening to this kid?" Dracar reached for him, but Jesper immediately turned, and with the flick of his hand, sent Dracar to his knees.

"Jesper!" I screamed again, but I knew better than to use my hands.

I chose to summon the whips instead.

He laughed as the whips came to life, flickering in my hands, but that laughter belonged to something far more sinister—more ancient.

"He's being possessed by the blade!" I yelled to Dracar, who was situated on his knees, holding his chest as if Jesper had been stealing the air from his lungs. I couldn't help him—I needed to retrieve that blade.

His eyes flickered to me; a frenzy stirred within them unlike his normal madness. His lips curled into a feral grin, and his voice was sharp and menacing when he spoke.

"I have become it—I have become *power*." He chuckled again, that otherworldly tone lacing with his. I had tossed the whip at the blade, but his grip on it was tight.

He then decided to lunge for me.

I hardly managed to dodge him, and I swung the whip again—but this time, he did the unthinkable: he caught it mid-snap.

His hands pulsed with a deep red glow, one that almost looked like blood. His hand still burned from the flame as I saw his flesh curl underneath the heat, but he did not flinch. He violently yanked the whip forward, pulling me to my knees and scraping my free hand against the floor.

"Get up," he growled.

The serpent on Dracar's armor caught my eye, my flames illuminated it as they began to coil up my arms. I turned for only a moment so my eyes met Dracar's, and he was mortified at the sight of me.

I scrambled to my feet, and my chest heaved as I summoned another whip, the flames roaring to life in my hand. Jesper stalked toward me, the predatory gleam in his eyes unrelenting.

My palms were coated with my own blood, but I could feel the tissue mending as I moved. I lashed with both whips this time, their flames dancing wildly as they struck Jesper, but his grip remained on the blade; I could see his skin burning where the whips struck.

"Mirage," Dracar said weakly as he stabilized himself just feet away from me. I had to will myself not to look at him. I couldn't imagine his confusion…

Jesper let the whips go as he began to charge at me again, his hands reaching for my throat—his grip on my vocal cords forced guttural sounds from me. We struggled like that until his knee came up to my gut, knocking the wind from me. I managed to break his hold, and I staggered backwards. I heaved for a moment, worried I was going to hit the floor—when I heard him breathe those words again.

Those fateful words.

"*Drasick–*"

"No!" I flipped the whips out again and used all of my strength to wrap them around Jesper's arm and shoulder. The smell of burning flesh filled the air, and he loosed a raw, guttural sound that made my stomach twist.

For a moment, I felt terrible.

I wanted to release him—but I couldn't.

The blade clattered to the floor, and as it did, Jesper's head fell backwards, the magic draining from him and back into the jewel that sat in the hilt. The light drained from his eyes as he collapsed to his knees, his breath catching.

"Dracar, the blade!" I huffed, keeping the whips around Jesper, but they stopped eating at his skin.

Just like the apple.

I had willed the flames to stop burning.

Dracar lunged for the sword. I ran to Jesper's side and looked at his wounds; they had healed over.

"I'm sorry—I'm so sorry." He spoke breathlessly as if the words physically pained him to say.

"It's okay." I pulled him into an embrace, unsure of what else I could do.

"Oh Mirage…" Jesper started, "I would never—" He pushed my

shoulder back and touched my throat softly. I reached for his hand and held it between my own.

"It's okay."

Dracar stood over the top of us now; the blade sat perfectly between us.

"What was that?" he said, his voice shaky.

"Dracar." I was stunned at his decision to hold the blade so close to my throat.

My protector.
My best friend.
My brother.

"No…" He trailed off, as if stifling a sob. Dracar did not show emotions—not even to me.

"I can fix it with time—I just need time." He inhaled deeply as he stared down at me.

"Dracar, what are you talking about?" I tried to rise to my feet and reached a hand for him, but he brought the blade up between us, letting it sit just inches below my chin.

"I thought you might have died. I saw what was in those woods," he started, keeping the blade held at my throat. In fact, he inched it closer, allowing it to rest on my jaw.

"I followed that carriage, and when my men and I made it to those woods, those *things* nearly killed all of them." He looked at Jesper now.

"The Reavari," I whispered, slowly raising my hands upward to push the blade down from my neck.

"Don't…don't move. Please don't move." He nearly whimpered as he spoke. I raised my hands upward so that he could see my bloodied but healed palms.

"Dracar, we are *both* Tessiah—mother made a deal with a God. We were *made* this way," I said, my hands still signifying my surrender.

"Bullshit. I am *nothing* like you." The blade pressed into my skin, the metal kissing my jawline.

He began to ramble, like that of a madman—words pouring from his lips with no true meaning attached.

"They have brainwashed you. Whatever they told you is a lie, and you know it." He continued to push the sword into my skin; I could feel hot droplets of blood falling.

"Remove your blade from her throat." Jesper spoke now, his voice cautious yet warning.

"Shall I put it to yours instead?" He shot Jesper a look laced with malevolence—a gaze normally reserved for my father.

"Yes, if you must put it somewhere," Jesper said softly, rising from the floor and allowing his hands to remain in the air as mine were.

"Mirage, listen to me," Jesper spoke softly, gently.

"That blade can *kill* a God—it *will* kill you." He spoke with pure sincerity. Even in the moments where I dare say he resembled someone bearing empathy, he did not use that tone.

I reached a hand to my throat and the blood still fell.

"You won't heal. It was forged by a God." Jesper still spoke in that serious tone.

I felt a panic consuming me now as I felt the open wound under my fingers.

"You're okay," Jesper said softly.

I was rooted into place; I couldn't grasp the situation which unfolded before me.

"Come, you're okay." Jesper's voice was soft as he pulled my arm. His voice sounded muffled through the fog that settled over my mind.

This was not the reunion I had craved.

I absentmindedly pulled from Jesper's grasp and reached for Dracar; but the doors bursted open, and in came the raging sea of guards to seize us.

CHAPTER
THIRTY-FOUR

I could feel their armor biting into my bare skin as they forced my hands behind my back, their blades at the ready. I glanced at Jesper, who went willingly, so I followed his lead. We were taken down many corridors, past many grand rooms, some which still had my mother's essence about them.

We eventually made it to that horrible staircase.

The one that went deep beneath the earth to the dungeon cells—where we were thrown into the same cell; our hands unbound.

"Well, use your magic," he said plainly, leaning his back against the stone wall.

"What?" I snapped at him; admittedly, I was beginning to lose my temper.

How could Dracar throw me down here?

I inhaled deeply and made an effort to call upon my whips.

Nothing.

"I—I can't," I stammered. I started to feel hysteria settling in my bones.

"Hah—I can't tell if he's a genius or the dumbest man alive." Jesper softly let his skull hit the wall behind him as he laughed. But his laughter was anything but amused.

"It's Sifrune—all these cells are made of Sifrune." He sighed deeply, clearly irritated.

"Good thing Sifrune doesn't stop ritualistic magic then, huh?" I turned to him now, a frenzy sparking deep within me.

"Oh no, princess—that Shard drained me," he said too calmly.

"Should I be concerned that doesn't bother you?" I shot at him, my hands wrapped around the Sifrune bars.

"It doesn't bother me because we'll be fine." His eyes were now completely closed.

"Whatever," I shot at him.

"Would you like to tell me what happened back there?" I asked him as I turned to face him fully now.

"The power of creation is the power of corruption," he huffed, seemingly unamused by my question.

"I meant without speaking to me in riddles."

"I *meant* the Shard of Aetheris holds the power to create. By that, I mean it can create new Gods—new Tessiah, blah, blah, blah…" His eyes were now opened, and he was glaring at me as he spoke. I sank down beside him.

"What is that *thing* going to do to my brother?" I felt panic, washing over me.

"That *thing?* Hah—one of the most powerful objects in the universe, you mean. But anyways—nothing. Your brother is clearly Vulkram's scion." Jesper looked at me lazily now, the exhaustion from earlier overcoming his features.

"What does that have to do with anything?" I felt my gaze hardening on him as I spoke.

"Vulkram, the 'unbreakable' God? The God of the Forge? His scions don't have the ability to be corrupted by that sort of power.

Gods you need a history lesson…" His eyes began to drift shut once more.

"I am a scion too, though. Would it corrupt me the same way?" I asked.

"Probably. You are Arudia's, not Vulkram's." His eyes were completely closed again, but I reached for his jaw, pulling his gaze to mine as I spoke.

"Why the *fuck* would you grab that blade if you knew what it would do to you?" I snarled when I spoke, "Why would you endanger all three of us if you knew that would happen!"

"Did you seriously believe that I kept it in my hands of my own free will?" He reached up and shoved my hands from his face.

"It called to me, and I *couldn't* put it down. I wouldn't have endangered either of you intentionally!" He fired back and rose from his place to stand at the cell bars.

"I'm sorry," I inhaled deeply. The words felt hard on my tongue.

"Hmm," he grumbled in response.

He ran his fingers up and down the bars, and they rang with a metallic sound in response. We sat there for a while in complete silence, the only sounds coming from dripping water in nearby cells.

"My father gifted Dracar that blade, though." I spoke to no one in particular.

"And?" Jesper responded drowsily.

"*And?* Why would my father have the Shard of Aetheris?" I said.

"He probably didn't know what it was, darling. Someone likely gave it to him, and a coward has no use for a blade." Jesper removed his outer coat and draped it on the floor in front of him.

"Now, if you'll spare me your questions I wish to get some rest." He smiled briefly before turning away from me to lay on the floor.

I continued to stare out of the cell.

I continued to replay the moments in my head of Dracar's trembling blade at my throat.

He feared me.
   His own flesh and blood.

I tried to shake the despair and betrayal that stirred within his eyes.

Did he not see me anymore?
   When his eyes met mine… did he not see his own?

Jesper's even breaths filled the air around me, and I sighed in response. I merely ran my fingers against the hard stone of the floor, which had apparently disturbed him.

"Are you not going to rest?" he mumbled, draping his arm over his eyes.

"How can I?" I shot at him.

"You should still be recovering anyway," he mumbled again, hardly coherent.

"From what, exactly?" I snapped at him again, my patience wavering.

"I siphoned you—that *literally* drains your life force…I mean, you regenerate, just didn't expect it to be so quick." He turned over again, groaning as he did.

I could feel horror washing over me. I could recall Kaneira telling me something of the sort, but now her words all felt hazy now.

"What do you mean?" I asked through panicked breaths.

"It *means* your magic *is* you. I can use your life as a source to use my magic, so I did. You have God's blood. You're fine," he said nonchalantly.

"You could kill me doing that!" I shouted at him, now standing over where he lay.

"I *could*, but Gods—I would never," he uncovered his eyes to face me, a sincere look overcoming his features.

"How would you know you've gone too far?" I said breathlessly, fury and fear pulling my vocal cords into a higher octave.

"I can feel it," he said plainly.

"So could you feel that it *felt* like you were killing me back there?" I seethed.

"Yes, I could. I *cannot* use my natural magic without a source. The eleventh was my source…would you prefer I drive myself mad and kill us both?" he shot back, but his eyes did not match the hostility in his voice.

He stared up at me now, his eyes wide and apologetic even as he spoke in a vicious tone.

"Whatever," I huffed and sat down beside him.

I could feel my body shivering from the cold that seemed to be seeping into my bones. The walls were slick with moisture, contributing to the thick, damp air that clung to my skin like a shroud.

As I sat there, the chill became more and more merciless, stinging my skin like it was burning me.

I looked at Jesper, who had already slipped into a peaceful sleep. The flame from the lanterns flickered above his head, casting shadows over his face.

The cell did not afford us much space, so I lay just feet away from him, shaking from the cold that wrapped around me like a blanket.

I let out a silent sob, covering my mouth with my hands so as to not wake Jesper, who slept at my side. I watched the tears fall past my nose and onto the cold stone beneath me into a small puddle.

"Mirage?" Jesper said softly, and I could tell he had sat up. I chose to remain silent, making an effort to still swallow my cries. He placed a hand on my shoulder, and I continued to shiver beneath his touch.

"You're freezing," he mumbled. I could hear him fumbling about with his clothing, but I faced away from him. He draped the cloak he had used as a bed over my shoulders and mumbled something.

"Come here darling," his words trailed off as they escaped him in his drowsy state. He pulled my body into his, and I removed my hands from my mouth.

"Thank you," I whispered to him, unable to put up a fight in my depressive state.

"Mhm," he grumbled.

When I opened my eyes, I saw him standing before us, the hilt of his blade catching the surrounding flames from the lanterns.

"Dracar." My mouth was dry as I spoke.

"The doctor will be here soon," he said, his voice void of emotion.

"Dracar—" I stared at him for a long moment, positioning myself upright and removing myself from Jesper's touch.

"I'm not ill. Nothing has changed!" I pleaded to him, my raised voice jolting Jesper awake as he rolled to his back beside me, wiping his eyes aggressively.

"Oh hello, little prince, come to torture us now?" Jesper said sarcastically. Dracar's nostrils flared at his comment, and I shot him a look of disapproval.

"I have time. I can fix you." Dracar looked down at me. There was something gleaming in his eyes I did not recognize, and I thought I could place it as a feeling of superiority.

"Dracar, you can't *fix* me. I have magic, not some sort of disease! We're *both* Tessiah!"

"We are not the same," he said solemnly.

"You can bend fire to your will—we are *not* the same," Dracar said with sadness in his voice.

"I *am*. I am still me—your sister, your *twin sister*," I said softly to him. I was not afraid to beg for my freedom from this cell.

For my freedom from his hostility and rage.

If only he saw what I saw—knew what I knew. There's a beauty this kingdom cannot afford, a beauty reserved just for us, and if he had seen it—everything would change…

"You must come see what I have seen—you'll understand—"

"You want me to leave my kingdom? Leave *my* people? To see what exactly? So you can ascend to *my* place? Take *my* throne?" he spat at me.

"To see it all," I said silently. He stared at me for a long moment, his brows scrunching together as he did. I heard footsteps approaching us, slow and methodical, as if maintaining a rhythm.

Why did he suspect me to steal the throne?

"Doctor Mundrakir." Dracar stood and greeted him, a flicker of pain across his face as he did.

"Prince—oh…" The doctor said as he looked at me in the cell.

"Princess? What are you—"

"She's in here because she needs fixing, if you will," Dracar said, his jaw clenching.

"What sort of fixing, your highness?" The doctor replied.

"She has…a different kind of…*magic*..I need it gone." Dracar said in a hushed tone, and the doctor stumbled backwards a bit.

"That is impossible. I have been testing you since you were just children…She cannot have *any* magic…" The doctor spoke hurriedly and in a panic.

"I saw it."

"Your highness, I—"

"If you are about to give me some sort of excuse, save it. You've tortured us for two decades. Find a way." Dracar's tone was cold now. The doctor and Dracar continued to argue, and in the midst of their mayhem, Jesper grabbed my arm and pulled me into him.

"The second that cell door opens, use your magic," he whispered.

"What?" I challenged.

"What do you mean *what*?" he said in a hushed yell.

"I *mean* the second that Sifrune cannot hold you, do what you were made to do." Jesper squeezed my arm now, a gesture of reassurance.

I wasn't sure what he fully meant.

Part of me believed Jesper would relish in bloodshed, the other thought he wanted his freedom. However, they could both be achieved with magic.

DIANA

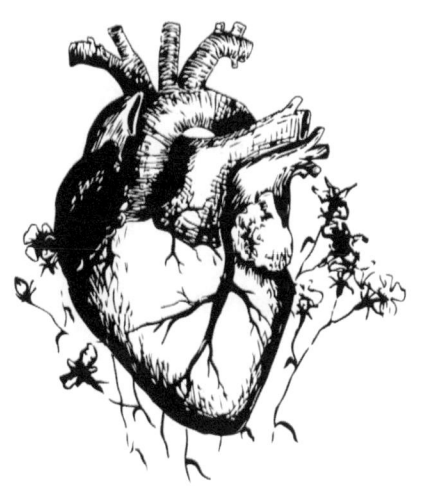

CHAPTER 35

DIANA

"Stygian," I grumbled, my head foggy and throbbing as I spoke.

I reached for his arm and gently moved it off of me so I could steady myself. We were in a closet of some sort, the darkness too consuming to see anything other than him.

"Stygian!" I yelled this time, gently shaking his body as he lay there. He groaned and turned to face me, his eyes collecting the shadows around us.

"Diana?" he mumbled, clearly also in a stupor.

"Mhm, it's me."

"Where the fuck are we?" He rubbed his eyes with his hands.

"Not sure—Jesper put us here for a reason though," I huffed, rising from the floor to search for a door.

"Jesper—why would he put us both here?" Stygian asked no one in particular as he also rose from the floor.

I began to rummage through the items in the closet, finding old armor, blades, flasks, amongst other random things.

I moved things around as I spoke, "If I had to make one good guess, I would say it has something to do with Mirage." I finally found a handle and pulled on it hard—but it was locked.

"Damn it," Stygian said, armor and other sharp objects clattering around him as he waded through the sea of metal.

"It's locked," I mumbled, fidgeting with it a little more as I turned to face him. I allowed frost to creep into the door lock, spinning it to open.

"Good plan," Stygian said as he attempted to stand upright without knocking more things down around us. I pushed the door open and found myself in Jesper's laboratory.

"No wonder no one found us." I raised my arm to my face to block out the incoming sunlight that was harsh on my adjusting eyes. We both walked out to find nothing of substance; the laboratory looked to be untouched. I led us over to the large wooden door with golden accents.

I reached for the handle, and when it opened, a body fell forward.

"Araya?" I said breathlessly, as I reached down to her. She looked up at me lazily and flashed me a brief smile.

"Diana?" She said softly, clearly disoriented as she looked up at me.

"What are you doing here?" I asked while helping her to her feet.

"Jesper—I tried to stop him." She turned to look at Stygian with wide eyes, "I'm sorry."

"What do you mean? What did he do?" I could feel my jaw clenching and my grip on her tightening.

"He took her, and they went to the tenth." She was defeated as she spoke, her tone carrying the weight of sorrow and fear. I had to make an effort to not let the shock rupture my composure.

"Why would he do that?" I felt my voice nearly cracking when I spoke.

"He knew she had God's blood, and he knew he could use that to wipe out the royalty of the ninth and tenth." Araya nearly broke into a sob, her inky hair swaying as she looked from Stygian to me.

"God's blood?" I gazed to Stygian as if to find any hint of knowing in his eyes. He merely shrugged as a response.

"She's a scion: her and her brother. Jesper learned it when he saw her wielding Arudia's whips. She was descended from a God. That's all I know." Her eyes were apologetic as she spoke.

"A scion," I said to the floor as I broke my gaze from hers.

I knew that Mirage was powerful, but God-descended? That was something I couldn't believe she kept from me...

I looked at Stygian now and linked my arms with Araya.

"We have to go and get her then." I sighed as I spoke, a bit fearful of the journey that lay ahead of us. We exited the laboratory space and found ourselves drowsily stumbling into a corridor that was swarming with castle guards. The clatter of their armor was deafening as they fell into step together, their marching feet following a rhythm like that of a heartbeat.

My head pounded as the morning light pierced my eyes. I repeatedly had to close them to stop them from throbbing under the weight of the sun's rays.

"Hey!" I yelled to a guard who was seemingly uninterested in me.

"Excuse me?" It turned now, and I realized that they were wardens.

"Princess!" The warden shouted, its spectral form swaying beneath the heavy armor that it was coated in.

The wardens were like ghosts; they existed half in the spirit realm and half in the material world—cursed would not be the right word, but they were certainly *odd* creatures...

The warden grabbed my arm and hurried me and Araya through the crowd. I turned back for a moment to see Stygian falling into step behind us, navigating the sea of gold and white armor.

"Your highness!" it grunted, gently pulling me forward before my mother.

"Mother." I began to briefly bow to her, but she rushed at me, and threw herself into me.

"My dearest," she cooed, her voice soft and thick.

"Mother?" I pushed myself from her gently and looked at her expression. She had been mortified and deeply unsettled.

"You were missing! Where were you?" she nearly yelled, but quickly pulled her tone into check.

"Jesper—he took us both," I nodded back to Stygian, whose mouth had formed a straight line as he looked upon Kaneira's face.

"He took Mirage—at least, I suspected..." she trailed off, and Hiver walked down to greet me. He pulled me into a tight embrace, deeply inhaling.

"I'm glad you're okay," he huffed, his eyes were dark, exhaustion discoloring the area underneath them.

"I'm perfectly fine, but I am unsure if I can say the same of you." I reached for the soft and blackened skin under his lashes and gently pressed my fingers to it, allowing a thin layer of frost to coat them.

He glared at me and pushed my hand down.

"I haven't slept," he grumbled; I pulled him back into a tight embrace as he finished his statement. When I pulled away, I turned to face my mother, who was gently caressing Araya's face.

"How, my child, did Jesper manage to take the *both* of you out?" Kaneira growled.

"He put me to sleep—I don't know what he did to her, but blood magic is damn solid magic," Stygian said solemnly and rubbed his eyes once more.

"He did the same to me. He caught me outside of my chambers before I was going to prepare myself for the ceremony," I said looking around the room for other familiar faces—I had been surprised to not see Lucius.

"He bested you both; I am rather impressed," she said with a bit of sincerity in her tone.

"I suppose the clever fox beats the mighty ram." She looked at me briefly before snapping her gaze to her dais, and she slowly approached it.

"So what do we do?" I asked her, a bit of frenzy leaking into my tone.

"What you've been trained to do: you will fight." She spoke in a rather unamused tone, as if she had expected this all along.

"Let's go then—I wish to not waste any time," Hiver said, his voice edged with irritation. I looked at Stygian, who shifted side to side.

"If you deem planning to be a waste of time, I fear your taste of victory will be as fleeting as your patience," Kaneira hissed at him, her temper also waning as we all stood.

She continued, her sharp tone easing, "You will take Samira." I nodded to her in response.

"Hiver, can you smoke us all into the tenth?" I asked him, my gaze meeting his.

"I can, but it will likely drain everything I've got," he responded.

"We can protect you," Stygian said curtly, giving Hiver a nod.

"You will smoke us into the kingdom then. I will send you two to wait in Mirage's chambers as I look for her. My presence will set off the least alarm should they catch me," I said to Stygian and Hiver.

"What of me?" Araya chimed in; her voice was sweet, yet laced with fear.

"You will go with them—"

"She will do no such thing," Kaneira interjected, her eyes narrowing on Araya.

If Kaneira lacked her supernatural strength, I suspect her tongue could cut down just as easily as her blade.

"I think she should come—she has access to the scripts," I looked at Araya, whose deep brown eyes were fixated on me.

"Access which was not officially granted by the Solarian," Kaneira nearly growled when she spoke.

"I'm Solarian either way—even if they haven't inducted me yet," Araya shot back, her eyes alight with something unfamiliar to her essence—*rage*.

Araya did not frequently wear hatred on her expressive face—though she told most of her thoughts through her eyes. They were large and brown, soft and warm. She radiated a calmness that Jesper did not match.

I could not fathom why she found herself always around him, enthralled by his disturbing presence. It was challenging to picture them as in love—but what else could give rise to this sort of sickness?

"Your call, Diana." Kaneira rested her chin upon her hand and cocked her head at me, awaiting an answer.

"I think she should come—she is invaluable," I said. Kaneira merely nodded in response, she did not fight me on it.

CHAPTER
THIRTY-SIX

We found ourselves in the armory, and as Samira entered the room; she was accompanied by another—*Natsu*.

"I think it is ridiculous to not include me," He huffed upon entering at her side. Samira simply stared and gave no comment on the matter.

"It's not about you. It's about the fact that Snow can only smoke so many of us into the castle," I said to Natsu, ensuring my tone was gentle as I spoke to him.

For years, he had valiantly stood at Samira's side. He would never let her go on such a dangerous mission without him. He loved her, and this was the only way he would tell her.

"You shouldn't come," Samira said plainly, her voice nearly void of emotion. Natsu spun to face her, his look was deeply perplexed as he did.

"What?" He said, his voice peaking in a way that indicated his pain.

"You shouldn't come—it is…" She looked at me as if I could somehow finish her thoughts.

"It is too dangerous," she eventually finished, but she did not face him as she spoke.

"I would *die* if something happened to you, Sam." His voice cracked as he spoke; he was holding back tears.

"And what should I do if you died anyway?" She shot back, a bit of anger danced upon her tongue. But she was careful with how she wielded that fury.

"Please, for the love of the Gods, kiss and be done with this." Stygian waved his hands in the air as he spoke, clearly irritated at the interaction unfolding before him. Samira's face turned bright red in response.

"I would," Natsu said softly, his eyes peering into hers as if begging to be let in. Samira's cold eyes speared his, sharp and unyielding, before she let out a subtle scoff and rolled her eyes. Then, she reached for his face and pulled him into a fierce kiss, wrapping her arms around him as if he would disappear if she slightly loosened her grip.

"Yay! Lovely!" Stygian clapped and maintained both sarcasm and genuine appreciation for the moment. I grinned at Natsu who turned to face me, his smile wider than I had ever seen it in the thirteen years of knowing him.

"Please, let me come," he pleaded, his eyes full of adrenaline and concern.

"Natsu, I would, but it will be too much to bring six—five is already going to be a hassle, especially for Snow." I looked to my brother who was grabbing his armor off the stand next to where Mirage's stood.

That helm fashioned of sun gleaming in the light that poured in through the high windows. I watched Snow's fingers gently trace his armor as he looked at Mirage's set. The look in his eyes was an unmistakable one.

Love.

I walked over to him, quietly enough to not startle him from his longing.

"We will get her back," I whispered to him, bringing a hand up to his shoulder. As I reached for him, he pulled away and gave me a harsh look. He didn't speak but merely shook his head. I watched his eyes wander past mine and lock onto Stygian.

"Do you truly believe that I would betray you?" I said in a hushed tone to Snow as his gaze found me again—this time it had softened a bit.

"I couldn't know," he said, turning away from me; it was clear he was deeply hurt. I didn't let him turn away, though. Instead I grabbed his shoulder and pulled him into a tight embrace.

"I would *never* do anything to hurt you," I whispered to him, and I felt his hands on my back. He squeezed but quickly pulled away, a brief smile stretching his lips.

He has always been told to play many roles.

I often served as a spy for my mother, slipping into places where I was never welcome. Hiver, meanwhile, became a master of many roles, donning the guise of countless men and characters.

I remember fleeing from the tenth the day he was to return. Kaneira had asked him to be cruel—to be cunning; he reluctantly agreed. He was asked to maintain the aura of mystery so Carlisle had no suspicions.

He was a greedy bastard, Carlisle.

I focused again on my own brother, his desperate blue eyes scanning the room before him.

"Of hollow and frost," I began—a promise we had shared since childhood that bound us in every moment of uncertainty.

"Everlasting, never lost," Hiver grumbled, but his lips spread into a smile that was a silent acknowledgement of the solace we found in each other.

Hiver leaned against the wall behind me as I unfurled a map that I was given many years ago. I looked at the others, and Stygian sat at the table, his legs spread while he weaved shadows between his fingers as if he were already bored.

Samira sharpened her frostbitten blade with her magic, though I never saw her use anything outside of her gauntlets. She frequently strapped her sword to her back, its blade following the trail of her spine as if it were a part of her.

The sounds of her magic on the blade made my teeth grind—such an unpleasant sound...

Araya found herself at the window, perched casually, her gaze fixed on the horizon which lay out before her.

I gathered my calm and spoke as clearly as I could, as if I were not daunted by what lay ahead.

"If Carlisle finds us, he will not hesitate to kill us," I said coldly, not allowing my voice to crack from the fear that welled in my stomach.

"He can certainly try," Samira said flatly, no emotion in her voice as she did. She situated the blade onto her back, where the sheath snapped itself over it. One by one, the small bones of it grabbed the sword to hold it into place. I shuddered every time I saw the bone cage—crafted by the damned. It was designed to succumb to the will of a Frostwalker: holding their blades, their daggers, their bows, or whatever weapon they chose.

It was made with real human bones.

"Some of us are more susceptible than others, but I agree, we can take him. We just cannot take all of his forces should he use them against us at once." I nodded at Samira.

Sometimes, I forgot she was not forged of frost entirely. Her demeanor was always cold—silent judgement laced her every expression.

"We will need to enter through the tunnels, which extend to about here—" I laid a finger to the edge of the castle, to the west of its grand gates.

"I overheard Jesper say something about Carlisle being absent from the tenth, but..." Araya chirped. She was quiet, her gaze avoiding ours as she looked around the room.

"How would he even know that?" Stygian said, his too calm demeanor diminishing as he spoke.

"His ravens, I'd assume?" Araya's voice was quiet, almost hesitant—as if she feared speaking too loudly might disrupt the fragile air around us.

Ravens.
Solarian magic.

I did my best to avoid Jesper as he frequently knew exactly how to make my nerves feel exposed in the worst way. I met him when we were thirteen years old, a week after his parents were executed. They were historians in the same way Lucius was. But they were a unique kind of Solarian—*Thrixes.*

They were the kind that could generate their own incantations; they didn't just record magic in the scripts, they *created* it. The scripts that Jesper now had full access to held the power to fell entire kingdoms—and it appeared he intended to do just that.

He must have been planning this for some time to know when Carlisle would be absent from the kingdom...

"Stygian, I need you to use your magic to make a distraction—light something on fire, use your shadows, I don't care. I'll leave you to make that decision. But just do it at the front of the castle and do your best to lead the legions *away* from us." I looked at him as I spoke, my gaze intensifying as I awaited his enthusiastic agreement.

"What if they catch me?" he asked. His question stunned me.

"They can't," Samira said softly, her deep blue eyes catching stray shards of light that flickered off of the blades that sat on the table before us.

She possessed a deadly sort of beauty.

Her eyes demanded submission—they were impossibly vivid and

captured all the light that dared find them. She reached for the map with a delicacy that was foreign to her persona.

"Once we reach the end of Aramore's tunnels, Snow will need to smoke you four in—I will go ahead and look for Mirage." I looked up and nodded at everyone. I found all of their eyes, took in all of their faces. I reached a hand back down to the map, my fingers tracing the black lines which belonged to the Easternmost wing of the tenth—where Mirage's chambers were.

"You need to get here." I continued to gently touch the lines on the map as I spoke.

"I'll come to you when I find her and let you know what we should do next."

"Are you saying we should improvise upon finding her?" Stygian scoffed, irritated at nearly every idea that was thrown out.

"What I am saying is that we shouldn't have a five-man search party going on as we enter a kingdom that would gladly hang our heads at their front gates." I could feel my jaw sliding to the side with agitation as I spoke.

"I want to go to her," Stygian said coldly, his usual sarcastic and light demeanor diminishing entirely as he spoke; his green eyes sparkled with determination.

"You shouldn't. It's too dangerous," I said solemnly. It killed me to refuse him—to tell him he could not go to the woman he loved.

"Shouldn't is poor word choice—*can't*." Samira eyes locked onto his, rivaling his determination with her own. Stygian glared at her, his dark green eyes blazing with anger.

For a brief moment, I feared he would rise from his chair and lunge for her—rather—make an effort to. She was entertained by his anger, as a smirk pulled at her lips.

"So when you find her, then what? Do you come back for us? Do you bring her to us, what?" Araya's soft voice rang out. She had stayed in her position at the window, fingering the fresh azaleas the wardens had placed just hours before. Her tanned fingertips were a stark contrast to the red as she graced the petals with delicate fingers.

"Hopefully, I can get her to her room, and Snow will smoke us back to the tunnels where we'll leave. I have to assume Jesper and her won't be too far apart anyways, so we will get him too." I tried to look upon her with kind eyes, but she did not see me.

She continued to set her gaze on the horizon—her mind was elsewhere—somewhere far beyond that of the horizon.

"Tomorrow we set out for the tenth," I said firmly, not allowing the fear to steal my breath away yet again.

"Tomorrow?" Snow's hands came down on the table as he spoke, his tone sharp.

"Yes, tomorrow—after we have all rested and prepared," I shot back at him, my temper wavering.

"I am ready to go now," Samira said softly, her voice lacking that authoritative tone she so frequently wielded.

"As am I," Snow agreed, he spoke a bit more calmly this time, his hands still palming the hard wood table. I slid my eyes to his, my chin tilted upright as I did.

"Tomorrow," I attempted to indicate that this would be the end of this discussion. I rolled the map in my hands slowly, and readied myself to exit the armory.

MIRAGE

CHAPTER 37

MIRAGE

"Hesitation will get us another night of sleeping in the freezing cold," Jesper hissed as I stared out at Dracar and the doctor who continued to yell at one another in hushed tones.

I watched the doctor throw his hands up in surrender as he reached a key into the cell's hole and slowly turned it.

It was open...
I hesitated...

When the whip came from my palm, it slashed at the doctor, lacerating the side of his face. The glasses he wore went crashing to the floor, and a blood-curdling scream erupted from his throat. Dracar immediately reached for his blade, drawing it upward toward me. I could feel myself burning with rage—with his betrayal.

"Put it down, Dracar," I hissed.

I had never felt this sort of anger before: the kind that consumed me entirely. I could hardly see what was in front of me—as if somehow the flames reached my eyes, tinting my vision red.

. . .

"I can't," he said softly. I flicked out a whip to reach for the blade, and as the flames wrapped around it, Dracar ripped backwards, his strength knocking me off balance.

"Don't do this," he croaked. But it was not fear in his voice—it was something else entirely.

"You would lock me away? You would make me sleep on the floor?" I continued to feel the rage build up in me, pushing me into a frenzy.

I hadn't a clue what had come over me, but I couldn't stop.

"Because I remember it all! I remember what she did to our mother—what she did to me!" he yelled, his blade still angled toward me as he took steps backward, attempting to put distance between us.

"What *she* did to *you*?" I spat.

"The fact that she nearly burnt a hole through my chest? Yeah! What *she* did to *me*." His labored breathing filled the air between us.

"She did it to activate your power, little prince," Jesper said from behind me—it seemed that he had also left the cell.

"To what?" Dracar inhaled quickly as I continued to approach him, the whips crackling at my sides.

"You are a special sort of Autumn-Kissed. You need sunfire to activate your magic!" Jesper yelled from behind me, and I could feel his presence on my skin as he approached.

"You, my darling, are getting a bit out of hand." His hand clasped down upon my shoulder, and I felt that terrible sensation again—the life actively being drained from me. I fell to my knees, coughing and gagging as if there were liquid pooling in my lungs.

"Jesper stop!" I croaked under the impossibly heavy weight of his hand. He merely stood over me, his golden eyes glowing brighter with every passing moment.

"As you wish," he said after a few seconds and released me.

"What the fuck!" I spun to him, my breaths strained as my chest rapidly rose and fell.

"You were about to kill your *beloved* brother, so I brought you down a few notches," Jesper said flatly. His tone lacked that usual lull of promise and charm.

"I would never," I gasped, still trying to push as much air into my lungs as I could.

I put my palms to the rough stone beneath me, the chill of it biting into my skin as if it wanted to remind me that I was in fact a prisoner.

Not just to this place, but to my blood.

Jesper then turned to Dracar whose blade was still raised, but I swear I could see him faintly tremble as he held it. Dracar's gaze shifted wildly between Jesper and I, confusion and pain warring in his autumn-toned eyes. He looked as if he were standing on an edge, unsure of if he should leap or retreat.

"You need to understand, little prince." Jesper hissed, but his voice was smooth, "You are Tessiah, whether you want to be or not. This is your *birthright*, this is who *you are*."

Dracar's hands clenched tighter around the tilt of his blade, his knuckles turning pale against the worn leather.

"This is *not* who I am. I'm a king—I'm *thee* king," he said as his eyes narrowed on Jesper—hatred fueling his expression.

"Don't be foolish." Jesper now stood inches away from that blade, and my heart raced.

A single fatal slice would end his life.

"You are a scion—a God-Born. Embrace it and you shall see the world bow before you." Jesper's tone was all too serious, not his usual demeanor.

"Bow?" Dracar spat at him, "I don't want the world to bow, and I want *my* throne and I want *my* family back!" His voice cracked, the raw emotion in it cutting the dampened air.

I flinched at his words, my heart tightening in my chest.

"Do you think I asked for this?" I had to stifle a sob as it reached my throat. I could feel tears fighting their way from my eyes.

"Do you think I knew what was happening when Kaneira nearly burnt a hole through *my* chest? Do you think I knew I could heal others with my blood? Do you think I knew what I would see when they took me? I thought they would *kill* me!" I screamed at him, but my voice wavered under the duress of the moment. I had wanted to sound strong—but instead, I sounded broken.

I could hear labored breathing and panting from behind me now, and I turned to face Doctor Mundrakir—he lunged for me, a blade at my throat.

"No you don't, you little bitch..." He said, his now broken glasses hung crooked on his face; I had to watch him out of the corner of my eye.

I tried to call upon my magic, but it was sputtering in my hands.

"Do you have any idea what the King would pay me if I returned you to him? Hmm?" The Doctor's crazed voice made me flinch.

"I will kill you," I whispered, trying to avoid the blade cutting into my throat as it bobbed.

"Not here you won't—and not now," he laughed maniacally.

I felt panic wash over me, and I dared not move. My eyes locked onto Jesper's.

"Maybe she won't... but I will," Jesper began to speak the incantation, his fingers spinning into certain motions as he did.

"Say another word, and I will slice her throat," the doctor said too calmly now, as if his body was already drained from the adrenaline.

Jesper froze, his golden eyes narrowing as his fingers hovered, poised to complete the incantation. His lips twitched, and though his voice became quieter, more measured, it lost none of its menace, "That would be the last mistake you ever make, *doctor*."

The blade against my throat pressed harder, a single drop of blood trickling down the flesh of my neck. I could feel my pulse thrumming wildly beneath the cold steel, fearful that my racing heart would force the blade further into my skin.

Jesper took a step forward, slow and deliberate, his hands lowering to his sides.

He spoke calmly—his voice as smooth as silk, "Your anti-magic does *nothing* to *me*."

Jesper's movements were almost too fast to follow. In a flash, he had closed the distance, his hand gripping the wrist that held the blade to my throat. The doctor yelped behind me, his hold faltering for a moment that allowed me to dart to the wall.

Jesper twisted the blade from his hand, sending it clattering to the ground, and then he drove his knee to the doctor's stomach. He crumpled with a groan, clutching his abdomen as Jesper towered over him.

"You know, I admire your courage, doc." Jesper let out a low laugh as he crouched down to his level, "I also admire how loud and wrong you are about most things." He reached a hand outward as he spoke and angled the doctor's face upward to meet his frenzied, glittering eyes.

His hand rose to his side, and in it a blade fashioned of blood formed in the palm of his hand. My breath came in short, uneven gasps as I watched Jesper loom over the Doctor, who whimpered beneath him.

"Jesper," I rasped, my voice shaky.

"Don't kill him." I shook my head at him as I spoke. Jesper responded with the tilt of his head, his eyes flicking to me. There was something almost playful in his expression, but it was tinged with cruelty.

"And why should I spare him? He was ready to kill *you*." I looked at him with vacant eyes; I had no answer. I just didn't wish to watch someone I knew—despite hating him—die.

Dracar silently came up behind Jesper, his blade angled at his back.

"Back into that cell—or I will kill you," Dracar said, pressing the blade into Jesper; he hissed under its pressure.

"Fun's over I presume, come princess." Jesper extended one of his hands out to me, and Dracar shot me a look of disapproval. I reached forward, allowing my hand to touch Jesper's, and he gingerly guided me to his side.

"You are *choosing* this," Dracar huffed, the hurt dancing in his eyes as he looked between Jesper and I.

"No, I was forced into this—by *you* of all people!" I turned to enter the cell, refusing to face him as I did. I pulled Jesper's hand, and he followed me.

"Lovely—another night of sleeping on the floor. Say, *Dracar*, could we get some more…comfortable sleeping arrangements?" Jesper said, gesturing about the stone cage we now stood in.

"Nope," Dracar said as he locked the cell; we now ended up exactly where we were before.

I shouldn't have hesitated.

"Why wouldn't you just put him to sleep or something?" I hissed at Jesper as Dracar left us in the dungeon.

"Darling, I was already pushing myself to my limit to save you from that *pig*," Jesper snorted when he spoke, nodding to where the doctor was just moments before scrambling to follow Dracar.

"Why didn't *you* try to tell your brother more?" Jesper retorted, clearly irritated by my lack of effort to initiate with my brother.

"Because I was completely consumed by rage—I…" I was afraid to finish that statement.

"You were nearly about to kill him," Jesper continued my thought as if he could read my mind as it spun.

"I wouldn't have…" I said as I put my back to the wall and slid down it. I wrapped my arms around my knees and squeezed as tightly as I could.

"As I said, you have her passion." Jesper used a gentler tone, one that starkly contrasted him in every single way.

"Why do you keep saying that? Passion means love, why would I kill someone I love?" I snapped, and tears began to stream down my face. Though shockingly, the warmth of them was welcome in the terrible chill of the cell.

"I fear you don't know what passion is, darling." I watched

Jesper frown through the blurriness of my tears, and he crouched down in front of me.

"Hatred and love are flowers which bloom from the same seed. You cannot hate something without first loving it—even if merely the idea. If you were indifferent, you couldn't be driven to hatred—to *rage*," Jesper said softly as his eyes remained fixated on mine. I could see the faint hue of gold through my tears.

"Gods, I am starved though, can we get any damned food down here?" he huffed, settling into a sitting position in front of me. I shrugged; I truly didn't know much of what the prisoners of our kingdom endured.

"I don't wish to die down here," I said through sobs.

"Die? There isn't a chance we will be dying down here. Perhaps a bit miserable for a while, but death is beyond us," Jesper said with a bit of a chuckle.

I lay against the freezing stone; it felt as if I were on ice. I let its chill seep into me, driving me to become infuriated with every passing moment. I spun to lie on my back, my gaze fixated on the damp ceiling that seemed miles above me.

I began mumbling to myself, recalling all of the memories and experiences I had over the last few months—searching for the moments that were void of Dracar. For the moments that he did not exist in my consciousness.

I thought of Stygian.
Of Hiver.
Diana.
Kaneira.
I even thought of Jesper...

Perhaps they had truly become my family; perhaps this one was meant to stay behind.

Hours must have passed as I lay that way, *seething*.

<hr>

"Ah, dinner—finally!" Jesper scrambled up from his position just beside me and went to the bars.

To my surprise, it had been *real* food—fit for royalty.

"Oh, thank you, cruel little prince!" Jesper praised mockingly. Dracar merely shot him a look of disgust and pushed the feast through the bars on small trays, one by one.

"So you'll feed us like kings but you won't allow us to sleep like even peasants?" I scoffed, pushing away the food Jesper placed beside me.

"It's probably poisoned, Jesper," I mumbled, hardly loud enough for Jesper to even hear me. His eyes found mine, narrow and playful, as if he were taunting me.

"Even better a reason to eat it—believe it or not I do not enjoy being a prisoner," Jesper said whilst shoving potatoes into his mouth. I looked at the glazed meats that sat before me, hunger consuming my every thought.

I couldn't recall the last time I had a proper meal. I averted my gaze from the array of foods now sitting in the cell with me.

"Eat it Mira," Dracar sternly spoke, his eyes cutting through the back of my skull like a blade.

"Mira is a lovely nickname," Jesper said quietly while continuing to gorge himself on the foods that sat freshly prepared. I could smell the meats and fruits, and my mouth began to water.

My strike of hunger would not last long.

"Eat it princess, you're starved too," Jesper shot, using the utensil to point at me as he did.

I hastily bit into the food, glaring at Dracar as I did. Jesper had encouraged me to tell him, more, so tell him more, I did. I explained the story of our mother, of Kaneira, of all of us.

"Are you fucking serious right now, Mirage?" Dracar said in a tone I could not place, his face displaying an entire array of emotions. He had gone through grief, denial, rage—all in a span of seconds, his eyes conveying every one to me.

"Deathly," Jesper said in response to him, those golden eyes gleaming with the excitement of the drama. Jesper then took this as his cue to contribute more of the story.

"Kaneira and your mother have known each other since they were children. They fell in love young, and your mother was married off to your jackass of a father, who kept her in a cage like a bird. Kaneira was always hers—she was always Kaneira's. It had to be her to kill your mother... it had to be *her* hands. All to save *you*. *You* who turned out to be a despicable bastard..." Jesper rolled his eyes as he finished his statement, his resentment of Dracar obvious to us both.

"And how do you know any of this?" Dracar pressed, both eager to understand as well as reject the new information.

"I saw it," I said simply, as if that could somehow answer every question that swam in his mind. He scoffed at me—a reasonable response for my terrible answer.

"That man who bought me, Hiver—he can reach into others' minds and walk you through their memories, if they wish it," I said to him softly, my tone begging him to believe me.

"How do you know they weren't making it all up? Creating an illusion of mother's past?" Dracar pressed, his gaze unrelenting—I didn't have the answer, not truly. But I trusted Diana, and Diana trusted Kaneira.

"Because I've met Kaneira. I've been with her this whole time—she rules the Eleventh," I admitted, instantly regretting it.

I hadn't a clue what that knowledge could do, what it could destroy...

Dracar's mouth fell open, the shock of my words overcoming all of his features.

"You were with that *beast*? That *monster!*" he yelled, rising from where he was seated.

"She is not a monster! She loves us Dracar, she *wants* us," I said shakily as I fought hard to suppress a sob. Yet the tears came to my eyes, fast and hot.

"She tricked you," He said coldly, his own eyes battling back the tears that threatened to go to war with his words.

"She *saved* me," My own tone hardened as I spoke.

"What you have become will destroy you—it will destroy *us*," His voice was laced with something dangerously close to grief.

※※※※※※※※

I hadn't a response for him; not a single word could get through to him—*I* could not get through to him.

For a moment, I thought he would cave entirely—to believe me, to free me. But he stood in place, as if rooted by some unseen force; his jaw was tight, and his eyes flickered with pain and sorrow. He inhaled deeply, his eyes closing as he faced me, and before they could open, he turned and left.

His footsteps echoed in the quiet as if they were retreating from more than just the dungeon.

He had retreated from me.

CHAPTER
THIRTY-EIGHT

Jesper sat beside me, taking in my tear-soaked cheeks.

I turned my head slightly, just enough to meet his gaze. There was no smugness in his expression, no hint of the man who thrived on wit and a sharp tongue—only sincerity in this moment.

"He may not come around now, but he will eventually. I just may need to put my kidnapping skill set to work." His lips turned upwards into the faintest smile. I let loose a giggle that radiated my sadness and appreciation for Jesper's commentary.

"He is struggling to comprehend the person you have become—the person you were *made* to be." He pulled me into a tight embrace then, his hands warm on my back.

"Someone dangerous, you mean," I scoffed, though it came out weak.

"Someone powerful and extraordinary."

His words settled into me, heavy yet comforting in some way. I didn't reply to him, but I returned his embrace, pushing my face into his shoulder and allowing my tears to soak his coat. I made an effort to speak, but I couldn't will the words to push past the lump in my throat. Instead, I leaned into his touch, letting the warmth of him seep into me.

"I know what it feels like—to be misunderstood, that is," he continued, his voice dropping to a whisper.

"You are not misunderstood, Jesper," I murmured, my voice trembling through the tears, "You're reckless and infuriating—and maybe even a downright criminal?" I allowed a slight laugh to escape through sobs.

He let out a quiet laugh, the sound low and warm.

"True, very true. But you still *see* me, don't you?" His voice held a sincerity. I pulled myself away from him—his golden eyes steady, unwavering.

"I do," I mumbled, allowing myself to still exist in the space just inches from him.

Perhaps I had come to appreciate his insanity.

"He will see you, too. Perhaps it will take a bit more…pushing," Jesper said, his thumb was brushing against my shoulder in a circle, a comforting gesture.

"You mean kidnapping?" I smiled.

"If you command it, princess." He returned my gesture.

"Thank you," I muttered.

"For what? I can't grab him yet," Jesper chuckled.

"For being a friend," I sniffled.

The night came quickly—rather, I presumed it was night as I felt unreasonably tired. I fell asleep with my head in Jesper's lap; he slept upright, his back pressed into the wall behind us. His arm was draped over my shoulders, his other buried deep into his pocket.

I woke in a haze, searching the darkness of the cell. For a moment, I was confused, unable to make sense of my situation and the world around me. I had just woken from a dream, and I had forgotten the comfort I derived from his face.

It was Hiver's face.

I didn't dream much, but when I did it was always *him* occupying my subconscious mind—or nightmares that plagued my conscious one.

I pulled myself up from Jesper, who was still out cold. His breaths shallow and even as sleep continued to keep him in its cold embrace. I tried to lay his head down in my lap so that he could take a turn at a more comfortable rest.

For once, I had not hated him.

For a moment, I watched him sleep, his face so pale in the darkness. Perhaps I was capable of convincing myself he was not the worst company.

I felt everything in that moment before sleep fully reclaimed me.

The cold bite of the stone beneath me, the damp and stale air that was heavy with the metallic tang of old blood, the faint flames that managed to survive even the darkest corners of the dungeon—I had felt it all.

But there was a silent comfort Jesper provided in this space, and part of me wanted to detest him for it.

CHAPTER
THIRTY-NINE

"Up." Dracar's voice was like steel, cold and hard.

I blinked myself awake, taking in his features as if for the first time. Jesper's head was still resting on my thigh, but I could feel his body jolt as Dracar urged us into consciousness.

"Ugh!" Jesper yelled before slinging his arm over his eyes to block out the imaginary sun from pressing into him.

"Eat," Dracar said simply. He was back to his typical self—using few words to speak. He pushed plates of battercakes and assortments of berries through the cell to us. Jesper must have smelled them, as he shot up and immediately reached for the food.

"Now we're talking, little prince!" He said gleefully as he began to indulge himself in the array of breakfast foods.

It was incredible that he managed to maintain a lean figure.

I watched Jesper scarf down his food happily, but then my eyes found Dracar's. I stared at him for a long moment, hoping my gaze would cut through him like a blade. I wanted him to feel my anger in every part of him.

His dark eyes flickered, barely masking the resentment roiling within them. He didn't look away, but I saw it: the faint twitch of his jaw, the tightening of his grip on the stone bench of which he sat.

He knew my stare.
He felt my eyes.

He didn't speak, though. He simply held my gaze; defiance and regret battling across his sharp features.

It wasn't enough—not nearly enough.
I wanted more.

I wanted his words, his admission, his guilt laid bare before me.
I wouldn't ask, though, He would need to offer it to me.
I needed his confession.

Rolling in my own fury, I shot a look to Jesper. Before I could stop the words from rolling off my tongue, I snapped at him.

"This is all *your* fault," I said softly, feeling instant regret upon allowing the words to slide out. He turned to me, completely dumbfounded.

"I suppose that is true," he said simply, his typical charm and wit now absent from his expression and tone.

"Do you believe in fate, Mirage?" Jesper said, his words perplexing me. I felt my mind spinning, and words failed me when my mouth opened.

"I—you mean, like Vidhi? How fate is death?" I said to him.

"Sort of—another concept related to it." He wiped the crumbs from his face and fully turned to me, speaking to me like Dracar was not on the other side of the bars.

"The Solarian believe that fate means something a bit more… *persistent*. That our lives are inextricably bound to one another," He stoped for only a moment before continuing, "they believe we are bound by some invisible threads. These threads bind us to one another, to moments, to choices."

"The Solarian believe that every action, every breath, every thought pulls those threads tighter—tangling them, weaving something more complicated than we could ever fathom," he continued, but my confusion persisted.

"The Solarian call these "threads", *Sunar. Dar Sunar un Anima*—or *the threads of life,* in old Tessian." He smiled, his eyes softening.

"Everything is by design. We were meant to be here, even if it is miserable for us now. Everything is meant to lead us to our final destination."

I turned to Dracar again; his eyes were shimmering with an unexpected interest that left me momentarily stunned. He had truly listened to Jesper's every word—no interruptions, no objections, just listened.

"What *exactly* are the Solarian?" Dracar said, both Jesper and I turned to him now. We shared a look of perplexity upon Dracar's interest. Though I thought it unwise to protest it.

"The Solarian are Seaura who were born on a solstice, meaning they belong to *two* seasons," Jesper said simply.

"What is *Seaura?*" Dracar asked again, the interest still shining in his eyes in the dim glow of the lanterns. Jesper and I turned to one another, our shared look of bewilderment overtaking our expressions—then Jesper allowed a joyful smile to pull at his lips, and I knew that he was more than willing to give answers.

"What *are*, little prince," Jesper corrected, but his tone was playful, excited, even.

"The Seaura are *us*—bound by a season, driving our magic to replicate the gifts of the two Gods: Rainier and Olym. Do you recognize those names?" Jesper spoke now as if he were a teacher telling a child about history for the first time.

"Vaguely," Dracar said simply to him.

Jesper went onto explain the complications of magic; which kinds belong to each season.

"Perhaps I do believe in fate," I said after he concluded his rant. I may have considered the idea that we were all bound by some forces we could not see, but that did not mean I enjoyed two nights on the cold stone. He reached a hand to mine and squeezed, enthusiasm sparking in his eyes.

"Though fate is not particularly kind," I murmured, brushing my fingers on the cold stone beneath me. This discomfort—this hollow ache in my chest—was part of the design—the fact that tomorrow was not promised to me, yet I had hoped for it to come.

"What *am* I?" Dracar finally said, shattering the fragile silence that hung around us.

"You, little prince, are actually quite special. You and your sister both," Jesper started, his eyes flickering again with that playful edge, the excitement of sharing the history he knew so well.

"You and Mirage are what we call *scions*. You carry out the mortal will of Olym's first born children."

"Whose will?" Dracar now sounded afraid.

"For you, Vulkram, the God of the Forge. The 'unbreakable' God —hence why you can wield that lovely object without falling to its corruption." Jesper rested his chin upon his hands as he nodded to Dracar, who allowed his sword to rest against the bench.

Since arriving, this was one of the few times that sword had left his hand.

"What of Mirage?" Dracar finally said, his voice even more on edge than before.

"Mirage is the scion of Arudia, th—"

"The Goddess of the Flame," Dracar said softly, interjecting.

"Indeed, so you know of her then?" Jesper's expression melted into something else now.

"My mother used to tell us stories of Arudia. How she was a warrior and fierce spirit…" Dracar's voice cracked when he spoke, as if the memory of Mother pained him.

"Arudia is also the Goddess of Passion," Jesper spoke softly, mirroring the fragile cadence of Dracar's voice with a careful precision.

Dracar studied me now, his eyes boring through me as if I were not constructed of flesh, but rather glass. I tilted my head at him, trying to examine his expression to determine what was driving his gaze—why he stared at me so intensely.

I finally felt my rage melting away, as if I was not seething just an hour or so before. I felt myself coming to understand my brother again, and perhaps his gross overreaction to what I—*we* have become.

DIANA

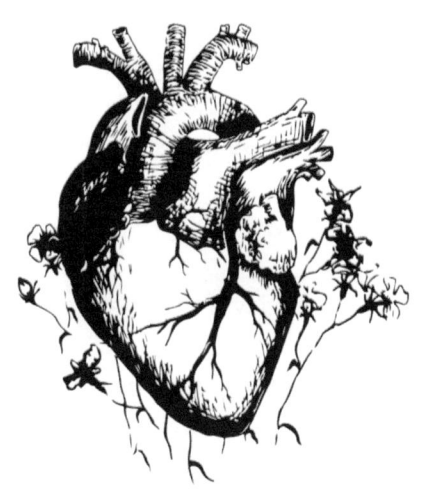

CHAPTER 40

DIANA

The morning sun nearly blinded me.

Olym's soft golden fingers instead took the form of talons, clawing me into a waking state. I felt its harsh scratch seep through me, the unwelcome heat crawling beneath my flesh attempting to thaw what could not be melted.

My courage.

"Snow!" I yelled as he lay face down on the couch of my chambers.

"You slept in here all night?" I rose from the bed now, reaching for him as he lay so peacefully on the white velvet.

"What was I supposed to do," he mumbled, and the phrase hardly came out a question.

"Okay, well up, up!" I gently shook his shoulders to urge him to rise from the long chair he took so comfortably to.

"Give me a minute," he grumbled, shoving his face further into the velvet as he groaned.

"I will begin counting down," I threatened.

"Please don't," I could hardly hear him now but could make out his plea.

I went over to my mirror, and I looked at the magnolias and olives which sat upon the vanity, fresh and lovely on the senses. Occasionally, the flowers reminded me of Aramore—of the lovely garden she tended in life.

She was life.

I began to brush up my hair and pull it into a single braid that fell down my spine.

I admitted that I was fearful to enter The Fang again; though I was never troubled by the Reavari, my brother had been. I hated those woods—the trees that inhabited them, the…*creatures*…

I turned to find Snow still face down on the couch. For a moment he looked to be dead, not even his breaths moving his body as he lay.

"Up, now," I scolded, though I admit I could have used a gentler tone as I spoke. I heard him mumble something incoherent and groan loudly, then he pushed himself up from the chair. I watched him leave the room in silence, nearly dragging his feet as he left.

I turned to my armoire and pulled the tight white suit we wore beneath our armor. I slipped into the suit, zipping its side up to tighten it to my body. I worried what would become of me if I needed to kill someone today…

I grabbed the twin karambit daggers from the bottom of the armoire and fastened them to my belt. I would adjust them later when I put on my armor. I took one last glance at the magnolias as they sat still upon the vanity, their untouched beauty eliciting a silent ache in my chest.

I walked the corridors in silence, not seeing another soul. The dawn still clung to the horizon. I took deep breaths as I walked, attempting to steady my raging heartbeat and erratic breathing. I was not one susceptible to panic, but that seemed to be all I could feel now.

I had prayed to the Gods Araya was right about Carlisle's absence, that I would not have to face that beast today.

I had hated him with every fiber of my being.

I could easily dedicate the rest of my existence to finding ways to exterminate him, but death would be too easy a punishment for someone as sick as him…

I reached Torvain and took the terrifying green of his great eyes, as if for the last time.

"Hello Torvain, may I access the armory?" I asked politely, my smile curving toward my eyes.

"Diana Frozain, daughter of the crown, I wish you victory in battle. *Nihiryn.*" Torvain's thunderous voice filled every silent nook of the corridor, shaking it like a storm. My mother truly had a knack for giving us the most obvious last names.

"Thank you, Torvain," I said quickly as I pushed past the giant door to enter the armory.

His words rang in my skull, and I could nearly taste what they meant…

The unmistakable tang of blood.

I saw them all before me as I pushed into the armory. The sun spilled into the room—this time more warm, less predatory as it did. Samira's eyes caught mine first. She sat before the hearth that so rarely was fed fire, her blade resting across her knee as her legs sat perfectly crossed.

Her armor caught every shadow in the room as she sat out of the reach of Olym's touch. She held a whetstone in one hand, methodically sharpening the edge of her dagger. Her movements lacked their usual fluidity—they were slower, almost hesitant.

Snow stood near the pool, adjusting the straps of his frost-embellished armor. His plates looked nearly enchanted as they gleamed under the golden hues of light.

His blue eyes were fixated on the map that was glued to the wall before him. I watched his fingers trace something on the map, but I couldn't tell what.

Stygian took to the weapons rack which held bows of every kind.

I had found Araya in the same place as yesterday, her eyes glued to the horizon in the distance. I thought of going to her—to console the worry she so clearly wore on her face. I looked at her reflection in the glass.

She had already been prepared for battle, her legs lined with daggers; her armor a deep red color as if fashioned from rubies, glittered in the light. I realized that the armor she wore was not her own —but Jesper's. Her breaths came out silently as she continued to stare blankly out of the window.

"Good morning!" I felt my tone was too cheery for what awaited us, for the potential peril we would have to endure. Samira's eyes slid up to mine and she stopped sharpening her blade for just a moment.

"Well? Let's go," Stygian said in his typical sarcastic tone.

I was the last to put on my armor.

For a long moment I stared at the helm, the horns of the ram shining in the sunlight from above. I traced my fingers along them.

As I lost myself in the thoughts of the day I was pulled back into reality by the lull of her voice, "I want to be the one to get him," Araya said softly, she was pleading, not only with her voice but also her eyes.

"Okay," I mustered with a smile that didn't reach my eyes. I didn't have the heart to stop her from pursuing him—the person she spent every waking moment with.

Sometimes, love was a sick thing.

Sometimes, it morphed into the kind of obsession that would drive you to your death.

CHAPTER
FORTY-ONE

We walked in silence to the front gates, my heart racing with every step.

It had been a while since we used a carriage pulled by horses. It was too risky to use our magic—we needed every drop we had.

I heard the beat of their hooves as they pulled us forward, the carriage bouncing slightly as it hit the gravel and rock. I looked up at him, his white hair catching stray light that made it into the carriage on his side. He didn't look back at me but kept his eyes fixated on what lay ahead—*The Fang.*

When the trees surrounded us, I couldn't take eyes off their bark bloodied with the red sap.

I hated the bloodwood trees.

I hated passing them every time I came through this cursed forest. The trees that symbolized the lost souls of the damned, forever imprisoned in the roots of the earth. I swear I could hear them breathing as we passed them, their leaves stealing oxygen from the air as their immortalized souls inhaled.

I felt my stomach turning with every jerk of the carriage. The hours felt like they were stretching into days—the impossibly long minutes melting into an amount of time indiscernible to me.

These woods maddened me.

"Halfway," Samira said curtly, her eyes canvassing the trees we passed, looking for even a glimpse of our enemies.

After a few moments of silence, we heard it.

The sound of the horse's screams was deafening.

I saw its bone mask as it threw itself at the carriage.

"You're fucking joking," Samira mumbled, the bones of her sheath clicking and releasing that frosted blade.

The carriage stopped.

"Stay put," Samira said coldly as she kicked open the door, her blade readied. I watched her walk to the horses, of which I could only see parts of through that window; it was too small to see them both. I saw her walk around them, her hand petting up their necks to their ears.

"They're both fine!" She yelled to us in the carriage. I kept my eyes fixated on the area just outside the door she had left open.

She would openly challenge death—and should they fight one another—I believe she would win.

Then its mask appeared at the door, its head tilted at us. Those despicable fangs jutting from its mouth like daggers.

"Where is the God-Born?" It hissed, its voice distorted, as if possessed.

"We don't have a God-Born," Samira's voice had an edge as she spoke—one that made my bones ache. As the creature turned to face her, she raised her blade, slicing it in half from the shoulder to the hip. Araya shrieked as its body hit the ground, both halves splitting upon its lifeless body falling.

I could feel the blood draining from my face. I looked out the door at the body of the Reavari, as well as the blood it splattered into the opened carriage. I noticed then Samira had taken out a cloth and was wiping her blade. She tossed the bloodied rag out of the carriage to the ground.

"Okay, let's go," she huffed.

I could hear their screams outside.
  I knew they were coming.

I allowed my fingers to trace the hilts of the karambits that sat at my back, waiting for a reason to pull them. I felt my heart racing with every thump of the carriage.

"They're looking for Mirage," Hiver choked, his words coming out muted.

"But you already knew that, didn't you," Samira said, an edge to her voice.

I watched Hiver's face turn pale, his jaw clenching.

"Why did they attack *you* in that carriage?" I turned to him, my emotions running wild, and I struggled to keep them in check as I spoke.

"They didn't..." he trailed off; I watched his throat bob as he kept his focus on the bloodwoods outside of the window. I reached for him, gripping his arm with enough to force his eyes to meet mine. He turned slowly, his eyes holding a secret I was desperate to know.

"You became her," Samira murmured, her eyes now turned to Hiver who still refused to make eye contact with me.

"You *what*?" I said breathlessly.

"You knew they were after her, and yet you said nothing!" I snapped now, my emotions getting the best of me.

"What would you have me say! I didn't want her to become a target!" he yelled back at me, his eyes wild.

"And yet she did anyway," I seethed, my teeth clenched now.

"I'm sorry." His breath caught when he spoke, as if he were stifling a sob.

Snow never cried—at least not in front of me.

"You almost died to save her." Stygian's voice broke the silence, rather shattered it, "Why?"

"I don't know..." Hiver continued to avert his gaze from everyone in the carriage.

"Perhaps because you knew you loved her the moment you laid eyes upon her—maybe even before then." Samira's voice cut, but not me. I watched Snow's eyes grow wide and his throat bob.

The threatening screams and scratches of the Reavari potentially saved him from having to respond to her. When we stopped, Samira jumped from the carriage—I hadn't a clue how long we sat in silence as she cut down creature after creature.

She finally came back into the carriage.

Her armor was drenched in blood, as was her face. She hauled herself back into the carriage, the blood leaking off of her onto the leather, staining it with the red streaks.

"Let's go," she said, and for the first time ever, her voice cracked a bit.

CHAPTER
FORTY-TWO

The remainder of our journey through The Fang went the same. Samira's armor was painted entirely red by the time we reached the outskirts of the tenth. In a matter of hours, she had become a reaper.

We reached the tunnels by foot, leaving the carriage at the edge of the castle after freeing the horses.

"I lead," Samira said, pushing her way to the front of us while Stygian went to the front of the castle.

The tunnels went on for eternity, weaving tightly to the point where I was fearful a single body could not pass between the stone. There was little light down there.

Occasionally, Araya would scramble to look through scripts to find lighting spells, but they were typically reserved for the Autumn-Kissed Solarians.

I watched Samira's back as I walked behind her. The frostbitten blade was still slick with the blood of Reavari. Her movements were steady, purposeful. The jagged stone walls occasionally pressed in on us, as if the world was threatening to swallow us whole. I could hear Araya straggling behind, flipping through pages in the darkness.

"Just keep moving; forget the scripts. The lanterns are enough." Samira said in response to the ruffling of pages several people behind her.

"What's this?" Samira's voice rang as she halted, suddenly enough for us to physically run into her. She turned, and though I couldn't see her eyes, I could feel her glare on my skin. I could faintly see her hand tracing the walls, as if something was on them.

I felt them too.

Carvings.

"Lucius," I breathed.

"He must have carved these tunnels." Samira's hand continued to delicately move along the wall—along the carvings.

"We should keep moving." Hiver's voice grew irritated as we paused.

Samira grumbled a response, then pressed forward.

At the end of the tunnels, there was a continued darkness—it should lead to the wing before Mirage's. We pressed through to a final wall: hard, but not stone. I touched it with my hands, unsure of how to open it.

"Surely, it's locked from the outside?" Araya said as she pressed forward to also lay her hands upon the door.

I passed through the wall as if it were air. I couldn't tell where we were. I pulled back on my physical form as I investigated—when I noticed a latch that was intricately carved of gold. I tugged at it lightly, and the giant wall slowly parted, just enough for a person to pass.

The room I now stood in was dark—terribly dark. The evening was falling upon us, but it still felt *off*. We all retreated from the passage, and I pulled the golden latch again to shut the wall to how it was before. We all stood in the darkness, our breathing the only sound.

After a few moments of silence, I heard guards marching—no—running.

"Fire! Fire!" they yelled, their voices raw with panic.

"How unoriginal," Samira scoffed and slowly approached the door leading to the halls beyond.

"Wait!" I hissed, trying to keep my voice low enough for the guards to not notice us.

I turned to face the window, where the evening light barely shined through the soft yellow curtains that cloaked them. I approached them slowly and swung open the cloth that hid the great windows.

I then realized exactly where we were.

The Queen's Chambers.

Carlisle had allowed no one to enter it since Aramore's death. This room was entirely off limits to *everyone* in the castle—including his own two children.

The footfalls of the guards eventually faded into nothingness, and Samira swung open the door. She peered out into the hallway, which was almost entirely empty now.

"This way," I motioned for the three of them to follow me to Mirage's chambers. Part of me had wanted her to be in there: untouched, unharmed. The more rational part of me knew that was wishful thinking.

We found our way to her chambers without any interference. Samira plopped herself onto the bed, an exhaustion overtaking her features as she did. I decided to search for Mirage. I left the chambers and passed through wall after wall in search of her.

. . .

I eventually made it to the kingdom's war room.

At some point, one might have believed this room was a relic of a kingdom that once valued strategy over drunken indulgence. Time had dulled its grandeur, leaving behind a space that whispered of conquest and battle, but never saw either.

A massive table dominated the center of the room, its surface etched with a fading map of Moterrian. The edges were worn and smooth from countless hands tracing borders and marking strategies, though now it sat covered in a thin layer of dust. A suit of armor stood sentinel beside it, cobwebs stretching from its helm to the spear held tightly in its grip. I allowed my fingers to follow those delicate webs but did not disturb the spider that inhabited them.

Then I heard footfalls behind me, but it was too late for me to retreat. I could only hope the familiarity of my face would save me from whatever guard stumbled upon me.

"Hello, Diana." His voice was grating to my ears, erupting a fury inside of me. The door must have been barely ajar—he saw me in here.

"Where is my lovely bride? Surely she's with you?" His voice made my teeth grind as I turned to face him—and he was in a military uniform.

"Did daddy's money fail to afford you freedom from required service?" I said, taking in the green and white uniform that cloaked him head to toe—completely clean, not a single crinkle from battle.

"Don't think I look good in a uniform?" Jamen rasped.

"I think you'd look better in a casket," I growled at him, reaching for the karambits that sat at the back of my waist.

"Don't." He pulled out a weapon unfamiliar to me—fashioned of metal and curved in a unique way. It was pointed at me, and it appeared to have an opening in its end. I kept my fingers situated around the hilts of my daggers, ready to pull them. I heard the metal in his hand click with the brush of his thumb, and I loosened my grip.

I hadn't a clue what I was looking at.

I reached instead for one of the smaller daggers and launched it at him. it clipped the shoulder of his uniform; the green slowly turned red from the blood that spilled through.

He yelped, reaching for where the dagger had nestled itself into his flesh and pulled it out, grabbing his arm as he whimpered in pain.

"You *bitch*," he muttered, pulling the steel upward, and he pressed his finger to something that released a small ball of fire. The sound it released was deafening. I managed to raise a wall of ice between us, the small fire ball barely being caught inside it. I saw now it was not fire, but another piece of metal, small and pointed. I gazed at it for a moment, utter confusion overcoming me.

"You're a witch!" he snarled and raised his metal slinger again at me; I wasn't sure my ice was capable of holding these *things*, especially as he inched closer.

I shot a dagger fashioned of ice at him, and it whirled past as he sidestepped it. I heard it hitting metal behind him, swords and blades clattering to the ground.

I was at a disadvantage from a distance.

I needed to get closer.

The metal object whirred and clicked again under the movement of his thumb, and I saw that it held eight slots where the metal pieces departed.

He had seven left.

I bore through the ice quickly, my body manifesting in front of the shield, and I pulled another dagger from my other hip. I lunged for him, scraping his thigh with it. He stumbled for a moment, managing to maintain most of his balance. A metal piece had escaped the contraption, but it missed me. He swung down at me with the metal weapon, hitting me hard upon the cheekbone. My vision swam under the blow, but I reached for another dagger on my calf and swiped for him.

His hand came down upon mine, pushing my blade downward; he angled the weapon at me now, that hole inches from my face.

Another metal shard would come barreling toward me.

I drove my body into his, my shoulder catching his midsection as I threw him to the ground, wrestling to get to the top of him—to pin him down. He managed to break loose from my grip, throwing a punch at my face. I blinked erratically from the force of his fist. Then, he thumbed the metal to make it whirl and click once more before firing directly at my shoulder.

This time, he did not miss.

CHAPTER
FORTY-THREE

It was oddly warm as it ripped through my flesh.

The pain of it was unbearable.

I reached for where the metal had entered my body, the heat of it made it sting more. I screamed and raged under it, pulling at where it had lodged itself.

"Never seen a gun before, *peasant?*" Jamen said as he rose to tower over me.

Gun? What the hell is a gun?

I roiled with the pain and felt the metallic stinging of blood on my tongue. I reached for the corner of my mouth to see it spilling slightly from my lips. I had to do something; I could feel the wound making me weaker, unable to fight. He grabbed me then, flipping me onto my back.

"I can't decide if I should leave you here or bring you down to the dungeon to rot," he said coldly, a despicably wicked smile tugging at his pale lips.

I had to get this thing out of me, but pulling it with my fingers was not enough. I quickly thought through all of the options—of every scenario where I could survive this thing in my shoulder. It hurt to draw breaths, even shallow ones.

> I couldn't die here.
> If it took defying the Gods, so be it.
> *I would turn my blood into ice and push it out.*

It whispered beneath my skin, a soft hum, like a song almost. I hardly summoned it—it rose to the surface for me, bending to my will. I could smell the faint scent of lilacs as it turned my blood solid; it flooded my veins with an icy burn. My magic crawled through my body, desperate to act out my will. I could feel the frost around my heart, slowing its beats. I could feel it dimming the heat in my shoulder, replacing it with a biting chill that made me shudder.

My nose dripped with blood.

I could feel my magic protesting me—stopping me from healing a wound as that wasn't my power. I could feel my body suffering under the weight of my magic.

The metal resisted my frosted blood, but I did not stop. I let it consume me—the power that welled within me. I would use every last drop if I needed to… and maybe then some—part of me felt my mind slipping, confusion rippling through me as the magic was.

I could feel it slowly moving forward, almost out of my flesh. I could also hear and feel the ice cracking around it: my newfound skin. The shard of metal left me, falling to my shoulder first, then to the floor beside me. I let out a guttural sound—a groan of sorts as it did. The power I felt was wild and unruly—unlike the magic I had typically used, which was measured and responsive.

It both hurt and didn't at the same time.

The ache was distant and muffled as if I were meant to be crafted of frost instead of blood. I was fearful to look down at where I had willed myself to become another element entirely.

I could feel blood soaking one side of my face; My nose dripped from the force of the magic, while my mouth poured red from the unsettling closeness of the metal to my lungs.

"Up, *handmaiden*," he said mockingly, the object pointed between my eyes as he stood over me. I groaned and called to my magic, but it remained still, humming where my shoulder had mended itself with ice.

I knew this would be a costly choice.

MIRAGE

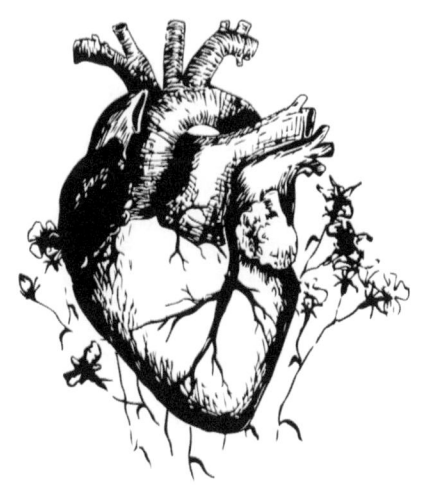

CHAPTER 44

MIRAGE

I could feel the ghost of a smile pulling at my lips.

Jesper was more than happy to tell Dracar all about the Solarian, the Tessiah, and the Gods. It brought him more joy than anything else seemed to. I felt a bit of hope dancing in my chest as I watched Dracar lean into the bars, fascinated by everything Jesper had to say.

Still, his words echoed through me now.

What am I?

What a loaded question.

Maybe I had become both my past and present, an amalgamation of words and phrases assigned to me—to my identity. I didn't know who I was or who I had become, but I *had* to assume I was where I was meant to be the entire time.

I didn't know if I was ready to choose my own identity—to choose my own fate. I wasn't sure if I could even begin to understand what stirred within me beyond the magic: my hopes, my fears, my love—my *hatred*…

I had hardly seen Dracar hopeful—that foreign look on his face that twisted his features in delightful ways. I had longed to see him happy, but hopeful was just one step off. I continued to watch them talk to one another—about beliefs, the Gods, their lives in the Eleventh.

Then I heard a struggle.

The heavy breathing and groaning of two people coming down to us.

Dracar turned his head, standing from the cell to see who would come down...*what* would come down. I saw the pure white metal before I saw her face. Her long blonde hair, tied into a braid, whipped around to the front of her as she came down the stairs, a man holding her arms behind her back.

"Diana?" Jesper's voice was surprised as he spoke, rising from in front of my brother. Her eyes were wild and brimming with anger. Dracar stood, his blade angled inches from her throat as he spun to meet her face.

"Dracar," she choked as she pushed back into her captor. I couldn't muster a sound; I couldn't even say her name. I was shocked and horrified, and it only got worse with every passing minute.

"There's my beautiful bride!" Jamen exclaimed from behind Diana. He shoved her forward and kicked her behind the knee, sending her to the ground. Her armor was streaked with blood and dirt.

Jesper immediately placed himself in front of me, as if to stop Jamen's pursuit—but those eyes were hungry.

Jamen sauntered forward, unbothered by Jesper's intimidating figure looming before me.

"I'd move." His wicked smile revealed his too white teeth. I noticed the red stain that destroyed the shoulder of his uniform. I allowed my gaze to fall to Diana's face, which was cut and already bruising.

Her eyes were soft as they reached mine, the lilac of them shimmering in the low light of the dungeon.

"Jam—I will not hesitate." Dracar held his blade with a steady hand, its tip pressing gently against Jamen's throat.

"Neither will I," he muttered, and pressed a finger to the metal object he held in his left hand.

I've seen that *thing* before.

I've seen it in ink—that was.

I remember my father investing in Voryn's inventions. He was constantly at the castle, speaking with architects and designers to bring to life his weapons. I supposed this *thing* was the first of his inventions that was functional; I thought he called it a *revolver*.

He pointed it at Jesper who held his hands upward toward his head. Jesper tilted his head to glance at me behind him, those golden eyes shimmering.

"Touch me," he murmured.

"What?" I whispered back. He looked at me again sidelong, not fully turning his head.

"Touch. Me," he growled. I hadn't a clue what he was thinking or what he had planned. He truly didn't give me a reason to *not* trust him, so I reached my hands around his waist.

"*Drasickar Blerium, Fordaseur Lockardis,*" Jesper mumbled it quietly, I might have been the only one who could hear him. His hands twisted above me, and so did my insides. I held myself up, fighting against the pain that rippled through my body. I felt like I was turning into dust—that my body was collapsing in on itself. I groaned as I gripped his waist, using his body to keep myself upright.

"Jesper—" I wheezed as I gripped him, forcing myself to remain on two feet.

"Don't let go," he huffed between incantations. I let my head crash into his back as I fought against my impending death if he kept pushing.

Then there was a deafening bang.

"Ah, fuck!" Diana's unmistakable yelp echoed through the stone encased walls.

"Diana!" I heard my brother's muffled scream. I lifted my head from Jesper's back, but the world spun violently around me. I kept my hands steadied onto him.

"You're okay…It's okay you did well," he whispered as he spun to face me, pulling my arms into him so that he could steady my almost limp body. I didn't have the energy to keep myself upright; I felt my head falling forward, as if sleep were coming to claim me.

"*Zertost…*" were the last words I heard him say before the blackness consumed me.

CHAPTER
FORTY-FIVE

I woke with a cut arm and Jesper pouring my blood into one of the leftover cups.

"What're y—"

"Shh, it's okay. Just rest," he murmured, his tone nearly willed me to rest my eyes again—to find myself falling into the sweet embrace of sleep. I could hardly see her, but I could make out the white metal and golden hair.

She had been lain onto Dracar, her face wincing with pain. I could hear him mumbling to her as he pushed the loose golden locks from her face.

I could hardly make out the scene before me, but I noticed her touching her stomach, the white of her armor stained with a sea of blood. I could hear her labored breathing cutting through the stillness of the dungeon like a blade.

"Diana—" I croaked, and I attempted to jerk forward, but Jesper pulled me back into him as he drained the blood from my wrist.

"I am helping. Just give me a moment," Jesper's voice was calm as he pushed my chest down with his palm.

I could feel my breaths becoming erratic and labored as I struggled beneath him, desperate to throw myself at Diana.

"I need you one more time," he frowned at me from above before gripping my wrist gently.

"*Drasickar Movond Eskost*," he whispered as he waved his hands in several motions above her wound. She yelped but didn't scream, and a small piece of metal hit the ground.

I had become a husk at this point, hardly able to keep my eyes open, let alone scream or struggle against the horror of the siphoning magic.

It felt like years ago since I last heard Voryn's voice, but I can vaguely recall him referring to the metal shard as a *bullet*. Diana began to violently cough, and as I turned to face her, I noticed blood sputtering from her mouth, covering her face.

"It's fighting me," she groaned, hardly able to say the words as the blood coated her throat.

"Pardon me, darling," Jesper said as he carefully removed me from his chest and helped me lie down on the floor. His voice was sweet when he spoke, and I could hear the concern lingering in his tone.

"What did you do?" Jesper said to her softly. I could see him hovering his hands over her body as if to find something—his hands faltered over her shoulder.

"*Solathrix*? Diana!" Jesper's voice was warning—his tone was aggressive but managed to keep its gentleness.

"What would you have had me do instead? I couldn't breathe!"

"It's solid," he said matter-of-factly.

"Because it's ice," Diana hissed.

"Ice? To *heal*?" Jesper rasped in a hurried whisper.

"Yes," she huffed.

I heard them continue to argue for a few moments as my consciousness faded in and out. The world around me shifted in and out of darkness, as if shadows lingered around my vision. I could see Jesper's hands suspended over her side, and her screams erupted, laced with despair and agony.

"You're hurting her!" My brother snapped.

"I am *helping* her," Jesper shot back, his voice calm as he spoke.

I then realized it was my *brother* holding Diana.

My brother was in the cell with us.

The blackness claimed me as I fought against it, its current unrelenting as it pulled me under its soft dark waves. I could not fight off the sleep that came for me.

I dreamed of him again.

The white of his hair flashing before me. The way his lips felt on mineSomething about Hiver just felt so *right*. I felt myself being ripped back into consciousness—his words still echoing in my mind as I saw the dim light of the lantern swinging above me. I woke to Jesper's face looming above mine.

"Bad dream?" he said, a hand reaching to my cheek.

"Not quite." I shot up, and felt my head throbbing as I did. I reached my hands to my hair which was damp with sweat and the wetness of the cell.

It took my eyes a moment to readjust to my quick movements, as the world around me blackened and shook. I crawled over to Diana, who was still blurred in my vision as my surroundings were still coming into focus.

She was still covered in blood, but fast asleep in my brother's arms. He was positioned with his back against the wall and her body largely pulled into his. I watched Dracar's chest rise and fall as he held her tightly in his sleep.

"How much time has passed?" I asked Jesper who still sat several feet behind me.

"A day? Perhaps? No one has come back down here since that little prick." Jesper scoffed.

"I'm starved," he mumbled.

My mind swam as I readjusted to the world around me, and. I noticed the lack of sword on my brother's hip...

"If you were there that day—if you saw my brother's sword—would you know what was in the hilt?" I asked, but Jesper looked incredibly confused. He raised a brow at me before his expression melted into understanding, "Yes? I would have known it was the Shard within it—just as I did here—why do you ask?"

"I was thinking of Hiver...I think he saw the Shard when he ate a Clariflux..." I admitted.

"Did you eat a fruit?" He asked.

"Yeah I–"

"What did you see?"

"I saw a funeral—for my uncle. It was my mom, Dracar, and I—" I sucked in a breath, "then...the shadows came." I trailed off and started to reach for my arms, fearful those shadows would strike at me again.

"Shadows? Was that a real memory?" he pressed.

"Sort of... I remember the scary shadows when I was a child—they made me cry at the funeral rite... but in the Clariflux vision they attacked me—made me feel mad."

"I don't see that as helpful information, darling." Jesper sighed and sat down beside me.

"Under her veil, I saw my face taking form in place of my mother's—it seemed that she was *turning* into me." I spoke softly, knowing that the information was useless.

"Under a veil?" Jesper sounded breathless as he spoke.

"I mean yeah, it was a funeral—my mother wore a black veil." I said.

"A veil that could make shadows attack and change the face of the woman wearing it?" Jesper stood abruptly, pacing the room with a restless energy, nervousness radiating from him in palpable waves, "That fucking bastard—"

"What?" I could only hear his mumblings.

"He has the Veil, too." Jesper's expression went cold, as if he had seen a ghost—perhaps he had become one in that moment.

"The Veil–"

"Of Phantasm, another Talis item—another *fucking* Talis item…" Jesper trailed off as he paced about the small confines of the cell.

"Okay, okay," He reached down to Diana and shook her arm a bit, her eyes slowly fluttering awake under his touch.

"Get up." He was a bit more stern as he spoke—more stern than I had heard him in the last few days.

"What is your problem, Jess?" She rubbed her eyes harshly.

"This sick fuck has two Talis items; we have to get out of here right *now*," Jesper said frantically, reaching an arm out to guide her to her feet. Dracar had caught wind of the discussion, his eyes also heavy with sleep.

"Why are you here?" I asked him.

Dracar looked at me dumbfounded, "Because I have a big heart, apparently," he grumbled.

"What do you mean *two* Talis items?" Her eyes widened with horror as she looked upon Jesper's face. His features were sharp and edged with concern as he looked down at her—at her bloodied armor and skin.

"He has the Veil, too," Jesper said with fear laced in his tone.

"How do you know that?" She still spoke softly, despite the new threat presented to her.

"Mirage saw it at *Summundor*. Your brother saw the Shard. The Clariflux wanted her to know that there were *two* items here." Jesper huffed.

"We have to go get the others–"

"Others?" I questioned Diana, "Who else came with you?"

"Samira, Stygian, Snow, and…" She sucked in a hard breath as she faced Jesper, "And Araya…"

"You brought *her*? *Here*? To this *death trap*!" Jesper snapped. The fury that clung to his aura was like nothing I had ever seen before. He was blazing with an anger I was not accustomed to—even for myself.

"She came for *you*!" Diana sniped back, her voice hoarse. Jesper's expression immediately fell into pain.

"Can you use your magic to get us out of this cell?" Diana said to him, her voice softening.

"I can't continue to siphon her." He nodded to me.

"I'd need a fruit," he sighed.

Him and Diana continued their bickering in aggressive whispers, arguing about the items, our escape, and the others who were likely in peril above us.

CHAPTER
FORTY-SIX

I heard heavy footsteps coming down the dungeon stairs, and we all turned to face the source of them—expecting another one of our friends to be brought to us by the guards.

Jamen was leading him down the stairs, hands bound behind his back, but unscathed unlike Diana was.

It was Hiver.

"Hiver—"

"Hello, Princess," he said in that familiar lull that had me reeling for him. I wanted to throw myself at him, to feel my body melting into the warmth of his. His eyes were flickering with a light that was both tender and devastating.

"See, I thought this would be fun." Jamen's voice was low and cruel as he spoke.

"I'm going to hang your little boyfriend for the King." His words struck like a blow. I could feel the panic rising within me, threatening to consume me.

"You'll regret it, *flusk*," Diana spat.

I had never heard the word aloud. The word that was derogatory to mortals—a reminder that they were not housing any magic in their flesh—just breakable bones and skin that would tear without fixing itself.

"And what can you really do behind those bars? Hm?" he teased—he ran the tip of the sword against the bars as he spoke.

Diana turned to face Jesper, desperation in her eyes.

"Perhaps I'll take you as a bride too—surely I could at least get enjoyment out of fucking you," he snarled at her, and Jesper's eyes were blazing with that familiar fury—the same kind he displayed upon learning Araya was here...somewhere.

Dracar was the one who spoke.

"I'll happily rip your fucking throat out the second you put your hands on her," he growled.

"Unless you can bend metal—you won't be doing any such thing," Jamen pressed the blade to Hiver's throat.

"Shit—the Shard," Jesper whispered under his breath—primarily to Diana.

"Well, we have important matters to attend to," Jamen sneered as he wrapped a hand around the back of Hiver's neck, "See you all later?" His laugh was wicked.

"Jesper, please just get us out of here." I held out my arms for him to take, so that he could use whatever necessary to make my plea a reality.

"I can't, Mirage," he said solemnly.

"I don't care if it kills me," I replied. Dracar shot me an intense look of disapproval.

"Can't you use *me*?" He said after a moment of contemplative silence.

"Indeed, I can little prince—but I fear the issue is not any shortage of God's blood. I am extremely limited in my own magic... the well is dry," Jesper rasped. His voice raw with emotion.

"We can't wait!" Diana cried out. Her desperation was mingling with fury to create something entirely unlike her.

"What would you have me do, Diana?" Jesper spoke in a low tone.

"Anything! That fucking maniac is going to kill my brother!" She began to pace the cell.

Her eyes were frenzied, deepening into a purple color that was foreign to her. Her jaw was clenching so hard I feared her teeth would crack under the pressure.

"There's another way out, and I am taking it," she huffed, sitting on the ground with her legs crossed. I watched her pull out a dagger from her back—a karambit. She sliced her wrist and took the blood between her two fingers.

She looked at it for a long moment—as if these were her final moments of sanity, marked by the blood she had spilled. I watched her reach her bloodied fingers to her forehead, marking a symbol I had been familiar with.

It appeared to be a moon with an arrow through it.

She lay on her back, chanting words that were deeply etched into my memory.

"Diana." My tone came out like a warning, but she did not open her eyes, and she did not turn to me.

"Diana!" I yelled again. Jesper's eyes widened at me, as if he did not understand what had been unfolding before him—*what* she had been doing.

She was embodying her God.

CHAPTER
FORTY-SEVEN

"Diana stop!" I barked, like an order.

She was completely entranced as she lay there.

"I don't recognize this spell," Jesper said, gripping my arm as I approached her. He stopped me in place and held me there. He continued, but his voice dropped to a lower tone as he did, "But you do—*How?*" His eyes were piercing on mine. It was not just a glance—it was a revelation, as if he could see every memory that swam in my consciousness.

"I saw Kaneira use it—I saw her use it to save *us*." I swallowed hard as I looked at Dracar.

"What did it—what is she doing?" Jesper spoke with a lethal calm.

"She is channeling a God—*her God.*"

"*Rainier*," he breathed, and took a step backward as if the wind had been knocked out of him by my answer.

"What can I do to stop her?" I reached for him, as if my grip would steady him.

"I don't know." He was terrified—an expression that was foreign to him.

He was not the type to wear fear on his face, but it had masked his features in this moment.

I looked at Dracar, who had knelt down beside her, stroking her cheeks softly and removing the loose strands of hair behind her ears. My mind swam, and I somehow felt like I was back at the beginning—being introduced to magic, what it meant, who it made me.

I felt something raw and consuming inside of me, like the moment a hurricane meets the shore—the elemental clash of a storm. I tried to think quickly—to think of how to stop her. I replayed the memory in my mind of Kaneira lying there as Lucius performed the magic necessary to make her a vessel.

My mind began to race faster. I had watched Diana's fragile body filling with an infinite, unyielding power, and I recalled Olym's demand for payment—how he could not even spare a daughter from the terrible cost to wield his power.

Diana would need to kill the person she loved the most.

What if that were the very person she was now trying to save?

I watched her skin begin to glow, as if her veins had been filled with moonlight. I watched her head as the bloody moon began to crystalize, turning into a bright purple crystal—an amethyst, maybe?

It had woven itself into her skin.

"Diana, stop this. Stop this now," Jesper warned. He also leaned down at her side, gently holding her hand in his own. His eyes panicked as they roved over her changing body. The moonlight coursed through her like blood.

"I cannot stop," she said. Jesper's eyes fell to mine, pleading for answers I could not even begin to give him.

Her voice came out low and distorted, a complete subversion of her usual tone, "I was told this was a last resort. If it means his life is on the line–" I watched her eyes flicker open and closed in quick motions, and when I caught a glimpse of them, they were flooded with a blueish-white light. I felt fear crushing my chest as I was paralyzed, unable to move or speak. I merely watched in awe as Diana became a God.

"What do we do?" I asked Jesper after many moments of contemplative silence. He turned to face me, his expression was unreadable.

"We allow her to become a conduit of chaos." He said as his eyes slowly closed. It seemed that he was praying in that moment—to what or *whom*—I could not know.

"You're going to just let her embody a literal *God*?" Dracar snapped, his voice almost sounded sarcastic as he raged. I flinched—nearly feeling his words were punches.

What would I have thought should I have heard these words leave his mouth just a few months ago? What terror and anger would this have evoked from the scared mortal girl...

The flusk...

"There are people I love up there..." Jesper nodded and threw his hands to the ceiling above him.

"People I would die for, and she is our only way out. So yes, *dar lihiteir prince*, I will be letting her embody a God." He had spoken the old language as he glared down at Dracar, his words almost like a spell, commanding him to cease his protests.

Dracar pursed his lips in response, his nose twitching with anger as he gazed up at Jesper.

Diana shot upright, a sharp breath tearing from her lungs as her eyes snapped open once more. The soft, lilac fields that once bloomed there—gentle and sweet—were gone, replaced by the unearthly glow of raw power. II hadn't noticed the change in her skin—something unlike what Kaneira had experienced. Her skin had frosted, her lips nearly blue. She looked as if she were reborn of ice. The faint glow of her veins still pulsed through her as if she were actively being pumped full of this…*power*.

"Niece and nephew!" she said in a terrifyingly distorted tone. She smiled wickedly, her eyes hard as she looked upon Dracar and I.

"No hello?" Rainier thundered through her.

"I know you're not all mute," Rainier trilled, his words seeming to be spun of silver and starlight.

"The God of Justice," Jesper breathed, the words hardly audible as they parted his lips.

"A fake Solarian," Rainier quipped. Jesper merely grimaced at the comment.

"Move now, children." That distorted voice rang out. Before I could react, the God wrapped his now delicate hands around the bars and ripped them open, as if they were not made to keep our kind inside. My eyes widened as I turned to face Jesper. He merely shrugged in response.

Diana's possessed body approached the stairs, but before she ascended them, she faced us and gestured for us to follow.

CHAPTER
FORTY-EIGHT

The stairs scraped beneath our boots, the grit grinding softly with each step.

The three of us walked in silence behind Diana, occasionally exchanging glances to one another as she murmured to herself.

The light of day was jarring.

I had not seen the sun's rays in several days.

Jesper continued to look at Diana with both a mix of reverence and defiance. I wasn't sure which was more dangerous when dealing with a God. I could swear I saw Dracar twitching, his hand desperate to hold a weapon. Eventually, Jesper reached out, forcing me to come to a stop.

"We have to get that Veil." He spoke hurriedly but solemnly.

"How do you suppose we do that?" I whispered back to him, hoping the God that walked just a few feet before us could not hear our frantic exchange.

"We will get that first," Diana said without turning to face us—rather, *Rainier* said. Jesper's face went pale.

"I think I know just where to find it, too." The God took a sharp turn, those eyes glowing almost like lanterns leading the way.

We came up to a familiar wing of our castle—*mine*.

"I don't think it would be here," I said softly, almost fearful of protesting the will of a God.

"I think it would be," Rainier smiled, a grin that felt so wrong on Diana's face. He—*she*—I wasn't even sure at this point—swung open the doors to reveal the damage of my room in the light of day.

When we last stood in here, my brother had held a blade at our throats.

"The others aren't here." Diana's voice came out distorted, but I could tell in that moment it was her speaking.

"What do you mean?" Jesper asked, an edge in his voice.

"I mean–" Diana's neck twitched a bit, as if she were wrestling for control.

"I mean they were here—I told them to wait here." Her impatience was overpowering.

"The Veil," Rainier thundered over her. To watch two people warring within the same body was an alarming scene. Diana turned to the wardrobe where I had been loitering, gazing at the blood on the ground, and reached for the handle.

Inside of the wardrobe were some of my favorite gowns, of all sorts of colors. I smiled for just a moment as I looked at the varying fabrics. Then her hand reached outward, moving them all down violently and revealing the veil I had seen my mother wear at the funeral.

"The Veil of Phantasm." Jesper's breath hitched as he spoke. He pushed past Dracar and I to stand at Diana's side, passing a loathing glance at the God then reached for the Veil. She reached forward and grabbed it first, stroking it gently as if it were a priceless artifact—though I suppose it was.

Jesper's eyes narrowed on the God, now inhabiting a woman whose beauty alone could kill—and whose deadliness needed no divine help.

"What is with those constant death glares?" I asked him once Diana was out of ear shot.

"I've heard about his so-called 'justice'," Jesper hissed, breaking from my loose grip around his arm and angrily following in Diana's footsteps.

The further we walked, the narrower the corridors became, as if the walls were pressing in on us. The sunlight faded into dim streaks through high windows, casting long, fractured shadows that danced with our movements. They seemed to almost recoil in fear from the God of the Night. A celestial incarnate—a God who promised to bathe the Earth in his soft glow for as long as his brother radiated his warmth.

We could hear the clatter and chatter of guards in the throne room as we approached it. I watched Jesper reach into his pocket to pull out a small vial with a dark red substance—one I had recognized as my blood. He drank the vial down, his eyes glittering in that ethereal glow of borrowed power.

"I hope he's worth the cost," Rainier smirked.

"Always," Jesper spat, his words, cold like steel as they cut through the tension of the air.

We reached those horrible doors.

What lay beyond them were memories that would forever stain my consciousness.

I was sold away in this room.

"You first, *incindica*." Diana's otherworldly voice rang as she reached for me.

"What—why?" Dracar's voice wavered as he spoke.

"Because that vermin is expecting her." Her eyes stayed fixated on Dracar as Rainier spoke.

She truly was *possessed*.

I walked through the doors and felt the gazes of everyone in the room searing into me. My skin felt dirty—stained under their predatory glares. I frantically searched the room for him, that white hair, the man who saved me...

My cruel salvation.

He was front of the room, a noose around his neck as he stood upon a box. His eyes were wide when they met mine and he began to tug at the ropes that bound his hands behind his back. Jamen circled the box with Dracar's blade in hand.

"My lovely bride, you are *just* in time," Jamen exclaimed. I could feel my fire swimming in my veins, begging to be released.

I could burn this room to the ground right now.

I *should* burn this room to the ground right now.

"Well come on! Come!" Jamen said all too cheerfully, extending a hand to me to join him up near my father's dais.

I froze.

"I know your little friends are out there. Tell them to join us too," Jamen smiled, almost looking sincere for a moment, like he might be capable of any human emotion.

At that comment Diana stepped through the door first, that power radiating off of her in waves. The air around her body seemed to crackle with intensity. Her frost-laden skin caught in the light like shattered glass, her hair unbound from her braid, cascading in waves as she walked forward.

Jamen's sick smile faltered a bit as he beheld her.

"Get me the handmaiden," Jamen commanded, and the guards did as he said, sweeping toward them.

"No! No! You follow my commands!" Dracar thundered. The guards did not listen as they rushed in. Diana swiftly surrounded the three of them in a dome of ice. The walls of the dome grew long spikes of frost that jutted outward, impaling the guards all the way through.

I shrieked in horror as they fell, the blood spilling from their mouths to interrupt their guttural cries and final mutters of prayers before meeting whatever Gods they worshipped.

"Enough!" Jamen yelled, and the remaining guards instantly stopped their useless pursuit.

"Or I'll gut this bastard," Jamen said wryly, pressing the blade to Hiver's exposed stomach.

The guards then turned their attention to me.

I felt their metal gauntlets wrapping around my arms and pulling me upward. I thought to release it then, to release my magic, but something was stopping me. Perhaps it was my subconscious speaking to me, asking me to wait. Thrashing underneath their grips, I could feel the flames welling to the surface, nearly exploding from my skin. I had to save my magic; Jamen had no idea I had it.

I let them take me up to Jamen. I looked away from him, just staring at Hiver whose eyes were fixated on me. He was anchoring me at this moment, the only reason I did not allow my magic to consume me.

Diana let down her ice dome, the soldiers retreating in fear from her.

"Good, good," Jamen said coldly. I stood at his side, unwillingly. Jesper continued to creep closer to us, his movements like that of a cat's—gentle and unheard—yet predatory. Those glowing eyes of his burned with an intensity that I feared deeply. Jesper was incredibly powerful—even more so when angered.

I felt Jamen's hand clasp around the back of my neck, as if to steer me to face what he wished me to see. He bent down and smelled my hair, his nose brushing against my cheeks as he did. I thought to strike him…

"You have me, now let him go," I croaked from the strength of his grip on me.

"Why would I do that?" Jamen laughed. I could feel my eyes twitching with fury as he held me there.

His lips came to my ear, his voice laced with venom as he whispered, "I cannot wait to fuck you, Mirage," he let loose another chuckle. My nostrils flared as I faced away from him, the opposite direction of Hiver.

"I cannot wait to see you try," I mumbled.

"Hmm? What was that? I wouldn't talk back to me..." He held the blade up and let the gem sparkle in the sun.

"You lot seem *really* worried about this blade..." Jamen's focus turned to Diana in her possessed state.

"It was an instrument made to kill. Perhaps I can show you if you come down to me," Rainier warbled.

"How easy." Jamen pulled out the gun again, stowed in a holster on his back. He pointed it at the unamused God.

"Go ahead, fire it," Rainier said, his calmness as lethal as the tempest of power simmering beneath the surface of that borrowed body. Jamen cleared his throat and allowed his thumb to brush what appeared to be a lever before firing it directly at Diana.

"No!" Hiver yelled from his post, but he didn't dare to struggle too much.

"It's okay," I murmured to Hiver at a volume I hoped only he would hear. He looked down to me, his gaze panicked, but something in it settled, as if he trusted me.

I watched the bullet connect with Diana's stomach, near the spot it had hit earlier. Rainier hissed but hardly responded to the metal that entered her body.

"Oh come now, did you think that was enough to kill a *God*?" Rainier's authority required no theatrics, yet he performed anyway.

"A *God*?" Jamen let loose a nervous chuckle, his grin faltering for just a moment as he beheld Diana. The glow of her eyes, the moonlight that made her skin glow, the crystal that had taken to her head—it had to be obvious she was *not* Diana at this moment. Perhaps someone like Jamen was incapable of recognizing it.

"A God?" Hiver echoed Jamen, shadows of worry etched deep within his eyes.

"She used the spell Kaneira used," I said to him, and before I could get his response, Jamen grabbed my arm, pulling me so hard into him I felt my vision swim for a moment.

"What do you know about this?" He questioned.

"I know that is *not* Diana—not right now at least," I managed to say to him, averting my gaze from his. He grabbed my jaw, forcing my eyes to meet his, but even as he pulled my head to face him, I kept my eyes focused elsewhere.

"Look at me," he said through gritted teeth, his voice thick with frustration and simmering fury.

"No," I said clenching my jaw, the word hardly able to make it through my own set teeth.

"Fine, don't wanna look at me? Hmm? Look at *him* then." Jamen yanked me by my hair, pulling me closer to Hiver as he took the blade and sliced it across Hiver's exposed abdomen. Hiver strained beneath it, his muscles tightening as he swallowed the scream that fought to escape his throat. He squeezed his eyes shut, as though blocking out the world would help keep the pain down.

"No, no, okay!" I yelled, grabbing Jamen by his shoulder and spinning him to me.

"Okay, you win. Whatever you want, just leave him be." I choked back tears as I spoke.

"See? That wasn't so hard." He reached a hand under my chin and pulled my gaze to his.

"So much anger in those beautiful eyes—I'll break that spirit of yours." He said with such gut-wrenching sincerity.

"Okay," I said in hardly more than a whisper.

My magic was begging to be freed—to coil up my arms and forge whips of flame to wrap around Jamen's throat. To force him to his knees to beg for his life—but I feared what he could do to my friends. I couldn't risk their lives for revenge.

I wouldn't.

Then the throne room doors groaned open.

She stepped through with a head in her hand—a woman who was carved by the wrath of the Gods. Her armor and flesh coated in blood like a second skin as she walked through, unbothered by the neck dripping fresh blood onto the floor around her.

Samira.

CHAPTER
FORTY-NINE

Her eyes were alight with a fury that would certainly make even a God fall to their knees.

The guards immediately went to seize her where she stood as the head of their fallen comrade hung menacingly from her left palm—she let it fall to the ground, its blood splattering the marble floors. The first guard to reach her was instantly struck down by her blade at a speed I could hardly register. He stopped for a moment once the sword made contact, his body completely still, before falling into three pieces onto the floor.

"I will kill you all," she said hoarsely as if her throat, too, were coated in a layer of blood. Behind her, Araya stepped delicately over the bloodied mess of one of the guards. My eyes were fixated on the entrails of the man on the floor before us. His intestines sprawled out from his midsection across the white marble.

I turned to Hiver who was horrified, but simultaneously at ease looking upon the carnage caused by Samira's hand. She pulled her blade along the inside of her elbow, removing the blood from it as she stood there unamused.

"Rainier," Samira breathed, her eyes lacking the coldness for just a moment. Instead her eyes widened upon taking in Diana's features. I could not read her expression as her eyes roved over Diana's body—from the moonlight-kissed blood in her veins to the gleaming crystal and those unearthly, glowing eyes.

Samira raised her blade up and attempted to strike it down over Diana's skull, but Rainier quickly massed a wall of ice above her head.

"Perhaps we watch this play out, yes?" Jamen snickered as he tilted his head toward me.

"*You.*" Samira choked as she raised her blade again, this time it connected with Rainier's side—*Diana's side*. Diana's pale hand reached to where the blade had nicked, the blood cascading down to the armor that sat just beneath the exposed spot.

"You cursed me!" Samira yelled, her blade swinging wildly as Rainier attempted to divert the blows.

She seemed to be winning.

"Sam, stop!" Hiver yelped. He hesitated in his movements because should he struggle too much, he may have hung himself. I scanned the room quickly, searching for Jesper as I was sure he was one of the only people capable of stopping Samira in her blind rage.

"You have the ability to bind souls—that is a *gift!*" Rainier fought against her furious blade, but seemed to be failing.

Samira was driven by a rage that I could not fathom. Every time I thought I'd seen the edge of someone's breaking point, I now realized they hadn't even brushed the abyss where Samira now stood.

Every move of her blade was driven by something so primal within her that she was hardly making the decisions.

Frost climbed up to her, coiling her wrists until they formed gauntlets of ice—her signature weapon. I could hear an unsettling clicking sound as her blade found its way against her spine, where I imagined a sheath was. Samira's nostrils flared as she stared down her opponent, ready to rip apart the flesh of her friend.

Before I could think a second longer, I allowed the whips to come out.

I grabbed Samira's wrists as she pushed in toward Diana. Her wild eyes met mine—those *hungry—insatiable* eyes. She continued to approach Diana, and I noticed then she was freezing the whips up to me. I immediately broke them as the frost crept upward as if she were frosting my actual arms.

"Ah fuck," I huffed as I allowed the whips to fizzle out. At the same time, I struggled to turn my gaze hardly an inch to see Jamen holding the blade up to me, just inches from my chest.

"You, too?" Jamen sneered.

I allowed the fire to climb up my arms, coiling around me like snakes. I could feel my eyes blazing as if my flames were begging to free themselves from every part of me.

I could hear Samira and Rainier bickering in the distance, Araya was searching for Jesper. The guards stood frozen at a distance, awestruck by the sight before them as icy blows sent scattering frost about the room.

He managed to jam the hilt of the sword into my temple—my head swam as I tried to keep myself upright. His fist then connected with my jaw and my teeth clashed against each other. I could still feel the weight of Jesper's siphoning in my bones, as if he had permanently taken something from me to use his blood magic.

Jamen came closer to me now, swinging Dracar's blade but just missing me as I turned to create more distance between us. Yet, while my skin felt unscathed, I could still feel that he had caught *something* with his blade. When I turned back, I saw nearly half of my hair lying on the ground between us. My eyes flickered up to his, and he let a malicious smile tug at his lips.

I was no good in close combat.

I let loose one of the whips, grabbing at his leg and pulling him to the floor, but he gripped the blade so intensely his knuckles turned white. But being on the ground gave him more leverage, and he yanked the flaming whip into him, ripping me downward. He squeaked and grumbled under the heat of it, and I could see his hands burning where he pulled at it. I tried to release the whip to keep from being pulled closer to that blade, but it would not retreat.

I was attached to it.

"Fuck, fuck." I squirmed and thrashed for control of the whip, but he was physically stronger, and continued to draw me into him. I reached to my side where I usually sheathed a blade, but I was quickly reminded that I was unarmed. I couldn't even cut it. He then began to coil my whip around Dracar's sword, using it as a sort of anchor.

I tried to command it to squeeze tighter, to cut off the blood circulation to his hand, to force his ligaments to snap under the weight of my flame. I relished in his pain, the screams of agony that clawed from his throat as he continued to try ad tie the whip to the sword.

He reached for his side and out came the revolver and he fired it into my shoulder. I hit the ground with a thud, the fire sputtering in my hands.

"You *bitch*." Jamen's eyes were glistening with the sheen of unshed tears, each one threatening to spill, but his madness refused to let them. I inhaled sharply, struggling to back up to put distance between us, but I couldn't fight him off with that blade in his hands. I ended up falling as I made an effort to escape him, and I knew I could not outrun him. I was still weak from Jesper siphoning me—weak from the hard hit to my temple.

I was just too weak.

I looked up at Jamen as he towered over me, jamming the metal again into the other side of my face.

I closed my eyes as he raised the blade, ready for it to pierce my flesh. Ready to not be able to heal around the metal as it crashed into my chest. I could hear Hiver calling to me, my name coming off of his tongue in frantic screams.

I could hear the blade singing through the air as it came downward.

I made my peace.

I fought for my people.

I had tried to become the sun—to swallow my enemies whole in searing light—but instead, I had become a spark, snuffed out by a wind I could not overcome.

CHAPTER
FIFTY

I heard his cough before I opened my eyes.

I could see the tip of the blade as it exited his flesh toward me, his hand pushing me backward so that it could not pierce my flesh, too.

Jesper.

"Jesper!" I squeaked, his name catching in my throat as a sob erupted from me.

"No, no, no," I cried, the tears were coming fast and hot, searing my skin.

"Z-*zertost*," Jesper croaked, sucking in a horrifying screech of breath. Jamen fell before him, the blade clattering to the ground. Jesper made many horrifying and guttural sounds as he reached for the hilt of the blade.

"Leave it in, please," I squeaked, and moved as fast as I could around to the front of him.

I heard a shrill and blood-curdling scream erupt from the middle of the room. It belonged to none other than Araya.

"Jesper!" She ran quickly through the guards who tried to stop her, fading in and out of this plane as she did—just as Lucius had when he first manifested before me.

Araya flashed in and out in puffs of smoke before she appeared before us, her hands immediately finding their way to Jesper's cheeks.

"Jesper," she sobbed, hardly able to keep herself together. He reached for her face, pushing her midnight colored hair behind her ears.

"It's okay, my love," Jesper muttered, his lips turning pale.

"No, I can't lose you—I won't," Araya sobbed; her large, wet eyes stayed open, fixated on his face.

I pulled a dagger from Araya's leg and sliced my wrist. I brought my bloodied skin to his lips, but he turned away from me, refusing it.

"Pull it out, darling." He coughed and gestured toward the blade. I closed my eyes for a brief moment, and before I could reach for the hilt, Araya had slid it out of him.

She threw the blade backwards, as if it didn't matter at all—as if the Shard were merely a piece of glass nestled into the hilt of a random sword.

"No, no!" Her cries were shrill and deafening. I felt I could hear her heart breaking with every passing moment, and it felt like mine was too.

"Jesper," I whispered, offering my blood to his lips again.

"It is no good. The blade was crafted to kill—not even you can heal–" He violently coughed, unable to finish his statement before the blood erupted from his throat. He weakly reached an arm to where the blade had gone directly through him. The floor around us was blanketed in blood.

"Use me—use my blood, my magic—anything!" I cried.

"I can't. I don't have the–" he rasped, struggling to suck in breaths.

"You're dying too fast…" I breathed.

He didn't have the energy, the magic, or the time to save himself.

"I love you… please. I love you." Araya crooned as she pressed her head against his. He reached his free hand to the back of her head, grabbing a mass of her hair in his fingers as he allowed his eyes to drift shut.

"In a thousand lifetimes, I could never love anyone more than you, my darling." he coughed, more blood leaving his mouth as he struggled to breathe.

Araya pressed her lips to his, kissing him hard. He pulled her head down into him as tight as he could, her hair wrapped around his bloodied hands.

"Please...don't leave me, Jesper." Her tears fell onto his chest when she pulled away.

"If this were the end of a life I got to spend with you, I would do it all again," he muttered. His words came out slower now, his eyes hardly staying open as he sat there. I came to Araya's side as Jesper opened his arms, inviting us to both say our farewells.

We shared a quick look of despair before both falling down into him, allowing him to wrap his arms around the two of us.

"Thank you," I cried into his chest.

"I've become the martyr I always wanted to be," he laughed softly, but immediately winced and wheezed.

"I love you—as a friend, as a martyr," I laughed and sobbed into his chest.

"I love you too, princess," he rasped

"Thank you for everything Jesper," I said through tears.

"No, thank *you*, for letting me be your friend," he smiled.

"Put me to sleep, Araya," he said, petting her head with soft strokes. He could hardly speak through his labored breaths, but he managed his final words to Araya.

"Look for me in the stars, my darling. They will always shine for you," he murmured, his breaths becoming more shallow as death loomed over him.

"Okay—I love you," she sniffled before rising slightly from his body.

"I love you more than anything, Araya." He said softly. She moved her hands to form some sort of sign before saying the word I now knew as sleep.

"*Zertost*," she wept as the word came out. Jesper's eyes gently closed—his final smile stayed on his face.

I couldn't remove myself from him.

I sobbed for a few minutes, but Araya had stopped. She sat back on her heels, her face haunted by the death of her lover. Her breaths came in shallow, broken gasps, as though her lungs were still catching up with her grief. I watched her sadness fade as her breaths grew deeper, steadier—then sharper, as her anger began to swell.

She rose to her feet as I sat over Jesper's body, watching as she sauntered over to Jamen.

"Get up you fucking pig." The words felt strange on her tongue —unfamiliar and heavy, as though they didn't quite belong to her. Araya had a sweet and expressive face.

Her large doe eyes felt only capable of carrying joy in them, but watching her now, I was fearful.

"*Ketsya*," Araya said, and he sucked in a desperate breath as he breached consciousness.

"*Rastark dar vaek leirs maskar. Mache fortund dar jagur.*" She slowly took the shape of another creature as she spoke—large and black.

A jaguar.

I watched her rip Jamen apart, starting at his throat. Those powerful jaws clasping around his weak human flesh. I watched her cover the floor in his blood. In the place of screams he merely sputtered streams of red from his throat where she had removed his vocal cords. He thrashed beneath her as I watched in horror. I made an effort to keep myself from vomiting, but I failed.

So much blood.
Too much blood.

Too much carnage.

※

Samira at some point had stopped her attempts to murder Rainier, and she immediately came to us as Araya continued to rip Jamen apart, shredding his flesh and muscle indiscriminately. She used her powerful jaws to pick him to the bone, his tendons and organs strewn about his body. I watched Samira place a hand on the back of Araya who was frenzied in her pursuit, growling while she continued to tear into his flesh. Samira's eyes stretched with horror—an expression she never once wore.

In the body of the jaguar, her eyes were still large and brown. She turned to face Samira, blood staining her black coat. Samira merely shook her head with fearful eyes as she looked upon the beast Araya had become. I heard a whimper come from the beast as she stepped over the carnage she had created. Samira's mere presence seemed to sober her frenzy. She came to Jesper's side, where she curled up and rested her great feline head upon his body. For a moment, I thought Samira might shed a tear as she rushed over to Jesper's side, pulling his limp hand into hers and pressing two fingers to his throat. It was clear what she was looking for, but I knew she would not find it.

The world around me felt like it was turning in slow motion, muffled screams and cries interjected with the clattering of armor.

From the corner of my eye, I could see Diana striking down soldier after soldier as if unphased by the weapons they wielded. I made a lazy effort to look for the blade, but didn't see it where Araya had thrown it.

I watched Samira's movements, slow and methodical as she stroked Araya's fur, her entire body coated in blood. I could hardly see the pale skin that existed beneath it. Diana and my brother cut down soldiers in the throne room as they continued their never-ending pursuit.

My hands were covered in the blood of my friends.
My mind was shattered.

I could never unsee Jesper's dying breaths, his last words, his final kiss to the woman he loved.

He died for *me*.

Diana eventually cut Hiver down from the noose that his neck was trapped in, freeing him completely. I felt his arms come down around me, but I couldn't even turn to face him.
I couldn't remove my eyes from Jamen's mutilated corpse either.
I couldn't unhear the sputters from his throat in his final moments.
I couldn't un-*feel* his touch on my neck—on my hair.

"Mirage," Hiver spoke softly in my ear and pressed his nose to my cheek.
"Look at me, don't look over there," he cooed softly, pulling my chin toward him. I could finally see his eyes as he searched mine. I could see his head was bleeding now, his white hair stained with blood. I couldn't will myself to speak as I reached a hand to where his skin had been cut open.
"No, no," he spoke softly, stroking my cheeks as he looked upon my face with compassion.
My mind raced with a million things to say. None of which I could force to come off of my tongue. I stared at him for a long moment, seeing the sea swim in those sapphire eyes.
He pulled me into a tight embrace, my chin resting on his shoulder as he squeezed me. I pulled away from him soon after, rather abruptly. I needed to tell him now, I needed to feel his lips on mine.

My salvation, my sanity, *my...love.*

I pressed my lips onto his. I could taste his blood and the salt of his sweat as I did. His hand came to the back of my head, pulling me into him as I kissed him. I started to cry as I did, the tears falling to our lips for both of us to taste. He slowly pulled away, looking at my face with deep concern.

"What's wrong?" he asked, gently caressing my cheeks.

"I love you," I blurted. The words felt odd as they left my tongue, as if I had allowed my heart to be ripped from my chest. I had hardly ever allowed myself the luxury of complete vulnerability. Hiver coaxed that reaction from me, the safety of his gaze, of his touch.

His eyes widened, his lips parting slightly as though the words had stolen the air from his lungs. A flush bloomed across his cheeks, and for a moment, I feared he had forgotten how to breathe. I felt my brows knitting together and I breathed heavier. I could feel myself shaking with fear and despair, my body quivering as I beheld him.

"I love you, *my* princess." He took my hands into his and kissed my knuckles. I threw myself back into him, pressing my body into his as we embraced each other. I wept into his shoulder, and he rubbed my back with tender hands.

"Everything is okay," Hiver whispered into my ear as he continued to make soft circles in the middle of my back. I sobbed so hard I could feel myself becoming nauseated.

I felt the tears mixing with the blood that had dripped from my cheek, where Jamen had hit me with the hard steel.

I could feel Hiver kissing the top of my head as he cradled me in his arms. He rocked me back and forth as if the world around us did not matter. His warmth reached through my tattered clothing, warming my soul from the cold that it had endured these last few days.

⁂

"There has to be a way to reverse it," I said through tears.

"Reverse what?" Hiver said softly, looking down upon my face as I pulled away from him.

"His death." I felt the words sticking to my tongue—as if they were not meant to exit my mouth.

"No, no. There's only one object on this Earth that can reverse death," Hiver said.

"Is it one of the five Talis items?" I asked.

"Mhm, Arakos's Star," he said solemnly.

"Then I'll get it," I responded. The look of horror and shock on his face was unlike anything I had seen him exhibit before.

"You'll never find it," he whispered, not meaning to be discouraging, but truthful.

"I'll have to try," I murmured back, the words hardly able to leave my throat that was left raw from the sobs.

He brushed the loose strands of hair from my face, his fingers lingering at my temples as if he were trying to will my heartbeat to slow beneath his touch.

The world around me felt distant, like I was trapped behind a glass wall. The sounds began to reach my ears muffled, warped, as if the air had thickened around me. Time itself seemed to stutter and drag, each second stretching into an eternity of sorrow and tragedy. I felt Hiver's fingers pulling at my flesh to try and dig out the bullet that was making it near impossible to breathe.

CHAPTER
FIFTY-ONE

My brother made it to my side, blade angled at my throat.

"Dracar?" I croaked. His eyes were glazed over with a fury unlike him.

"I can't let you leave," his words came out choked.

"Dracar." I said again, as if my cry could sober him from whatever had possessed him to hold a weapon under my chin.

I could feel my nose twitching; all of my sadness, the despair, was forging itself into something entirely new.

My newfound heart, reforged in fire.

My newfound heart that was bleeding with desperation, with rage, with anguish. I could feel my skin turning hot, burning from the anger and sadness. A fire erupted all around me, pooling itself around my arms and at my back, but Dracar pushed the blade into my neck, drawing the smallest drop of blood.

"You traitor! You coward!" I cried at him, reaching for where my skin had broken.

I had no one to save me now.

No more Jesper—no more blood magic.

"You're dangerous, Mirage." Dracar spoke with such an *emptiness*.

"So are you!" I panted, "So are you."

Hiver stood before him, eyes blazing as his magic erupted at his fingertips—the sparkles radiating from his skin like diamonds.

"Stay out of my way."

"Touch her again, and you die." Hiver replied, his tone cold and harsh—like a winter storm.

"I'm the only one who can make that decision, no?" Dracar's steely tone was grating on my ears. I sat there before him on my knees, my magic useless in the face of a God forged weapon. I frantically scanned the room for Samira or Araya, but they and Jesper's body were gone, and to where I could not know.

I had prayed for them to come out of the shadows, to save me, to save *us*—but I was damn near out of hope to spare. I had never in my whole life felt more betrayed than this moment, than where my brother held me hostage.

"You can't leave—I have to—" Dracar choked on the words as he gazed down at me, a pain searing through me as the blade punctured the skin. He, like Diana, appeared to be at war with himself.

"Back. Up." Hiver said again, and at his side now was a great large creature, one I had come to know as Glacien. Dracar withdrew the blade from my neck and pointed it at the giant beast, whose fangs were as long as daggers.

"What the hell is that?" Dracar gasped, a fear taking his features hostage.

"*That* is Glacien," Hiver smiled, "And he will rip you apart." Glacien growled at Dracar, who continued to take steps backward from me as the wolf stalked him.

"None of you understand. None of you! None of you even love her!" Dracar shouted, a madness taking hold of him.

"I love her." Hiver started, face contorting into a frown as he spoke, "I love her more than anything." I felt the tears pouring from my eyes, like a tidal wave. Yet I'm all but washed as I drown in this sea of salt—as my hands are covered in my blood.

"None of you. None of you. None of you!" He screamed out, blade outward as Glacien continued his predatory stalk.

"*Diakto.*" Hiver raised a hand, and Glacien returned to his side, his demeanor softer than that of when he approached Dracar—the bloodthirsty wolf now just a happy dog as his tail thumped beside Hiver.

"We're leaving, now," Hiver reached a hand down to pull me up from the floor where I still sat and cried.

"Not yet." Rainier's voice rang out, hands frosted over to form blades.

DIANA

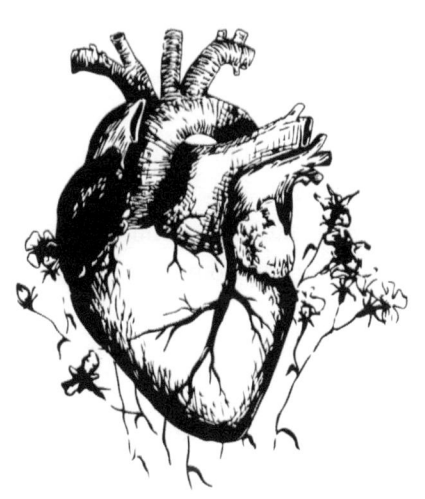

CHAPTER 52

DIANA

I was no longer in control of my body.

"There is a price to pay," Rainier's voice quaked through me.

I thought I was willing to pay whatever it cost to save my brother—to save my friends, but I had not been told.

I remembered when Kaneira had taught me the spell. The memory was hazy when I started to summon Rainier; but now, when the most control I had over my body was to think, the memory was crystal clear.

"It's guarded by the Solarian, and even most of them can't be trusted with access to it." She smiled at me, something devious hiding in her expression.

"I trust you'll use it wisely. Only when you have no other options." A seriousness overcame Kaneira as she spoke: something almost solemn.

"Of course," I responded, a smile tugging at my lips.

"I am serious, Diana. The cost is very high." Her tone was somber.

KINGDOM OF THE SUN

. . .

I had fought against Rainier. I had fought against his magic that had taken over my body—nearly consuming me. I struggled to even get a few words out as Hiver stood in front of—*us*.

"You want me to kill the person I love most?" I strained as Hiver gripped our shoulders, panic washing over his features as the icy blades protruded from my hands.

"You knew there was a steep cost... but you didn't care." Rainier's voice boomed over mine.. I hardly recognized the distorted tone that emitted from my body.

"Diana, what the hell did you do?" Hiver gripped our shoulders harder now, his nails digging into me.

I looked over his shoulder at Mirage, who had turned to face me—her eyes glazed with terror.

Free me, please.

I pleaded in my mind, desperate for his reply. There was a pause—a long deafening silence in my mind where I felt nothing but the cold grip of Rainier around my consciousness.

You called to me, Diana. You cannot summon ruin then mourn its arrival.

The weight of the words that echoed into my skull sank into me like a set of fangs. I didn't know the cost. I didn't know it would be someone I loved.

I called to you to save my brother, not to pilot my body and refuse me freedom!

I screamed in my own head. I could feel the wall of frost that divided Rainier and I in my mind—a literal sheet that split my body into two consciousnesses.

I won't harm Hiver, but you must kill the boy.

Rainier's otherworldly voice trilled in my skull. I could feel his magic coiling around my soul, threatening to steal it from me entirely. I could feel Hiver's touch on me, as if for a moment it was just me in this body. I could feel myself staring at him, searching those blue eyes.

"He—" I choked on the words as I spoke, hardly able to gain enough control to use my voice.

It was night incarnate who wielded my body now—the God who brought the death of winter and the life of spring.

He was numbing the parts of me that still fought against him, clawing for control. My own magic, the quiet pulse of winter I had carried since I was a child, felt muted beneath the crushing weight of a God's magic.

I wouldn't let him win.
I would never hurt Dracar.

"He wants me to kill Dracar!" I screamed at Hiver. I felt Rainier tilting my head, and saw through my own eyes but from a distance, as though I were a passenger in my own skin.

It was Mirage's eyes I met first.

I watched her experience several phases of grief as her brother now stood over her—Mirage tried to stand, but he immediately brought the blade down on her, piercing it through her thigh. Her guttural cries sounded as if they were ripped straight from her soul.

"Stay down—" Dracar commanded, and she stared up at him through teary eyes.

Even Rainier hesitated upon hearing her screams splinter the air around us.

Dracar then approached us, blade at the ready.

"Don't make me fight Diana—you *coward!*" Dracar snarled.

"The only coward is *you*," Rainier hissed, and it came to blows.

I begged Rainier as he moved my body with a perfect precision, dodging every swing of the great blade.

Sacrifice...

Rainier raised my hand upward, forming a sword of my own, forged of the ice from *our* power.

"Dracar, run!" I screamed as I fought off the power that consumed me. The power that was piloting me to walk toward him.

I could hear Mirage's screaming sobs as she held the wound on her thigh—where the Shard had impaled her.

The Veil—give her the Veil.

Rainier said to me. For a moment, I had some control again, and reached into my armor and pulled out the black veil. I stared at it for a long moment, really looking through my own eyes as myself for the first time in what felt like an eternity. My limbs ached as he willed himself aside for me to give her the Veil. I tossed it to Mirage, who looked at me bewildered.

"Please," I managed before Rainier had fully taken control again.

"I'm sorry love, but I always take my toll, in blood or in souls." Rainier warbled as he approached.

I looked toward my brother with pleading eyes—I had hoped that beneath the frozen exterior of a God, he could see me—he could *feel* me pushing back. Hiver's eyes widened in horror, and he lowered his hands. I pursued Dracar despite my begging cries to Rainier to leave him—to *spare* him.

He would not fight me.

I clung to that look. That fleeting look, that fragile thread of love that wove itself in his brightly colored irises.

"Of hollow and frost," he said as he took a knee, his eyes shimmering with hope.

I couldn't use my voice.

I had hoped that he could feel the words echoing on the walls of my skull, searing themselves into my consciousness as I felt a single tear shed from my left eye.

Everlasting, never lost.

MIRAGE

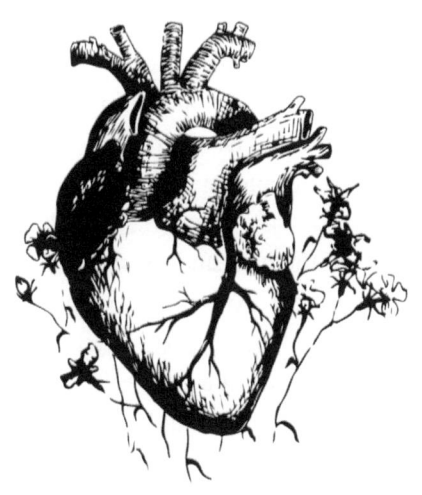

CHAPTER 53
MIRAGE

I could hardly breathe.

The pain didn't just stay in my leg—it radiated outward, searing up my spine and down to my toes like an uncontrollable wildfire. It throbbed, a heavy, sickening pulse that felt as if the wound itself had a heartbeat. The warmth of the blood spilled over my skin, slick and hot, as if agony itself had been pouring from the wound.

Diana then threw me the Veil and its shadowy form rippled as it came down hardly a few feet from me. I managed to pull myself to it, biting my lip to hold in the screams I wished to free from my tongue. The Veil shimmered like moonlit smoke—like a silken expanse of shadow and starlight. I could swear I felt it breathe in my hands. I could hear it whispering to me as I held it in trembling hands, begging me to wear it.

Don the Veil.
Don the Veil.
Don the Veil!

The shadows cried out to me, desperate for use—but I was not Tenebris—I could not wield shadows.

As I began to raise my shaking hands to place it upon my head, I caught a glimpse of Hiver's sudden movements.

I watched as he fell to his knee out of the way of Diana, who was pursuing us with hungry, yet entreating eyes. I felt that some part of her was in there—some part of her was fighting against the God that was seeking out *his* definition of justice.

"Please don't," I croaked. The words hardly came out as more than a gasp.

Wear it, child. Command the shadows.

The voices sounded almost as if they were inside of me, as if they were whispering to me in only my mind.

"Hiver?" His name scraped out of me, broken and trembling. My body felt like it was folding in on itself, every breath a struggle, every movement sending another jolt of fire through my leg.

I couldn't heal from the Shard of Aetheris.

I started to feel helpless, hopeless even, as she approached. My friend, my *sister*, now a God of frost and darkness. Hiver looked over to me, his face pale and streaked with dirt and blood, but his eyes burned with anguish.

"I can't fight her—I can't," he rasped, his voice fraying at the edges.

"I won't do it." His voice barely louder than a whisper.

I merely stared at him, the pain in my leg nearly consuming me entirely. I tried to rise to my feet, and as I did, a sharp cry swelled in my chest—reverberating through my body. It felt like my skin was tearing more with every movement I made, but I found my footing and stood in front of Dracar, who was paralyzed in the face of the

God who sought his blood. As I stood straight, I could feel the flames coiling up my arms. I stared at her through blurred eyes as tears were stinging my skin, but I could hardly notice them as my body hummed with magic.

I raised the Veil to my head and put it on.

At first, the world around me was deafeningly silent.

Then all at once, I heard a thousand screams, threatening to rupture my skull.

I reached for the Veil, but couldn't pull it off.

I heard them chant in an eerie harmony—words that were all too familiar to me.

> *Reality will fade under the shadow's grip,*
> *The fleeting sensation, an illusory slip*
> *The cost is hidden, the truth a pyre,*
> *Your newfound heart reforged in fire.*

But then they continued.

> *Command the shadows become the light,*
> *Sunfire's spirit, the dawn's first flight.*
> *Shadows can only exist from the sun,*
> *Scion of Arudia, we...are...one.*

I could feel the shadows weaving into my body. I watched their tendrils, thin and precise as they wove into my torn flesh. I screamed as I reached for my leg, which I could hardly see as the shadows danced around it, binding the muscle and skin with seamless darkness. I felt a strange, icy pressure—not pain, but a cold feeling that spread outward from my wound, numbing everything it touched. The shadows then began embedding themselves *into* my flesh. Seeping into the wound and burying themselves within me.

It had almost entirely closed, and on top of it, the shadows wove what appeared to be a marking over the freshly closed skin. Thin, obsidian-like veins radiated from the shadowy stitching, tracing delicate, branching lines across my skin like cracks in glass, shimmering faintly when touched by the light of my fire. I snapped back into reality after a few moments of the shadow magic infecting my body, then I looked up at Diana. I allowed a whip to flip out at her, but Rainier caught it, turning his head ever so slightly, as if amused by my attempt.

My jaw tightened, but I didn't move. My hand hovered for a moment, and I could feel the screaming shadows pulsing in my veins. I held my hand out, allowing the shadows to coil around my outstretched fingers. My flames continued to dance along my arms, caressing my skin in a soft orange glow. Shadows wove themselves into the fire's embrace, lulling to me a haunting symphony of light and darkness. From their union, I could feel my heart straining to beat under the weight of my newfound power.

From my hands, I managed to forge a blade made of shadows and flame.

I stared at it in awe for a moment as Rainier extended a leg, kicking me in the chest. I briefly lost my footing before pulling the blade up to my face. I could feel the shadows humming in my skin, just as my flame magic had. Whatever horrible power this was, I *needed* it. I tightened my grip on the shadow blade as a dull throb vibrated in my ribs. Diana was upon me again, her form a blur of frost-laden rage. Her fists came down like steel, every strike precise and heavy as she blew me backward.

I managed to parry one of the blows with the shadowy blade, but Rainier reached out and grabbed it with a bare hand—in his other, a blade forged of frost came swinging toward my head, and I ducked underneath.

I kicked at the God's feet—he hit the ground hard, but as he did, a laughter erupted from him—a laughter that was chaotic and cold.

He was back on his feet, but before I could react, another fist came crashing down onto my cheek.

I fell to my knees before the God.

"I'm not here for *you*, niece," his voice trilled, threading through with the sharp, feminine lilt Diana's voice took on when frustration burned beneath her words.

Blood sputtered out of my mouth onto the floor as I loosed a violent cough. I quickly flicked out one of the whips, catching Rainier's leg. I ripped at it as hard as I could, but those ethereal eyes turned to me, devouring me. He approached me slowly, reaching a hand down to my throat as he lifted me from the floor.

"Please, stop!" Hiver yelled, a hand wrapped around Diana's forearm. His eyes were imploring as she turned to face him, completely devoid of emotions, before releasing me. I fell to the floor, fighting off the black spots that danced at the edges of my vision as I struggled to gasp for air.

"No!" I yelled as her hand came down around Dracar's throat instead, pulling him up from where he sat paralyzed on the ground.

"No, please!" I yelped.

"Kill me! Take me instead!" I rose to my feet, staggering as I made it to Rainier's back. I placed my hands on his shoulders, still gasping for air. My vision was hazy from the pain. I raised the shadow-wreathed blade upward, except this time it was not to swing, but to surrender.

"Kill me instead," I said through labored breaths, the sting of blood on my tongue.

I couldn't let someone else die.
  Not when it could have been me.

For a moment, I thought I saw Jesper's face instead of Dracar's —golden eyes gleaming with sorrow and fear.

I saw him there.

I saw that blade go through him.

I saw his hand against my chest, pushing me backward.

I saw all of him.

In a blind rage, I struggled to swing the blade again; this time it connected with Diana's midsection and she hissed under the weight of the blade. In place of blood, shadows looked to be leaking from the wound. She let out a primal scream as she fell to one knee, but steadied herself.

"I can spare him for you." Rainier's garbled voice rang out over the singing of the dark magic that squeezed my lungs and heart. I dropped the night-cloaked blade, the shadows screaming as it fell to the ground beside me.

"No!" Hiver yelled, but Rainier raised a hand upward, and a mist surrounded Hiver as he was lulled into a sleep, his body hitting the ground with a heavy *thud*. Dracar sat on the ground, choking from the steel grip of Diana's possessed body. He was on his hands and knees, blood erupting from his throat as he arched over the ground. Desperate breaths ripped through him.

But he was alive.

Rainier forged a frostbitten sword over the top of me, and I saw no clarity in those immortal eyes, no regret for what he would do to me. The blade descended almost in slow motion. The shadows surged up from me, trying to protect me, but I released them.

The blade sank into my chest.

The pain was instantaneous—deep and all-consuming. The cold spread through me like a flood, smothering the fire that was just moments before burning so fiercely in my veins. I gasped, a sharp and moist sound as the frost lanced through my ribs—through me. I could feel my pulse stuttering, weakening with every passing beat.

"I'm—sorry, Dracar," the words clawed their way up my throat, wet and ragged. Dracar's eyes met mine for one last time, terror and sadness spilling out in the form of tears. The taste of blood coated my tongue.

"Goodbye, little bird," Rainier said.

He is alive.

I thought as I fell to the ground, the blade still lodged in my chest. I felt the cold stone beneath me as the scent and taste of blood overwhelmed my senses. My vision blurred while the world dimmed.
Maybe death was like falling asleep.

THE TESSIAH WILL RETURN.

www.ingramcontent.com/pod-product-compliance
Ingram Content Group UK Ltd.
Pitfield, Milton Keynes, MK11 3LW, UK
UKHW041304180426
11947UKWH00009B/679